The Path of the Dead

THE PATH OF
THE DEAD

Caroline Benton

Constable • London

In memory of Kay

Constable & Robinson Ltd
3 The Lanchesters
162 Fulham Palace Road
London W6 9ER
www.constablerobinson.com

First published by Constable,
an imprint of Constable & Robinson Ltd 2006

A copy of the British Library Cataloguing in Publication
Data is available from the British Library.

ISBN 13: 978-1-84529-269-0
ISBN 10: 1-84529-269-3

Printed and bound in the EU

Chapter One

It was a warm night. Or rather morning. A Wednesday morning in July, two weeks into a heatwave. I'd discarded the duvet and was sleeping beneath a sheet when at 3 a.m. I got a phone call from HQ.

'Miss Tavender? This is Control. We have a three-pump fire at Danner Road, Exeter, possible persons reported. The Officer in Charge has requested your attendance.'

I'm not my best at three in the morning, especially when I've only been asleep since two. I struggled to sit up.

'Sorry, give me that again.'

'Come on, Gus, get it together.' I recognized my friend Lisa's voice. 'A three-pump fire at Danner Road. Possible persons –'

'Yeah, I got all that.' I threw my legs over the side. 'Okay, I'm on my way.'

I reached for my jeans, apprehension knotting my stomach. Possible persons reported is a Fire Brigade euphemism for persons possibly dead. It was the last thing I wanted to hear. Death might be an inevitable part of my job but that doesn't mean I have to like it. Previous fatalities were still vivid in my dreams.

Minutes later I was out the door, my camera bag slung over my shoulder, avoiding the shadows as I hurried to my car. I gunned the engine, radioing to HQ as I sped away. Already I suspected arson.

Danner Road is a cul-de-sac on the opposite side of town,

in one of the sleazier parts of the city. It's a road where GBH is a way of life and policemen walk, if forced to walk at all, in twos. You don't park a car in Danner Road, come back five minutes later and expect to find wheels. Probably you won't even find the car. It's full of social drop-outs and DSS families who've been evicted from their council houses for habitual non-payment of rent and other minor misdemeanours, like smashing up the doors and furniture for firewood when the weather turns cold. There are more hoax calls from Danner Road than from any other part of the city.

But tonight it was the real thing. Kids, most likely, getting a cheap thrill with a can of kerosene and a lighter nicked from the old man with the shop on the corner. Hoaxing wears thin after a time.

I probably sound unsympathetic, but it's hard not to be when your friends and colleagues are going out each day risking life and limb to put out fires deliberately started, only to have bricks thrown at them and Christ knows what else, and to run the risk of further booby-traps left inside the building, their sole intention to maim and kill. And when you have to photograph the aftermath of violence and rage, like the torched house of an eighty-five-year-old widow who lost everything she owned and cherished because she'd dared to complain about the neighbours' noise. Or the old man who'd been duffed up by a gang of twelve-year-olds and left handcuffed – where the hell do twelve-year-olds get handcuffs? – to his bed for two days for the sake of three pounds twenty.

And these are by no means isolated incidents.

Life in a sleepy West Country town.

Life at the turn of the millennium.

Danner Road resembled a fairground when I reached it. I could see the flashing blue lights two streets away, their stroboscopic glow sending the rooftops into stark relief.

I pulled in at the end of the road, grabbed my hard hat and jammed it on my curls.

The street had been sealed off by orange tape and despite the hour a small crowd had gathered. I pushed through them, flashed my identity card at the constable on duty and ducked under. The ground was a mess of hose-reels, water and debris. I made for the furthest pump and gestured at the fireman in charge of communications. He leaned down to hear me over the noise.

'Brigade photographer,' I yelled. 'Can you book me in attendance?'

He gave a thumbs up.

'Who's the Officer in Charge?'

'DO Wiltshire.'

'Will you let him know I'm here?'

He nodded and spoke into the two-way radio hanging from a cord round his neck.

'Delta one-four, Delta one-four, from three-two-one, over.'

A couple of seconds and Leo's voice crackled back. 'Three-two-one, go ahead, over.'

'Brigade photographer in attendance.' He listened a moment then looked back. 'He says to wait here.'

'What's going on?' I asked. 'Any casualties?'

'Doesn't look like it. The place was empty, boarded up. Neighbour thought she saw someone going in but they must've come out again or BA would've found 'em.'

I nodded. The breathing apparatus teams were nothing if not thorough.

'More likely kids,' he added. 'Still, better here, I suppose, than somewhere else.'

I thought of the old people's home that had been set alight for fun six months before and silently agreed.

The radio crackled again and he turned away. I looked towards the house. Until that night it had been a red-brick turn-of-the-century terrace, derelict but salvageable. Now it was a shell. Part of the roof had caved in, taking with it a large chunk of the roof next door. Smoke and steam

7

issued from the void, drifting upwards between the blackened rafters. More charred wood, the remains of the boarding, formed a jagged edge to the dark holes where windows had once been.

I pulled a camera from my bag. I was too late for the flames but I could still get the aftermath. I took some shots of the front of the building, a couple more of firemen reeling in hose, then noticed a white helmet with two black stripes moving towards me, beneath it a pair of coal-dark eyes in a face blackened by soot. Divisional Officer Liam Wiltshire, Leo to his mates, heart-throb to the numerous secretaries and women in the Control Room. The Officer in Charge of the incident.

Normally Leo's a charmer; tonight he was all business. He dropped a hand on my shoulder and steered me nearer the house.

'Okay, you know the score. A lot of people are clamouring to have this whole street pulled down. When the place is vented I want you inside. Shoot anything that looks like a fire hazard, show the Brigade clearing up. Let people see where the budget goes, okay?'

'Yes, sir. Was it arson?'

'What do you think? Anyway, I'm getting the lighting in now.'

He barked commands into his radio and moments later firemen were entering the building carrying spotlights and tripods, trailing long lengths of cable that connected them to the pumps. I waited until the interior was ablaze with light, then adjusted my hard hat and went in.

There is no smell quite like that of a building after a fire. Charred wet wood, years of accumulated filth and soot drenched in water, steaming brick and stone. An acrid, dank smell that lodges in your throat and stings your eyes. Tonight it mingled with another smell – petrol. It hit me as soon as I walked in, pungent and unmistakable, so strong the place must have been awash. Whoever had torched it must have really wanted it to burn.

I picked my way into what had once been the living

8

room. The powerful lamps were unmerciful, revealing every ugly detail of its squalor and dereliction. Wallpaper still adhered to some of the walls, an enormous geometric design of swirls and squares in orange, white and brown. But it was torn, dirtied by fire, streaked by the gallons of filthy water that had poured in through the roof. The stripped areas were a riot of graffiti. Instructions to 'Kill the Pigs' rubbed shoulders with derogatory terms for individuals, gang logos and crude drawings of grossly inflated genitals.

In the mud on the floor lay bottles, lager cans and assorted junk. More junk was piled in a corner. Against the far wall was a half-burnt polyurethane foam settee. I took wide-angles of the entire room then moved in for the details.

The kitchen was equally squalid. Doorless units housed a filthy enamel sink piled high with crusty pans and crockery. Broken china crunched on the floor. A thick layer of brown grease surrounded the space where the cooker had once been. Filling the gap was a rusty child's pram.

I finished one roll of film and loaded another, then went back into the hall. Here the stench of petrol was at its strongest, presumably the seat of the fire. A fireman was descending the ladder that ran up through the well in place of the burnt-out stairs.

I said, 'Okay to go up?'

He checked the ladder's stability. 'Yeah, but watch where you're walking. Make sure you keep to the edge.'

'Will do.' I slung the camera across my chest and began to ascend. Above my head I could see the stars.

'Hope you've got a strong stomach,' he called after me.

The landing was deep in broken slates and sodden chunks of plaster. Straight ahead was the bathroom. My nose wrinkled involuntarily as I peered in. The cistern and basin had been ripped from the wall and smashed; the lavatory used long after the water had been disconnected. The bath had clearly been used for the same purpose, and water from the hoses had turned it to slurry. I held my breath, took the necessary shots and beat a hasty retreat.

There were just two bedrooms, neither of them large. The bigger was at the front. On the floor that remained were two badly charred mattresses, each with a soggy mound of what I assumed was bedding. It may have been clothes. Odd bits of furniture had survived – the remains of a chest of drawers, something that could have been a wardrobe, half a chair. A mirror, still retaining a few shards of glass, was propped against the wall. Cans and bottles were everywhere, of every conceivable brand and size. Squatters? A wino's retreat? A crack house?

I was busy recording when voices sounded on the landing and DO Wiltshire entered, followed by his second-in-command.

'How's it going?' he asked.

'One more room, sir.'

He nodded and continued to survey the wreckage. I left him to it and headed for the back room.

Here it was the same story. More cans strewn across the floor, screwed-up wads of foil, a double mattress beneath a knot of cloth. This time I could make out the remains of a pink eiderdown, a dun-coloured blanket. A partially burnt melamine wardrobe had a fist-hole through its door. In the middle of the party wall was a six-foot metal shelf unit, stacked upon it the amorphous remains of half a dozen car tyres.

I've long since ceased to be surprised by the bizarre things one finds in burnt-out houses but these looked particularly incongruous. Probably the proceeds of a robbery. I zoomed in for a close-up, trying to catch the brand. What I caught was an outline of something on the wall behind.

I lowered the camera, squinted. It looked like some sort of frame. Cautiously I edged towards it, my back against the wall, testing the floor at each step before giving it my full weight. The unit was on casters. I touched it lightly with the back of my hand – warm but not hot – and gave it a tug. It slid to one side – not far, but enough to make my stomach lurch. The frame marked the edge of a door, barely four feet high, with a key set very low down.

'Sir!' I called as I took more shots. 'There's something you should see.'

Without waiting, I dragged the shelving clear and turned the key. The door swung towards me. I jumped back to avoid possible flames. But it wasn't flames that came out, only a smell – the sickly, cloying smell of charred human flesh.

I reeled back, gagging, my hand over my mouth. *'Sir!'* I screamed. *'Casualty!'* I took a breath, steeled myself, then turned back to record the horror on the floor.

The body was just inside the door, face down, its head towards me. One leg was slightly bent; the face, what was left of it, mercifully hidden. It had no hair. Few clothes either, though from its size and shape I guessed it was a man. The left arm was outstretched and ended in a grizzled charcoal claw just inches from the door.

I was rapidly running off shots when the DO burst in.

'What the hell . . .!' He pushed past me, brushing me aside. 'Jesus, get her out of here!'

Strong hands grabbed me and dragged me away. I know I was protesting. Minutes later I was sitting outside, nursing a mug of tea, listening to talk about delayed shock and counselling. Someone suggested I spend the rest of the day at home.

'No way!' I said, with a forcefulness that surprised even me. Home was the last place I wanted to be.

Chapter Two

It was the first time I had seen a burnt body. Most fire-related deaths are caused by smoke inhalation and it's rare to see a charred corpse. It's even rarer to see one *in situ*. No sooner does a pump arrive at a burning building than firefighters don breathing apparatus and go in, dousing the flames before them. They follow a strict procedure, tapping their way around walls, fanning out across rooms, feeling their way through every inch of space whether or not someone's been reported inside. The Brigade doesn't take chances. If a casualty exists, nine point nine times out of ten they will find it. But not if it's locked in a secret room.

Yet that, it appeared, was what I had found – a narrow windowless space, separated from the main room by a plasterboard partition. Heaven knew why it had been built. As a private, if joyless, sleeping area? For hiding stolen goods? Hiding people?

I had little chance to speculate. It was a busy time and work was piling up, though for once I welcomed the distraction. But late that afternoon I was forced to confront the scene again. My stills had been processed and I needed to check the prints.

The images were startlingly clear, revealing details I hadn't noticed at the time, small irrelevant things that brought an oddly personal touch to the pervading squalor. A bright rectangle of wallpaper in the living room where a picture had once hung. A flower pot on the window sill in the kitchen. A tiny blue and orange Outspan sticker on the metal unit that had concealed the door.

A gold stud in the ear of the corpse. How the hell had I missed that?

I stared again at the crusty blackened lump that had once been a human being. On the back of the head and shoulders were irregular pale strips, showing where the charred skin had contracted and split as a result of excess heat. Another strip circled the wrist of the outstretched arm clawing for the door.

A locked door, barricaded from the outside.

He might not have made it anyway, I told myself, remembering the foam settee directly below. Six inches might as well be six miles when toxic fumes are replacing the oxygen and smoke is filling your lungs. Nevertheless, it was this final gesture that I found most disturbing, the desperate, futile, failed bid for life. Whoever he was, I could only hope he was well and truly dead before the flames reached him.

It was nearly five when my door opened and Buzz Beecham's head appeared.

'Tosser wants you, Gus.' He paused. 'You okay?'

I nodded. I wished they would stop asking.

He fumbled with the knob. 'We've all been there, you know. First one's always a shock. I mean, if you want to talk . . .'

'I'm fine. Honestly.'

'Well, you know where I am.'

The door closed and I sank back in my chair. I felt exhausted, at least ten years older than my thirty-one years. Despite a shower, I still felt tainted by the squalor and not for the first time wished my flat had a bath. A long soak would have felt more cleansing.

The corridor was empty when I set off through the rabbit warren that is Fire Brigade HQ. A one-time Georgian country house, its grandeur has been destroyed by unsympathetic division into numerous poky offices. I stopped at the door marked *Senior Divisional Officer John*

Enticott, and knocked. After the customary few seconds a husky voice told me to enter. Despite the open window, the magnolia-painted office was shrouded in cigarette smoke. SDO Enticott waved me to a chair.

'Sit down, Augusta.'

I winced. Tosser always uses my full name. It's his way of reminding me of my position – or my position as *he* sees it, a woman in a man's world. When women were finally accepted as firefighters, I'm told he did not react kindly.

He was sitting behind a standard-issue teak veneer desk, the piles of papers and writing implements arranged with neat precision on top. He didn't stand up. His companion did. Leo Wiltshire looked fresh as a daisy – if daisies come in macho six foot two hunks – with not even a tell-tale smudge beneath his eyes to indicate a disturbed night. He said nothing, merely looked, eyebrows raised, then flashed a don't-you-wish-we-were-alone smile and sat back down. What really hacked me off was that part of me, despite all reason, did.

'That the photos?' Enticott held out a pudgy hand.

He tipped the glossy 8×10s on to his desk and began to sort through, lips pursed, brows lowered over piggy dark eyes. The contrast between the two men was so marked I almost felt sorry for him. Even sitting down they looked like a straight man and his patsy.

Tosser is about five foot six, the minimum height for entering the Brigade, and since his promotion to SDO, and hence pen-pusher, is well on his way to becoming as wide as he is tall. Grizzled grey hair, convict-short and patchy, sits like a bristly fuzz on a head narrower at the top than at the bottom, where the starched white collar cuts into numerous folds of chin. His uniform fits him like Tom Kitten's blue coat.

Leo, by contrast, is lean and athletic, and makes his uniform look like the latest Armani. Perhaps it is: I wouldn't put it past him to have it specially made. But what price image when you're on the way up? Already he's the youngest DO in the county and it's my guess he'll

14

be Chief within ten years. You can always tell a high-flyer in the Brigade. They speak, as they say here, in joined-up writing, an undeniable plus in an institution where all senior officers are promoted from the ranks. Also, their shoes shine just that little bit brighter.

Watching and listening to Leo it's easy to see why he's done so well. Compared with most officers he speaks in copperplate script, forming coherent sentences which he delivers with just the right degree of authority to get him noticed. He wears leadership like he wears his uniform, with conviction, inspiring the kind of trust that, as a child, I was taught to have in policemen. And as for his shoes . . .

I glanced down at the feet just visible round the side of the desk. If I'd been closer I could have seen myself smiling.

Tosser slid him the first batch of photos. 'Where was the seat of the fire?'

'Bottom of the stairs. Burnt them right out.'

'And there's no doubt it was arson?'

'Smelled like a tanker had dropped its load.'

Tosser fingered a shot of the corpse lying in front of the door and shook his head. 'Nasty. Poor bastard almost made it.'

'Not with that shelf unit blocking the door. It was the only exit.'

'And locked from the outside. So are we talking murder?'

'Looks that way. Depends if whoever struck the match knew he was there. And if that same person turned the key, and why.'

'Do you think he would have been dead before the flames reached him?' I asked.

Leo glanced up. 'It's impossible to say for certain before the PM, but in a sealed room, with that sofa below, I wouldn't have thought there was much doubt. The fumes would have got him. The flames would have come later, after the roof caved in and let in air.'

15

It was what I wanted to hear. It didn't mean his death would have been painless but at least it would have been quick.

'Damn shame BA didn't find him.' Tosser stubbed out a cigarette. 'Sloppy search?'

'Not as far as I'm concerned.' Leo pulled a sheet of paper from a folder. 'I've drafted a rough plan. The room, for want of a better term, was a three foot wide windowless strip down the party wall, the entrance hidden by shelving. They had no way of knowing it was there.'

'What about length of walls? There must've been some discrepancy.'

I saw Leo tense. 'Working only by feel, with the disorientation one gets in a smoke-filled room –'

'Yeah, yeah, I know all that. But I have to ask. You can bet your arse there'll be an enquiry.'

'Sir, I interviewed the BA team myself immediately after the discovery and I'm satisfied they conducted the search with their usual diligence. As the photographs show, the rooms held obstacles. No single wall had a clear run.' He glanced across at me. 'It's fortunate I summoned the photographer, and that she's provided us with such an accurate record.'

'Damned shame she moved the shelving,' muttered Tosser. 'Next time, Augusta, touch nothing and call an officer, you hear? Your job is to take photos, nothing more.'

My fists clenched. 'I know my job, sir.'

'Yeah? So how come there's no shots of the false room?'

Leo coughed. 'I'm afraid that's my fault, sir. I instructed her to leave.'

'Leave? What the hell for? If she can't cope she shouldn't be here.' He glared at me across the desk. 'No concessions, Augusta, you understand?'

'I wasn't aware I'd asked for any.'

'Don't!'

He broke into a hacking cough, pulled out a handkerchief. 'So who've the plod put on it?'

'Simon – er, DI Furneaux,' Leo replied. 'He's liaising with myself and Dick Tucker.'

'Good. I want it in competent hands. I will, of course, offer any assistance I can.'

It was all I could do not to smirk. The Brigade policy of promoting from the ranks results in some interesting and improbable appointments. Tosser's was a prime example. He hadn't earned his nickname for nothing.

The phone rang on his desk and he picked it up. 'SDO Enticott.' His eyes travelled across to me. 'Yes, she is. Right. I'll pass the message on.' He replaced the receiver. 'There's a horse trapped in a gully. Dartmoor. Specialist Line Rescue's been called.'

I glanced at my watch.

'Problem?' he asked slyly.

'No, sir.' Already I was on my feet.

'Better get on then. Details with Control.' He turned back to the photographs.

I spun on my heel and let myself out, even managed to close the door quietly. *No concessions!* The prick knew I'd been up most of the night. Well, if he thought I was going to plead tiredness he could think again. I wouldn't give him the satisfaction. If it meant propping my eyes open with matchsticks, I would answer the damned shout.

The sky was a Mediterranean blue as I headed down the A38 towards Plymouth, the windows of my car open, my hair doing a dervish-dance in the breeze. I could feel myself relaxing with the miles until I felt calmer than I'd felt all day. My main concern was that I wouldn't get there in time to catch the action.

I'd been trying to film the Specialist Line Rescue team for several months and it was proving surprisingly diffi-cult. The crew had been formed by a group of firefighters in Plymouth to deal, as the name suggested, with any emergency requiring the use of rope – injured climbers trapped on a cliff face, animals left stranded by rivers in

17

flood. But Devon is a large county, and time and again the rescues were being successfully carried out by local crews long before the Specialists reached the scene. It had made for a certain rivalry and earned for the members the somewhat unfair nickname of Dopes on Ropes. But their intentions were commendable, and dramatic rescues were always good for PR. I was happy to give it another try.

Especially on Dartmoor. I've always loved wild, open spaces and the 365 square miles of mostly untamed upland acts like a magnet. I first visited it as a child with my parents and I've been coming back ever since, in recent years with my camera. It's an artist's paradise, one of England's last great wildernesses, an uncompromising wasteland of stunning light and vast dramatic skies. What better place to unwind.

I was approaching the Drumbridges roundabout. Ahead of me the skyline was dominated by the imposing outcrop of Hay Tor, one of the best-known landmarks on the moor. It's also one of the most visited. The proof was visible even from here in the straggle of well-worn pathways leading to the summit, like the rivers of a delta converging at the sea. I left by the slip road and headed north towards Bovey, branching left at the fire station to begin the long climb on to the moor.

A turning to the left took me to Haytor Vale. Some wilderness! The car parks were heaving, the queues at the ice-cream van twenty yards long. Everywhere people were shouting, laughing, kicking balls, flying kites, picnicking beside their cars. The herding instinct at its most overt. For the umpteenth time I wondered why they came – why, of the millions of annual visitors, so many stay within a hundred yards of their cars. Not that I was complaining. It leaves the rest of the moor exactly as I love it, wild, desolate, bleak – and empty.

Leaving the Hay Tor circus behind, I headed west through some of the most dramatic scenery on the moor. Tors towered above me on either side, Rippon on my left, the aptly named Saddle Tor on my right. Ahead of me loomed Top Tor and Pil. This was the land made famous by Conan Doyle in his story of the ghostly hound and it never failed to thrill. Even the names evoke mystery – Seven Lords Lands, Blackslade Mire, Bonehill Rocks, Hangingstone Hill.

On into Widecombe, destination of Uncle Tom Cobbleigh and all. The place was heaving, cars and people jostling nose to tail. A coach had become jammed in the centre of the village and I was forced to wait behind, locked between milling bands of tourists, their Bermuda shorts bulging over one too many clotted cream teas. The sneaky eyes of a hundred lurid pixies leered at me from ye endless Olde Worlde Gift Shops. But finally I was through, heading into what, for me, was unknown territory.

The narrow lanes were snarled with traffic and I lost count of the times I had to reverse, but after a few miles the number of cars dwindled until it was just an occasional backpacker edging to the side to let me to pass. I drove for another ten minutes before pulling into a gateway and unfolding the OS map across the wheel. If the grid reference I'd been given was correct I knew I should be close, but it's notoriously difficult to give an accurate reading on the moor.

The place I was looking for was an undistinguished spot half a mile from the road in an area known as Yarwell Brake. It was shown amid symbols for bracken and rough grassland, a pencil line of blue trickling between contours that almost touched. Beside it, two words in tiny print – *Mine (disused)*. A track ran towards it at forty-five degrees.

I found the entrance to the track half a mile on, barred a few yards back by a wooden gate. Parked inside was an RSPCA van. I pulled on to the verge behind a shiny new BMW, changed into walking boots, then hauled my equipment from the car and set off.

The track cut through closely cropped grassland for several hundred yards, then veered to the right and began to climb, finally disappearing behind a coppice of silver-trunked birch. Within minutes I was sweating. Despite the altitude the air was heavy with heat. Another quarter mile and I had to slow down. The birch had been replaced by conifers, a small plantation blocking the view to the right. To the left and ahead it was blocked by a hill. In front of me a thirty foot spur of granite jutted into the path, and skirting around it I almost collided with a blue and white sign. *Police – Slow.* Who were they kidding? Twenty yards on I found the fire pump belonging to the local crew.

The pump's door was open, a young fireman leaning against the side enjoying the sun. He looked about sixteen, fresh-faced and freckled, the skin on his nose and temples showing the first signs of burn. When he saw me he jumped, glanced uncertainly at the helmet and jacket thrown inside on the seat.

'Don't blame you,' I said. 'It's scorching.'

He grinned sheepishly.

I told him who I was and asked where I would find the crew. He jerked his thumb towards the plantation. 'They're down there. You can't see it from 'ere. There's like, you know, a gully.'

I looked at where he was pointing but all I could see was bracken, acres of it, stretching in a seemingly unbroken carpet as far as the trees.

'You're too late, though,' he added. 'We got 'im out.'

'Is he okay?'

'Far as I know. They're waiting for the horse box to take 'im away.'

'What happened to Line Rescue?'

The lad gave a snort. 'Beat 'em to it, didn't we. Put in a stop message to turn 'em back. Just shows, you can't beat a local crew when it comes to getting somewhere quick.' He puffed out his chest. 'You come all this way for nothing?'

'Story of my life,' I told him. 'Ah well, I might as well film him being loaded.' I turned away. 'And watch that sun, otherwise the vet'll be treating you, too.'

The lad smiled uncertainly and touched the bridge of his nose.

The bracken was waist-high, criss-crossed by sheep paths. I tried not to think of snakes.

'Watch out,' he called after me. 'It's bloody steep.'

Ten minutes later I saw what he meant. Abruptly the land dropped away, falling steep-sided into a deep ravine, a picture-postcard stream tumbling over rocks at the bottom. Gullies radiated from it on both sides, narrow grassy clefts cut into the hill. The old mine workings. Parked on the far ridge was a National Park Land Rover.

The Park Ranger was in the bottom of a gully, one of a group of men surrounding a small dark pony. With him was Chris Daggett, the RSPCA officer, a man in a check shirt, presumably the vet, and four firemen. I picked my way down, introduced myself to the sub-officer in charge and – polite formality – asked his permission to record the incident.

The sight of the pony brought a lump to my throat. Blood had congealed around a wound on its leg and a red-raw graze scarred its flank. It looked weak, on the verge of collapse, its head sagging almost to the ground. Chris saw my expression and came over.

'He'll be okay, Gus. We've got water and glucose into him. Though I doubt he'd have lasted much longer.'

'How did you find him?'

'Woman reported it.' He jerked his head at the opposite bank. 'She really put herself out.'

It took me a moment to spot her. She was sitting in the shade of a holly bush, camouflaged by her dark clothes. A book lay open across her knees and she appeared to be writing. A second later she looked up. She was about my age but model-thin, with dark hair bobbed at the shoulder. Something about her was vaguely familiar.

'Did she give a name?' I asked Chris.

'Kempe. Mrs Kempe. Why, you know her?'

'I'm not sure . . .'

The woman turned back to her book, then promptly

21

looked up again. Eyes darting between book and stream, she began to make marks. Not writing – sketching.

'Maybe I've seen her at the Art Centre.'

'Could be. I gather she's some sort of artist. That's what she came here for, to sketch. When she saw the pony she walked all the way back, drove to Widecombe and phoned for help – then came back, waited, and drove out in the Land Rover with us so we knew where to look. Not bad, huh? Even got the grid reference near as damn-it spot on.' He grinned. 'Good-looking, too. Could fancy her myself if she wasn't so tall.' He cocked his head. 'Sounds like the horse box arriving.'

I pulled out the camcorder as a tractor and enclosed trailer appeared over the ridge, and in the next half-hour shot some respectable footage as the pony was half-pushed, half-carried out of the gully and up the ramp.

'That's it then,' Chris said, snapping closed the tailgate. 'Off to a local sanctuary. Couple of weeks and he'll be back on the moor, to whatever fate awaits him.' He dusted himself down. 'Better go and thank the lady, see if she wants a lift back.'

The woman saw him coming and climbed to her feet. Heavens, he was right about her height. Chris isn't short but she towered over him by at least two inches.

I frowned: I *did* know her. Not from the Art Centre, longer ago. College?

An image flashed into my mind, of a tall, thin girl, hair hanging to her waist. She'd been in the year above me, came out with first class honours for wild impasto landscapes in sombre hues. A name balanced on the tip of my tongue – Julia? Joanna?

'The officer has my address,' she was telling Chris as I approached. 'No telephone, I'm afraid.'

An educated voice, clipped, slightly tense. The voice I remembered, too, and the finely drawn features, the flawless olive skin, the curious grey-green eyes. She'd been a strange girl, distant and aloof, choosing to shut herself off in her studio space behind a wall of easels and canvases. For a while we'd wondered what she was on, came to the conclusion it was a higher mental plane. And left her alone.

It seemed rude to do the same now. I waited until Chris had finished then wandered up and introduced myself. 'I think we were at college together,' I said. 'You were in painting, right?'

She regarded me suspiciously. 'I was, but –'

'So was I – well, part of the time. I moved between that and photography. I'm sorry but I can't quite remember your name . . .'

'Judith,' she said after a pause.

'Of course. Judith. So, Judith, are you living around here?'

'At – the moment.'

'Really? Whereabouts?'

She seemed reluctant to tell me. 'Swinlake,' she said at last. 'It's a village . . .'

'Oh, I know where Swinlake is,' I grinned. 'I'm there most weekends. My father lives there. Perhaps you know him – Bob Tavender?'

She shook her head. 'I know very few people.'

I could believe it if this was her normal response. Rarely had I encountered anyone so entirely lacking in warmth. I thought the years might have mellowed her but she was displaying the same chilly reserve she had shown at college. I decided to give it one more try.

'So – are you here to paint?'

'Partly.'

'Still doing landscapes, I see.'

'Yes, I . . .' Her eyes locked on my cameras. 'Are you a reporter?'

'What? Oh, heavens, no. I'm with the Brigade – or Devon Fire and Rescue Service, to give it its proper title.'

Her eyes narrowed. 'They employ you to make videos?'

'To record incidents,' I corrected. 'That's part of my job. The rest of the time I run their Media Resources department at HQ.'

'Why? I mean, why record incidents?'

I shrugged. 'Lots of reasons. Training new recruits, public information. A visual record in case things go to court –'

'Court? As in criminal court?'

'If there's an investigation. Why?'

Before she could answer the Park Ranger intervened, asking if she wanted a lift to her car. Judith glanced at her sketchbook, thanked him and shook her head. He turned to me.

'Please!' I said and shouldered my bags. It was a long walk back and my lack of sleep was beginning to tell. 'Well, it was nice seeing you again, Judith,' I lied. 'I'll look out for you next time I'm in Swinlake.'

She inclined her head, but didn't bother to reply.

'You knew her, then,' Chris said after the Ranger dropped us at the gate.

'From college.'

'Was she always that offhand?'

'Pretty much.'

'I wonder why? Still, she cares about animals so she can't be all bad. Not short of a bob, either.' He jerked his chin at the BMW.

'That hers?'

'Or hubby's.' He clicked his tongue. 'I must be in the wrong job.'

'You and me both,' I said, struggling to suppress a yawn.

Chapter Three

The department known as Media Resources sprang from humble origins. It began when a couple of unsuspecting firemen were handed cameras and told to take photographs for use in the training of new recruits. In those days all semi-skilled jobs were handled by uniformed personnel, many of whom were untrained and ill prepared. Skilled jobs, such as radio and telephone communications, were contracted out.

Until, that is, sometime in the eighties when one of the top brass realized skilled civilians could be employed for a fraction of the cost. It led to a grand reshuffle and new departments were formed, staffed by a fresh breed of non-uniformed employees, but always with a uniformed officer at the head (in my case SDO Enticott) to whom they were answerable. U and non-U. Gradually the departments merged, expanded or contracted in line with the changing climate, the growing need for economic awareness and PR. Media Resources is one of those that expanded – which is where I come in.

My official title is Media Resources Co-ordinator, a grandiose way of saying we deal with audio-visual aids. To help me I have three assistants – Liz Cossey, who was drafted in from Fire Safety and does most of the typing, Nick Williams, a good amateur photographer who acts as my back-up and shares the on-call, and a young lad called Ross Thompson, whose main asset is an unbridled enthusiasm for the Brigade. But for poor eyesight Ross would have been a fireman. I know how he feels.

Apart from audio-visuals, we also handle press releases, arrange talks, design and create publicity stands for local festivals and events and, not least, edit *The Beacon*, the monthly Brigade magazine. Not exactly high-powered stuff. But in my capacity as photographer I'm allowed to attend incidents and for that I'll put up with the rest. Without it I wouldn't have lasted three months let alone three years.

I would put up with a whole lot more if they but realized it. My father was a fireman and loved the Brigade with a passion that verged on obsession. It rubbed off on me. I've got photos of myself aged three wearing a helmet twenty sizes too big, going vroom-vroom at the wheel of a pump, and countless similar ones taken over the years – even one showing me strapped to the platform of the extending ladder a hundred feet above the town. My tenth birthday present and I still don't know how Dad wangled it. My mother hit the roof when she found out.

It never occurred to me that I wouldn't one day follow in Dad's footsteps, nor that I was a girl and that all the firemen were men. And Dad to his credit never disabused me, gauging the times, guessing that things were changing and that sooner or later women would be allowed in. They were, but not yours truly. Like Ross, I was prevented by poor sight.

Perhaps we should have anticipated it, my mother being myopic in the extreme, but when I was twelve and my eyesight began to change, the bottom fell out of my world. At first I told no one, just moved nearer and nearer the blackboard at school, but finally I could disguise it no longer and I was forced to wear spectacles, horrid things in plastic frames. In time I progressed to lenses, and now the modern miracle of laser surgery has made even those a thing of the past. But for me the miracle came too late. It was the end of a dream.

For Dad, too. In some ways I think he was more disappointed than me. The Brigade was his life – would be still if he hadn't been invalided out following a fatal RTA

– and he'd looked forward to me carrying on. I couldn't help feeling I'd let him down. But life goes on and eventually I settled for my other love, art. With few regrets. I took to photography like the proverbial duck to water, from the first having an instinctive feel for the camera and what it can do. Though I never imagined when I went to college that it would take me full circle and I would wind up here. Again, it's Dad I have to thank.

'Gus,' he said on the phone one evening, 'there's a job in Devon just crying your name.'

I was in London at the time, still smarting from my break-up with Dougie, my live-in partner of four years. My job was undemanding and tedious, my flat more than I could afford. I was ready for a change of scene. But Devon?

'I'll die of boredom,' I told him.

'Rubbish!' he said. 'There's enough action here even for you.'

He was right. And three years on I'm still here, attending incidents, albeit in an unexpected role.

Though I'd still rather be wielding a hose than a camera. I wonder what Freud would make of that?

The letter arrived on my desk on Friday.

> *Higher Verstone,*
> *Swinlake.*
> *Wednesday.*
>
> *Dear Gus,*
> *Forgive me if I seemed a little distant when we met this afternoon, but it was quite a surprise after all this time. I soon regretted the lost opportunity (to renew our acquaintance) and am writing in the hope that you might call in – perhaps when next visiting your father? I shall be here on Sunday afternoon if that's convenient.*
> *Please try.*
> *Judith*

I stared at it in astonishment. I'm not sure what surprised me most, the fact that she wanted to see me, or that she even remembered my name. Renew what acquaintance? She hadn't remembered me from Adam!

I had no intention of going – even if I'd wanted to, I couldn't spare the time – and it seemed only fair to let her know. I picked up the phone, then realized there was no number. The directory showed no Kempes listed at Swinlake, and I was about to call Directory Enquiries when I remembered her words to Chris. 'No telephone, I'm afraid.'

And too late to reply by letter.

Well, too bad. I'd tried. She would just have to wait for me in vain.

The following morning Dad rang. 'Hi, Gussie,' he said brightly. 'How's my little girl?'

'Grown up, Dad. And you?'

'Fine. Will I be seeing you this weekend?'

Always the same question. 'Not today,' I told him, 'I'm on call. How about tomorrow evening?'

'Oh, Gus – I've got a gig.'

I smiled. Dad plays accordion for a local Morris dance team. He made it sound like he was playing Wembley Stadium. 'Which hot-spot is it this time?'

'Don't be cheeky. The Square in Chagford, then the green at Nattersleigh outside the Ring of Bells. Want to come along?'

I muttered something non-committal. Folk music just isn't my thing. Shame, really, they're a nice bunch of people. A few nerds, but I guess everything has its share.

'Afternoon, then,' I said. 'But it'll probably be late. If I don't get some work done soon, my exhibition in October will be mostly blank walls.'

'Well, don't ruin a shot on my account.'

'I won't. Oh, by the way, I met a neighbour of yours the other day. Judith Kempe?'

'Kempe, Kempe . . .' I could almost hear the cogs turning. 'Don't know anyone by that name. She give an address?'

28

'Somewhere called Higher Verstone.'

'Verstone? Good Lord! That's old Miss Hillas's place. I didn't even know it had been sold.'

Hillas? 'That was Judith's maiden name,' I told him. 'She must be a relation.'

'Must be the niece. Well, I'm damned. So how come you know her?'

I told him about college, the incident with the pony, and how Judith had gone to a lot of trouble to report it.

'That figures,' Dad said. 'Must take after the old lady. She was mad about animals, poor soul.'

'Why poor soul?'

He clicked his tongue. 'You've got a memory like a sieve, girl! Harriet Hillas, died out on the moor. Last, when was it, April? Fell down a quarry, not found for four days, by which time – oh, you remember!'

'The old lady with missing limbs?'

'That's the one. Missing presumed eaten. One foot gone plus most of her right arm, and what was left pretty badly chewed. Fancy you not remembering.'

I did now. It had happened at the time of the flu epidemic, when I'd been almost permanently on call. I hadn't seen my father for nearly a month. 'They claimed it was the Beast of Dartmoor,' I said, recalling the sensationalist headlines, the subsequent spate of new sightings.

'*Beast!*' Dad gave a snort. 'If you ask me it was good old Reynard. It was a hard winter. Food's food.'

I pulled a face.

'Sad though, her going like that. She was quite a character. Had to be to live up there. You say your friend's married? Well, let's hope her husband's with her. Desolate sort of place if you're not used to it. I often wonder how the old lady survived.'

'Did you know her?'

'Only to pass the time of day. She wasn't one for idle chit-chat, liked to keep herself to herself.' His voice lightened. 'So tell me about this pony rescue?'

'I'll tell you tomorrow,' I said. 'After I've seen Judith.'

'You're going up there?'

'I wasn't, but – yeah, maybe I will.'

'Intrigued, huh? Why doesn't that surprise me? Ah well, you can tell me about her, too. Kempe, you say . . . I wonder if she *is* the legatee? Better ask Monty, see if he knows.'

I cast my eyes to the ceiling. And they say *women* are gossips.

No sooner had I hung up than it started, blasting through the walls, the daily intrusive helping of my neighbours' music. I checked my watch – ten thirty. Early for them considering they'd been listening to the same stuff at three that morning. I knew, because they'd made sure I was listening too. I was beginning to know how my mother must have felt when I'd been going through my heavy metal phase, hour after hour of Van Halen hammering from my room.

But never so late. And never this *loud*.

The volume went up a notch. Sex Pistols. Rave from the grave.

Wishing them in there with it, I grabbed my bag and went out. Compared to my flat, Sainsbury's would be like the Celestial City.

It wasn't, but I'd known it worse. I pushed my trolley along the aisles, taking my time choosing salady things, fresh herbs and cheeses, before moving on to frozen foods, where I grabbed half a dozen Linda McCartney specials for when I couldn't be bothered to cook. Not exactly haute cuisine but at least they don't taste like damp cardboard.

At the bread stand I met Etta, Tosser's secretary, arm in arm with her new fiancé. Darryl, she told me proudly, was manager of an electrical store. I already knew, she'd told me before, more times than I cared to count. Darryl grinned and looked me up and down the way a new fiancé shouldn't, while Etta tested loaves with her left hand, bouncing light from a sapphire solitaire.

'You had a late shout,' she said, dropping a floury cob into her trolley. Then, leaning closer, 'They identified that body.'

'Danner Road?'

She nodded. 'Sounds like the police had their eye on him. Some guy called Trevor Collins – least, they're pretty sure that's who it is.'

'Young?'

A shrug.

'Know why they were they watching him?'

'I'll let you know on Monday.'

I smiled. The secretarial intelligence network, known facetiously as SIN, stretched between all three emergency services and operated with remarkable efficiency. For some reason it included me, presumably because I'm a woman, a civilian, and the occasional operator of a PC. I wasn't complaining. There was little the secretaries didn't know, or couldn't find out if they set their minds to it, including proposed departmental changes and the all-important cuts in budget. Most of the information they would willingly pass on – until it was something hush-hush when they closed like clams.

Etta prodded a doughnut. 'Did you see Leo before you left?'

I nodded.

She glanced around for Darryl but he'd wandered off to the lager display. 'He fancies you, you know.'

For a moment I thought she meant Darryl. She must have seen my confused look.

'Leo Wiltshire!' she exclaimed. 'Stands out a mile. Want to watch him, Gus, you know what he's like.' She gave another covert glance. 'Not that I'd mind a night in the broom cupboard with him before finally tying the knot. Something to think about during the long winter nights, eh?'

31

She winked conspiratorially. Theirs promised to be a great marriage.

'No room to lie down,' I told her.

'What? Oh, you!' She hit my arm. 'Anyway, must go. We're off to Budleigh for a bit of skinny-dipping. You got anything planned?'

'A few hours in my dark room.'

'With anyone nice?'

'Only my enlarger.'

'Do I know him?' She gave a snort, looked around to see if Darryl had heard. He was still studying cans. 'What about tonight?'

I gave what I hoped was a canny shrug but Etta wasn't fooled. She bit her lip, gave me a look of pained sympathy.

'You need a fellah,' she said, jerking the trolley and heading off to collect her own.

I snatched a baguette and made for the checkout.

By eight that evening I was beginning to think she was right. I felt irritable, tetchy, hemmed in by four walls. Nothing on the box and the music from next door still blaring like *Apocalypse Now*. If I didn't get out soon I would scream.

But where? A sorry state of affairs when my only option on a Saturday night was to visit my father. My own fault, I suppose. I'm no Julia Roberts but – let's have no false modesty here – I'm not unattractive. I'm slim, go in and out in the right places, and my face is okay apart from my nose, which resembles a ski jump. At five eight I deter the shorties, but what the hell, I prefer tall men. The truth is, since Dougie I haven't been looking, and those that have found me just haven't appealed.

Also I was missing Lisa. The only real friend I'd made since moving to Devon, she was in a similar situation, footloose and fancy-free after a break-up, except she'd been married to hers. For the past couple of years, when her shift work in Control allowed, we'd been taking in concerts, going to plays, hanging around in pubs. Until two months ago when she met John, since when I could count our evenings together on one hand. A tiny part of me was envious.

It's not often I get like this. Normally I'm happy with my own company, needing solitude like most people need air. I have no trouble amusing myself, rarely if ever get bored, and usually have far more things I want to do than hours in which to do them. But just occasionally the loneliness creeps in and I crave companionship. Tonight was one of those occasions.

Cooling off in the shower I considered my options. More photographs? A walk along the canal?

Not wise. Only last week a woman had been raped there while walking her dogs and the guy still hadn't been caught.

A lonely drink in a city centre pub?

I shuddered. I've never been good at sitting around doing nothing and the thought of spending the evening staring at a drink whilst fending off guys on the make made my toes curl. I'd rather stay home with a book.

But not with this noise! It was really beginning to get to me. Even over the shower I could hear it, could feel the vibrations coming up through my bare feet.

I dried quickly, climbed into jeans and a T-shirt and dragged a comb through my dark curls. The steam had turned them to corkscrews. I tossed a coin – heads the Art Centre, tails the Globe, the Brigade hangout, the only two places where I was likely to meet someone I knew. It came down tails.

I'd just reached my front door when the music stopped. Silence. It closed over me like a shroud. I paused, my hand on the latch, hardly daring to breathe. Beneath me a door slammed, rattling the walls, and voices shouted in the street. I ran back to my window and looked down.

There were six of them, four guys and two girls, plus two large dogs sniffing the garbage piled high in their yard. One girl had spiked-up black hair, a battery of silver rings clipped through ears, nose and lip. The other had hair the colour of neat cochineal. Both wore black. Spiky's loose top had slipped from one shoulder to reveal two large tattoos – one a skull, the other the word *Blood* in Gothic script.

She looked up and I automatically drew back. I needn't have bothered. Whatever the glazed eyes were seeing I doubted if it was me. I wondered what she was on. Only last week an ambulance had arrived to cart off yet another OD – a sixteen-year-old, according to SIN, called Michele Graves. The previous month's casualty had been only thirteen.

A few mumbled words from a tall guy with a pock-marked face and the men took off towards the city centre. The women followed. A whistle and the dogs followed too. I sank back against my desk and closed my eyes.

The silence was almost tangible, drifting around me, cushioning me from the world, and I could feel myself unwinding, like hair that has been bound tightly all day and suddenly let fall. The urgency to leave had vanished. Hell, it wasn't companionship I craved but quiet, a stillness I could control.

Suddenly I felt exhausted. I padded to the kitchen, poured a glass of wine and carried it up the narrow stairs to my room. By nine thirty I was in bed, tucked up with the latest Minette Walters, determined to savour this unexpected treat to the full. I must have read all of two pages before falling asleep with an ease I'd almost forgotten. And one thought prominent in my mind. Whatever the difficulties, however great the cost, somehow *I had to sell my flat!*

Chapter Four

Long before I reached it I knew what Higher Verstone would be like – an ancient weathered farmhouse built of huge blocks of granite, with tiny deep-set windows, doors that make you stoop, and a whimsical collection of out-buildings that would send me scrabbling for my camera. I couldn't have been more wrong. What confronted me at the end of a two-mile stony track was a square Victorian house of unbelievable dreariness.

Even on a summer's day it looked depressing. The walls were grey ashlar, the roof of shallow-pitched slate, with chimneys jutting at each end like ears. Only two things broke its symmetry: a bay window to the left of the door and a large ornate conservatory on the far side.

But if the house was dull, the view it commanded was sensational. From its elevated position on the slopes of Ver Tor, it faced south across Wykemans Cleave, a vast tree-lined valley gouged by the river I could hear tumbling far below. Beyond the Cleave, moorland stretched as far as the eye could see, distant tors sticking like jagged teeth above the skyline, their outlines blurred by the shimmering after-noon haze.

A high wall, green with lichen, separated the property from the track. Halfway along was an iron gate. Rust came off on my hand when I pushed it open and climbed the half-dozen steps to the terrace. Clearly little had been done since Miss Hillas's death, and already weeds were pushing up through cracks in the slabs and brambles making inroads from the sides. A rogue buddleia was playing host to a bevy of brown butterflies.

In front of the house, a line of half-barrels and granite troughs held dead plants and thriving weeds – dandelions, herb robert, the ubiquitous willowherb – and in the trough nearest the door, a small black and white cat was warily monitoring my approach.

I stretched out my hand. 'Hello, puss.'

It took off like a bullet from a gun.

'You won't get near Badger,' said a voice, and when I looked up Judith was standing in the doorway, her feet bare, a white cotton shirt tucked into tight blue jeans.

'What happened to his ear?' I asked.

'I've no idea. It was missing when my aunt found him.'

More missing parts? 'Your aunt was Miss Hillas, right?'

Judith frowned.

'It's okay, my father knew her.'

'Oh. Of course.' She stepped back, held open the door.

The hallway was dark and smelt of unlived-in houses. Or maybe it had always smelt like that. The door on the left was open, and sunlight filled the room beyond, a billion dust motes dancing in its beam. The room looked like a film set for a Victorian melodrama. All the trappings were there – the overstuffed furniture, antimacassars, oil lamps adorning lace-covered tables. An over-the-top Gothic mirror bounced our reflections from the opposite wall.

'Hideous, isn't it.' Judith had seen me staring. 'My aunt bought the place furnished and hardly changed a thing. The house didn't interest her. She only bought it for the view.'

'Are all the rooms like this?'

'More or less. It's quite a museum piece.'

I whistled silently. Under the dust, the trappings appeared in mint condition. If Judith had inherited this lot, she was a rich lady indeed.

I followed her along the hall, past a bulbously carved side table flanked by two uncomfortable-looking chairs. The walls were dark, lincrusta up to dado, mottled wallpaper above, and hung with even darker paintings, land-scapes mostly of dramatic mountain scenes in subfusc hues. Judith's early inspiration? She pushed open a door at the far end, letting out a cry as a dark shape shot past our ankles and vanished under the stairs.

'Wretched cats! I'll never get used to them.' She brought her hand to her chest. 'I'm sorry, can I get you a drink?'

I told her something long and cold if she had it. Judith nodded and ushered me through the door. Another time warp, this time a dining room, dominated by an almost life-size portrait above the mantelpiece of a fierce bewhisk-ered gentleman in country garb, a liver and white spaniel lying at his feet.

'Portly Pomp,' Judith murmured.

'I'm sorry?'

'The original owner, Pommeroy Butler, MBE. We always called him Portly Pomp. He terrified me as a child, his eyes follow you.' She waved towards a door to his right. 'The conservatory's through there. Go on in, I'll fetch the drinks.' She turned away. 'Oh, I forgot – Geoffrey's in there.'

So she wasn't alone. Why had I assumed she was?

'Speak to him by all means,' she added, 'but don't touch – *whatever* he tells you.'

I froze. *Touch?* I had assumed Geoffrey was her husband. Belatedly I turned to ask the obvious but Judith had already gone, her footsteps echoing across the hall.

I looked back at the door and felt myself shiver. The room was depressingly dark, the windows facing north on to the rock face from which the plateau had been hewn, their glass obscured by a greenish-black slime. The place was filthy, dust covering every surface, grit and fluff lying in long rolls at the edge of the floor. Spiders had been at work on the ornaments and from the corners of the ceiling cobwebs hung like wispy grey shrouds. Yet Judith's aunt hadn't been dead that long – three months at the most. The room looked as though it hadn't been cleaned for years. I wondered about the state of the kitchen. Thank God I hadn't been invited for lunch!

I jumped as a clock on the mantelpiece chimed the hour. I was beginning to feel like Pip on his way to meet Miss Havisham. Had Judith's aunt also been jilted by a lover, I wondered fancifully? Did that explain her lonely choice of home? Well, as long as she hadn't done him in and kept him, like Norman Bates' mother, beyond the next door.

Corpses don't talk, I told myself crossly. They did to Norman, said a little voice.

For heaven's sake, Tavender . . .

I grabbed the handle and pushed open the door. Heat met me like a wall. So did the smell, a mixture of warm compost, geraniums and cats' pee. In the centre of a brick floor, half a dozen basketwork chairs that had seen better days were grouped around a rattan table. Cats curled in two of them, an enormous fluffy grey and a skinny tabby. Neither of them spoke.

But someone did, in a voice curiously seductive.

'Well, *hel-lo* there.'

Seductive – but not human. I spun around. Staring at me through the brass bars of a cage was a brilliant green parrot.

I laughed out loud. 'Geoffrey?'

He side-stepped along the perch, tilted his head to one side. 'Geoffrey's a flirt.'

'I bet you are. I bet you have them falling at your feet.'

'All fall down.'

He was a charmer, as vivid as bog-grass, with boot-button eyes above a lethal hooked beak. He moved to the side, thrust his cheek against the bars. 'Tickle. Geoffrey won't bite.'

'I'm not sure I believe you, Geoffrey.'

'Don't.' Judith had come in carrying a tray. 'He doesn't bite like he doesn't tell lies, isn't that right, Geoffrey?' Her smile, the first I'd seen, transformed her face. Relaxed, Judith Kempe was beautiful. 'Actually he only bites strangers, and only when in his cage. Loose, he's one big softy.'

'You let him fly around?'

38

'Of course. Believe me, the cats give him a wide berth.' She set the tray on the table. On it were bottles of gin, tonic and Perrier, ice cubes and glasses. She dislodged the grey cat and sat down. 'This was Aunt's favourite room. Mine, too. Freezing in winter, of course.'

But in summer like a furnace. Already I was beginning to feel like a damp rag, sweat starting on my brow and sticking my shirt to my chest. A yard from my ear the parrot shrieked.

I helped myself to a Perrier. 'Mind if we go outside?'

'What? Oh, if you prefer.'

I waited while she sloshed more G than T into a tumbler then followed her out. Beyond the conservatory was a smaller side terrace flanked by a low stone wall, just right for sitting on. The grey cat reached it before us and sprawled languidly in the sun.

'Dimpsy,' Judith said, sitting beside it and stroking the pink fur of its tummy. 'It's the local word for twilight.' The cat crawled on to her lap and placed its paws on her chest.

'How many cats are there?'

'Just four. Five if you count Edward, but he only appears now and again.' She averted her face as it tried to lick her nose. 'When I was young Aunt had quite a menagerie, but as she grew older she became more cautious.'

'Animals make a lot of work,' I agreed.

'It wasn't that. She didn't want to leave them stranded should anything happen to her.'

'Was she expecting to die?'

'As much as anyone does at eighty-two.'

'I mean, she wasn't ill . . .'

'Good God no! Sound as a bell. Would probably have outlived the lot of us if she hadn't been pushed into that quarry.'

The bottle stopped halfway to my lips. 'Pushed? I thought her death was an accident.'

'Oh, it was, according to the inquest. But they didn't have the relevant facts. And at the time neither did I.' She extricated the claws, lowered the cat to her lap. 'Since then – well, certain things have come to light. There's no question it was murder.'

I stared at her blankly. This was something my father hadn't known. Why hadn't we seen it on the news or in the papers?

'I had no idea,' I said, genuinely shocked. 'That's terrible! Are they deliberately keeping it quiet?'

Judith frowned. 'Is who keeping what quiet?'

'The police. Presumably they've reopened the case?'

She gave a snort. '*Police!*'

This time it was me who frowned. 'Are you not happy with the way they're handling it?'

She stared down at the cat, absently stroked the silver-grey fur. 'I haven't told the police.'

'But I thought . . .' I broke off. A distant warning bell had begun to toll.

'They would laugh me out of the station. The things I've discovered would never convince them. All they're interested in is hard evidence, incontrovertible proof. But *I* know it wasn't an accident. My aunt was a very frightened old lady.'

'Frightened?' I looked at her sidelong. 'Of – what exactly?'

She paused. 'I don't know.'

The bell was getting louder. I inched away. Had Judith lost the plot? I thought of the girl I had known at college, her unwillingness or inability to make friends, the self-inflicted isolation. Had that early strangeness been a forerunner of deeper instability?

She turned suddenly and met my eyes. 'Oh, I know what you're thinking. That I'm delusional. That my lift's not reaching the top floor. And that's precisely what the police will think. As far as they're concerned my aunt was a senile old woman who strayed too close to the edge, and if I go in claiming murder they'll see me as a neurotic relative who can't accept the truth.'

I shifted uneasily. 'Not if you have something to back it up.'

'No? You didn't meet the detective! People joke about policemen being thick, but my God! Aunt would have been appalled. To think she was relying on the likes of that!'

'Who was he?' I asked. 'Do you remember his name?'

'How could I forget? A Detective Inspector Edge.'

I tried to suppress a smile.

'You know him?' she demanded.

'By reputation. But they're not all like Edge, Judith. Perhaps if you approached one of the others –'

'Who? Who would you recommend?'

'Me?'

'You know them! Who should I approach?'

'Hey, I only know them through work –'

'Exactly. On a professional level.'

I almost laughed. 'I'd hardly call an occasional half in the Globe, and a formal good morning when they happen to come to HQ, a professional working relationship.' Her brow furrowed. 'I don't work for the police, Judith, I work for Devon Fire and Rescue. I have no more influence with the plod than – well, your aunt's cat.'

'But what about court?'

'Court?'

'Criminal court. The photographic evidence, the investigations.'

Oh, God. Suddenly I understood. My invitation had nothing to do with college or renewing acquaintance. It was simply that Judith needed help and she thought she'd found the answer in me. My appearance on the moor must have seemed like a gift from the gods.

'I think you've put two and two together and made five,' I told her. 'I don't go to court: my photographs do. All I provide is a visual record. Occasionally – and I mean occasionally – I meet members of the force, but that doesn't mean I have any clout. And I'm certainly not involved in investigations.'

Her eyes narrowed. 'Not at all?'

'Not at all.'

'I see.' She let out a sigh. 'So much for making assumptions.'

'I'm sorry.' Why was I apologizing? 'Look, if there's anything else I can do . . .'

She started to shake her head. 'Actually, there might be. I wonder . . . Those things I mentioned, the things that have convinced me. Would you look at them? It wouldn't take long and –'

'How would that help?'

'You're not involved, you could give an unbiased opinion. See if you think I'm justified.'

'And if I don't?'

She shrugged the question away. 'I really would appreciate it. To be frank, there is no one else I can ask.'

'What about your husband?' I assumed she was still married.

'Stuart?' Judith gave a laugh. 'He liked my aunt about as much as she liked him. If I told him someone had pushed her into the quarry he'd probably say, "Great, bully for them."'

'Then perhaps he did it.' *Careful, Tavender . . .*

'Oh, he's probably capable,' Judith replied matter-of-factly, 'but he was miles away, in London. The gallery won't *run* without Stuart Kempe.' She picked up the cat, placed it gently on the ground. 'But someone did, and I want to know who. So would you?'

'Now?'

'Aunt always said, there's no time like the present.'

Chapter Five

We returned the way we had come, passing from the inquisitive stare of the parrot to the dour gaze of Portly Pomp. Crossing the hall, Judith said, 'I suppose I should tell you that all this is now mine. Aunt Harry left me everything. Well, apart from a few small legacies but nothing of any account. I imagine that makes me prime suspect – is that the correct term? Though I'd hardly be crying murder if I'd committed it.'

She led me through a baize-covered door at the rear of the stairs and into a stone-flagged passage. Beyond was the kitchen and I knew at once this was where Miss Hillas had spent most of her time. Unlike the other rooms it was cosy and welcoming, fashionable in its outmodedness. In the fireplace was an Aga, that modern icon of genteel country living, but this one wasn't for show. It was old, functional, its cream enamel chipped, and blackened by smoke above the firebox door. A stone sink under the window was flanked by wooden draining boards, above which hung plate racks in faded Gustavian blue. In the centre of the room a large table was surrounded by an assortment of Windsor chairs, and littered at one end with the detritus of an old lady's life – RSPB magazines, cookery books, biscuit tins, jars of biros, an open basket of sewing things. I was aware of more dust but only the accumulation that comes from day-to-day living, a tidiness barely kept under control. Judith's aunt had battled with housework in the only room that mattered and won, but it had been a close thing.

For the first time I was getting a sense of the woman who had lived here. The rocking chair in front of the Aga, the overstuffed sofa with its patchwork quilt, the delicate watercolours of the moor. On one of the dressers a colourful collection of china hens, cockerels and geese strutted, pecked and sat on nests of eggs that would never hatch, and for some reason the sight of them saddened me. I regretted not meeting the woman to whom they belonged.

Judith leaned across the table and began rifling a pile of papers.

'These legacies . . .' I said. 'How much is nothing of any account?'

'Five thousand each to a couple of local charities, fifteen thousand to June Weblake at the farm. She's been looking after the cats since my aunt's death.'

'A generous reward for looking after cats.'

She shot me a disparaging look. 'That's not why Aunt bequeathed it! She'd known June for more than twenty years. She was extremely fond of her.'

I made a mental note not to be flippant. 'Is that the farm at the end of the track? The one with the scrap cars?'

'I'm afraid so. Aunt called it Cold Comfort. The cars belong to June's son. Gary,' she added scornfully.

'You don't like him?'

'He takes after his father.'

I let that pass. 'And is the money to be paid after the sale of the house?'

'Not necessarily.' She pulled a paper from the stack. 'My aunt had other investments.'

So – the estate was a large one. Even so, hardly amounts worth killing for. I said as much to Judith.

She shrugged. 'I suppose it depends how desperate you are.'

'Meaning you suspect June?'

'Good God no! She's the least of my worries. It's this lot that concerns me.' She shoved the paper towards me. 'Ever heard of the Chadwickes? At the so-called Sacred Oak Institute?'

44

The name rang a bell. 'Are they the people who bought Wickleigh Manor?'

'That's them. And promptly changed the name to Sylvanus Lodge. Can you imagine? A name that's been in existence for four hundred years, wiped away at a stroke. Aunt Harry was furious, told them so in no uncertain terms. She tried to stop it but – well, by then it was too late.'

'So what's the problem?'

'Read it.'

The paper contained a few lines written in blue ink and began with an unfinished sentence: *Should Judith not inherit . . .*

Beneath was a list of what I assumed were the beneficiaries, the amounts of the legacies detailed alongside. But the figures were higher than the ones Judith had quoted.

Dartmoor Preservation Society – £15,000

Dartmoor Wildlife Protection – £15,000

June Weblake – £50,000

I looked up. 'Fifty thousand?'

'Exactly. More than triple. Does that make it an amount worth killing for?'

She had a point. When does murder became a viable proposition?

'I thought you trusted June.'

'I don't trust her family. But this isn't about them. Read the last part.'

And what of the remainder? Who deserves or would appreciate Verstone? Alas, I can think of only one.

There was an inch gap, then: *Sacred Oak Inst.*

'You see?' Judith said angrily. 'A draft will. Leaving everything to those charlatans.'

I shrugged. 'Your aunt must have approved of whatever it is they do there.'

'*Approved?*' Her eyes flashed. 'She despised them – loathed everything they stood for. She wouldn't give them the time of day, let alone everything she held dear. The very last time I spoke to her she mentioned them, two days

45

before she died. Referred to them as "those dreadful people at the Manor". Is that the way to describe someone to whom you're considering leaving your estate?'

'You were here before she died?'

'No, no, she telephoned. From the village. She did from time to time. I remember . . .' She broke off, wiped her hand across her cheek. 'Her voice sounded shaky and I asked if she was ill. She assured me she was fine. And like a fool I believed her.' She gripped the back of a chair. 'Next thing I know the police are at my door, telling me there's been an accident. Some accident!'

'So what are you suggesting – that the Chadwickes were forcing her hand in some way?'

'I'm not sure. Something. Hell, I don't know!' She moved around, slumped into the chair.

'So what exactly *do* they do up there?'

'Hm? Oh, run residential courses. They claim to be a study centre – for Spiritual and Ecological Awareness or some such grandiose title. You know the sort of thing – pay us a monumental fee and we'll put you in touch with your innermost resources whilst saving those of the planet.'

I smiled. 'And your aunt wasn't into that sort of thing?'

'Not the way they offer it. Oh, I don't mean she wasn't "ecologically aware" for want of a better term, but she considered it an attitude, a way of life, not something you spend a small fortune to learn about on a seven-day course. She claimed there was only one thing the Chadwickes are aware of and that's this.' She rubbed her thumb against her fingers.

'I seem to remember my father saying much the same thing,' I told her, 'though he was less polite.' Money-grabbers and intellectual wankers, if I remembered correctly. 'Have you ever met them?'

'Once, when Aunt and I were out walking. Alden and Zara – apt names, don't you think? She's American. That's where they were before moving here, West Coast needless to say. Alden does most of the talking, though it's mostly pretentious waffle. Etherealspeak, Aunt called it. She

46

claimed they were so high on spiritual enlightenment their feet barely touch the ground.'

'Handy for the bogs,' I quipped. 'I take it you weren't convinced?'

'Neither of us were, though I can see how they persuade the gullible. People like that always have a strong following. I suppose they pander to a need. People want to believe there's some good in this shitty little world, some meaning to all the cruelty and madness.' She sighed. 'It's a pity they don't put their energies into making it a better place.'

'They probably think they are.'

'By filling the coffers of the Chadwickes?' She gave a grim laugh. 'Anyway, you can see why that was a shock. The idea of leaving everything to them!'

I frowned. 'Assuming that *was* her intention. To be honest, I'm not convinced.'

'You don't think it's a will? What *else* is it? *Should Judith not inherit . . .*'

'Oh, clearly the first part is, but look how she's written *Sacred Oak*. It's larger, at an angle, like it was scribbled in a hurry.'

'So?'

'So maybe it was written at a different time. Suppose your aunt wrote the first part and left it lying on the desk. Later, needing to jot something down, she grabs the nearest thing to hand. If she'd written *See bank manager* or *Pay milkman*, you wouldn't have given it another thought. Instead she wrote *Sacred Oak* and threw you into a panic.'

Judith snatched it from my hand. 'Why would she need to write *anything* about Sacred Oak?'

'I don't know.'

'And who's the "one" if it's not them?'

'Another relative?'

'There *are* no other relatives.' She was becoming impatient. 'My parents are dead and I was an only child. My aunt had a brother but he died, as they say, without issue. We're not exactly a prolific family.'

I sighed. 'Well, I still think you're reading too much into it. It's too ambiguous. You asked for my opinion and frankly, if this is all you're basing it on –'

'Of course it's not! My aunt left diaries.' She jumped to her feet. 'They're in the bedroom. I'll fetch them. Then you'll see why I'm worried.'

I glared after her. So why hadn't she shown me those in the first place?

Irritated, I stood up and crossed to a roll-top desk. Above it hung two watercolours showing views of distant tors. They were exquisite, the brushstrokes fluid and economical, the use of colour restrained with none of the muddiness common in amateur daubs. I looked down at the signature – *Harriet Hillas*. So her aunt had been a painter, too.

Next to the desk was a large bookcase, the contents much as I would have expected. Numerous books on Dartmoor, the West Country and natural history. Fiction filled the upper shelves, classics mostly with a few lighter novels thrown in – Conan Doyle, Dorothy L. Sayers, Ngaio Marsh. No paperbacks. The lower shelves were more varied, with tomes on gardening, psychology, mythology, the arts; an ancient Mrs Beeton. And then I saw them, the books from her childhood. The illustrators' names leapt out at me – Rackham, Wain, Greenaway, Dulac. Legends from a golden age. When Judith returned I was sitting cross-legged on the floor, poring over magnificent chromolithos of Wain's anthropomorphic cats.

'I see you've found Aunt's books,' Judith smiled. 'Wonderful, aren't they.'

I nodded wistfully and reluctantly replaced it on the shelf.

She had brought two diaries, last year's and this. She handed me the former. The relevant entries were marked with small scraps of paper, the earliest 10th October: *June visited me today in a dreadful state. That poor woman. She's worried about Gary (again) but won't say why, though I sense*

48

it's something serious. I pray it's not the same thing that is worrying me.

'Thing?' I asked, but Judith shrugged.

I turned to the next marker. Two days later, the 12th: *My apprehension is mounting. I'm sure I'm right. But what to do? Who can I tell? Who will believe me?*

And on 13th November: *No more doubt, I overheard them talking. Should I tell Judith? Perhaps if I watch, try to establish a pattern . . .*

A month later, 17th December: *That wretched man! I met him on the moor today and confronted him. The callous brute laughed. He claims I have no proof, which is sadly true, and claims I won't find any. But he's wrong. I shall find it if it kills me.*

'Proof of what?' I asked.

'She doesn't say.'

'And the callous brute?'

Judith hesitated. 'It could be Tom Weblake, June's husband. I've heard Aunt refer to him as a brute. But I can't be sure.' She handed me the second. 'It continues in here.'

The first marker was 5th February: *A and Z, same place. A coincidence?* And four days later: *They were there again, confirming my suspicions. It can't be allowed to go on. But how to stop it? I'm tempted to call Judith but am loath to worry her. She already has too much on her plate. I'm not even sure she would believe me, might view it as the befuddled ramblings of a senile old woman. The police certainly would. Ah, the unfairness of it! Age is indeed a burden.*

Quickly I turned the pages, aware of my own misgivings, to 15th March: *Sound travels a long way on the moor. I almost wish it didn't. Things are even worse than I imagined. What kind of world are we living in? There is evil everywhere, even out here. My only consolation is that my time here is almost spent, though I am not yet ready to shed this mortal coil. There is too much still to do. I must find a way of stopping it or I fear I shall not rest easily.*

I turned to the last entry – and caught my breath. The words were barely legible. There were just three sentences, stark in their simplicity. *Have horrible feeling he saw me. I can't stop shaking.*

I am so afraid.

Judith said quietly, 'And the following day she was dead.'

I perched on the corner of the table and read through the entries a second time. I'd never previously given much thought to old age. It was simply a stage one reached, too far in the future to concern me personally. Yet what must it be like to know you are of sound mind, but to know with equal certainty that your fears will be dismissed and ridiculed merely because you have lived longer than those around you? The knowledge that your sight and hearing are less sharp than they once were, your memory less reliable, your body not working as efficiently, must be nothing compared to the indignity and humiliation of being dismissed as a fool. It gave new insight and meaning to the term second childhood. Children, like the old, are rarely listened to.

'Old ladies shouldn't live in fear,' I said.

'No.' She took the book from my hand and closed it. Then, as if reading my thoughts, 'I know how this looks, but my aunt wasn't senile. Mercifully. It was her greatest fear, the one thing she dreaded about getting old.'

But was that a reason to dismiss it? It was true the entries had been clearly written, by an old lady all too aware how such revelations would be judged. Except there *were* no revelations, not really, no mention of the whos and whys. Was that in itself suspicious?

I didn't envy Judith. As far as I could see, she was in a cleft stick. Accept her aunt had suffered from the senility she dreaded, or believe she had discovered something that ultimately led to her death. I wasn't sure which way to lean myself. How much worse if I had known and loved her.

'What made you think it was Tom Weblake?' I asked.

Judith sighed. 'The use of the word brute.' She pulled out a chair, indicated for me to do the same. 'He's an awful man, vulgar, disgusting. Drinks like a fish. And when he's drunk he gets violent.'

'With June?'

'Aunt thought so. Often there were bruises. Not that June would admit it, of course. There was always some plausible story – she walked into some farm machinery, tripped over a rug. But I gather that's quite common.'

I nodded. 'Might that be what she confronted him about?'

'It occurred to me. It would certainly explain why he laughed. If June denied the abuse and refused to press charges, there would have been little Aunt Harry could do.'

'And you say the son takes after him?'

'Unfortunately. I haven't seen him for years – well, not to speak to – but he was always a troublemaker. At school it was bullying and petty thieving; later street-fighting and stolen cars. Last year he was in court for beating up a student. Gary claimed he was provoked and his friends backed him up. He got away with a suspended sentence.'

'Sounds like a great guy. Is it possible he was knocking his mother around, too?'

Judith stared at me aghast.

'It wouldn't be the first time,' I said. Nor, sadly, the last. I'd seen too many cases of domestic violence during my time with the Brigade not to give it credence. But there was another possibility that was bothering me, a different kind of violation. Too often domestic violence and sexual abuse went hand in hand. 'Are there any other children?'

'A daughter, Lorna, a few years younger. She must be about sixteen. But she's nothing like her brother. It's a true case of like mother like daughter; like father like son.'

I kept my darker thoughts to myself. 'Is there any connection between them and the Chadwickes?'

'Gary. He works part-time at the Institute. Odd jobs, mostly, he's reputedly good with his hands. He worked here once – a long time ago, before he left school. Aunt didn't really need him, but she thought if he had money of his own he might be less inclined to steal. Alas, it wasn't

51

the case. Things kept disappearing – money from her purse, a portable radio – until eventually she was forced to speak to June. All hell let loose and Gary stopped coming, but . . . Oh, I can't believe it. Not his own mother!'

'Your aunt did mention June was worried about him.'

'She also mentioned Alden and Zara, and how do they fit in?'

'She only mentioned initials.'

'They're hardly common ones.' She rubbed her hands on her thighs. 'God, why wasn't she more specific!'

'What I don't understand is why she didn't tell *you*,' I said. 'What did she mean about you having too much on your plate?'

For the first time Judith looked uncomfortable. 'We were very busy. At work. Stuart and I own an art gallery, Kempe Hillas Fine Art. Not Cork Street exactly, but fairly success-ful. At the time . . . well, to say things were hectic is an understatement, which is why I've only just come down. It's the first chance I've had since the funeral. Stuart couldn't even get away for that.'

From what she'd told me, I doubted if he wanted to.

Judith stood suddenly and reached across the table. 'One last thing. They might not be relevant but . . . well, it's more your line than mine.' She extracted a black envelope from the heap of papers and I recognized the logo of a local film-processing firm. She tipped out the photographs and fanned them across the table.

I leaned forward. Each showed a nondescript stretch of moorland with neither landmark nor focal point to draw the eye. A couple had interesting skies but I sensed more by accident than design. So too with the people. Distant specks of colour suggested walkers but they were too far in the distance to be relevant. They appeared as incidental as the skies.

'Well?' Judith asked.

'They wouldn't win prizes for artistic merit.'

'Exactly. So why did my aunt take them?'

I smiled. 'Not everyone knows what makes a good picture.'

'Aunt Harry did. Have you seen her paintings?' She waved her hand at the walls. 'She had a natural gift for composition. If she'd wanted to photograph landscapes, she would have done it a damn sight better than this.'

'So what are you saying, exactly?'

'That maybe she had a different reason for taking them. Look.' One by one she turned them over. Each had something written in the top right corner. 'Grid references and dates, presumably when each shot was taken. All between January and March. Odd, don't you think?'

'But there's nothing in them. They're just boring bits of moor.'

'Precisely my point.' She swivelled her head, squinted. 'Unless there's something I'm missing.'

'If there is I'm missing it too.' I sat back. 'I wouldn't lose sleep over them, Judith.'

'No? What about the diaries? Would you lose sleep over those?'

'They – would worry me most,' I conceded.

'Thank you. That's all I wanted to hear.' She began collecting up the prints.

I glanced at my watch. 'Look, I really must go. My father will have given me up for lost.'

'Of course. And thank you.' She slipped the photos in the envelope. 'Just one last favour. Would you take these with you?'

'Whatever for?'

'You're a photographer. You might see something I missed.'

'There's nothing *to* see . . .'

'Please?'

Unable to think of a good reason for refusing, I surrendered and slid them in my bag. 'Better leave you my number,' I said, and jotted it down.

Judith came with me to the car. The sun had moved

round to the west, making silhouettes of the tors and plunging the gorge in shadow. It was hauntingly beautiful.

'What will happen to the house?' I asked, flapping the car door. The interior was like an oven.

'I'm not sure.' She was staring out across the Cleave. 'I love Verstone, always have – had hoped one day to live here. But now . . .'

'Your husband wouldn't want to?'

Her laugh carried no humour. 'If you knew Stuart you wouldn't ask. To him the countryside is an irritation one has to cross in order to get from one town to the next. He's only ever spent one night here, shortly after we were married. He and Aunt – well, let's say it wasn't a meeting of like minds. Since then I've always come alone.' She glanced back. 'We do have other things in common – art, music. I enjoy the city too.'

I smiled. 'So how long will you be staying?'

'As long as it takes, I suppose. To learn the truth, finish what she started. I want my aunt to rest easily.'

'Well, be careful.'

'Oh, I intend to be.'

She stood watching me as I pulled away. Why had I told her that? Did I really believe there was a murderer on the loose?

I prayed not for her sake. She was far too vulnerable. A lone woman in a lonely house, three miles from the village, without a phone.

Chapter Six

The two miles of track were a sobering reminder of Judith's isolation. There was no sign of human habitation until sunlight glinting on metal warned me I was approaching the farm. Curious to see the Weblake homestead, I pulled in opposite the entrance and cut the engine.

It wasn't an impressive sight. The gateway, despite the dry weather, was a deeply rutted sludge of mud and dung – the gate, long since parted from its hinges, lying in the hedge, barely visible beneath nettles and goosegrass. The cars, some little more than rusted shells, began just inside the entrance and continued on both sides of the drive – if you could call such a mudsplat a drive – as far as the house. More lay in an adjacent field. The ground between was littered with spare wheels, mangled body parts, and enough loose tyres to stock an entire chain of Kwik-Fits.

Beyond it was the farmhouse, a bleak edifice of grey rendered walls broken only by a rogue spray of ivy at the far end. It was as drab and decrepit as its surroundings. The roof had lost several slates and part of the ridge, and must leak like a sieve during the violent Dartmoor storms. It was a rural slum within the bounds of the National Park and it reeked of poverty.

But farmers are a shrewd breed, putting every penny under the microscope to ensure the pounds look after themselves, and I knew better than to assume penury. The shabbiness was more likely to be caused by laziness than a shortage of cash. It was easy to understand why Miss Hillas had felt sorry for June.

I was about to pull away when a door opened in a ramshackle barn. The man who came out was fiftyish, unkempt, stocky. Tom Weblake? Somewhere inside a dog whined. He yelled at it to shut up and slammed the door, then turned towards the wall and began to pee. Quickly I started the engine and pulled away.

I was still thinking about the Weblakes as I approached the junction and to this day I don't know how I missed the car. Or rather, how it missed me. It appeared from nowhere, squealing around the corner, throwing a cloud of dust in its wake. I jerked the steering wheel and swerved to the left, clunking over stone and grit before grinding to a halt on the verge. The car didn't even slow. Red Porsche, I registered, male driver, then listened with mounting anger as it roared off up the track.

'Maniac!' I screamed through the window. '*D'you think you own the bloody road?*'

My heart was pumping adrenaline – I hate fuckwits who drive like that. I've spent too much time at incidents recording the aftermath. And why the damned hurry? Where the hell was he going that he needed to be in such a rush? I doubted he was a walker and he hadn't turned in at the farm. The only other property on the track was Judith's.

Stuart? It wasn't impossible. He sounded like the type who might drive a Porsche. In which case, I'd made a timely exit. The last person I wanted to meet was an artyfarty Porsche driver getting his feet dirty visiting the space between towns.

The dust was finally settling, most of it on my windscreen. I hit the washer, smiling nastily as the wipers churned it to mud. With luck he'd crack his sump on the way up.

Okay, I admit it – I don't like Porsches. Especially not red ones. It was a red Porsche that invalided my father out of the Brigade. Ridiculous, I know – cars don't kill, their owners do. But the association lingers, fuelling an unjust dislike of both car and anyone behind the wheel.

The driver responsible for my father's injury was a guy in his thirties. Stoned out of his brain, he hit the central reservation of the M5 doing close on the ton, causing a twenty-car pile-up with five dead. He was still alive when the fire crew reached him, trapped in the wreckage, and while waiting for him to be cut out my father crawled in to offer comfort and check his wounds. Dad gashed his hand in the process though at the time he barely noticed. It was something he had cause to remember later. The driver's injuries were severe and he died before reaching the hospital. But by then his legacy was secure. He'd left a sword of Damocles hanging over my father's head, the blade inscribed HIV+.

It was nearly five when I drove past the church and entered the village. My father's house is the last but one on the far side, a wisteria-draped turn-of-the-century cottage – prettyish, provided you don't compare it with the other houses in Swinlake. This is arm and a leg country, where the council tax alone is as much as some people's rent and most households have at least two cars, one of them a Range Rover. They need it to tow the horsebox.

Dad bought Tynings with his insurance money. At first I thought it a dreadful mistake. As long as I'd known him he'd been a townie, enjoying all that city life has to offer, not least the camaraderie of his mates at the local pub. Yet suddenly he was casting all aside and opting for the rustic idyll, in a community of the rich and successful where wealth is the only thing that gets you in. I was convinced it would be a disaster. And so it might have been, had it not been for his next-door neighbour.

A widower like himself, Monty Beal is a retired school-master with a passionate interest in gardening. To my astonishment he's passed it on to Dad. My father, who until he bought Tynings had done little more than mow his few square yards of lawn, had within a month begun creating a Garden of Eden in the acre of land around the house, and now can be heard discussing moss roses and hybrid teas whilst poring over the latest catalogue from Thompson and Morgan. Life is indeed curious.

It was in Eden that I expected to find him but only Hewitt came bounding to meet me, barking and tail-thumping a welcome. I found Dad in the kitchen, struggling to squeeze an orange with his left hand. His right was swathed in a clumsily wound bandage.

'Now don't start fussing,' he said, before I had a chance to speak. 'It's a cut, nothing serious.'

'You look like you've lost half your hand!' I dropped my bag on the table. 'How did you do it?'

'Letterboxing.' He clicked his tongue. 'Some idiot had smashed a bottle and chucked it in the hole. Don't worry, I cleared everything up!' He reached for another orange.

'Here, give me that . . .' I snatched it from his hand.

Dad stepped back, leaned against the dresser. He's a tall man, a little over six foot, but carries the height well. Slimmer now than he used to be, the once-dark curly hair mostly grey. But at least it covers his head – no bald spots for Dad. I once heard him joking that he could still 'pull the birds' should he be so inclined, and though it's difficult to be objective about one's parent, I've a sneaky suspicion he's right.

'So what's this about you finding a body?' he said as I handed him the juice.

'My, the jungle drums *have* been busy.'

He didn't smile. 'First one, wasn't it? Well, no use pretending you get used to it.' He glowered. 'Sometimes I wish I'd never recommended that job.'

'And miss out on all the grisly details?'

'It's not funny, Gus. It's a rough place, Danner Road.'

'You'd know, of course.'

'I have my sources.' He sipped the juice. 'Do they know who it was?'

'Unconfirmed, some guy called Trevor Collins.'

'So how come you found him?'

I told him he could continue the inquisition in the garden, and led the way outside.

We sat under the rustic pergola, built the previous spring to catch the evening sun. Already it was draped in clematis, the delicate blue flowers hanging like tiny lanterns above our heads. As always Dad wanted every detail – the layout of the house, contents of the rooms – and listened without interruption as I filled him in. His eyes were fixed on a clump of lupins though I knew he wasn't seeing them. He was right there in the house with me, tapping around the walls, making his way through the smoke-clogged rooms. Vicarious firefighting. He missed his work more than he would say.

The subject finally exhausted, we moved to the pony incident – which in turn led to Judith.

'So is she the niece?' he asked.

'Niece, sole surviving relative and main beneficiary.'

He whistled softly. 'What's she like?'

'You mean apart from being stunning?'

'So looks and money, too. Well, well. Sounds like a lucky girl.'

Right now, I wasn't so sure. 'Dad,' I said, 'what do you remember about Miss Hillas?'

'What, character you mean?' He puffed out his cheeks. 'I'd say she was strong, independent, outspoken. Could be abrupt – I don't imagine she suffered fools gladly. She was passionate about the moor, I know that.' He chuckled. 'And could she walk! I'd like to think *I'd* be as fit at that age. . .' He broke off sharply, realizing what he'd said. 'You know what I mean,' he shrugged.

I know, Dad. 'Did she change much before she died?'

'In what way?'

'I mean, she wasn't senile . . .'

'*Miss Hillas?* Good God, no. Sharp as a razor. Why, her niece say she was?'

'Just the opposite.'

'So why ask?'

'It's just . . .' Hell, where did I begin? 'Judith's got it into her head her aunt's death wasn't an accident. She seems to think she was murdered.'

Dad's mouth opened and closed. 'What on earth makes her think that?'

I told him about the things she'd shown me, this time saving the diaries until last. He winced when I mentioned the final entry.

'And the day after she was at the bottom of a cliff?'

I nodded. 'Does that sound like dementia to you?'

He pulled a face but didn't commit himself.

I snapped a leaf from the clematis, began tearing it with my fingers. 'How long before her death did you last see her?'

'Not long – three or four days? Met her out near Scorhill.' He paused. 'Come to think of it, that was a bit weird. Maybe she wasn't talking about the sheep.'

'Sheep?'

'Hang on, let me think . . .' His brow was a concertina of lines. 'I'd taken Hewitt for a walk, out near the circle. It was a bitterly cold day. I came over the hill and there's Miss Hillas, sitting on a rock. Didn't recognize her at first, not till I got closer. When I did I called out, told her she'd get a chill sitting still like that. No response. I thought, my God, she's had a heart attack, but before I could get to her she turns around. "Do you believe in evil, Mr Tavender?" she says. Well, I ask you! How do you reply to a question like that?'

'How did you?' I asked, as something tingled at the back of my neck.

'Mumbled something about watching the news, I expect, though I'm not convinced she heard me. "It's everywhere," she said, "even on the moor." I couldn't think what she was talking about until I saw the sheep. It was Hewitt who found it, I had to virtually drag him off. The thing had been savaged. Its throat was ripped out, blood and wool everywhere. Anyway, knowing how she felt about animals I assumed she meant that. Maybe she didn't.' He ran a hand through his hair. 'I thought at the time it was an odd word to use. Nature's cruel, I know, but you'd hardly call

it evil. To me that suggests something calculated, malicious
– the work of two legs rather than four.'

'Any two legs in particular?'

'Heavens, no – at least, none that would take it to those
lengths. There were some whose fur she ruffled but –'

'About what?'

'The moor, mostly. As I said, she was passionate. Wanted
it left wild, not ploughed up and reclaimed, which didn't
always endear her to the locals. But I don't think she got
in anyone's way. More a case of making her feelings
known and a bit of campaigning with the DPS. The Dartmoor Preservation Society,' he added, when I frowned.
'The ones you say she left money to.'

'Do you know Tom Weblake?' I asked.

'I know of him. Why? Is that who Judith suspects?'

I rolled my hand. 'Miss Hillas thought there was violence at home.'

'I didn't know it was that bad, though I'd heard he's a
nasty bit of work.' He grimaced. 'Even so, it's one hell of
a step from that to killing an old lady.'

We sank into silence, both absorbed in our thoughts.
I scattered the remains of the leaf and started on a new
one, staring towards the horizon, shielding my eyes as the
sun emerged from beneath a branch. In a neighbouring
field a horse whinnied. It was a perfect summer evening,
in a perfect corner of England – difficult to imagine anything sinister taking place nearby. In fact, the more
I thought about it, the more bizarre it all seemed. Miss
Hillas might not have been senile but she had been old, her
faculties not what they were. A freezing day, a patch of ice
. . . Even if she *had* discovered some nefarious practice,
there was no reason to suppose it led to her death.

Dad cut across my thoughts. 'Has Judith shown the
diaries to the police?'

'No, she thinks they'll laugh at her.'

'Could well be right. So what's she going to do?'

'Make enquiries herself, I think. Try to learn the truth.'

Dad frowned, rubbing his chin. 'You do know this isn't

61

your problem, Gus?' I nodded. 'Then be sensible, don't get involved. It might sound harsh, but you've a lot on your plate right now.'

Where had I heard that before?

He glanced at his watch and I suddenly remembered the gig. 'What time are you leaving?' I asked, picking up the glasses.

He held up his bandaged hand. 'Can't play like this, can I?'

'Oh, Dad . . .' Judith's problems had pushed it from my mind. 'Have they found someone else?'

He whistled silently, looked towards the heavens. I knew that look of old.

'No way!' I cried, leaping to my feet.

'Gussie –'

'No, Dad, I am *not* standing in! Have you any idea how long it is since I played?'

'Just for tonight. What harm can it do?'

'What, other than make me look a complete berk in public?'

'Don't underestimate yourself. I wouldn't ask if they could get anyone else.'

'What about Keith?'

'In Portugal with his family. And Barry's on the Norfolk Broads. Believe me, I've tried everyone. If you don't play they'll have to cancel.'

I turned away, counted to ten.

'Just this once, Gus . . .'

'You said that last time, when I got lumbered with the Christmas ceilidh. Which now I think of it *is* the last time I played!'

'Crying shame!' he muttered. 'You could knock spots off half the guys on the circuit.'

'Yeah, well right now I could knock spots off you!' I glanced down at my shorts.

'You don't need to worry about clothes, Mike's bringing a spare kit. He's about your size so –'

'Oh, I see, fait accompli! Christ, Dad . . .'

'Well, I knew you wouldn't let them down.' He sneaked another look at his watch. 'Though if I were you I would do some practice.'

I stormed into the kitchen, snatched up Dad's accordion and ran through a few tunes. My fingers felt like sausages. Even simple four-fours defeated me, acquiring time signatures that would have defeated Dave Brubeck. 'Bit rusty,' Dad muttered as he wandered past.

Of course I'm bloody rusty, I wanted to yell. I haven't played since December!

It's not laziness that stops me practising. I just don't like the accordion. I play, quite simply, because Dad plays, having picked it up as a child, through watching, listening and having a go. My greatest regret is that he hadn't played sax.

I was making a pig's ear out of 'Shepherd's Hey' when Mike Taylor arrived, armed with the kit – white shirt, black britches, baldrics in purple and yellow and – God help me – a red and white spotted hanky to knot around my neck.

'Think she'll be all right?' I heard him ask as I went up to change.

'Fine!' Dad said. 'Playing comes second nature.'

Oh really?

The first set was a disaster. I fluffed the opening number, skipped ten bars in the second, and played the third so slowly the guys could have nipped off for a pint between leaps. God knows why the crowd applauded. I wasn't even sure why they were still there. By the time we reached the second venue I was beginning to relax, still fluffing the odd note but at least keeping the right tempo. Which was just as well. The Ring of Bells is an olde-worlde pub in a picturesque village, and like most of its kind has become trendy. Designer-labelled twenty-somethings were everywhere, braying loudly and knocking back designer beers. How they were going to react to a group of men old enough to know better, wearing bells, ribbons and flower-decked top hats, was anybody's guess.

We assembled on the green and I launched into the first dance, 'Swaggering Boney', expecting to finish to mild applause. Instead we got cheers and foot-stomping. I turned to see who was responsible and my heart sank, taking most of my street cred with it. The noise was coming from a bunch of officers, among them Leo Wiltshire.

Some plod were there too, two of whom I recognized – DI Simon Furneaux and DS Phil Twigg. Of all the pubs, in all the towns . . .

I was planning various ways to kill my father when one of them called out. 'Hey, Gus, d'you know "Purple Haze"?'

Station Officer Martin Secombe.

'Sure, Marty,' I yelled back. 'I'll play if you dance.'

Hoots of laughter followed as they tried to push him forward. Life was going to be hell on Monday.

The light was fading when the performance finally ended and the team, all men together, headed for the bar. Reluctantly I followed, wishing I'd brought my car so I could have driven straight home. The Brigade contingent had drifted away after the first few numbers, I hoped back to town. But no, the first person I saw was Leo, standing at the bar. He noticed me and beckoned.

'Think that deserves a drink,' he grinned when I managed to reach him.

'Thanks. Half a shandy.' I dumped the accordion case between my feet.

Leo looked me up and down. 'Didn't know you were into the folksy scene.'

'I'm not. I stood in for my father.' I lurched forward as someone tripped over the case.

He held me longer than was necessary. 'Perhaps you should sit down before there's an accident.' He nodded towards a corner. 'Phil's grabbed a table.'

I found it squashed against the wall by the entrance to the loos. No Brigade, just Furneaux and Phil Twigg, plus a closely guarded third chair. Phil saw me and let go.

'Hi, Gus, grab a pew. Leo can find another. Want me to take that?'

She swung the case over the table like it was balsa wood, muscles cording her arm. Her daily workouts were legendary. Though she's inches shorter than me, if caught in a tight spot I'd be happy to have her with me. Task done she sat back down, ran her hand over urchin-cut blonde hair. 'I didn't know you were into –'

'I was doing my father a favour, okay?'

She grinned.

'What are you lot doing here anyway?'

'Blame him.' She jerked her head at Simon. 'Reckoned he needed a change. Looks like half the county had the same idea.'

Simon gave a half-smile and twisted in his chair. He was backed against the wall, too big for the narrow space. Since I'd arrived he'd been scanning faces at the bar, but now the slightly hooded grey eyes drifted to mine. His hair is lighter than Leo's but not by much, and longer than when I'd last seen it, falling across his forehead and visible behind his ears. I wasn't sure if it was a fashion statement, or if he simply hadn't had time to get it cut.

He glanced up as Leo arrived with the drinks. The two of them are best buddies, something I've always found strange. They're a similar age and physically have a lot in common, but personality-wise they're like chalk and cheese. Leo's the upfront type, what you see is what you get. About Simon I knew nothing. Whatever light he might have he keeps firmly under a bushel.

'Damn woman's nicked my chair!' Leo muttered. 'Better sit on my lap.'

'Behind you,' I said. 'Someone's leaving.' His was one lap I was *not* going to bounce on.

It's not that I'm immune to Leo's charms. Far from it. He has intelligence, good looks, a great body . . . And a wife. I'd never met her but she had my sympathy.

He was at it within seconds, flirting with the women at

the table behind. Phil caught my eye and winked. 'So how goes it?' she asked.

'Okay.' I sipped the shandy. 'Any news on that body?'

'Body?'

'Danner Road. Was it who you thought?'

'Did we think it was someone?' Simon spoke for the first time.

'I heard some guy called Trevor Collins. Also that you were watching him.'

'He was known to us,' Simon conceded.

'Do you know how he died?'

'No – and if you don't mind, I'm off duty.' He stood abruptly, rocking the table, and disappeared to the loo.

I pulled a face. 'Touchy.'

'Ignore him. He's probably premenstrual.' Phil lit a cigarette.

I grinned. 'Have you really not had the results of the PM?'

She gave a shrug.

'Hey, it was me who found him, right?'

She glanced towards the loo door. 'Smoke inhalation, okay?'

'Anything else?'

'Isn't that enough?' She inhaled deeply, blew smoke out the side of her mouth. 'Don't lose sleep about him, Gus. Guy was a toerag. You name it, he was into it – pimping, GBH, extortion. A real choirboy was our Trev. Furneaux knew him from way back, used to be on his patch in Plymouth. Fuck knows what he was doing up here.'

'Extending his empire?'

She gave a snort. 'Didn't have the nous. Always did the dirty for others, including Furneaux's *bête noire*. Villain called Rayjay,' she added when I raised my brows. 'But that's history. He's long gone.'

'Inside?'

'Disappeared. About twelve years ago. Rumour has it he's in the foundations of the new chemical plant they were building at the time, but Furneaux thinks different.'

'About what?' Strong hands pressed down on my shoulders as Simon squeezed past.

'Rayjay. The concrete waistcoat.'

He eased into the chair. 'Why are we talking about him?'

'Putting Gus's mind at rest about the toerag she found.' Another long drag. 'Furneaux here thinks Rayjay skipped the country, ain't that right?'

His face remained deadpan. 'Two, three million on the street buys a lot of travelling.'

'Assuming he had anything to do with it. Drugs were never Rayjay's thing.'

'You saying he had a conscience, Twigg?'

'I'm saying he was a gambling man, gambling and prostitution.'

'Come off it, he was anything that made money! Finger in any number of pies. Bastard would have sold his own mother.'

Phil grinned. 'Wouldn't get much for old Joyce.' She turned to me. 'His mother worked Union Street. Still does, though Christ knows how she gets any takers. Talk about lived-in.' She stubbed out the cigarette. 'Anyway, past history. No longer our concern.'

A gong signalled last orders. 'One for the road?' Leo asked behind me.

'My round,' Simon told him. 'Same again?'

Leo swung a chair up beside me and straddled it, arms resting along the back. Close enough to smell the alcohol on his breath. 'I hope you're not driving,' I said.

He shook his head, nodded towards the bar where a sullen-looking youngster was standing alone nursing a glass of orange juice. 'New recruit. Found him in the Globe and invited him along. Thought he'd really joined the big boys till he realized why he was here.'

'Bastard.'

Leo grinned. 'By the way, I think someone wants you.'

I turned to see Mike Taylor gesturing wildly and pointing at the door.

'Boyfriend?'

'Lift.'

'Knew I should have brought my car.' No smile this time, just a sultry meaningful stare.

No way, Jose!

Though I knew what Etta meant about those long winter nights.

Mike dropped me at Tynings and I quickly changed from the kit.

'So how did it go?' Dad asked when I came downstairs.

'How d'you think!' I snapped. 'Don't *ever* do that to me again.'

He stuck out his lower lip. 'Accept a peace offering?' He plucked a pile of old newspapers from the hall table and thrust them into my arms.

'Wow, Dad, you shouldn't!'

'Don't mock. They're the reports of Miss Hillas's death. Found 'em in the garage.'

'I thought you wanted me to leave well alone?'

'I do, but no harm reading about it.'

I told him the gift was accepted and hugged him goodnight.

Halfway home the tiredness hit. I tuned to a classic rock station and sang along to keep myself awake, praying that when I got there my neighbours would be quiet. Fat chance! Their house was ablaze with light, every window open. How else would they ensure the music reached the entire street?

Walking up the path I felt a wave of anger. Why did the men in the neighbourhood let it go on? Why didn't they bash in the door?

Up in my bedroom I hammered on the wall. My neighbours hammered back. I stuffed plugs in my ears and dived beneath the pillows. If someone had placed a grenade in my hand at that moment, God help me I would have lobbed it in.

Chapter Seven

I had little time to think about Judith during the next few days. The following week some top brass *Sapeurs Pompiers*, French firefighters, were visiting HQ and Media Resources was planning their schedule. But as so often happens when I need time in the office, the incidents came thick and fast – a fire in a listed building, an overturned tanker on the motorway, two particularly messy RTAs, plus another abortive attempt at capturing Line Rescue. Nor were things helped by the weather. The continuing heatwave had become oppressive, with a distinct smell of thunder in the air. People were getting tetchy, including me.

By Thursday I was beginning to panic and knew I would have to work late. It couldn't have come at a worse time. At seven that evening some prospective purchasers were scheduled to view my flat, which meant the agent would have to show them around. He didn't sound pleased when I called him. As he'd made clear when I approached him the previous Monday, with neighbours like mine I shouldn't anticipate a quick sale.

Thinking about the flat did little to improve my mood, and when Etta looked in on her way home to ask what I was planning for my holidays, I almost bit her head off. I quickly apologized but she was clearly put out. More proof that I needed a 'fellah'.

I finally arrived home sometime after nine, armed with an Indian takeaway, and settled in the kitchen. Separated from next-door by the stairway, it's the quietest room. Searching for the mango pickle I noticed the old newspapers, lying in the corner where I had first left them. I put them beside my plate and read while I ate.

The first was dated 13th April. Miss Hillas had made the front page.

MUTILATED BODY FOUND ON MOOR

A woman's mutilated body, discovered yesterday afternoon at the foot of Veniston Quarry on Dartmoor, has been identified as that of Miss Harriet Hillas (82) of Higher Verstone, Swinlake. The body, thought to have lain undiscovered for several days, was found by James Holroyd (27) of Furzebrook Close, Tavistock.

'I was walking through the quarry when my dog ran ahead, barking,' he told our reporter. 'I thought he'd found a dead sheep, but when I got close I saw it was a woman.'

The mutilations have been attributed to animal predation. 'Any body, human or animal, left lying on the moor is open to attack,' said Park Ranger Geoff Henderson, one of the first on the scene. 'Predators make no distinction.'

Miss Hillas, who lived alone, was a keen walker and a familiar figure on the north moor. 'We think she simply strayed too close to the edge and slipped,' said a police spokesman. 'In this weather there may have been ice on the stones which she failed to see. It was a tragic accident.'

When asked about the mutilation he assured us that foul play was not suspected. It was, he claimed, 'the work of animals, probably foxes', though already speculation is mounting as to whether this is the latest attack by the so-called Beast of Dartmoor.

Miss Hillas leaves a niece, Mrs Judith Kempe, who lives in London.

The following day's headline was predictable – BEAST SPOTTED NEAR SITE OF BODY – and explained how a woman from Okehampton had seen a large black animal resembling a cat lurking in rocks just north of the quarry. I smiled. It didn't take much for the Beast to rear its ugly head. Others are reputed to live on Exmoor and Bodmin,

70

and heaven knows how many other desolate tracts of land. Advocates claim they are pumas, escapees from a zoo, and perhaps they are – perhaps there's a whole troop of them out there. There must be if the other sightings were to be believed. Within forty-eight hours a big cat had been spotted at Hameldown in the east, Ivybridge in the south, and plumb in the centre on Beardown Tor. Unless, of course, Puss has seven league boots.

The remaining papers contained reports of further sightings, arguments over the Beast's existence, and a blurred photograph purporting to be the Beast eating a lamb. It could have been anything from the family cat to a bin liner blowing in the breeze. Miss Hillas's death had been entirely eclipsed by speculation and was barely mentioned, except in the last rag which gave a brief report of the inquest, with its verdict of accidental death.

I drank coffee as I washed up, watched half an hour's television, and took myself off to bed. My neighbours were relatively quiet – not silent, but the decibels were at a level that didn't damage the ears. I read for a while and switched off the light. Five minutes later the telephone rang.

Groaning, I picked it up, expecting to hear a chirpy voice from Control. The voice that greeted me was tense and breathless.

'Gus? Thank God! I was afraid you wouldn't be in.'

'Judith?' I dragged myself up.

'Yes, it's . . . I'm sorry – about the time. But I had to call. There's been a burglary. Someone broke in and –'

'When?' Suddenly I was wide awake.

'This evening. I went for a walk and coming back – I was nearly at the house when I saw someone. Running away. He must have heard me and –'

'How do you know he was a burglar?'

'The kitchen window. It was forced, a plant knocked over. There's nothing missing – at least, I don't think there is. Most likely I disturbed him.'

'Have you called the police?'

'Not yet. I've only just come out. I was afraid to leave

71

before in case he was hanging around. I waited until it was dark and walked.'

'You *walked*?'

'I couldn't use the car, he would have seen the lights. I sneaked out and kept to the shadows.'

'You need a phone!' I said, my mind spinning. 'Look, you can't walk all the way back. You'd better spend the night at my father's.'

There was a pause. 'Don't be silly. He doesn't know me.'

'He knows of you. And believe me, he'll be only too happy. I'll call him now, explain what's happened. And when you get there, ring the police. No arguments,' I added when she started to protest. 'Do you know where he lives?'

I gave her directions, and as soon as she'd rung off called Dad. So much for not becoming involved!

I intended to phone from work next morning to see how they got on, but in the event there wasn't time. The visit by the *Sapeurs Pompiers* had been brought forward and we were running around like headless chickens, trying to do several days' work in one. I was arranging the final details of the slide show when the estate agent called. When, he asked sarcastically, were my neighbours likely to be quiet?

Before eleven in the morning, I told him, except on signing-on day when it might be as early as ten.

'Nobody views houses at that hour,' he said coldly, and went on to explain how the previous evening the prospective purchasers had been greeted by so much noise they refused even to go in. Had I, he asked, consulted Environmental Health?

'We're on Christian name terms,' I snapped and slammed down the phone.

A moment later it rang again. Control this time, informing me that Line Rescue had been called to a cliff rescue near Hartland. I had little choice but send Nick, my

second-in-command. Sod's law said he would get the shots
I'd been after.

I worked through my lunch hour, stopping twice to call
Dad. No reply. Nor was there when I finally arrived home.
I grabbed a sandwich and disappeared to my darkroom –
alias second bedroom, window blacked out – and an hour
later tried again. This time he answered.

'Gussie,' he said, 'that poor girl.'

'What happened?' I asked. 'Did she call the police?'

'They were up there this morning. No doubt about the
intruder. Dirt on the window sill and the weeds below had
been trampled. Makes you wonder if there's something in
all her wild ideas.'

'She talk to you?'

'Late into the night and again this morning. *And* I've
seen the diaries. She brought them with her, didn't want to
leave them in the house.' He paused. 'I know you told me
what was in them, yet somehow, seeing it all written down
. . .' He made a noise like a shudder. 'Strange though, don't
you think? I keep asking myself, Why now?'

'Why now what?'

'The burglary. The place has been empty for three
months. Why attempt it now when someone's living there?
Anyway, I've told her we'll keep in touch, it's the least we
can do. We're the only people around here she knows.'

I found myself nodding. But were we? Suddenly
I remembered the car.

'Dad,' I said, 'does anyone around you drive a red
Porsche?'

There was a moment's pause. 'There's that sculptor fellow. An American, lives out at Holt Mill. Joe something-or-
other. Why, have you met him?'

'He almost met me. Nearly mowed me down at the end
of Judith's track.'

'Lucky for him he didn't!' Dad muttered. 'But don't get
any wild ideas about him being the burglar. From what
I hear he's loaded.'

'I just wondered if Judith knew him.'

'May do – you arty types seem to find each other. Anyway, about this weekend. Will we be seeing you?'

We? 'It depends on the weather,' I said, glancing towards the window. 'On whether the storm breaks.' Even as we'd been talking the sky had darkened, and heavy clouds were massing above the rooftops in Vale Road.

'Let's hope it does, it might clear the air.' He paused. 'De Zaire, that's his name. Joe de Zaire.'

'Like the ski resort?'

'Hm? Oh, Val d'Isère, hadn't thought of that. No, two words – de, then Z-A . . . actually I'm not sure how you spell it. Rhymes with dare. Anyway, do your best. You know I like to see you.'

After the goodbyes I wandered to the kitchen and took a bottle of iced water from the fridge. So Judith's intruder had been genuine, I mused, filling a tumbler. Unless, of course, she had staged it herself. It would be easy enough to do – stomp on a few weeds, rub dirt on the sill – and it would certainly lend weight to her claims. God, I was getting cynical!

I took the glass to the sitting room and picked up a book. Collapsing into a chair I heard the first faint rumble of thunder.

The storm broke shortly after midnight, waking me with a crash that had me leaping up in bed. Minutes later the heavens opened, hurling a deafening torrent on to the slates above my head. The neighbours compensated by turning up the volume. Thunder and rap. My anger was approaching that of Thor's when, at a quarter to one, the power went out.

'Hallelujah!' I cried and snuggled beneath the duvet where, grinning smugly, I let the downpour lull me to sleep. Never had a storm seemed sweeter.

I was on the road by six, heading for the Shovel Down Longstone, one of Dartmoor's ancient megaliths. Prehistoric stones feature strongly in my work and were to be a major theme in my exhibition. I had been planning today's shot for a long time but had been waiting for the right sky. With luck, the aftermath of the storm would provide it.

I parked as close as was possible and climbed out. The chill air was a shock after the weeks of sun. I changed into wellies and, weighed down by cameras and tripod, set off towards the stone, boots squelching and sucking in the waterlogged ground.

The moor was like an enormous sponge being squeezed by a giant's fist, water oozing from every pore, channels that only yesterday had been dry as dust now filled with gushing water. Above my head clouds scudded across an opal sky, blinding and translucent, while ahead of me parallel rows of stones five thousand years old directed me towards the skyline. Walking beside them brought a deep sense of history. Why had they been placed there? What strange rites had they witnessed? It was a primeval land-scape, lonely and mysterious – and I felt elated.

The wind picked up as I crossed the ridge, and by the time I reached the Longstone ominous clouds were sweeping in from the south. The slender granite menhir towered above me as I circled around, choosing my position. Satisfied at last, I sprung the legs of the tripod and planted it on the ground. I took preliminary meter readings, adjusted the settings, and began to wait.

And wait. Clouds passed over and were replaced by others, and soon spits of rain were dampening my face. I covered the camera as the pattering grew louder, watched dispiritedly as the far horizon vanished into grey. This was the part I hated – the uncertainty, the utter lack of control.

I was starting to feel cold and stuffed my hands in my pockets. Began to pace. Still there was no let-up. Kes Tor to the east had been swallowed by mist and the valley was about to follow. I began to jog, first on the spot then in ever-widening circles, my eyes on the ground to avoid rabbit holes and stumps of gorse. Which is how I noticed the letterbox. To those in the know, the small pile of carefully arranged stones was a giveaway. With no better reason than to pass the time, I squatted down and began lifting them out.

It was Monty who first told me about Dartmoor's letter-boxes, shortly after Dad moved to the village. The two of us had driven one Sunday afternoon to Bonehill Rocks, but had turned back when we saw the number of people. There were dozens of them scouring the hillside, mostly bent double, Berghaused bottoms thrust towards the sky.

'What were they picking?' I asked Monty when we returned home.

'Nothing, I shouldn't think,' he laughed. 'I expect they were letterboxing.' And he proceeded to tell us about the bizarre phenomenon peculiar to Dartmoor that began almost a hundred and fifty years ago.

It all started at Cranmere Pool, a remote spot on the north moor. In Victorian times it had become a Mecca for stout-hearted walkers. One such stalwart gentleman, proud of his achievement, left his calling card stuck inside a bottle. Subsequent walkers did the same, and soon they began to add messages and the date of their visits. In time the bottle was replaced by a box, and over the years others appeared, in similarly remote locations. And thus an elite clique was born, of those with enough stamina and courage to explore the wilder reaches of the moor.

Not so any more. Nowadays you can trip over half a dozen boxes without straying more than a hundred yards from your car. The purpose, it seems, is no longer to arrive but to acquire, to collect as many as possible irrespective of where they are. Visit any popular location, on any half-decent afternoon, and you'll see letterboxers, groping under rocks and bushes in their quest for yet another prize. At weekends they arrive in droves, armed with maps and compasses, and for the dedicated there are books, badges, clubs – even, God forbid, websites. For hundreds, maybe thousands, it's become a hobby. For some it's an obsession.

And what is this prize for which they'll battle through rain, sleet and blizzard?

A rubber stamp. A rubber stamp placed in a waterproof container and hidden inside a hole.

Exactly when it metamorphosed into its present state I'm not sure, but recent years have seen a staggering increase in the number of boxes and I wasn't surprised to find one near the menhir. There were probably several more if I cared to look. I removed the final stone and thrust my hand into the dark cavity beneath the rock, much as my father must have done when he encountered the glass. Inside was a screw-top container, the plastic too clean for it to have been there long. I removed the lid, turning my back on the rain to protect the contents, and tipped out the stamp. Also inside was a rolled-up notebook. There was an example of the stamp on the first page, a simple line drawing of a retriever. Beneath it someone had written, *Ben's Box. In memory of Ben, loving friend, companion and keen letterboxer. Died 2nd July, aged nine years*. It had only been out a couple of weeks, but already the book contained thirty or more entries.

Letterboxing works like a swap. Most letterboxers carry an individual stamp of their own – for the most part professionally made – plus an inkpad to wet it in. When they find a box, they leave their personal imprint in the book and take the box's imprint in return. It's these that form the collection and I've heard said some run into thousands. Not being a letterboxer I don't own a stamp but I wrote in the book anyway. Or rather drew – a quick biro sketch of a camera lashed by driving rain. I dated it, returned it to its hole, and replaced the stones.

No sooner had I done so than the heavens opened. Even the Longstone had vanished in the mist. The world had become a grey featureless void that was growing darker by the minute. I've been caught like this before, barely able to find my way back, and it's not a pleasant experience. It was time to accept the inevitable and call it a day.

Before returning to Tynings I decided to visit Judith.

I could kill two birds with one stone, beg a hot drink and hear the latest on the burglary. I arrived to find a flashy car parked outside – not the Porsche but a midnight blue Mercedes sports. Could this be Stuart?

I sprinted to the front door and knocked. No one answered, but I thought I heard voices coming from the conservatory. I walked along the front of the house. The glass was misted with condensation but I could still make out two figures, a man standing a little way inside, his back towards me, and Judith in the centre, half turned away. I'd raised my hand to tap when the man began to shout.

'For Christ's sake, you must be able to get *something* against all this.'

Whoops! I started to back away when the parrot screeched.

'Fucking bird!' the man yelled. 'If you think I'm staying here with that noise . . .' He spun on his heel, saw me at the window. 'What the hell?'

I gestured apologetically, indicating that I would leave. Judith shook her head and pointed at the door.

I met her on the threshold. 'Sorry, I did try knocking . . .'

'That's all right. Stuart arrived unexpectedly. Please – come in.'

'I can come back later . . .'

'Please?'

I kicked off my boots.

'You're soaked,' she said calmly. 'Let me take your jacket.'

I shrugged it from my shoulders as she introduced us. Stuart was older than Judith, probably late forties, tall, slim and immaculately tailored in beige trousers, a cream silk shirt, a racing-green cravat. Almost handsome, with ink-black hair swept back from a high forehead, dark eyes, a well-shaped nose. It was the mouth that let him down. It was curiously wide, the thin lips tilted at the corners, the points beneath his nose exaggeratedly defined. He

78

reminded me of someone but for the life of me I couldn't think who.

We nodded curtly, assessing each other across the rattan chairs. He looked as though he'd like to kill me, but perhaps that wasn't surprising if I'd arrived in the middle of a row. Perhaps also that's why he didn't speak. Alas, introductions over, neither did Judith, and for what seemed an age we stood mutely facing each other, like characters in a spaghetti western waiting for someone to draw. All that was missing was Moricone's music . . .

Laughter bubbled inside me. If someone didn't speak soon . . .

I was saved by the parrot – an ear-piercing screech that had Stuart glaring at the cage. It was Judith who broke the silence, finally asking if I would like a coffee.

'Thought you'd never ask,' I said, moving to a chair.

'I'll make it,' Stuart snapped. 'Get some peace from that infernal bird!' He stormed out, slamming the door behind him.

I glanced at Judith. 'If this is a bad time . . .'

'Not at all, I'm glad you came.' She took the chair beside me. 'I wanted to thank you for the other night. Your father's a kind man. Has he told you what happened?'

'He said the police found evidence of an intruder.' Clearly the subject of the argument was taboo.

She nodded. 'They tell me there have been several robberies in the area recently, thefts from isolated houses for the most part during the day, and they think this was the latest attempt.'

'Sounds logical.'

'Except I now know who it was. The man I saw running?' She glanced towards the door, lowered her voice. 'I haven't said anything to Stuart but yesterday, coming back from shopping, I saw Gary, messing with one of the cars. It was *him*, Gus, I'm certain. He was even wearing the same clothes.'

'Have you told the police?'

'How can I! He's June's *son*, and already on a suspended sentence. Besides, nothing appears to be missing.'

'This time,' I said. 'How do you know he won't come back? That he's not responsible for the other robberies?'

She gave an indifferent shrug.

'So you're just going to let him get away with it?'

'I thought I might have a word with June.'

'Like your aunt did?' No wonder louts like Gary got away with so much.

Judith chose to ignore me. 'What I don't understand,' she said, 'is why he's waited until now. As your father pointed out, the house has been empty since April.'

I swallowed my annoyance. 'Could be he's only just found a fence. Most burglaries these days are commissioned. If someone's in the market for Victoriana, this is an Aladdin's cave.'

She stared down at her lap. 'Unless he was after something more specific. I wondered . . . you don't think he was after the diaries?'

'Oh, for God's sake! How would he have known about them?'

She shifted uneasily. 'I told June – when I first found them. At the time I saw no reason not to. It was only later I thought about Tom.'

'Would she have told Gary?'

'I doubt it. But he might have overheard. I'd gone to see her at the farm.' She looked up defiantly. 'I didn't say much, only that they existed and that Aunt was worried. I might have said frightened. But I wanted to know if she had confided in June. Needless to say she hadn't. June was no wiser than I am, it was a complete shock.' She glanced again at the door. 'Oh, whatever is Stuart *doing* out there? I don't suppose he can find things.' She levered herself from the chair. 'Come on, we might as well make it ourselves.'

The baize door swung quietly to behind us as we padded down the passage. Despite the change in weather, Judith was still barefoot, and with me in my socks we made virtually no noise. The kitchen door was open and I followed her in, almost crashing into her when she suddenly stopped dead. Across the room, Stuart was crouched at the desk, rooting through a drawer.

'What the hell are you doing?' Judith demanded, her voice like ice. 'The will's with the solicitor, if that's what you're looking for.'

Stuart climbed languidly to his feet. 'Naughty boy!' he murmured, slapping one hand with the other. 'Caught with my fingers in the till.' His gaze shifted to me. 'You see how my wife trusts me?'

Without further words Judith spun on her heel, eyes blazing, and stormed out, leaving me standing like a dummy. For the first time Stuart smiled and suddenly I knew who he reminded me of – the Master of Ceremonies in the film *Cabaret*. It was the same nauseating grin. To my horror he swivelled a finger at the side of his head. 'Her aunt was the same, you know – completely gaga. Still want that coffee?'

My skin crawled. How could Judith have married a creep like this?

'Well?' he asked, moving towards the table.

'Not any more,' I said, and followed her out.

I found Judith by the back door, sitting forward on a bench as she laced up some walking boots. 'Where are you going?' I asked.

'Out.' She stood up, stamped her feet.

'Want me to come?'

'Do what you like!' She grabbed a red waterproof jacket and slammed out through the door.

Well, stuff you! I thought, my anger rising. Better still, stuff the pair of them. I had better things to do than act as buffer for their marital spite. What kind of marriage did they have, for Christ's sake? Not one made in heaven, that was for sure. Unless they were the sort who got off on public squabbles, in which case they could find themselves a different audience.

I returned to the conservatory, ignored Geoffrey's invitation to tickle and pulled on my boots. Outside the rain had stopped but mist still enveloped the house. I could barely see across the terrace. I was starting towards the car when she called my name. Turning I saw a red jacket emerging from the mist.

'Forgive me,' she said, 'that was uncalled for. I *would* appreciate some company.'

I hesitated for a fraction then walked towards her. It looked like the hot drink would have to wait.

Chapter Eight

Wet bracken brushed against my legs, clamping my jeans to my skin. Ver Tor was awash. Flash floods had torn deep gouges in the soil, forming conduits for the water hurtling down from the heights. Far below the river thundered.

Judith appeared to know where she was going, though how she could tell was beyond me. Visibility was abysmal, everything but our immediate surroundings hidden by fog. It was as much as I could do to keep the red jacket in view. Higher up, bracken gave way to rocks, and soon we needed hands as well as feet to haul ourselves up. I'd long since lost all sense of direction, had no idea where we were in relation to the house. All I knew was we were still climbing.

Moisture clung to my hair, formed droplets and trickled down my neck. The temperature of the air was rising. The wind too was gaining force, and soon the mist began to disperse. Nowhere do conditions change more rapidly than on the moor and within half an hour the air was clear, a timid ray of sunshine pencilling through. Where it fell, colour sprang from the rocks, lichen whorls in orange, ochre and blue. Quartz crystals glistened like diamonds.

The red jacket had long vanished from view and I was wondering whether to call out when, rounding a promontory, I found myself on a swathe of grass. It was a mini plateau, backed by a wall of rock about eighty feet high. White clouds were rushing towards it, making it appear to topple forwards, like some massive tidal wave hurtling towards the gorge. Giddiness overcame me and I lowered my eyes. At the bottom of the cliff stood Judith. Instinctively I reached for my camera. Her coat was a splash of blood against dark stone.

I wandered across to the edge and peered over. It was like standing at the edge of the world. Wykemans Cleave appeared to be on fire, mist rising in vertical smoke-like plumes along its length. Nearer, below where I was standing, I could see the roof of Higher Verstone. It looked like a doll's house. From its direction came the sound of a car.

'Is Stuart leaving?' I asked.

Judith had come to stand beside me. 'I imagine so.'

Without saying goodbye? 'Is he going back to London?'

'Cornwall. He's visiting a painter we show.'

We listened as the car descended the track, and once or twice I caught the glint of chrome. Beside me Judith sighed.

'I'm sorry about just now. Stuart upset me. He's not always . . . It's worry. It affects people in strange ways.'

'What's he worried about, you being here alone?'

'No, he – Well, that too, I'm sure but . . . Mostly it's the gallery. Recently there have been one or two problems.'

'Financial?'

She hunched a shoulder.

'Is that why he wants to borrow against the estate?'

I saw her stiffen. 'So you heard. I wondered if you had. In that case there's little point denying it. Yes, he wants to borrow, but unfortunately it's not possible. Stuart doesn't believe me.' She gave an ironic smile. 'A lack of trust on both sides, I'm afraid.'

'Are the problems serious?'

'About as serious as it can get. We stand to lose everything – the gallery, our home. One minute everything was fine, the next . . .' She broke off, stared down at her feet, shuffled the loose stones with her boot. 'You know how it is – one artist goes out of favour, another doesn't realize potential. Next thing you know, you're mortgaged to the hilt. You probably won't believe this, but at this precise moment I don't have a bean.'

I almost laughed. 'Those cars . . .'

'Keeping up appearances. It's a miracle they haven't been repossessed.' She kicked a stone, sent it skimming over the edge. 'Sometimes I think the banks *want* us to go under. They fall over themselves to lend you money, but look out if something goes wrong. They're like sharks, harmless until they scent blood, and right now they're circling for the kill.' She swept strands of hair from her face. 'If it wasn't for Aunt's inheritance they would have foreclosed long ago. It's only the promise of that that's keeping them at bay.'

'And you really can't borrow?'

'There are complications. Besides, that would mean even *more* interest and if it continues to drag on . . .' She gave a shrug. 'There are limits to how much they'll risk.'

I watched her a moment longer. 'Why did you say Stuart was capable of killing your aunt?'

The eyes snapped round. '*What?*'

'The other day. You said –'

'Oh God!' She averted her head. 'It was a joke, a throw-away comment. Stuart couldn't – oh, that's ridiculous! Do you think I would still be married to him if I believed that?' She shook her head and gave a sad little laugh. 'You really have no idea, Gus. At the time Aunt died, Stuart was in London, working all the hours God sent trying get us out of the mess. He barely had time to sleep, let alone come down here. What you witnessed just now is the result. The pressure's changed him, he's a different man. There are times when I barely recognize him.'

I frowned. 'But if you were in that deep, couldn't your aunt have helped?'

'She didn't know. I told her we were swamped with work. I couldn't bring myself to mention the debts. Partly pride, I suppose . . . Mostly I didn't want to worry her.'

I looked away. Everyone not wanting to worry everyone else. Plates so full they were in danger of cracking. Was it possible Stuart had?

I tried to imagine him, working around the clock,

becoming more and more desperate as the debts mounted higher. And not so far away in Devon a wealthy old lady, an old lady he disliked, his wife the sole beneficiary. Would the temptation have proved too great? Could it be something more heinous than money worries that had wrought the change?

Beside me Judith shivered. 'It's getting cold,' she said. 'Let's go back.'

We left our boots at the back door and returned to the kitchen. The desk drawers were closed, a half-drunk mug of coffee abandoned on the table. Lying beside it was a camera and out of habit I picked it up. It was a 35mm Olympus, fully automatic, in appallingly bad condition. Several scratches scarred the body and there was a deep dent in the side. I would be surprised if it still worked.

Judith was filling the kettle. 'Is this Stuart's?' I asked.

'What? Oh, no, that was Aunt's.' She crossed to the stove. 'It's a miracle it survived.'

'She had it with her when she fell?'

'Must have done. It was returned with her things.' She bent down to riddle the Aga.

I turned the camera over. The window was showing empty. 'What happened to the film?'

'Film?'

'I don't imagine she carried an empty camera.' I flipped open the back to make sure.

'Perhaps she had a new roll. Hadn't got around to reloading it.'

'Did it show up on the list of possessions?'

Judith straightened. 'I've no idea, I've never seen a list. I was in London so June kept everything at the farm until . . .' She froze. 'God, you don't think –'

'I think we don't jump to conclusions,' I said quickly. 'It could easily have been lost in the quarry.'

'Not if it was in the camera!' She crossed to the table and snatched it up, as if by doing so the film might magically appear. 'Suppose someone stole it? That could be why she was killed. If it contained evidence . . . Hell, why didn't I think of it before? I need to see the list, see if one existed. But I'm loath to ask June. Do you think the police would have a copy?'

I told her I would find out. Yet another question for SIN.

Judith went off to the bathroom, and while she was gone I took another book from the shelf. *Fairy Tales* by Sir Arthur Quiller-Couch. The illustrations were by Dulac, every one exquisite. Judith returned with something in her hand.

'I found this in the library,' she said, putting it on the table. 'Thought it might interest you.'

It was the Chadwickes' brochure, a glossy white-covered booklet with an illustration of an acorn and oak leaves a third of the way down, drawn in the style of an ancient herbal. Below it was the title, printed in a rich dark green. *The Sacred Oak Institute – An International Centre for the Promotion of Spiritual and Ecological Awareness.*

'Very tasteful,' I said. 'Must I read it now?'

'Heavens, no. Take it with you, browse at your leisure.' She brought the coffee to the table.

I stuffed the brochure in my bag. 'Oh, by the way, message from Dad. He said will you please ring Telecom. He's worried about you not having a phone.'

'I know, he told me. But I'm afraid it's out of the question. Stuart made enquiries and in our present circumstances . . .'

'What about a mobile?'

'They don't work. He tried that too. Something to do with strength . . .'

'Field strength.' It was the answer I'd expected. 'It means the signal's weak, probably no direct line of sight between here and the transmitter. It's a huge problem on the moor.' I glanced at the window. 'It would probably work up on the Tor.'

'Oh, I don't doubt it,' she smiled. 'But we both know it's quicker to walk to the village.'

*   *   *

By the time I left it was raining again, and with no hope of getting the photograph, I drove to Tynings. Dad was in the garden, swathed in a hooded jacket, checking the damage wrought by the storm. I left him to it and headed for the kitchen. There was someone in London I wanted to call.

I found the number in my address book. 'Phillip Mawson, please,' I told the receptionist, and spent the next few minutes listening to strains of Debussy while wondering if I was doing the right thing.

I also wondered how Phillip would respond. Unlike Judith he'd been a close friend at college, though I hadn't seen him now for a number of years, not since we'd lunched together at the Royal Academy. We'd promised to keep in touch but, as so often happens, it had dwindled to a card and a few lines at Christmas. I wasn't sure how he would take to a request out of the blue.

At last the music cut. 'Phillip Mawson.'

'Phillip?' I said. 'It's Gus Tavender.'

'*Gus?* Good God! How are you?'

I told him I was fine, and we indulged in a few minutes' small talk, bringing each other up to date with the changes in our lives. His work as advertising manager at *ArtView*, a magazine carrying gallery listings, was going well, but his tempestuous six-year relationship with Reuben was finally over. There was now a new man in his life, Carl, a 'real sweetie' though it was early days. I wished him luck and, as soon as it was polite, posed my question.

'I want to pick your brains,' I said. 'What do you know about a gallery called Kempe Hillas Fine Art?'

There was a pause. 'I know who you mean. The Hillas part was at college with us. Remember that strange girl in the year above? What was her name . . .?'

'Judith.'

'That's the one. Real loner. I think the Kempe half is her husband. From what I remember they deal in contemporary stuff, though on a pretty small scale, no major league names. Why? They offered you a show?'

'It's a possibility.' So was anything.

'Hm.'

'What's that supposed to mean?'

'Nothing. Really. I'm sure it'll be fine.'

Clearly it wasn't. 'I'm reading between the lines here, Phillip,' I said. 'If there's anything I should know . . .'

'I'm not sure there is. Truly. There've been one or two whispers but –'

'What kind of whispers?'

'Nothing I'd want to pass on. But as it's you . . . Look, give me your number. I'll ask around, make a few enquiries, okay?'

I hesitated. 'Is it going to stir things up?'

'Why? You met up with her again?'

'Yes, as a matter of fact.'

He chuckled. 'Always who you know. Don't worry, I'll be discreet. Though I will say this. If there *is* something dodgy and word's out, nothing I don't say or do will make a blind bit of difference.'

Chapter Nine

The following day I was on call. Officially someone (namely Nick or myself) must be available at all times of the day or night to answer emergencies, camera at the ready. But most officers are considerate and we're rarely summoned out of office hours – unless the incident is serious, unusual or politically sensitive, as in the case of Danner Road. On Sunday all was quiet until late afternoon.

I spent the morning cleaning the kitchen, a chore long overdue. Housework's not my strong suit and there were things in the fridge even I didn't recognize. All the while my mind was on the Kempes, and something Dad said the day before. It was after my phone call to Phillip Mawson. I'd told him about my meeting with Stuart, the argument I'd overheard, hinted there might be money problems. Dad thought for a moment.

'So he had the perfect motive,' he said astutely. 'Might be better for Judith if he *were* responsible.'

'What?' I cried.

'Sorry, that came out all wrong. All I meant was – if Miss Hillas *was* murdered, Stuart would have done it for the inheritance and soon he'll have what he wants. End of story. But if it was because of this other business . . . Well, if Judith starts ferreting around she could be putting herself in danger. Someone who's killed once won't hesitate to kill again.'

A cold shiver ran down my spine. 'Are you saying you believe her?'

'Let's say I'm keeping an open mind.'

The fact that he was even considering it was enough.

I finished in the kitchen and started on the sitting room. Books and magazines were strewn everywhere. They have a strange habit of attaching themselves to me whenever I sit down, so every so often I'm forced to round them up and tidy them away. Under a catalogue of art materials I found Miss Hillas's photos. They gave me the perfect excuse to stop.

A second examination left me none the wiser, though this time I took it further and fetched a magnifying glass from my darkroom. The most exciting thing it turned up was the rear end of a sheep, half hidden by a rock. I had just resumed the housework when something thumped against the party wall, and a moment later it started – reggae this time, full volume. I switched on the Hoover to mask the noise, and when it didn't bopped around to the beat, like the woman in the advert.

There was so much noise I almost missed the telephone. It was Control, informing me there had been an accident on the motorway north of Junction 29. Persons reported.

I wasn't surprised there had been an accident. Sudden rain after weeks of dry weather makes road surfaces greasy and turns them into skidpans. My heart raced unpleasantly as I drove up the slip road: despite my work, I'm not happy at the sight of blood. The vision that greeted me was a test of my endurance.

A caravan had jack-knifed while overtaking a pick-up. It had hit the central reservation and bounced backwards, flipping the tow-car and depositing it upside down on the cab of the truck. A transit had ploughed into the back. Other vehicles had swerved and collided.

The paramedics and fire crew were already at the scene. I approached the Officer in Charge and held up my camera. He gave a cursory wave.

'Who's in the car?' I asked a passing fireman.

'Family of five. Mum, Dad, three kids.'

91

'Alive?'

'Just about.'

'The pick-up?' I looked at the flattened cab.

He held up two fingers.

At that moment the cutting saw started, drowning the sound of the mother's screams.

I left when the final ambulance pulled away and drove to the Globe. I needed a drink. I also needed company. It was still early, with just one car in the car park as I crossed the tarmac to the mock-Tudor façade. A banner advertising The Carvery fluttered above the porch.

The landlord was polishing glasses, a low-band VHF radio tuned to police frequency crackling at his side. His hand went out to switch if off, stopped when he saw it was me. His face puckered into a thousand creases.

'Gus! Long time, no see. How's tricks?'

'Hi, Pete.' I climbed on to a stool, shrugged.

'That good, huh?' He leaned across the counter, took my hand. 'Want to sail away for a year and a day, to the land where the –'

'Just a drink, Pete.'

He frowned. 'Been on the motorway?'

I nodded.

He held a glass to the whisky and raised his brows. Hell, why not.

'You eaten?' he asked as he slid it in front of me.

'No thanks.'

'You should. We've got some nice chilli sans carne . . .'

I winced. Why did that sound like chilli sans carnage? 'Just the drink, Pete.'

'You know best.' He looked up as a crowd of youngsters barged noisily into the lounge. Wrong company.

'Mind if I take this in the dining room?' I asked.

'Be my guest.'

Only one table was occupied. A couple in their thirties sat by the window, gazing into each other's eyes across

92

rump steak and French fries. I squeezed on to a settle in the far corner, rucking the turkey-red cushion on the polished wood. The table was set for four, mock-Georgian silver on a pink linen square over white damask.

Murmurs carried from across the room, too quiet to decipher. Pity – a spot of eavesdropping might have distracted me from the images crowding my mind. I could still see the white pick-up with the flattened cab, the green and red sign on its side. *Rosamunda Nurseries. Roses are our speciality.* I knew it well, had been there with my father, could still smell the moss roses with their age-old complex blooms. In a few days' time they would be twined into a wreath.

'Mind if I join you?'

Miles away I jumped, spilling whisky on the cloth. Simon Furneaux was staring down at me, his head slightly to one side. 'Pete said you might like company.'

I forced a smile, waved him to a chair.

'I gather it was pretty nasty up there.'

'Two dead, seven injured, three of them kids.' I stared at the whisky, swirled it in the glass. Bit my lip. And suddenly, without warning, it came pouring out. 'You know what really bugs me about this job?' I said angrily. 'The pointlessness. Everyone's there helping – you lot, firemen, ambulance – and what am I doing? Taking photographs! Essential, or what?'

Simon eyed me steadily. 'You know it is. That's why you do it.'

'Try telling that to a mother whose kids are injured and trapped. Jesus! I tell you, sometimes I feel like a ghoul.' I took a long swig of whisky. 'Guess I'd be no good working for the tabloids.'

'Glad to hear it,' he said. 'The day you get blasé, it's time to get out.'

A waitress appeared, holding a pencil and pad, and hovered by our table. Simon cleared his throat. 'You eating?'

I shook my head, told him to go ahead.

He turned to study the blackboard, treating me to his profile. He has a straight nose and firm chin, today with a hint of stubble. Not the sultry good looks of his best friend, but an interesting face nonetheless and not unattractive. A tiny scar I'd not noticed before ran from the corner of his eye to just above his ear. I wondered if he was married. Rumour had it there had been a wife but his current status was a mystery. A man who kept his private life private.

He settled on the roast beef, then did a quick retrieving act when the waitress dropped her pad. She blushed as she took it, scurried to the other table.

'Day off?' I asked.

'That a joke?' He pulled out a packet of cigarettes. 'Mind?'

'Not if they don't. Still on that rape case?'

'That and a dozen others.' He flicked a Zippo and the smell of petrol wafted in a nostalgic cloud.

I fiddled with a concertinaed napkin. 'Sorry about the outburst.'

'Don't be. Makes a change to meet someone human.'

'That bad, huh?'

His expression said it all.

I sat back. 'While you're here, can I ask you something? Personal belongings found with a dead body. Would your lot have a list of effects?'

'I take it we were involved?'

I nodded. 'The old lady who fell into a quarry. Dartmoor, last spring.'

'I remember. Edge was on it. Who wants to know?'

'A friend. She's next of kin, the niece.'

'Why – something missing?'

'She's not sure. Possibly a film. A camera was returned empty.'

He looked at me sidelong. 'Eighties, wasn't she? Slipped on some ice.'

I knew what he was thinking. 'The list?' I prompted.

'I dare say there's a record somewhere.' He checked his watch, glanced over his shoulder.

I flattened the napkin with my fingers. 'I don't suppose
. . . There wasn't anything odd about the case, was
there?'

'Odd? In what way?'

'Her death. It being an accident.'

'Why do you ask that?'

'Oh, just some things my friend found. Her aunt kept
diaries and . . .' I hesitated. I hoped I wasn't going to regret
this. 'Some of the entries have made her uneasy. It sounds
crazy, but the aunt thought something was going on. On
the moor. Presumably something illegal.'

'She say what?'

'No. But she does say she confronted someone.'

'And?'

'And nothing. He laughed at her.'

'I meant did she give a name?'

I shook my head, and I saw the corner of his mouth
twitch. 'It's not funny, Simon. She was a very frightened
old lady.'

'And now your friend suspects foul play.'

'Wouldn't you? Look, I've *seen* the diaries. If it was my
relation –'

'Okay, so what exactly did the old girl say?'

I repeated what I could remember, all too aware of the
dearth of facts. Judith was going to owe me big for this. I'd
barely finished when the waitress arrived with his food.
Simon smiled his thanks and earned a simpering grin in
exchange. Maybe he'd been taking lessons from Leo.

'So what does your friend plan on doing?' he asked, as
he shook out his napkin and tucked in.

'Keep her eyes open. Try to find out if there was anything in it.'

He nodded, then laid down the knife and fork. 'Want my
advice?' He reached for his beer. 'Tell her to forget it.'

'I'd be wasting my breath.'

'Then more fool her.' He glanced at the window as a
Morgan turned into the car park. 'She was an old woman,
Gus. Bad weather, walked too far –'

'*She walked all the time!*' The couple at the window turned to stare. 'She was on the moor every day,' I said more quietly.

'Then she should have known better.' He'd started eating again.

'Judith won't give up,' I told him. 'Especially since the burglary.'

'What burglary? Shit!' he muttered when his mobile rang. He slammed down the knife and fork, checked the number. 'Sorry, I'll have to take this outside.'

Another couple were coming in as Simon left, and they were shortly followed by a group of four. Soon the place would be filling up. I decided to leave when Simon returned. But five minutes later there was still no sign, and tired of watching gravy clot I returned to the bar. Buzz Beecham had arrived and he and the landlord were ogling two girls in cut-away shorts flaunting it at a far table.

'Anybody there?' I asked, passing my hand in front of his eyes.

'Gus!' he exclaimed. 'Where did you spring from?'

'Is Furneaux about?' I asked. 'His food's beginning to look like something from Motorway Services.'

'D'you guys ever get to eat a complete meal?' Pete muttered, gesturing at the waitress. 'He took off. Said to tell you he'd be in touch. Oh, and he left this.' He pulled a card from under the counter, his eyes twinkling. 'Reckon he's hoping *you* might call *him*.'

'Fancy another?' Buzz said, dragging his eyes from the girls and pushing forward my glass.

I told him no thanks. Far be it from me to come between him and his fantasies.

Monday morning the French firefighters arrived and lined up for the welcoming photographs. In full regalia, the Chief Fire Officer and his Assistant exchanged gifts with their opposite numbers, and I captured them in a tableau of frozen handshakes and paralysed smiles. The Chief's secretary was doing her best to translate the agenda – lunch at HQ, followed by the slide show in the afternoon.

'Wonder what the Frogs'll make of the Brigade canteen?' Nick chuckled beside me.

At the first lull I went to find Etta.

'Feeling less crabby?' she asked as I perched on her desk.

I mumbled something about the weather.

'You know what you need . . .'

'Information.'

'Uh?'

I told her about the list of effects. Etta pursed her lips. 'That'll be Jenny,' she finally decided. 'I'll see what I can do.'

'Thanks.' I slid from the desk. 'Oh, anything more on Trevor Collins?'

Her eyebrows lifted. 'Who?'

I knew that look. It meant SIN had closed up, that the case was hush-hush. 'What's going on?' I asked.

She shrugged, glanced towards the door. 'But I reckon you opened a can of worms when you unlocked that door.'

'Any worms in particular?'

She shook her head, began to type.

'Well, thanks for the other.'

'No problem,' she said, all sing-songy again. 'Have a nice day.'

Whatever the French thought of Brigade food, they clearly weren't happy with a one-hour lunch break. The minutes dragged on, and as presenter of the slide show I was left hanging around. To kill time I read the Sacred Oak brochure. It began with a description of the house and grounds, words like *restful*, *pastoral* and *meditative* much in evidence. So too in the summary of the Institute's aims, headed *A Future Consciousness*. The study programmes allowed a generous amount of *time for reflection* – cheaper than hiring lecturers? – and there were several photos of students becoming aware. A few lines under the heading *Accreditation* waffled persuasively but said little.

I turned to the list of courses. *Green Politics and a New World Order . . . Gaia, a Message for Mankind . . . Listen to the Goddess . . . Creative Spirituality through Art and Music . . .* Yeah, yeah, yeah. Each bore a mugshot of the visiting lecturer, all but two male. Most looked like successful businessmen, apart from one who resembled a female impersonator. A small paragraph at the end, entitled *Living in the Community*, prettily packaged the fact that you'd be fending for yourself. No chambermaids or kitchen staff at Sylvanus Lodge. It was DIY on a rota basis, sharing thoughts of enlightenment whilst peeling the spuds.

The final page gave the cost of the courses. I gasped. I hadn't imagined awareness came cheap, but four figures to do your own cooking and cleaning had to be a wind-up. I was still reeling when the telephone rang. It was Judith, wanting to know if I'd looked at the brochure. I told her she must be psychic, that I was reading it now, still trying to take in the prices. She told me to turn to the bottom of page nine.

'Why?' I asked.

'Just look.'

The course was entitled *Myth, Memory and Creative Imagination*, and began the following Friday.

I frowned. 'You're not thinking of going?'

'I wish I could, but unfortunately they know me.' She paused. 'Actually, I was rather hoping you might go.'

'*Me?* That's a joke, right?'

'I was afraid you might say that. But it's only a weekend. Two days –'

'No, Judith. No way!'

'At least think about it. I'll pay. Your father did say you've a holiday coming up –'

'And I'm not spending it at some muesli-and-sandals holiday camp!' I snapped. 'Judith, I've an exhibition in three months and I desperately need to work. I'll be spending the entire two weeks working. Besides, I thought you were broke. Where are you going to get that sort of money?'

My door opened and Buzz appeared, held up five fingers. I mouthed okay. 'Look, I've got to go, Judith. Sorry, but the answer's no.'

I slammed down the receiver, shaking my head. If nothing else, you had to admire her cheek.

And persistence. Late that evening she called again. Not being on call, I almost didn't answer. I was curled in front of the television with a glass of whisky, watching a re-run of *London's Burning* that I'd missed first time round. It was late, I was comfortable, and the plot was building to the climax, flames leaping into the night sky and a wall threatening to collapse. I wanted to see what happened. But the phone kept ringing. Keeping my eyes on the screen, I lowered the volume. 'Hello?'

'It's Judith. Please don't put down the phone.'

I hit mute. 'What's happened?'

'Nothing. I'm in the village. Do you have someone with you?'

'Only the television. Why?'

'I have a proposition.'

'If it's about the Institute –'

'Please listen. I realized after we spoke that – well, it was unfair to expect you to give up your holiday, not without some form of recompense. So I thought –'

I sat forward. 'Recompense?'

'For your time. I shouldn't have –'

'You're offering to *pay* me? I don't believe I'm hearing this! What happened to the debts? You have a money tree up there or something?'

'Of course not, I'm not offering money. I'm offering you a deal. You go there, look around, ask questions, and if you find anything –'

'Are you out of your mind? What d'you think I am,

some sort of private investigator? I wouldn't know where to start, Judith. Besides, this isn't about money, it's about time, which right now is a precious commodity. So forget it, okay? And please don't ask me again. There's nothing you can offer that will change my mind.'

There was a pause. 'Not even my aunt's books?'

Chapter Ten

'Sacred Oak Institute. May I help you?'

It was a woman's voice, husky, with a strong American twang. Zara Chadwicke?

'I hope so,' I said. 'You've a course this weekend, *Myth, Memory and —*'

'That's right. You want to join us?'

'Do you still have a place?'

'One moment, I think you might be in luck.' I heard the rustle of paper. 'Yes, we have a last-minute cancellation. Somebody up there's smiling.'

'Aren't they just,' I said.

'So may I have your name and address?'

I repeated it slowly so she could write it down.

'You're local,' she said, sounding surprised. 'Most of our visitors come from much further afield. May I ask how you heard about us?'

'Your brochure was in the library.'

'Of course. Now regarding payment . . . Normally we require a deposit but at this late date . . . Perhaps if you settle in full when you arrive?'

I assured her that was fine, and she went on to explain how I was to arrive at seven to settle in, after which there would be an informal get-to-know-each-other in the 'Encounter Room'.

'And have you special dietary requirements?'

'I'm sorry?'

'Macrobiotic, vegan . . .'

'I'm vegetarian,' I said.

'Oh, we all are here. Simple basic food to nurture the soul. Well, I think that's about it. We'll look forward to seeing you, Augusta. I'm so happy we had a place.'

'It was meant to be,' I said, my tongue prodding my cheek. At least she hadn't told me to have a nice day.

My two-week holiday began the following Friday, but first I had a birthday to get through: 1st August, the reason for my name. I arrived in the world shortly after midnight, with what I now consider perfect timing. A day earlier and I'd have been named after my grandmother, Florence. Flo Tavender?

Cards decorated my filing cabinet, mostly smutty cartoons or jokes about age. Others stood on the mantelpiece at home, including one from my ex-partner, Dougie. I was tempted to burn it when I saw his name, and would have done had it not been a Bill Brandt. The bastard knows my weaknesses.

I stared down at the brochure lying on my desk. The course ran from Friday evening to Monday morning and promised a visiting lecturer from Canada, one Magalie Vosper. For the umpteenth time I read the blurb.

Using the medium of their choice, participants will be taught to probe the innermost reaches of consciousness, and from the rich imagery within to recreate, in abstract or concrete form, the feelings generated by . . .

Blah blah blah. What was the term Miss Hillas had used – etherealspeak?

But what the hell, it was only two days. The books would be with me a lifetime.

There are some mornings when I think I'll never get out of bed, usually when I've been up half the night at a shout. The morning after my birthday I had no such excuse. I'd spent the previous evening with Lisa – just the two of us, just like old times – and we'd taken in a play by a well-known touring company. During the interval we met friends in the bar and afterwards returned to their place for a nightcap. Too many, as it turned out. During the night an Alien had clamped itself to my forehead and sunk its tentacles deep behind my eyes.

I crawled to the edge of the mattress, rolled out and landed heavily on my knees. I felt as if my skull had cracked. Was I really going to work like this?

Somehow I made it, praying for a shout to get me outside. Never had the phones been quieter. By eleven I was desperate and, inventing an excuse, drove into town, where I spent an hour recuperating in a café. Several cups of strong Colombian later I returned to my car, via a slight detour to the street market. I needed a persona for the coming weekend. Having no idea what Sacred Oakians wore, I plumped for ethnic, and bought a couple of items from the Indian stall – a pair of long silver earrings made of jangly coins and a bracelet of woven leather thongs. Something told me I needed to blend in.

Back in my office I found a computer printout on my desk. The inventory of Miss Hillas's effects. I ran my finger down the list, then double-checked to make sure. No mention of a film. The camera was described as empty.

I heard nothing from Judith for the rest of the week, though on Friday a cheque arrived to cover the fee. I hoped it wouldn't bounce. At five that evening I said goodbye to my office. My holidays were upon me. Two whole weeks of photography and painting and, because I was spending them at Tynings, two blissful weeks without noise. But first there was the Institute to get through. I thought Judith would have rung, if only to wish me luck.

I returned to the flat, packed a holdall for Sacred Oak, plus a suitcase to leave at Dad's. A quick bite to eat, followed by a shower, and I changed into loose cotton trousers and an Anhouki top. I fixed the earrings, knotted the bracelet at my wrist, and took a final look in the mirror. Hippy chic? Lord knows, it was too late to care. One last check and I was off, heading west in search of enlightenment – though I doubted it was the kind the Institute had in mind.

Sylvanus Lodge lay at the end of a long drive bordered by rhododendrons. It was a classic small manor house, with mullioned windows, a row of steep pitched gables and tall slender chimneys. Centre front, steps led up to a crenellated porch. Much of the façade was covered with Virginia creeper, neatly clipped around doors and windows. Sunlight lit the tops of the chimneys but the rest of the house lay in shadow, shielded by a wall of dark pines that cloaked the grounds in privacy. The perfect retreat.

Fronting the entrance was a large well-kept lawn, an ancient oak tree standing proud in its centre. The Sacred Oak? A sign saying *Visitors' Parking* directed me to a courtyard at the rear. I pulled in between a shiny new Rover and a vintage Daimler, which told me a good deal about the clientele. My Brigade Escort looked as out of place as a bottle of ketchup in a ritzy hotel, and I wondered if who arrived in what was being noted.

Before I could reach the front door a man tripped down the steps, his hand extended in greeting. Suntanned face, orthodontic smile, dark hair hanging past his shoulders in guru-like locks. I guestimated mid-forties, then did a quick reassessment when he came up close. The hair was peppered with grey, the neck deeply lined. Early to mid-fifties but wearing well.

'Alden Chadwicke,' he beamed, clasping my hand in both his own. 'Welcome to Sylvanus Lodge, Augusta.' He laughed at my bemused look. 'Don't worry, I'm not psychic. It's simply that everyone else has arrived.'

'Am I late?'

'Not at all. The others were early.' He lifted my hand, peered at the leather bracelet, then met my eyes. The stare was hypnotic, making it difficult to look away and equally difficult not to. Finally he released me and swept up my bag. 'Come, you must meet the others. I think we can promise you a *stimulating* weekend.'

The hall stretched the full width of the house, linenfold panelling hugging the lower walls. At the far end a wide staircase dog-legged upwards. A floor-length window on the half-landing was filtering coloured light through panes of stained glass.

'A later addition,' Alden said, following my gaze. 'Victorian, most likely. But beautiful, don't you think?'

I said, 'It's a very beautiful house.'

'Indeed, we were lucky to find it. Or *destined*, if you listen to Zara. She believes the oak tree grew especially for us, knowing that one day we would come and appreciate it as it deserves.'

'And you?'

'I admire her conviction.' The dark eyes crinkled.

He must have been handsome in his youth, before excess weight softened his features. Even now the eyes promised seduction. If Lisa were here she'd be nudging my arm and whispering, 'He'll play!'

'It requires a lot of upkeep,' Alden was saying, 'but it's well worth the expense. Can you imagine a more perfect environment for study? Ah, here's my wife now. Zara? Come and meet our final guest.'

I'm not sure what I was expecting. Certainly not what I saw. My first impression was New Age. She was an extraordinary woman, almost as tall as Judith, with a gaunt face, Nancy Reagan cheekbones, grey-blonde hair cut in a shoulder-length fringed bob. Like her husband, she appeared younger from a distance. She came gliding towards us, her feet invisible beneath a flowing homespun robe. I braced myself for the inevitable brushing of cheeks, but she stopped a few yards off, brought her hands together as if in prayer and bowed her head.

'Welcome to Sylvanus Lodge, Augusta. I hope your stay will be a pleasant one.'

The voice on the telephone.

'I'm sure it will,' I said.

Alden clapped his hands. 'Right, well I must get back to the others. Zara will show you to your room. Please join us when you're ready.'

His wife swept past me and up the stairs. I picked up my bag and followed. The landing was large, three corridors leading off. A sign on the first said *Administration*. The second was roped off, barred by a *Private* sign in a wrought iron stand, presumably the Chadwickes' quarters. Zara coasted into the third. Bare walls and an oak-board floor, covered by an almost threadbare runner. The only furniture faced us at the far end, a dark wooden chest bearing a single brass bowl, hanging above it a framed mandala.

Rooms opened on both sides and I hoped they were better furnished than the corridor. For what they were charging the least we should expect was a private bathroom, with asses' milk spewing from solid gold taps.

'Where did you live in America?' I asked Zara's back.

'Los Angeles. The City of Angels.'

'That's something of a misnomer these days, isn't it? My American friend refers to it as the City of Freaks.'

'A somewhat narrow view,' the woman replied brusquely. 'I prefer to think of it as a City of Vision. It attracts a great many original thinkers.'

Nice start, Tavender.

She turned left at the end, briefly pointed out the bathroom – so much for the en suite – and started up a much narrower flight. It seemed I was to be up with the gods.

'I was thinking more of crime,' I said. 'The murders, drug abuse, violence . . .'

'But isn't that why we're here? If the world wasn't in such turmoil, places like Sacred Oak wouldn't be necessary.'

Of course.

We had arrived under the eaves. Zara pushed open a door and stepped back into the shadows. 'Our rooms are simple, perfect for contemplation. Please join us when you're ready. You'll find us in the Encounter Room, off the main hall. All doors are clearly marked.' She turned, then paused. 'I trust you will find the weekend stimulating.'

106

I closed the door behind me and dumped my holdall on the narrow bed. The room was spartan. A small chest of drawers doubled as a bedside table, and held a white lamp with a plastic shade. The only other furniture was a wooden table and chair. No wardrobe, no carpet, just a hand-woven dhurry on unpolished boards and a couple of coat hangers dangling from a hook on the door. Beneath the hook a printed notice informed me of the fire drill. If the alarm sounded I was to return the way I'd come – unless the fire was on the stairs, in which case I was to continue along the passage to a fire escape. It was comforting to know there was one. Old timbers like this would go up like matchwood.

I looked down for the key. No key.

But of course there wasn't. Trust would be a byword at Sylvanus Lodge.

The booming voice was already in full spate when I entered, and all eyes were on the speaker, a bald, round-faced man in a fawn linen suit, half an inch too tight. He was gesturing dramatically.

'. . . and that is what has been missing in the latter years of the twentieth century. Art has become sterile, mainly because of its divorce from spirituality.'

I crept in unnoticed and did a quick head count. Thirteen, including Alden and Zara. A pleasant little coven.

'But can we be so sure it *is* divorced?' said a thin woman with buckteeth and wispy hair. 'Can we presume to know what is in an artist's mind?'

'We can *see* what is in his mind,' said Bald-head vehemently. 'Simply by looking at his work. It should have *soul*, *passion* . . .' He brought his hands to his chest. 'It's the *soul* that is missing in contemporary art. Put a modern painting on the wall and you might just as well hang a – a photograph.'

I gritted my teeth. Two minutes into the course and already I was confronting the same old prejudice.

'Can a photograph not have soul?' I enquired, and all eyes turned.

'Augusta.' Alden stepped forwards. 'I didn't see you come in.' He had changed into blue trousers and a white Nehru-collared shirt. He looked like a masseur. 'Our final seeker, ladies and gentlemen. Augusta, allow me to introduce you.'

Names sailed over my head as my fellow 'seekers' smiled and nodded hello. Only two sunk in. Bald-head's name was Fraser Ashley-Jones, and a large lady wearing a bell tent was called Jenny Carey. I only remembered hers because during the introductions she jerked her head at Fraser and winked.

'So tell us, Augusta.' Alden spread his hands, giving me the floor. 'Can a photograph have soul?'

I jutted my chin. 'I know I can be as moved by a photograph as by a painting.'

Away to the side, Jenny muttered, 'Hear, hear.'

'Oh, come now, young lady.' Fraser bestowed a supercilious smile on the room at large. 'Surely you can't believe that, merely by pointing a camera and pressing a button, one can achieve the same meaning . . . emotion . . . depth,' he rolled his hand, 'as in something created from the heart, brushstroke by agonizing brushstroke, over a period of weeks, months – sometimes years?'

I felt like yawning. 'Yes, I do,' I said. 'A camera is merely the medium of expression. It's the artist who creates the image, not the machine.'

'And are you speaking as a photographer?'

'Photographer *and* painter.'

'But I suspect photographer foremost.' Without allowing me to reply he turned back to his audience. 'As I was saying, art divorced from spirituality . . .'

'Pompous ass,' said a voice in my ear.

It was Jenny Carey. She directed me to some chairs, lowered herself with a sigh. 'Somebody ought to step on him. He's been droning on like that for the past half-hour and not one original idea. All rehash.'

'Who is he?' I asked.

'A writer. Of sorts. He's *self*-published half a dozen books – *In Search of Spiritual Aesthetics*, that sort of thing. You can see why they call it Vanity Publishing.' She hooted loudly, earning a disapproving glare from Fraser, then leaned back in the chair, legs spread wide beneath the fuschia-coloured tent. Her humour was infectious. It may be a cliché to label fat people jolly but I couldn't think of a better word. Blue eyes twinkled in the full-moon face, above a snub nose sandwiched between rosy cheeks. A Mabel Lucy Attwell character turned sixty.

'He was here last time I came,' she continued. 'I almost turned tail when I saw him tonight.'

'You've been here before?'

'Several times. Got to do something with the old man's money.' Another hoot. 'It's the same with those two over there, making fools of themselves over Alden.' She nodded towards the fireplace where the women stood one each side of their host, gazing up adoringly as they clung to his words. 'You'd think at their age they'd be less obvious.'

'Who are they again?'

'Laura, the one in the floral trousers, claims to be a painter. The other – God, she shouldn't wear yellow – is a poet named Mildred Naish. It's his eyes, of course, the threat of sexual conquest. I'm surprised you're not up there with them.'

I shook my head. 'Not my type.'

'Nor mine. Too sure of himself. Lucky for him, eh?' She slapped her thigh, gave another bellow.

I said, 'Zara must be a tolerant lady.'

'Oh, don't you believe it. Watches him like a hawk. Every few minutes her eyes sweep the room. She's pretending to check on the guests but she doesn't fool me. An inch out of line and look out!'

I smiled. 'Sounds like you know them pretty well. They're from Los Angeles, right?'

'That's where they met. Lord knows why they came back here.'

'Back?'

'Oh, they're not American, my dear.'

I frowned. 'Zara is, surely?'

Jenny laughed. 'Don't let the voice fool you. Accents can be acquired. If you ask me, our hostess is as American as clotted cream.'

'She's English?'

'I'm sure of it. Cornish, at a guess. I'm a local girl myself, you see, brought up just across the Tamar. *Plus* I have a very good ear. Sharp on accents and never forget a conversation – useful qualities for a writer.' She leaned closer. 'Also, I once overheard a slight contretemps between her and Alden. In anger people forget.'

I thought of Dinah, a girl I'd known in London, whose clothes and accent screamed Sloane. Until she lost her rag, when she was as English as a koala.

I looked at where Zara was sitting, on a large sofa next to a middle-aged man in a purple bow tie. She appeared to be listening intently but every so often her eyes drifted away and did a quick scan of the room.

'You see?' said Jenny.

I grinned. 'So what about Alden? Is he local too?'

'Ah, now Alden's more interesting – something of a chameleon. English, certainly, though where exactly . . . If asked to guess I would say Home Counties, but I'm not sure I would want to commit myself.'

I didn't press it. There would be plenty of opportunity for that in the next couple of days.

'So what do you write, Jenny?' I asked, changing the subject.

'Write?'

'You mentioned useful qualities for a writer . . .'

'Oh, no, no – that wasn't in this life.'

'I'm sorry?'

'That was in a previous existence – when I was a contemporary of Jane Austen.' She touched my arm. 'Do you recall any previous lives?'

'Er, no, I . . .'

'Then you *must* try regression therapy. I've a wonderful man. Remind me to give you his card.'

I managed a smile. And just when I thought I'd found someone of like mind.

I wasn't sure who to approach next. The lady with buck-teeth had joined Alden's little coterie and Fraser was out of the question. I focused on a man in a grey suit. He'd been alone since I arrived, sitting at the undraped window and contemplating the night sky. But as I started towards him Zara jumped up.

'Not Mr Brewer,' she whispered. 'He doesn't speak.'

'Oh, I'm sorry,' I said, 'I didn't realize. Poor man.'

'Not can't – won't. He's taken a temporary vow of silence. Come, I'll introduce you to Dr Claybourn.'

It was the man with the bow tie, a painfully thin man with a long face, a thatch of dark hair, a prominent Adam's apple. Add a top hat and he would have passed for the Mad Hatter.

'Call me Leonard,' he said, patting the sofa with a skeletal hand.

'Leonard's a therapist,' Zara informed me before drifting away.

'Not regression . . .'

'Psycho.' He smiled. 'I see you've been talking to Jenny. Do I take it you don't subscribe?'

'Not entirely.'

'Me, neither. Nor, incidentally, do I agree with Ashley-Jones.'

The way to a girl's heart! Doc Claybourn turned out to be not only pleasant but knowledgeable, and we ended the evening discussing the work of Robert Mapplethorpe, about whom he knew considerably more than me. Several times I caught Alden watching me. Zara was watching him. The Doc, needless to say, was watching all three of us. I bet he didn't miss a trick.

At last the party broke up and I climbed the two flights

of stairs to my room, jamming the chair under the door handle in lieu of a lock. I undressed quickly and climbed into bed. Sweet dreams were not forthcoming. The mattress was a two-inch strip of foam on a solid base. I'm not sure about nurturing the soul, but it was certainly capable of numbing it.

Chapter Eleven

The Saturday morning lecture was held in the library. It was smaller than the Encounter Room, with bookcases lining two walls, an arched stone fireplace on the third and the fourth mostly taken up by window. Small tables faced the fireplace, two chairs to a table. Jenny was sitting near the front but when she beckoned I pretended not to see, sat instead by the man who didn't speak. Standing by the bookcases, Fraser was already pontificating, holding open a thin volume for Buckteeth to see.

'You will notice I mentioned precisely that on page fourteen, where I was attempting to show . . .'

So it was one of his. I didn't doubt it had been donated.

Doc Claybourn arrived last and took the chair in front of me, and shortly afterwards Zara coasted in. Fraser and Buckteeth hurried to their chairs.

'I hope we're all feeling refreshed?' Zara asked, and after a few half-hearted murmurs, 'Then let's set out on our path of discovery.'

She launched into a flowery account of the aims of the course, then passed neatly over the fact that the visiting lecturer had been delayed and would only be with us on Sunday. She hoped we wouldn't mind, therefore, if she gave the lecture herself. More murmurs. Clearly she hoped to achieve miracles because by Sunday, she promised, all *manner* of magical things would have happened to us. We would be staring deep into our souls, have become familiar with the language of memory, be adopting a new, more personal approach to artistic creation, all of which were steps on the path towards wholeness and integration. Or that was the gist. I drifted off after the first few minutes, grimly reminding myself of why I was there.

I'd gone to bed wondering if I was out of my depth. Now I was sure. I had no idea what, if anything, I was looking for, nor how to go about finding it. Already I'd been here fourteen hours and what had I learnt? That Alden fancied a bit on the side, and his wife's accent was probably false. And that from a woman who believed she'd been swanning around Bath with Jane Austen. Yet Judith had made it clear she expected results – no info, no books. I had a nasty feeling we would both be disappointed.

Gloomily I tuned back in. Zara's talk had drifted to colour symbolism, how certain colours conjure moods and emotions in the conscious and unconscious mind. Familiar territory; I'd covered it in my first year at college. Black, symbolic of death, mourning and earthy dark secrets; white, the symbol of purity, illumination and light. The masculine principle, the feminine realm. All basic stuff. The psychotherapist was doodling on a pad, looking bored.

We moved on to red, token of the emotions, anger and sexual excitement, and this time Zara wanted examples.

'Wine,' offered Fraser. 'Our Lord turned water into wine.'

I wasn't sure which token it was supposed to illustrate but Zara seemed pleased. 'Indeed he did,' she said. 'And what a symbolic gesture that was. Anything else?'

'Menstruation,' said Buckteeth and Fraser winced.

'Ah yes, the blood of life itself. The ultimate symbol of the Feminine. Augusta?'

I jumped. 'Um – fire?'

'Fire. Good. The element of destruction. Red is the universal symbol for danger, because fire kills.'

Tell me about it!

I listened with growing disbelief as she dredged up all the clichéd references – tongues of fire, burning in hell. How did they get away with it? I could have learned all this and more during half an hour in Waterstone's basement. For seven ninety-nine I could have bought the book. When she touched on dream symbolism I almost laughed out loud. Fighting a fire, she informed us, represented a subconscious need to calm the sexual passions. I must remember to tell the guys at work.

When we broke for coffee Doc Claybourn sidled up, disillusionment in his eyes. 'And are you *fired* with enthusiasm after Zara's little talk?' he asked.

I told him to hush or her ears might burn. Something told me he wouldn't be coming back.

The period before lunch was much the same, more superficial stabs at dream imagery, archetypes, and the collective unconscious propounded by Jung. Half an hour's revision and I could have given the talk myself. When she finally wound up it was with the hope that her talk had been *stimulating*, clearly the Sacred Oak buzzword, and the suggestion that from now on we examine and use our dreams for creative expression. The afternoon, she concluded, would be a time to 'absorb and reflect'.

Beside me Mr Silent's stomach rumbled. It was the first audible contribution he'd made since he arrived.

Lunch was a do-it-yourself affair of salad and rice. No Zara, though Alden arrived soon after we started and squeezed on to the bench beside me. At once Buckteeth began bombarding him with questions about local folklore, apparently a continuation from the night before. I was half listening to them, half to Mildred and Laura who were discussing the poems of Ted Hughes, when Alden mentioned Veniston Quarry. My ears pricked up.

'In medieval times,' he was saying, 'the law stated that the dead be buried in their own parish churchyard. For a large area of the moor that meant Lydford on the western edge. Imagine, carrying a coffin in winter across such treacherous terrain. Mists, bogs, no roads, few if any bridges –'

'"Eight miles in fair weather, fifteen in foul,"' I cut in, quoting some ancient source I had long since forgotten. 'You're talking about the Lych Path.'

He swivelled to face me. 'I forgot you were a local girl. But you're right, the Lych Path. Otherwise known as the Path of the Dead.'

'I didn't know it ran past Veniston Quarry,' I said. 'I thought it was further south.'

'The main one, perhaps. But consider the area we're talking about. Clearly there had to be offshoots.' He picked up an earthenware pitcher, poured water into his glass and without asking topped up mine.

'Isn't Veniston where that old lady died?' I asked casually.

'Miss Hillas, you mean? Yes, it was. Dreadful tragedy.'

'What happened?' Buckteeth asked, sitting forward.

'Oh, one of those foolish accidents.' He filled her glass too. 'An old lady out walking, icy weather, strayed too close to the edge. She slipped and fell to her death.' Buckteeth winced. 'It's lucky she was found, as a matter of fact. The bulk of the quarry's flooded. If she'd fallen into the water . . . well.'

'Did you know her?' I asked.

'Oh yes, she lived not far from here. Remarkable lady. In her eighties and still walking every day. They say walking brings inner calm and Miss Hillas was a shining example.'

'Did she ever stay here?' Buckteeth asked.

'Alas, no. To be frank – well, I'm not sure she approved of us. I'd hoped, given time . . . But there, we mustn't dwell on the past.' He looked pointedly at his watch. 'So do we all have plans for this afternoon? Augusta?'

'Colour photography,' I said, squeezing my legs over the bench. 'Normally I use black and white.'

'Sounds like Zara's talk has inspired you. Will you be working in the grounds?'

'I doubt it. I want to use water and reflections.' I paused. 'Maybe I'll visit Veniston Quarry.'

'Well, you'll certainly find reflections there.' He swivelled on the bench, blocked my path with his legs. 'It's an interesting choice – going down to the water. You do realize it's symbolic?'

'It is?'

'Of spiritual and psychic rebirth.' He brought his hands together, touched the fingers to his chin, then looked up, held my eyes. 'You must take care. This could be a critical time –'

'Did I hear you say you were going out?' Mildred jumped to her feet and reached for her cardigan. 'Mind if I come with you?'

'Actually, I do,' I said, thinking quickly. 'I'm sorry but . . . you'll understand if I say I need to be alone?'

Mildred looked miffed but didn't argue. This wasn't the place to question spiritual necessity.

Before going anywhere, I wanted to see Dad. He hadn't been happy about me visiting the Institute, and the least I could do was let him know I was okay. Hewitt's early warning system must have alerted him because he arrived at the door before me.

'Thank God!' he breathed, almost dragging me inside. 'I've been out of my mind. You're not going back there, you hear?'

'Whatever's the matter?' I asked as he bundled me into the kitchen.

'This! This is the matter!' He snatched a scrap of paper from the table and thrust it towards me. 'Judith got it. Last night.' He was breathing fast. 'I went up there, to see how she was. When I left it was on the floor.'

'Floor?' I repeated lamely.

'Hall floor. Just inside the front door.'

I sank down on a chair, read it through again. My hand was shaking. The paper had been torn from a cheap exercise book, a pulpy beige stuff with faint blue lines. The message was written in pencil.

LAY OFF. YOUR FREINDS TO.
WE DONT WANT NO MORE ACIDENTS.

'I take it we're the friends,' I murmured.

'Who else does she know?' Dad pummelled his fist on his thigh. 'Bastard must've delivered it while I was there. If I could get my hands on him . . .'

'You're sure it wasn't there when you arrived?'

'Of course I'm bloody sure! Stuck out a mile.' Dad rarely swears, not in front of me, a sure sign he was troubled. 'It was me who picked it up,' he growled. 'Didn't read it, just handed it straight to her. Then I saw her face . . .'

'And you didn't hear anyone?'

'Not a peep. I don't reckon they came by car. If they did, they didn't park close. Judith reckons it's Weblake. Someone barely literate, no doubt about that.'

Or someone who wanted us to think that. 'Well, it wasn't the Chadwickes,' I said. 'I was with them all evening.' I frowned. 'Why haven't the police got this?'

'With you up there? Don't be daft!'

'*You haven't told them?* Christ, Dad . . .' I shot to my feet.

'What are you doing?'

'What you should have done!' I rummaged in my bag for Simon's card, hurriedly tapped out the number. 'Simon,' I began, before realizing it was a message. Impatiently I hung on for the beep. 'It's Gus Tavender,' I then said, trying not to sound shaky. 'That friend I told you about? She – *we* – have received a threatening message. Please get back.' I followed it with Dad's number and address.

'Who's Simon?' Dad demanded.

'DI Furneaux.'

'You told the police about Judith? What did they say?'

'He. He said to forget it. Perhaps now he'll have second thoughts.'

118

Chapter Twelve

In the nineteenth century, when Veniston was in full production, a moorland railway hauled stone from the quarry to the road. Much of the granite ended up in London, some reputedly in London Bridge. Now all that remains of the railway is the raised grassy embankment, a favourite route for walkers. I expected to be one of dozens and was pleasantly surprised when I passed only a few, mostly coming the other way.

Walking allows you to think, and today most of my thoughts were on Dad. I had left him in the middle of a fairly heated row – inevitable, I suppose, given the circumstances. It was the same old story, whose needs to put first, and needless to say concerned the Institute. He insisted I stay with him. I insisted on going back.

'Why?' he'd demanded. 'Why put yourself in danger? You've called the police, now leave it to them. Miss Hillas is *dead*, Gussie!'

'But Judith isn't,' I said. 'Don't you care about her?'

'Not nearly as much as I care about you.'

A lump had risen in my throat. I could see what this was doing to him. But it was no longer just Judith, the note had made it personal. I didn't like being threatened. I didn't like *him* being threatened.

'Remember what you used to tell me?' I said. 'Your work wasn't about fighting fires, it was about saving lives. There's nothing more important, you used to say, and for years you put your life on the line –'

'That was different!'

'Was it? You did it for *strangers*, Dad – people you'd never met. Yet now, when it's you, me, Judith . . .'

'God damn it!' He turned his back. 'You always were a feisty little madam. Why must you be so damned headstrong?'

'Maybe I take after my father.'

'Oh, so now it's *my* fault!'

And so it went on, ending with me storming out, slamming doors and speeding away. Trying to ignore the look on his face as he watched me from the path. Remembering it now made my gut churn. My father had been a handsome man in his youth, strong, robust, the hero of my growing-up years and a pillar of strength throughout my mother's illness. But the fear in his eyes when I left was a harrowing reminder of how the roles had changed. Was what I was doing fair?

His last few years hadn't been easy – leaving the work he loved, coming to terms with the disease – and I admired the way he had handled it. From the start he'd tried to be positive, reading everything that came to hand in order to make choices, reach informed decisions, finally arriving at a philosophy that was right for him. His beliefs are very simple. Disease thrives in a sympathetic environment, i.e. an unhealthy run-down body. Ergo, make the body as fit as possible and it will keep disease at bay. He creates this 'hostile' environment by adhering to a healthy diet, plenty of relaxation, daily though not excessive exercise, and the avoidance of stress – a natural approach that might not work for everyone but has had a profound effect on him. It's the stress that occasionally creates problems and frequently I'm the cause, never more so than now. The last thing I wanted was to tip the balance.

But I have a life too and I can't always bow to his demands. Hell, did he think I *wanted* to return to the Institute? So why did I still feel guilty? If there's one thing I've learned in the last few years, it's the fine line between selfishness and individual need.

*   *   *

120

The ground to the north had been rising, and as the track curved right I saw a sharp vertical edge. I had reached the quarry. I struck off through a landscape of overgrown spoil heaps and ruined buildings, past granite corbels and ancient winding gear, still bolted to its concrete plinth. Ahead of me was the entrance, a giant cleft in the shape of a V. Beyond it the walls of the quarry loomed in a precipitous horseshoe curve.

Reeds and bog cotton warned me the entrance was waterlogged, so I climbed higher, finally found a path. From somewhere within came the shouts of children. Minutes later I was looking down on a mirror-glass lake. Alden had been right about the reflections. Cliffs looked back at themselves around the edge, while the centre mirrored the sky – a deep intense blue, the colour of a Madonna's robe. Two-thirds of the way around a narrow shelf of rock projected into the water, and it was here the children played, a boy and a girl, carefully watched by two adults.

It was a scene begging to be photographed and I pulled out my camera, reeled off half a dozen shots. I'd zoomed in for a close-up when the boy threw a stone. It landed with a plunk, sending up a shower of silver droplets, and I caught them while they were still in the air, the little girl clapping her hands with glee. Pure serendipity.

The adults had produced a towel and were drying the children's feet. They must be on the move. I waited for them to leave before making my way to the ledge. The ripples had long since faded, leaving the water clear and undisturbed. For a few feet beyond the shelf, rocks were visible beneath the surface, then nothing, only the fathomless murky depths. I realized with a jolt that this must be the spot where Miss Hillas had come to rest. Everywhere else the walls dropped sheer to the water.

Yet despite the grim connotations it was intensely beautiful, the crevices in the cliff forming dark shadows against the sun-warmed rock. And that blue! According to Zara, blue was the colour of intellect, intuition and spiritual energy. I would probably need all of them in the next couple of days.

I took some Polaroids – something to show the group on my return – then reverted to the Nikon and finished the film. The new rolls were in my bag at the rear of the ledge. I wandered back, sat down and began to reload . . .

Something plopped into the water nearby, and when I looked up ripples were radiating just right of the shelf. I tilted back my head and stared up at the rock face. Christ, it was high! I tried to imagine the place in winter – chill grey light, the lake dark and threatening, water dripping from the rock face frozen into ice. And that's when I noticed the silence. No voices, not even a bird call. I was entirely alone. Normally that's something I relish. So why did I suddenly feel uneasy?

I sat forward, craned my neck. No sign of movement on top. Stones must be falling all the time, I told myself, and yet . . .

Another splash.

I squirmed round on to my knees and replaced the camera in my bag. Something hit my arm. More of a sting than a pain, yet when I looked down blood was forming a thin red line. For a moment I watched it, more surprised than frightened. And then I heard the noise.

I didn't need to look up. Only one thing could sound like that. Without stopping to think, I threw myself along the base of the cliff. The undercut was tiny but it was all there was. I squeezed in tight, covered my head with my hands, cringing in terror as the stones came crashing down. From the depths of my childhood came the words of a hymn – *Rock of Ages, cleft for me* . . .

Oh God! Please God, no . . .

When the large rock hit the ledge, the shock ran through my body. I'm pretty sure I screamed. A moment later came the aftermath, an icy wave of water that soaked me to the skin. After that, silence.

I'm not sure how long I lay there, probably only seconds,

122

but it seemed like a lifetime before I opened my eyes. Cautiously I tested my limbs. Everything *seemed* okay . . .

Craning upwards, I crawled out. Nothing broken, just a couple of nicks on my calf. Somebody up there smiling?

Or pushing. Had the rock fallen on its own?

Teeth chattering, I climbed to my feet. The ledge was littered with debris – stones, rock shards, sodden clumps of grass – and where the boulder had landed was a deep jagged gouge. The water beyond was a swirling brown soup, bubbles still rising to the surface. It must have bounced off the rock, causing the wave.

I looked around for my bag, found it coated in dust but apparently intact. I didn't bother to check. Snatching it up, I hurled it over my shoulder and, heart thumping, legged it back to the entrance.

Never have I been so glad to see people. Half a dozen were milling around the ruins – not close, but a comfort nonetheless.

Had it been an accident?

Dartmoor's a dangerous place, I told myself. Disasters happen all the time. Rocks fall, fog descends, mineshafts cave in . . .

I wasn't convinced. Only one person had known I was coming here, Alden Chadwicke. Had this been another warning?

Knowing I wouldn't rest until I found out, I climbed to the top of the quarry. The rim was unfenced, grass running right to the edge. A few feet back it had been worn into a path. I followed it rigidly, gauging my position against the opposite walls. At least the hillside was barren, there was nowhere for anyone to hide.

The source of the landslide wasn't difficult to find. The shallow depression lay to the left of the path, a patch of dark earth, damp, threaded with etiolated plant roots. The grass was gouged between there and the rim, where large clumps of it had been torn away. A larger gouge on the opposite side showed the spot where the rock had been

123

levered. Whatever had lain there, it had not moved on its own.

Heart pounding, I looked around. The nearest people were at the bottom of the slope, two men in blue anoraks heading my way. I ran down towards them, hailing them when I got close, and asked if they had seen anyone at the top of the quarry. They stared at me as if I was mad.

'Up there.' I pointed. 'Someone just started a rock fall.'

'When?' asked the taller of the two. His companion's eyes were again on the ground.

'Fifteen, twenty minutes ago?'

'God, we were miles away. How d'you know it was deliberate?'

Before I could answer his partner gave a yell, and I watched helplessly as they flung off rucksacks and sank to their knees. Out came the impedimenta – inkpads, note-pads, a rainbow of felt-tip pens . . .

I left them behaving sadly and began the long walk back to my car.

The evening meal had already started when, showered and changed, I entered the refectory. If Alden was surprised to see me he hid it well. 'Ah, here she is,' he beamed. 'We wondered where you were. Successful afternoon?'

'Interesting,' I said, and took my place on the bench.

To my surprise I was ravenous. Fear must have honed my appetite. The food was surprisingly good – new pota-toes boiled in their skins, fresh-from-the-garden peas, green salad, courgette and nut crepes – and we toasted the chefs, Laura and Mildred, with an equally excellent wine. Donated by the Doc, I later discovered. Maybe he needed it to get through the weekend.

Fraser and I were down for clearing up and he obviously wasn't pleased. Who, I wondered, had thought of that one? I made a few stabs at conversation, then offered to finish alone, just to get him out of my hair. It took longer than I thought and by the time I entered the Encounter

Room the evening was in full swing. Etherealspeak was rife as sketches and poems were passed around or read out loud, and guests took turns to recall experiences and thoughts. When my turn came I followed suit, waffling about reflections mirroring the unconscious and the importance of colour in creating mood, and with the exception of Fraser it was warmly received. I felt like a fraud.

When the talk became general, Alden sidled up. 'Interesting photographs, Augusta. May I see them again?' I handed them across. 'Just look at that blue,' he sighed. 'Such power. Tell me, how did you feel when you were there?'

'Feel?' I was caught in another eye-lock.

'In such a deep, enclosed space. Did you feel uncomfortable? Confined?'

Only when the rock came crashing down!

'Relaxed,' I said. 'It was – very quiet.'

'So silence is important to you.'

'Isn't it to most people?'

'Not all.' His tilted his head 'Do you live alone, I wonder? I'm not trying to pry,' he added quickly, 'merely to seek a deeper understanding.' He released my eyes, turned again to the Polaroids. 'Such magnificent reflections. By their very nature a mirror image, of course, the opposite of what's truly there. I find opposites fascinating, don't you? Black, white; positive, negative – purity versus lust.' He lingered on the last word. 'I wonder why you chose to photograph *water* especially. Perhaps because it's a passive element?'

'I doubt if sailors would see it as passive,' I said. Nor firemen, come to that. Stand in front of a jet working at ten bars and it will knock you across the ground, possibly break ribs.

'Passivity can wield its own power, Augusta.' He breathed in, flaring his nostrils. 'Is that how you see yourself, as passive?'

'Hardly. Just the opposite.'

'They're two sides of the same coin, you know.'

'Really?' I had no idea what he was talking about. I dragged my eyes away, searching for an escape, and met Zara's gaze head-on.

'I think your wife wants you,' I said, and Alden drew back.

'She, er, probably wants me to circulate. But I think it's important that we continue this conversation. Why not come to my study – say, tomorrow afternoon?'

Dream on, I thought, giving my best non-committal smile. The last thing I needed was a hands-on experience.

The party broke up shortly after eleven and I returned to my room, though not alas to sleep. Tonight I had other plans. I changed into my black jogging suit and curled up on the bed, listening to late-night sounds – footsteps on stairs, doors closing, water gushing through pipes. My heart was thumping against my ribs. Was I really going to go through with it?

Walking back from the quarry I had decided to search the house. At the time – fuelled by anger, emboldened by bright sunshine – it had seemed like a cool idea. Now it seemed like insanity. If the Chadwickes *were* involved in some racket, they wouldn't be stupid enough to leave proof lying around. Worse, if they *had* engineered the rockfall . . .

But that was somewhere I didn't want to go. All I knew was I had to do something. Why else had I come back?

Midnight came and went. Never had time moved more slowly. In danger of falling asleep I paced quietly up and down, until a quarter past one when I could stand it no longer. I grabbed the torch and, checking everything was quiet, crept downstairs.

Moonlight was flooding through the windows, forming eerie dark shadows – the kind that dredge up childish fears of headless knights and clanking chains. I told myself to grow up. The only entity I need fear would be of flesh and bone and very much alive.

Boards creaked as I crossed the landing. Hell, everything creaked in a house like this. I continued on tiptoe and entered the corridor marked *Administration*. Four doors led off it, two on either side. The nearest on the right was marked *Office*. I opted for the one on the left and found myself in a storeroom. Closing the door, I switched on the torch. Shelves lined the walls, piled high with cardboard boxes. The labels told me they were replacement supplies, everything from typing paper to toilet rolls. I chose a couple at random and peered inside. The labels hadn't lied.

The next room along was a repository for art materials. More shelves held cartridge paper, tins of cow gum, plastic containers of poster paint and PVA. Easels leaned at rakish angles on the rear wall. Alongside a carousel projector were several boxes of slides. Again I read labels. *Visionary; Dream Landscapes; Icons; Ecological Disasters*. Random dipping pulled out a landscape by Samuel Palmer, a drawing by William Blake, a photograph of a dead seabird on an oil-slicked beach. No surprises here.

I closed the door behind me and tiptoed across the corridor. The door facing me bore a brass plate, legible even in the moonlight. *Alden Chadwicke, Director*. I tried the handle, wasn't surprised when I discovered it locked. The one place where I might have found something . . .

My optimism had sunk to nil when I crept back down to the office. I just knew that would be locked too. Amazingly the door opened, and I slipped inside, again risked the torch. How much longer would my luck hold?

How much longer would my *courage* hold?

The furniture was conventional and modern, as out of place here as at Brigade HQ. A teak desk in the centre held a computer, complete with modem. I wondered for a moment about switching it on, but decided against it. Anything sensitive would be protected by a password, and I had neither time nor knowledge to hack in.

Feeling more useless by the minute, I checked the drawers. Staple gun, paperclips, biros and envelopes – everything one would expect. The same with the unit under the fax machine. Sliding doors hid nothing more sinister than boxes of printer paper, replacement cartridges and pile upon pile of the Institute's brochures. A small box held used floppy discs. Could anything be learned from them?

Maybe – if I knew what I was looking for!

I moved to the filing cabinet. The top drawer was marked *Disbursements*. I flicked through individual files for Telecom, Insurances, Public Liability and other essential services. Was anything out of order? Could I identify it if it was?

Impatiently I closed it, moved to the next. *Visiting Lecturers* – slightly more interesting. The names were filed in alphabetical order and included several that I recognized – a high-up in the Green movement; a feminist writer; various artists, many based in the south-west. The final name leapt out at me – Joe de Zaire. The sculptor Dad had mentioned, the guy who nearly ran me off the road.

I pulled his file. It contained just two sheets of A4. The first listed times and details of his visits. There were quite a lot, seven in the last twelve months – though perhaps that wasn't surprising considering he lived close by. A further lecture was planned for September, entitled *Seeing, Shaping, Synthesizing*. How had I missed that in the brochure?

The second page was de Zaire's CV, though it took me a moment to recognize it. The document was anything but conventional. De Zaire had eschewed chronological format in favour of a jazzy free-thought narrative, but it made interesting reading. He claimed to have been born in New York in 'the mid-fifties, of parents of French/Italian/ Hungarian descent', but had left when he was three, his father, 'unskilled and something of a nomad', having set off around the States looking for work, dragging wife and son with him. Never long in one place, de Zaire had had little formal education, though he always knew he had 'artistic flair'. At fifteen, when his parents finally split, he took off on his own, determined to become a painter. Life was tough. After several 'shit-lousy jobs', chance landed him a place with a small metalworking company where he was taught to weld. He began piecing together off-cuts in his spare time, creating structures, and soon realized his future lay in three-dimensional art. Now his work could be found in collections throughout America. 'Wiped out by the razzmatazz of the West Coast art world', he had moved to England three years before, in search of a quieter life-style and the chance to 'attune with nature'.

By blasting around the lanes in a Porsche?

I wondered how much of the CV was true. It sounded like hype – but why not, if it worked? Hype didn't make him a criminal.

A sudden dimming of the torch reminded me time was limited. I replaced the file where I'd found it and moved on.

The third drawer contained names and addresses of students: the fourth, details of courses past, present and future. Nothing unusual; nothing suspicious. So much for my bright idea!

I was turning to leave when I saw a second door, in the wall separating the two offices. Direct access to Alden's room? To my surprise it was open, and a moment later I was standing inside. Moonlight poured through the window, falling on a large table, a Commonwealth armchair, a Knole sofa facing the fireplace and two leather wing chairs. Gilt-framed paintings adorned the walls, the largest above an ornate credenza. I didn't need to look to know what it contained – sherry, brandy, cut-glass decanters, more brochures. This was a room for show, a place to entertain privileged guests. A room that had been left open. I would find nothing here.

I backed out, closing the door quietly behind me.

The moon had moved round while I'd been searching, and now the corridor was in darkness. As I crept back across the landing, a timber snapped above my head. The noise ricocheted through the silent house like a gunshot, forcing my heart up into my mouth. Lord knows how I didn't cry out.

The upper stairs to my room were black as pitch, and rounding the corner I knocked against the fire bucket. It clanked loudly against its support. It was the final straw and, throwing caution to the wind, I pounded up the stairs. If that hadn't woken the occupants of the rooms, they must be enjoying the sleep of the dead.

Chapter Thirteen

The Sunday morning lecture was held in the Craft Room. Magalie Vosper, the visiting lecturer, was tiny, barely five feet tall, with tightly curled grey hair, a pink twin-set worn over a pleated beige skirt, sensible shoes and pearls. She looked like a vicar's wife come to sell the parish magazine. I put her in her late sixties and was astonished to learn she was seventy-eight.

In a gently lilting voice and an accent I couldn't quite place, she talked to us about her life, her faith, her hopes. Her life had indeed been remarkable. At nineteen she had left Canada and gone to France to work for the Resistance, returning after the war to enter a Benedictine monastery where she spent twenty years in contemplative study. Since then she had worked with aborigines in Australia, homeless children in Calcutta – and yes, she had met Mother Theresa – and finally the poor in El Salvador. Now, in her twilight years, she was living alone in a croft on the west coast of Scotland, in 'her own ring of bright water' with her animals, paintbrushes and pen.

Her talk could have been pompous, a narrative of self-worship; instead it was a gentle unfolding of a personal history, a natural unexceptional progression for someone in search of truth. Her tone was mesmeric and, although I couldn't subscribe to her faith, I could appreciate her dedication. I caught the psychiatrist's eye and smiled.

Later Magalie played music, Chopin and Vaughan Williams, telling us to close our eyes and drift. Later still we took up brushes and, with the music playing, began to draw. I found myself painting hills and trees, a stream, finally a bridge – the brushstrokes wild, the sky a turbulent mix of reds, oranges, purples and mauves. Munch's *Scream* minus the screamer. Magalie studied it for several minutes, her lips pursed.

'Do you think you will cross?' she asked at last.

'I'm sorry?'

'The bridge. I wonder what's on the other side?'

I laughed. 'Something good, I hope.'

She patted my shoulder. 'So do I, my dear. So do I.'

I was looking forward to hearing more that afternoon, but again I was disappointed. When lunch was over, she informed us, she would be leaving to catch a train. Faced with another afternoon of 'reflection', I decided to explore the grounds. The brochure had described the Lodge as 'slumbering in an air of reverential calm'. It could have added sunlight and birdsong. Perhaps this was what people paid for, the sense of unreality, the complete detachment from everyday life.

The rear courtyard was bordered by a long high wall. Jenny was taking up most of a bench in the corner, and not wanting to get caught in a discussion, I followed it the other way. A short distance beyond the house, an arched wooden door was let into the stone and, unable to resist it, I pushed it open. It led into a walled garden given almost entirely to vegetables, row upon neat row of spinach, beetroot, lettuces, leeks. No wonder the food had been so delicious. There were wigwams of runner beans, long trailing pumpkins, some of the biggest courgette plants I had ever seen. Herbs grew near the entrance in luxuriant green clumps.

Over to one side an elderly man was digging pink-skinned potatoes. His head was round as a football, bald on top, fringed back and sides with pure white hair. When he saw me he straightened. 'Lovely a'ernoon,' he called.

I wandered across, told him I was admiring his garden.

''Taint mine,' he said, in a sing-song lilt. ''Tis Mr Chadwicke's. Lovely man, Mr Chadwicke.' He nodded the whole time he was speaking, his head keeping time with his words.

'Have you worked for Mr Chadwicke long?'

'Oh, yeah, an' previous owners afore that. I gardens for lots of people.' He pronounced it gar-dins.

I smiled. His face was the colour of a walnut and almost as deeply lined. His expression was one of sheer contentment.

'Name's Wilfie,' he said, drawing a filthy handkerchief from the pocket of trousers several sizes too big and wiping his brow. 'Likes me gardens. Lovely place to be on a day like this.' He stabbed the fork in the ground. 'You like raspberries?'

Without waiting for an answer he set off towards a fruit cage, and I noticed he walked with a limp, slightly dragging his left leg.

''Ave what you want,' he told me, pushing open the mesh door. 'Mr Chadwicke won't mind. Lovely man, Mr Chadwicke.'

I brushed past him and got a blast of unwashed body. 'So who else do you work for?' I asked, choosing a bush several feet away.

'Oh, lots of people. Works all over. In village, up on moor.' He snapped a leaf from a redcurrant. 'Blister beetle,' he said, showing me a dark red blotch. 'They'm buggers.'

Maybe they were, but they weren't affecting the flavour. 'I don't suppose you ever worked for Miss Hillas?'

He looked round sharply. ''Er died.'

'I know.'

'Niece got it now.' He plucked another leaf. 'Yeah, us worked there. Lovely lady – 'ard but fair, like. 'Er talked, too – when we was working. Always talking. Reckon 'twere 'cause she lived alone. Wouldn't've used 'er voice, else.'

I bit back a grin. 'What did she talk about, Wilfie?'

'Oh, this and that – where she wanted things. Knew 'zactly what she wanted. Like Mr Chadwicke. Proper garden – not like some.' He screwed up the leaves, shoved

133

them in his pocket, and began to chuckle. 'Mr Zaire's garden – that's daft.'

'De Zaire, the American?' I was having trouble following.

More nodding. 'Still I just plants it, does what I'm told, and 'er seems happy enough. Want to try the strawberries?'

I told him I would burst if I ate any more, and in any case, I wanted to explore the grounds.

'Lovely day for a walk,' he called after me. 'Lovely a'ernoon.'

Indeed it was.

The ground beyond the garden had been left to run wild, and nettles and thistles grew chest-high. Umbrellas of giant hogweed were level with my eyes. From somewhere beyond rose a thin plume of smoke. A path had been hacked through the weeds to a slab of concrete, the remains of a bonfire smouldering at its centre. I picked up a stick and for some reason poked through the ashes. What did I expect to find – bones?

A brief burst of hammering came from beyond the weeds, no doubt one of the guests fulfilling a creative urge.

I paused. Or could it be the odd-job man?

I stared towards the source of the sound. It was coming from behind a line of giant rhododendrons. I beat my way towards them, trampling nettles and getting several stings for my trouble. Why hadn't I worn more sensible clothes?

I finally reached the shrubbery, chose a spot where it was sparsest and forced my way in. Whoever was hammering had begun whistling too. Ten yards in I paused, beyond the shrubs I had seen movement. Abruptly both hammering and whistling stopped.

A moment later I heard voices, men's voices, too low to decipher. Maybe it was the guests after all. I was stooping under a branch when one of the voices was raised in anger.

'Quit fucking around, will ya!'

I froze. *Not* one of the group.

'For Christ's sake! You want everyone to hear?'

But that was. Alden Chadwicke, and he didn't sound happy.

'No skin off my nose, mate!' laughed the first. 'Just get it, okay?'

'I can't just –'

'Listen, mate – I know about the old lady, right? And if you don't want someone else to find out –'

'You bastard!' Alden growled. 'One of these days . . .'

'You'll what, huh?'

'You'll regret it, Gary, you mark my words.'

'Yeah, right. I'm shittin' me fuckin' pants.'

The hammering began again, accompanied by more whistling, the odd line of words thrown in. *Money for nothing, get your kicks for free.*

Another of Alden's employees who sounded utterly content.

Shaking, I retreated through the shrubbery, barely able to believe what I'd heard. Blackmail – Gary was blackmailing Alden. About Miss Hillas. *I know about the old lady . . .* Judith had been right, her aunt *had* been murdered. And from the sound of it by Alden. At the very least he was involved. And somehow Gary had found out and had chosen to profit. Evil everywhere.

But what could an old lady have learned that warranted her death?

One thing I did know – Alden was angry. And anger makes men dangerous.

I returned to the house and dashed up to my room, pausing briefly at the roped-off corridor. If an explanation existed that's where I would find it, not in offices and rooms open to guests but in the rooms marked *Private*. But how, in heaven's name, could I gain access to those? Occupied at night, who knew when during the day . . . And still the questions kept coming. Was Alden acting alone? Did

Zara know? Did whatever Miss Hillas had learned concern the Institute? God knows how I would get through the coming evening.

My clothes had suffered from the foray so I ripped them off, changed into a white T-shirt and a flimsy cheesecloth skirt I'd last worn on the beach. Coming back down the stairs, the skirt trailed out behind me, and rounding the corner I felt it snag. The fabric had caught on the fire bucket. I stopped to pick it free. On the wall above the bucket was a fire alarm. *In case of fire, break glass.*

I stared at it. Fire. The one thing guaranteed to force them from their rooms. If someone were to raise the alarm . . .

No way, Tavender! Are you out of your tiny mind?

So why was I still staring?

Moments later I was retracing my steps, instead of going up went down. The servants' stairs, leading directly to the kitchen. There was a smoke detector on the stairs, another sand bucket at the bottom, a fire blanket and extinguisher beside the massive stove. Fire safety taken seriously. Outside the butler's pantry was a similar alarm to the landing, a small hammer hanging beside it for breaking the glass.

In a passage leading to a side door I found the main fuse panel and electricity meter, but no controls for the alarm system. Often, I knew, these are located near the main entrance so I made my way to the hall, hanging back when I heard voices. It was Laura and Buckteeth, heading for the library. I waited till they had gone and wandered in, gazed round admiringly. If anyone saw me I was planning some photographs.

I found the control panel to the left of the main door, partially hidden by a tapestry curtain. While 'admiring' the fabric, I eased it to one side. The panel consisted of a double row of lights and two switches. The pairs of lights, one red, one amber, were numbered one to seven, each referring to a zone of the house. If a fire started, the red light would flash for the appropriate zone, though without the accompanying floor plan there was no way of telling which was which. The amber lights would highlight a fault in the system. A wire led from the panel to a phone socket, which meant an automated system. If the alarm was triggered it would self-dial 999.

I did some quick mental calculations. The nearest station was staffed by retained firemen, part-timers who would have to rush in from their homes. One minute for the call to be relayed, five for the men to get from bed to the station, ten, maybe twelve, to reach the Lodge through the narrow, twisting lanes . . . Eighteen minutes, twenty at the most. Not long for what I had in mind.

My heart revved up a notch. What I had in mind was illegal. If caught I would lose my job, be dishonoured by the Brigade, most likely wind up in court.

I know about the old lady . . .

A sick feeling lodged in the pit of my stomach. The afternoon was rapidly losing its charm.

Cooking the evening meal had fallen to me and Mr Silent. I peeled onions until my eyes ran, while he sliced and tossed vegetables with such enviable expertise I finally asked if he were a chef. He shook his head.

'So what *do* you do?'

He eased the pan from the flame, glanced over his shoulder. 'Can you keep a secret?'

I nodded.

'I'm a GP.'

I laughed out loud. 'And the minute you mention it, people tell you their ailments?'

'Precisely. So now and then I like to escape. The vow of silence works like a charm.' He looked at me from under his brows. 'You won't tell?'

'Hypocrites ain't seen nothing.'

He chuckled quietly and returned to his courgettes.

The atmosphere on the final evening was more relaxed, perhaps because we'd grown more comfortable with each other. It began in much the same way, but around nine

Alden found some golden oldie CDs and pulled Muriel to her feet. Fraser looked appalled. I danced a couple of numbers with the psychologist and one with Mr Silent before the tempo slowed and Alden intervened. He caught my hand, drew me towards him.

He must have sensed my aversion because he murmured, 'Relax,' as his hand slid down my back. He brought his mouth close to my ear. 'Where were you this afternoon? I looked for you. I thought we were going to continue our talk.'

I gritted my teeth. 'Too late now.'

'Not necessarily.' His fingers stroked my wrist, toying with the leather thong. 'You're not far away. We could meet up. Why don't I give you a call?'

'I don't think that's a good idea.' I pushed against his shoulders. 'Save it for my next visit.'

'You're coming back?' His eyes locked on to mine. 'That's great. So which of our courses has inspired you?'

'The one with Joe de Zaire.' It was the first thing that came to mind.

To my surprise he jerked back. 'You know Joe?'

'I've heard of him. He lives near by, right?'

'Yes, he . . .' He glanced to the side. Zara was watching our every move. The hand moved from my back. 'Well, I'm glad we've inspired you enough to return, Augusta. I shall look forward to it. Now if you'll excuse me . . .'

'You need to circulate.'

'The joys of being the host.'

I watched him move away, wondering what had caused the sudden change. Chatting up one minute, cold shoulder the next. Fear of Zara? Or was it the mention of de Zaire? Whatever the reason, the result had been dramatic. But at least he was out of my hair. Would that I could always cool unwanted ardour so easily.

I realized Zara was still watching me and forced a smile. She didn't respond. Beneath the long blonde fringe her eyes remained cold.

*　　*　　*

Somewhere in the distance a church clock chimed three. Two hours since the party broke up; two hours for everyone to fall asleep. I wandered across to my window. During the evening clouds had sprung up, patterning the grounds in shadow as they drifted beneath the moon. With luck they would work in my favour.

When the clock chimed the half-hour I slipped outside, padded barefoot down the servants' stairs. The flagstones in the kitchen felt cold and clammy. I took rubber gloves from the draining board and pulled them on, then carried a chair to the passage, placed it beneath the fuse board and climbed up. A flick of the switch disabled the supply, creating an eerie silence as fridges and freezers ground to a halt. The alarm system, powered by its own battery, would be unaffected. Next, I unlocked the side door and replaced the chair, then hurried to the alarm outside the butler's pantry. Moonlight had stripped it of colour but the instructions were still clear. *In case of fire, break glass . . .*

Slowly I unhooked the hammer – then wavered, barely able to believe what I was about to do. Hoax calls are the bane of the Brigade, a serious punishable offence. What would my father say? My friends at work?

I thought of my anger at the note, my fear as the rocks began to fall, and smashed the hammer against the glass.

The wail was immediate and deafening, and for a split second I froze. Then adrenaline kicked in and catapulted me into action. Racing back up the stairs, I dived into the bathroom, just as I heard the first cries and pounding feet.

'There's no lights! What's happened to the lights!'

'Is it a fire?'

'Which way? Where do we go?'

I crouched behind the door of a cubicle, praying no one would hurt themselves in the rush. At least the moon was still shining to light the stairs.

Over the noise Alden was shouting. 'Is everybody out? Make for the hall. Assemble on the lawn.' Next moment the bathroom door opened. 'Anyone in here?'

I huddled up small; if he checked the cubicles I was done

for. He didn't and a second later I heard the door close. When fire threatens, people tend not to hang around.

When the only sound was the siren I left my hiding place and ran to the landing. The rope to the Chadwickes' corridor was down, the *Private* sign knocked over. I peered into the first room. One glance told me it was unoccupied. The door to the next was half-open and I was met by a cloying waft of perfume. Zara's room. It was chaotic, the bed a rat's nest, drawers half open, chairs and tables littered with clothes. Robes and more robes. Nothing of Alden's.

His room was next – ordered, very masculine, the clothes he had worn earlier folded neatly on a chair. Only the bed was shambolic, the result of a hurried departure. I could see why they had different rooms.

I checked my watch – already seven minutes gone. Where the hell did I start? I homed in on a chest of drawers and yanked open a drawer. Handkerchiefs, underpants, socks arranged in pairs. My body recoiled as I felt under, around, between. Never before had I searched someone's personal effects. Suppose Alden was innocent? How would I feel if someone did this to me?

I know about the old lady . . .

I slammed the drawer closed and moved to the next. More clothes. The same in the wardrobe – trousers, shirts and jackets on hangers, shoes and sandals on the floor, a row of ties on the back of the door. Was this to be another fruitless search?

I crossed to the bedside cabinet and slid open its drawer. More neckties, but this time in a jumble. Jumble? The sudden disorder jarred. I pulled one out, found it knotted to the next, and the next, like handkerchiefs in a conjuror's hat. Did Alden practise magic in his spare time? I stuffed them back, crouched down, opened the cupboard beneath. A pair of handcuffs and a riding crop rested on a pile of magazines. The covers said it all.

I sat back on my heels. So Alden got off on bondage. Well, whatever rocked your boat. Judging by recent media coverage, he wasn't alone. I could imagine it was something he would want to keep quiet – visitors might find it offensive. But enough to kill? And how would Miss Hillas have found out? No, there had to be something else . . .

Time was running out. I stared frantically around the room. On the far side of the bed a modern unit housed a sound system, television and video player. Video cassettes filled the shelf beneath. I skirted around, shielded the torch with my hand and ran it over the titles. *Pulp Fiction*; *Wild at Heart*; *Blue Velvet* . . . Gentle bedtime viewing. The last ones in the row bore no titles, only numbers, 1 to 14. Number 12 was missing. I touched the video player. Warm. He must have been watching it when the alarm went off.

I jabbed Play, then remembered there was no electricity. Nor was there any more time. As I knelt back my watch began to bleep. Out of time and out of options.

I jumped to my feet, then paused. I was damned if I would leave with nothing. I grabbed a cassette at random and made a dash for the door.

'There she is,' Jenny cried as I stumbled through the front door. Alden came rushing forward.

'Where were you? We were frantic! Didn't you read the drill?'

Everyone was talking at once. I stared from one to the other, feigned disorientation. 'I got lost,' I stammered. 'Couldn't find . . . The lights didn't work and . . .' If this didn't deserve an Oscar, nothing would.

'For heaven's sake!' Jenny steamed forward like a leviathan. 'Can't you see she's in shock?' She draped a massive arm around my shoulder. 'Come with me, we'll go and sit down.'

'Is she all right?' Zara had detached herself from the others. She turned accusingly on Alden. 'I thought you checked the upper rooms.'

'I did!'

'So where was she?'

'Is there a fire?' I asked, somewhat belatedly.

'Probably not,' Alden growled. 'Damn system up the shoot.'

Another glare from Zara.

'Surely the important thing is we're all safe,' Jenny said archly, and led me away.

She ushered me to a bench at the side of the lawn. 'Don't be too hard on them,' she whispered. 'They're in shock, too. They're the ones responsible for our safety.'

We had barely sat down when the pump swept up the drive. It crunched to a halt on the gravel and five firemen jumped out. Alden went forward to meet them. I knew what he was being asked. Was anyone still in the building? Had he smelt smoke? Where was the control panel? It wouldn't be long before they found the broken glass of the alarm.

Broken glass. Precisely what I was treading on.

Without warning I began to shake. Reality was hitting home. I leaned forward, rested my head on my knees.

Which is why I didn't see the white car come up the drive, its engine drowned by the noise of the pump. Nor did I bother to look up when I heard someone approaching. Not until Zara spoke my name.

When I opened my eyes I saw the hem of her robe, beside it a pair of polished black shoes, the revolving blue light reflecting in their shine. My head snapped up.

'Good God!' Leo Wiltshire exclaimed. 'It *is* you.'

'I couldn't believe it when I saw the name,' he grinned, as I walked with him to his car. 'Thought it was coincidence. I thought, it can't be *our* Gus, not here. Morris dancing's bad enough, but a place like this . . .'

'I'm allowed to go on a course, aren't I?' I was hugging myself against the cold, shivering in the aftermath and night air.

His brows lifted as he opened the door. 'Touchy, aren't we?'

I climbed in, told myself to act calmly. 'What are you doing here anyway?' I demanded, as he slid in beside me. 'No, don't tell me – you happened to be passing.'

'I was, as a matter of fact. On my way back from Plymouth.'

'Yeah, right.' Ambition never sleeps, not when you're after making Senior DO.

'So what was the course?' he asked.

'Does it matter?'

'Interesting?'

'Not particularly.'

Leo smirked. His eyes were on the fire crew who were coming back out.

'Have they found anything?' I asked.

'Doubt it. Someone playing silly buggers. Disabled the electrics, then smashed the alarm. Doesn't look like there's any other damage.'

'How did they get in?'

'Side door was unlocked. Though the boss-man – Chadwicke, is it? – swears he locked it. Anywhere else I'd say kids, but there aren't any for miles. My guess is one of you lot.'

'Us?' It came out as a croak.

'Makes sense. Any oddballs on the course?'

'How long have you got?'

He smiled. 'So how come you were last out?'

'Oh, you know – strange house, no lights. That place is a warren.'

'The others managed.'

'Don't rub it in.'

The smile widened to a grin. 'Ah well, better get someone to check the drill.' He grabbed the door handle, glanced back. 'I trust *you* had nothing to do with it?'

'You calling me an oddball?'

'You're here, aren't you?' He gave a wink and climbed out.

Chapter Fourteen

I left before breakfast and returned to Tynings. Still angry at my stubbornness, Dad tried to pretend indifference, but I could see the relief in his eyes. I left him to work it through and went up to unpack. In a pocket of the holdall was the videotape, the sole, and it now seemed pathetic, result of last night's escapade. Not only pathetic, but unbelievably stupid. Not content with raising a false alarm, I could now add illegal entry and theft to my list of crimes.

The memory of those last minutes brought an adrenaline rush. Running from Alden's room, dashing to my own, stripping off the jogging suit. The oversize T-shirt I use to sleep in was already underneath. From there I'd run to the bathroom and hidden the tape behind a radiator. I'd retrieved it on a last-minute visit to the loo before leaving the Lodge.

Looking at it now, I wondered why I'd bothered. It probably contained nothing more sinister than footage of students at work in the grounds or of the Chadwickes' time in LA. All I would have achieved by stealing it was to alert Alden to the fact that someone had been in his room, and he would have a pretty shrewd idea who. Who else had had the opportunity?

My hands were shaking as I stuffed the cassette in a drawer and buried it beneath a pile of jerseys. The ostrich principle – if you can't see it, it doesn't exist.

Yeah, right!

Two messages were waiting for me on the answering

machine, one from Phillip Mawson in London, the other from Simon Furneaux, both urging me to call back.

'Didn't DI Furneaux contact you?' I asked Dad.

'Briefly. He was in a hurry. Some other lad turned up for the note.'

I waited till Dad was out of the room and rang Simon's number but he was still unavailable. At *ArtView* I had more luck.

'Looks like I was right,' Phillip said, after apologizing for the delay. 'Kempe Hillas have problems.'

'Financial?' I asked.

'Dire, from the sound of it. But what's interesting is why.'

'Bad judgement?'

He gave a laugh. 'That's one way of putting it. Seems the husband sold a pricey painting to a collector, one Herbert van Eys. Turned out to be a fake.'

My fingers tightened on the receiver. 'Did Kempe know?'

'Claims not. Which might be the case – a good copy can fool even the experts. But van Eys didn't see it that way and threatened to sue. I gather there was a good deal of legal wrangling, which must have cost a packet, until finally they settled out of court, presumably to save the good name of the gallery.' He paused. 'One hopes the expense was worth it. These things have a way of leaking out.'

'Sounds like they already have,' I said.

'Oh, I don't think it's common knowledge – not yet.'

'You think they'll go under?'

'Depends. On whether there's some resource they can tap into. If someone's willing to bail them out, there's a chance they'll pull through.'

I thanked him for his help, assured him I wouldn't mention his name, and after promises to keep in touch we said goodbye.

'That your DI?' Dad asked as he came back in.

I shook my head. My mind was reeling. 'Dad, I have to go out.'

'*What?* You've only just come in!'

'I know.' I snatched up my keys. 'But I need to see Judith.'

'Can't you see her later? I want to know what happened up there.'

'It'll keep,' I told him. 'Remember what you used to tell me about patience.'

I'd hoped to see her alone but Judith had visitors. Not only was a red Porsche parked outside, but when I ran up the steps Wilfie was on the terrace, weeding between the slabs.

'You was at the Manor,' he said.

I nodded. I'd hoped he wouldn't remember. 'Is that Mr de Zaire's car?' I asked.

'That's right. Lovely motor.' He gazed down at it longingly. 'Mr Zaire showed us it runnin'. Real powerful 'tis.' He turned back. '*You* like cars?'

'As long as they go. Are they in the house, Wilfie?'

'Didn't see 'em go out.'

I took that as a yes and knocked on the door. Judith took her time answering.

'Oh, it's you,' she said when she saw me, and glanced over her shoulder. She leaned forwards, lowered her voice. 'Joe's here. The sculptor. Please don't say anything in front of him.'

'Like I would.'

'You know what I mean.' She stepped back. 'You'd better come in. We're in the conservatory.'

The first thing I noticed about de Zaire was his hair, a glossy dark mane reaching halfway down his back, caught at the nape with a band. That and his height. He was probably no more than six one or two, but his spare frame made him appear even taller. Black jeans hugged narrow hips and a black T-shirt moulded his torso. The one arm I could see bore a deep olive tan.

He was leaning in the open doorway to the terrace, his

back towards us. When the parrot announced our arrival he turned lazily around.

'Isn't he great?' He grinned widely. 'I just love that bird.'

There have been few men over the years for whom I felt an instant attraction. Normally it's something that grows out of knowing, deriving as much from personality as from physical appeal. Joe de Zaire was an exception. He was older than I'd thought from his rear view, probably forties, but he had that rangy, hungry look that I can't resist and a lean face verging on handsome. Or maybe it was his eyes . . .

I realized Judith had been introducing us.

'Another artist, huh,' Joe said, as he pushed away from the door and came towards me. 'Painter?'

Definitely the eyes. Dark, intelligent . . .

'Painter, photographer,' I told him.

'Yeah? What kinda thing d'you do?'

'Landscapes mainly, though –'

'This your inspiration?' He motioned towards the moor.

'Mostly.'

'Mine too, though few can see it.' He squinted into the sun. 'It sure is energizing out there. All that haze and shimmer . . . '

'Do you work in stone?'

'Metal.' He turned back. 'I'll show you if you like. Come to my studio, Jude knows where it is. But a quick buzz first, okay? I don't like to be disturbed when I'm working.' He glanced at Judith. 'Talking of which . . .'

'You're leaving?' she asked.

'Got to. There's this piece I'm working on that won't leave me alone, know what I mean?' He threw a wave at the parrot. 'See ya, Geoff.'

The parrot gave a cackle and Joe laughed. 'What a star!'

We watched through the windows as he swung himself over the wall and headed back to his car.

'Where did you meet *him*?' I asked.

'Oh, he used to visit my aunt.' She took a beer from the table, held it out. I shook my head. 'He heard I was staying here and called in. He's been a few times. Keeps asking if there's anything he can do to help.'

'You should have taken him up on it,' I said, as the roar of the engine drifted through the open door. 'You do know he lectures at the Institute?'

'He mentioned it. Oh, I see – you think I should have asked *him* to nose around.' She shook her head. 'I don't think that would've been a good idea. Two Americans, living not far apart. For all I know he and Alden could be bosom pals.'

'You're saying you think *Joe's* involved?'

'Heavens, no! He's a fairly well-known sculptor. Anyway, how did you get on? Did you –'

'In a minute,' I said. 'First I want to ask you something.'

'About Joe?'

'About a fake painting.'

Her mouth opened and closed. 'Fake? I'm not sure –'

'The one Stuart sold? The reason you're in this mess?'

I watched the colour drain from her face. She took a step backwards. 'How – Who told you?'

'A friend.'

'But no one was supposed . . . Oh God!' She sank down in a chair, gripped the arms. There was no need to ask if the rumour was true. 'So it's out,' she breathed at last. 'It's all been for nothing. All the wrangling, debts, worry . . .' Anger sparked in the green eyes. 'Well, thank you, bloody solicitors! Tell no one, they said, that way it remains secret. Some secret!'

'I don't think it's common knowledge,' I said.

'So how come *you* know? Hell, I need a drink!' She pushed herself from the chair, looked around, found the gin bottle beside the parrot's cage.

'Want to tell me how it happened?' I asked, as she half-filled a tumbler.

'It wasn't deliberate, if that's what you think!' She gulped the gin neat, winced, began to pace. 'Stuart bought the painting in good faith, sold it the same way. It wasn't his fault that . . . The problem is he's always dealt in

148

modern works. This was eighteenth century, not a period he's familiar with. Or genre. But the provenance was excellent, as was the price, so . . .'

'He saw the chance to make a killing.'

'He knew if he didn't grab it someone else would.' She stopped, rubbed her forehead with her hand. 'I'm sorry. This is taking some getting used to.'

She took another drink, came back to the chair. 'I said the price was good, and it was – but far more than we usually pay. Way out of our league, if I'm brutally honest. It meant an enormous loan, short term, colossal interest. But Stuart knew if he could sell it on quickly he could still make a sizeable profit. And he knew of this collector –'

'Herbert van Eys.'

Judith started. 'Is there anything you don't know?' She smoothed back her hair, ran her fingers around the neck of her shirt. 'But you're right – Herbert van Eys. God, I knew we shouldn't have done it . . .'

'So Stuart bought the painting,' I prompted.

She nodded. 'And as he'd predicted, van Eys lapped it up. So Stuart arranged things and the deal went through. It took longer than we expected – I swear the banks were holding back – but we still managed a comfortable profit.' She sighed. 'Stuart was still busy congratulating himself when the letter arrived from van Eys's lawyers. He'd had the painting examined by experts and they'd declared it a fake. The letter was to inform us of his intention to sue.'

'Just like that?'

'Just like that.'

'But mistakes of that kind must happen all the time. Couldn't you simply apologize, plead ignorance and return the money?'

'We didn't *have* the money. Stuart ploughed it straight back into the business. What hadn't been used to repay the loan was hanging on the walls of the gallery. Besides, that wasn't good enough for van Eys. He was convinced Stuart had tried to swindle him and he wanted to make us pay.'

'By going to court.'

149

'Exactly. And dragging our name through the dirt, effectively putting us out of business. But Stuart *didn't* know, I swear he didn't. He sold the painting in good faith.'

'Then why not let him sue?'

'You think I didn't want to? I *begged* Stuart. Let him go ahead, I said, we have nothing to hide. But Stuart wouldn't hear of it. Mud sticks, he said, and we couldn't afford the bad publicity. In retrospect, he was probably right. Van Eys had hired one of the best law firms in the country, better than anything we could afford. Even our own solicitors weren't sure we'd win. It was they who advised us to settle out of court. That way, they said, we'd lose a fortune but retain our reputation. If we went to court we would probably lose both.'

'But if it was a genuine mistake . . .'

Judith gave a watery laugh. 'I thought like that when all this started. Until I had a few facts pointed out. Would you trust twelve strong men and true not to be persuaded by the country's top wordsmith? At least this way we have a chance of struggling back, our reputation untarnished.' Her brow wrinkled. 'Or so I thought. It seems I was mistaken.'

'When did all this happen?' I asked, and for the first time Judith hesitated.

'In February,' she said quietly.

'And you received the letter . . .?'

'A month later, in March.' She met my eyes. 'Six weeks before my aunt's death – and yes, I do know how that looks. But *I* didn't kill her and nor, I swear, did Stuart. He might have faults but violence isn't one of them. Besides, as I've already told you, he couldn't leave London.'

'You sure about that?'

'Of course I'm bloody sure! Christ, if you knew what it was like back then. Phone calls, meetings with solicitors, paperwork going back and forth . . . It dominated our lives: there was no spare time. It was difficult enough me getting away, let alone Stuart.'

'Even so, your aunt's death must have seemed like the answer to a prayer.'

'Prayer?' She spun round at me, her face dark. 'If you must know, it was more like the final straw! The one stable thing in my life, snatched away. Later, yes, of course I could see how the money would help – but at the time . . .' Tears moistened her eyes and she turned away. 'And now this. All our efforts in vain.' She swallowed the last of the gin. 'You know what worries me most? How I'm going to tell Stuart.'

'Need you tell him?' I said. 'Why not wait and see what happens?'

'And let him hear from someone else?'

'It might not come out. No point in worrying him unduly.'

She sighed. 'Maybe. You could be right. Hell, I don't know!' Then, 'Who did tell you about van Eys?'

I shook my head. 'I gave my word, Judith.'

'Of course. So I just sit around and wait for things to erupt. Hell, Stuart can't even contact me . . .' More gin sloshed into the glass, though this time she added tonic. 'Just when you think it can't get any worse. Problems there, problems here, problems bloody everywhere! I suppose you're now going to tell me the Institute was a waste of time, too!'

'Depends how you look at it,' I said, knowing things were about to get a lot worse indeed.

Judith paced up and down while I explained what I'd overheard, only stopping once when I mentioned Gary's words. I saw a shudder pass through her body. I wondered whether to mention my searches but decided against it. I certainly wasn't going to mention the video.

By the time I had finished she was back in the chair, struggling to control her anger. 'I want that bastard behind bars,' she hissed. 'Both of them.'

'We don't *know* Alden killed her,' I pointed out. 'Only that he was involved.'

'Isn't that enough?' Another shudder. 'As for Gary . . .

151

How can anyone be so callous? He'd known Aunt all his life and he's capitalizing on her death. Capitalizing! Well, I hope the pair of them rot in hell!' Her knuckles whitened on the chair. 'It was probably Gary who brought that note. Blackmail, the burglary –'

She broke off and we both turned to the window. Outside a woman was laughing.

'Hell!' Judith muttered. 'It's June. She's come to do some cleaning.'

'Want me to send her away?'

'No.' She climbed shakily to her feet. 'Everything must seem as normal. I'll be fine.'

I went with her anyway.

The woman talking to Wilfie was thin as a rail, almost as thin as Doc Claybourn, the hands fiddling with the carrier bag appearing quite literally worked to the bone. When she saw us she hurried across.

'What a climb!' Her hand went to her chest. 'Never did like the heat. Shouldn't complain though, after all that rain back in May.' She put the bag on the ground, wiped her hands on a pink gingham overall. Once she must have been pretty, but her skin had become sallow. Her hair was a greying fluff of lifeless waves.

Judith introduced us. Her eyes hadn't once left my face.

'Bob Tavender's daughter?' she exclaimed. 'Well, there's a thing. Never would have guessed, 'part from the height. Expect you take after your mother.'

'So I'm told.'

'Like our Lorna. Just like me, people say she is. Gary too, though in other ways he's more like his dad. Funny how it works out. Take him over there.' She jerked her head at Wilfie. 'Mother was quite a beauty, by all accounts. Can't imagine, can you? Still, mustn't be unkind. Might seem daft, but he ain't so green as cabbage-looking. Not much passes Old Gam.'

'Old who?' I asked.

'Gam.' June clicked her tongue. 'That's what they call him, on account of his gammy leg. Not to his face, mind.

Still, he's a good worker, long as you don't get downwind.'
She squeezed the end of her nose. 'Don't mind what he
does or in what weather. Works all over, even for that
American what I just seen leave.' She chuckled. 'Bet he
fancies that car! Loves cars, does Wilfie.'

I said, 'Your daughter, Lorna. Does she have long dark
hair?'

'That's right, down to her waist. Why?'

'I think I might have seen her on my way here. Pink top,
jeans –'

'That'd be Lorna,' June beamed. 'Getting real excited
about Saturday, she is. You do know she's Queen of the
Revel?' She flapped her hand. 'But of course you do,
seeing as you're playing.'

'I'm sorry?'

'That squeezy thing.' She mimicked a concertina. 'Or so
your dad said. Didn't he tell you?'

'It – must've slipped his mind.'

'Probably savin' it as a surprise. Big event, Swinlake
Revel.' She turned to Judith, lowered her voice. 'Young
Kenny's in the tug-o-war. Hope things – you know. Any-
way, best get on. Start on the kitchen, shall I?'

I watched her hurry away. 'If she cleans like she
talks, I want her,' I said, and Judith managed a smile.
'Her daughter's very pretty,' I added. 'Is Kenny her
boyfriend?'

'Yes, but it's hush-hush.' She nodded towards the car.
'Thanks to Gary – again,' she explained when we were out
of earshot. 'For some reason he's taken a dislike to Kenny.
He's forbidden Lorna to see him.'

'You're not serious. Why?'

'June doesn't know – or claims she doesn't. All I know
is they meet in secret.'

'And Kenny goes along with that?'

'For Lorna's sake. June says he's a nice lad – gentle,
kind-hearted. Everything Gary's not.' Her eyes narrowed.
'What did she mean about you playing? Are you in the
procession?'

153

I told her about the accordion, said it was wishful think-ing on the part of my father. 'Don't worry,' I added, 'I won't be going.'

'Maybe you should. *Everyone* will be there.'

'Meaning the Chadwickes?'

'And Joe,' she replied, giving me a sly smile.

Chapter Fifteen

Clearly it was a day for visitors. I arrived back to find Simon Furneaux in the kitchen talking to Dad. Both stood up as I entered.

'At last,' Dad said. 'We'd just about given you up.' He turned to Simon. 'Well, I'll leave you to it then. It was nice meeting you. Should you want me, I'll be next door.'

I stared after him. 'Why the sudden departure?'

'I wanted to speak to you alone.' Simon cleared his throat. 'I apologize for arriving unannounced, but I happened to be in the area so –'

'That's okay.' I switched on the kettle. 'Has Dad made you coffee?'

He stared down at his cup. 'Actually it's some sort of tea.'

I smiled. One of Dad's herbals; I'd smelt it as soon as I walked in. I took down a second mug.

'I hear you've been away this weekend.' Simon moved up beside me. 'The Sacred Oak Institute, is that right?'

'I thought you were here about the note.' I pushed past him to the fridge.

'Your father's filled me in on that. Besides, he seems to think they're connected – that the owners might have sent it?'

'They didn't deliver it,' I said, closing the door and side-stepping back round him. 'I was with them the whole evening.'

'Any idea who did?'

'Do you?'

'Not yet, that's why I'm here.' He leaned back against the worktop, folded his arms. 'He told me why you were there, Gus. He was worried out of his mind.'

'I'm aware of that,' I said coldly. 'Sugar?'

He shook his head. 'Why couldn't your friend go?'

'They know her.'

'And now they know you.' For some reason he sounded angry. He watched me fill the cafetière. 'I gather the Chadwickes are American.'

'Zara might be. Alden's English. But that's where they were before, in LA.'

'Any idea how long he was out there?'

'None. Why?'

'I thought you were supposed to be sleuthing.'

I gave him a 'Very funny' smile, carried the coffee to the table and sat down.

He followed and perched on the edge. 'So what's the connection between Chadwicke and your friend's aunt?'

'I don't know.'

'But your friend thinks he murdered her, right?'

I nodded. 'And presumably so does the guy who's blackmailing him.'

I went through it all again, only this time Simon took notes. Occasionally he interrupted to clarify a point. 'Are you sure they didn't see you?' he asked finally.

'Pretty much. I couldn't see them.'

'That's not –'

'I'm sure.'

'Let's hope you're right.' He tapped his teeth with the pen. 'So how old's this Chadwicke character?'

I told him early fifties and gave him a brief description. He scribbled everything down. 'Don't suppose you noticed eye colour?'

'Blue.'

His brows lifted. 'That was quick.'

'I had plenty of opportunity to study them,' I told him. 'He's a habit of holding you in his gaze, locking on, a sort of full-strength penetration –'

'Okay, I get the message. So sees himself as a charmer. Do women find him attractive?'

'They appeared to.'

'Not you? Sorry – none of my business.'

'Not my type,' I said. 'Besides, there were enough women fawning over him without me adding to the crush. Plus there's an ever-vigilant wife.'

'Hampers his progress?'

'I imagine so, at least at the Institute. My guess is extramural liaisons. Matter of fact, he asked to meet me – though it could just be that I'm local.'

'I doubt that.' Simon smiled. He took a wallet from his pocket and pulled out a photograph. 'Could that be him? I'd better warn you it's out of date.'

'How out of date?'

'Twelve years?'

'Wow. Nice to know you lot are on the ball.'

I held the photo towards the light. It showed a man on what appeared to be a cabin cruiser, his lower half hidden by the bows. Dark hair cropped short, a Mediterranean tan, eyes narrowed as he stared into the sun. An attractive face with fine, even features. But not Alden's. I shook my head.

'You sure?'

'Nothing like.'

Simon clicked his tongue.

'Who is he?' I asked.

'Doesn't matter.' He reached out to retrieve the print.

'Not good enough, Inspector.' I snatched it away. 'I want to know what's going on.'

'That's what I'm –'

'Here to find out? Yes, you said that. So why do I get the feeling you already know?'

'If I knew, I wouldn't be asking questions.' He beckoned with his finger.

'But you suspect something, that's why you brought this.' I looked from him to the photo, back again. 'I don't think you happened to be in the area at all. I think you

157

made a special journey. Now why would you do that? And what made you think this guy was Chadwicke?'

His looked impatiently to one side. 'It was a long shot, okay?'

'Very long if it's twelve years. Why suddenly dredge . . .?' I broke off as something clicked in my memory. The conversation with Phil Twigg in the Ring of Bells.

'The *bête noire*,' I murmured. 'It's the guy you were talking about, isn't it? You and Phil. The one who disappeared, who you thought had gone to America. Ray something. Ray – Ray . . .'

'Rayjay,' Simon growled. 'Okay, it did occur to me. But clearly I was wrong, all right?'

'But why now after all this time?'

'I told you, a long shot. You mentioned Chadwicke being in the States –'

'That's bullshit, Simon! You didn't know of Chadwicke's existence until five minutes ago. And you just happened to be carrying the guy's photo?' Another memory stirred. 'That body I found – Trevor Collins . . .'

'Just leave it, Gus!' This time his voice was sharp. He beckoned again but I determined to ignore him.

'Phil said Trevor worked for Rayjay,' I continued. 'He dies in suspicious circumstances. We get a warning, then you turn up with this.' I met his eyes. 'You think they're all connected, don't you? The note, the body . . . So what's going on, Simon? Is Rayjay back, is that what this is about?'

'Just leave it, can't you?' He jumped to his feet and crossed to the window. 'I mean it, Gus,' he said, lowering his voice. 'You don't know what you're dealing with.'

The softly spoken words had more effect than if they'd been shouted. A shiver ran down my spine. 'What *am* I dealing with, Simon?'

He didn't answer.

'And why here? Why Chadwicke?' Now I was thinking out loud. 'There must be hundreds of men who've spent time in America, yet you home in on him. Why? Has he been seen in the area, is that it?' My eyes widened. 'God, is that why you came to the *pub*?'

Angrily he spun around. 'I was having a night out with my mates! It's allowed, isn't it?' He wiped his hand over his face, came back, took a chair. 'Look, Gus –'

'Don't bullshit me, Simon! I'm living here, remember?'

'Oh, I remember!' The hand raked his hair.

'So don't I deserve some sort of explanation? Some kind of warning? It's me who's going to be out on the moor all day. Alone. Miles from anywhere –'

'Okay, okay!' He held up his hands. 'I'll tell you what little I know. But if you so much as breathe a word . . .'

'You know it won't go any further.'

'It better not.' He stared at me long and hard. 'Jesus,' he sighed. 'Okay, a couple of weeks back a call came through to HQ. The caller asked for me personally, claimed he had information. Unfortunately I wasn't there. He wouldn't say what it was about, and wouldn't give his name, just that he was someone I'd known way back. A couple of nights later he called again and this time I caught it. It was Trev. I asked what it was about but he refused to talk on the phone, insisted we meet. I told him I needed more, kept on pressing, and eventually he coughed. Said it concerned our old friend Rayjay, who was, quote, "back from America and up on the moor".'

'Where on the moor?'

'Wouldn't say. Didn't trust phones. But it was enough for me to set up a meeting the following night. Trev never showed. Next morning I learned why.'

'The fire.'

He nodded. 'Someone got to him first.'

'You think it was Rayjay?'

'Who else? Oh, he wouldn't have done it himself, he'd have paid someone else. Rayjay never did his own dirty work.' There was a bitterness in his voice that spoke of unresolved history. I wondered how much he wasn't telling me.

He tapped his pocket. 'Mind if I smoke?'

159

I found him an ashtray. 'But what made you think Rayjay was Chadwicke? I thought from what Phil said he was a petty criminal.'

'You kidding?' He sat forward. 'People *disappeared*, Gus. Does that make it any clearer?'

I shuddered. It was clearer than I would have liked. 'But if that's the case, what the hell made you suspect Chadwicke? A villain like that playing spiritual guru? Come on!'

'Believe me, it'd be no problem for that bastard.' He blew smoke from the side of his mouth. 'Okay, potted history. Real name Raymond John Rickards, only child of Joyce Rickards, drunk, tom and part-time user. God knows who his father was, I doubt if Joyce did. So from day one young Raymond was fending for himself. But he had something old Joyce never had – a brain. Couldn't be bothered with school, habitual truant – instead, used to take himself off to the library and mug up on whatever took his fancy. Did an excellent job, too. He's remarkably well educated.'

I tried to interrupt but he held up his hand. 'While mugging-up there, he had a team of lads out on the street mugging old ladies. Trev was one of them, that's how far back they go. Mugging, thieving, nicking cars . . . The lads took the risks, Rayjay took the profits. By the time he was eighteen he was loaded, first legal car a Jag straight from the showroom, though by then he was into more *lucrative* scams.'

'Like?'

'Protection, slum landlord, you name it. Yet in all the years he was operating, not once was he convicted. Pulled in, questioned, a hundred times but always a foolproof alibi. As I said, others did the dirty. Several went down but they wouldn't name names – they knew what would happen when they got out. So no – Rayjay wouldn't have thrown the match. But playing spiritual guru? Right up his street. Impersonation was his forte. That asshole could pass as anything from a dustman to the local MP. He'd probably get off on the challenge.'

160

I stared again at the photo. 'Why not check his finger-prints just to make sure?'

He exhaled a laugh. 'I would if we had any. Got disappeared when he did, along with everything else. Must've had at least one of our lot in his pocket.'

I was still studying the print, trying to superimpose Alden's face, adding wrinkles and excess flesh, greying and lengthening the hair.

'Having second thoughts?' Simon asked.

'Not unless he's had plastic surgery.'

'That's not out of the question.'

'How about clutching at straws?'

He smiled. 'Frankly, I'd clutch at anything to get my hands on that low-life. He's a psychopath, Gus – no conscience. I mean *really* no conscience. No one's safe while that scum's around.'

It was a comforting thought.

'Sure there's no one else he reminds you of?'

I frowned. 'Something looks *vaguely* familiar but . . . Hell, it could be anyone – a famous actor, someone I once worked with . . .'

'Well, if you think.'

'You'll be the first to know.' This time I handed it back. 'One thing I don't understand. Why, if they went so far back, did Trev suddenly decided to shop him?'

'My guess is he got on Rayjay's wrong side, thought it was the only way to save his skin.' He laughed.

'What's funny?'

'The idea of someone getting one over on Rayjay. To be blunt, the minute you mentioned the blackmail I gave up on it being Chadwicke. No one would blackmail Rayjay and live to tell the tale.' He paused. 'Someone *working* for Rayjay however, now that would be a different story.'

'Doing his dirty work, you mean? Might that include killing an old lady?'

Simon shrugged.

A cold feeling lodged in my stomach as I remembered what I'd done, creeping around his house, searching the rooms. The person who had found Trevor's body – befriended Judith – who had turned up at the Institute out of the blue. The one who had questioned him about Miss Hillas, focused attention on the quarry . . .

'You see now why I told you to back off,' Simon was saying. 'You've already had one warning.'

I swallowed. 'Actually I might have had two,' I said, and told him about the rock fall.

He tried to remain impassive but I could sense his anger, though whether it was directed at me or Alden I wasn't too sure.

'Who else but Chadwicke knew you were going?' he demanded when I finished.

'No one. Well, I suppose the others at the table . . .'

'Names?'

I reeled off those I could remember. 'Do you think it was a warning?'

'I doubt they'd have lost sleep if it had crushed your skull.'

'I meant . . .'

'I know what you meant.' He stopped writing, leaned forwards across the table. 'For all I know it could have been kids, yobs with a sick sense of humour. Then again it might not. All we do know is the rock didn't move on its own, and personally, I'm not one for coincidences. Believe me, whatever Rayjay's into, he's gonna protect it – he'll do whatever it takes. What he won't do is sit around and let some meddling female fuck it up.' I started to protest but he grabbed my hand. 'You did what you thought was right and I admire that. But from now on leave it to us, okay?' His voice softened. 'I don't want you getting hurt, Gus.'

Well, at least we agreed on something.

He let go my hand and checked his watch. 'Now, unless you've any other surprises . . .'

'One,' I said. 'There's another American who lectures there, a sculptor, lives a few miles away. But don't get excited, this one's genuine.'

'You sure about that?'

Could pass himself off as anything . . .

'He's nothing like the photo.'

He took details anyway, then returned the notebook to his pocket. 'Right, you've got my number. Anything else you remember . . .'

'I'll get in touch,' I said absently, my mind already elsewhere. I was wondering just how radical plastic surgery could be in the States.

The evening dragged. Ten fifty and still Dad wasn't in bed. Normally he went at ten but tonight he'd stayed up, engrossed in a documentary about the war on some obscure channel. Before that it had been the news, before that something about gardening. I'd sat through the programmes with him, but registered little. My mind was on Alden's video, watched that afternoon while Dad was taking a nap. It hadn't been about the Institute, nor was it innocuous. It was blatant pornography.

Monochrome images filled the TV screen, but the images in my mind were of other scenes of brutality – sexual brutality, lewd and tawdry. A simulated cruelty, enacted for those who liked to give or receive pain. Which clearly Alden did – big time, if the other numbered cassettes contained similar stuff. But I hadn't known that when I slotted the tape into the machine, turned the volume low and sat back against the chair arm with my cup of tea. Maybe the title, *Just Punishment*, should have warned me.

The film opened on an empty room, cellar-like, with low ceilings and stone floor. Up high, a small barred window. Let into the wall were rings and lengths of chain. A man's voice mumbled something off camera and there was a shuffling sound, followed by what sounded like heels tapping on stone. The voice came again, pleading, and the camera panned to a doorway. It wasn't until the actors emerged that the penny finally dropped.

There were three of them, a man and two women. The man was on hands and knees; the women standing on either side, tall and blonde, with cut-away shorts and flimsy shirts knotted beneath silicon breasts. Their bodies were voluptuous, their features coarse and heavily made-up. One had hair scraped back into a bun, the other wore a military cap. On the front of the cap was a swastika. The man had a chain around his neck and Bun was dragging him like a recalcitrant dog, while Cap pointed a gun at his head and yelled words of encouragement, like, *Crawl, you scum! Eat dirt!* His progress was aided by occasional kicks from the toe of a thigh-high leather boot.

I felt like laughing. The production was amateurish, the acting pathetic. Did Alden really get off on this stuff? Of course he did, witness the toys in his nightstand. But who did he indulge his fantasies with? Zara? It was hard to imagine. Maybe he found his playmates amongst the guests.

Lucky escape, I thought, as the women dragged the man to his feet and slammed his face against the wall. A slight struggle and his wrists were secured with manacles fixed to the chains. The same with his ankles. Now they began to caress him – stroking, teasing, running blood-red nails across his skin. Bun dropped to her knees and rubbed her cheek against his leg. The man groaned – a signal for Cap to tear off her belt and wave it above her head before bringing it down across his thighs.

And so it went on – seduction, punishment, seduction – laughable and banal. Various implements were used – canes, whips, even a metal hairbrush – accompanied by taunts of humiliation from the women, begging and cries from the man. Why the hell did they do it? For money? Some personal erotic buzz? Still, it could be worse. At least they were adults.

I had seen enough and reached for the remote, but suddenly things were changing. The door to the right had crashed open and two men rushed in, and within seconds the women were overpowered, the prisoner released. I gave a wry smile. Even in fantasy, it seemed, women weren't allowed the upper hand for long.

But it wasn't only the power balance that had shifted. With the advent of the men the atmosphere had changed, become tense and aggressive. Suddenly it was no longer a game. There was nothing playful in the men's expressions, nothing amusing in the way the women were held down, stripped of their clothes and abused. Their faces betrayed a genuine fear. Had this been part of their contract?

Somehow I watched it to the end. It left me feeling grubby. I thought of the warm video player in Alden's room, heard again his words – *Passivity wields its own rewards*. Remembered the way he had stroked the leather thongs at my wrist, so innocently worn and, I only now realized, so grossly misinterpreted. How could I have been so naïve?

The dead screen flickered. Something else was starting. More of the same?

This time the scene was a bedroom, its walls draped in red velvet. Centre stage was a divan covered with black satin sheets. To the left a man sat reading at a small table, dressed in a smoking jacket, swirling liquid in a brandy balloon. His hair and moustache looked false.

There was a rap at the door . . . *My* door!

'Bob? Gus? Anybody home?'

Monty!

I leapt to my feet while hitting Eject, grabbed the cassette and kicked it under the sofa. The last thing I wanted to do was explain to Dad's neighbour why I was spending my afternoon watching sado-masochistic porn.

Dad's programme was coming to an end now, mono-chrome segueing to colour as a war veteran recalled events. Finally the credits rolled and Dad looked at his watch.

'Heavens, is that the time? I'm usually asleep by now, must have been the nap. You staying up?'

I nodded. I had the rest of a video to watch.

He picked up a book. 'Well, don't be too late.'

'Don't read too long,' I countered, and he grinned. Would I ever be anything other than his little girl?

Chapter Sixteen

Few adolescent embarrassments have persisted into adulthood, but watching scenes of explicit sex in the presence of my father is one that has. I made sure he was fast asleep before switching on the tape.

During the few seconds lost in stopping and starting, a second man had appeared, and I caught the words, '. . . trying to escape.' The man in the smoking jacket glanced up, and with slow precision placed a marker in the book and laid it on the table. His voice was younger than his disguise, silky smooth.

'Bring her to me,' he said. 'She will have to be punished.'

I groaned, knowing what to expect. Or I thought I knew.

The camera swung to the right and focused on an arched doorway. An identical doorway. Was this the same room, the barred window hidden by the drapes? I had little time to ponder. Next moment a young girl was pushed in. She fell forward and landed roughly on her knees.

My heart skipped. A *very* young girl.

The guard screamed at her to get up. She stumbled when she tried to comply – hardly surprising in such impossibly high heels – and when she finally made it, had trouble balancing. I wondered if she was drugged, but it was impossible to tell without seeing her eyes, and they were hidden by the black leather hood that encased her head like a second skin. Perhaps it was merely sense deprivation.

She wasn't entirely naked. Her slender body was laced

into a scarlet satin basque that ended just below the waist, exposing boyish hips, a small triangle of blonde hair. Her skin was smooth and unblemished, her breasts barely formed. *Too* young.

The guard disappeared and the man in the smoking jacket moved towards her, taking his time, slowly circling around. He tilted up her chin, touched her cheek, coiled his fingers in the blonde hair hanging from beneath the hood. At every touch she flinched.

'I hear you've been a naughty girl,' he crooned, though the glint in his eyes belied the honeyed tone. 'And what happens to naughty girls? They get punished.' On the final word he jerked the hair and her head shot back. A muffled cry issued from the hood.

I looked away, fists clenched. How had someone so young become caught up in this shit?

By the time I looked back her wrists were bound, the man flexing a schoolmaster's cane. She crumpled at the first hit. He raised it to strike again but before it made contact I'd hit Stop. Enough was enough.

I awoke next morning lying sideways across the bed in a tangle of damp sheets. It was barely light. I got up anyway, showered, and while eating breakfast scribbled a note to Dad. Hewitt guessed what was coming and was at the door before me.

Early morning is my favourite time for walking. There are few people around and the air smells clean and pure, like freshly laundered linen dried in the sun. I drove on to the moor, then drove some more, until pleading whines from Hewitt forced me to stop. He shot from the car like a bullet and careened around in circles, tail stuck out like a rudder, happy to be alive. It cheered me just watching him. He's a large dog of mixed parentage, with a black glossy coat, the only white the moustache under his nose. The same tache, according to Dad, as his former boss, ex-

Chief Fire Officer Guy Hewitt. I wonder if he'd be flattered to know the dog bears his name?

Energy spent, the dog slowed down and jogged happily at my side. We walked for an hour, mainly through pine woods, finally emerging on to open moorland. Suddenly everything was colour. Rowan trees dangled scarlet berries against the watery-blue sky, and heather and gorse covered the hillsides in purple and gold drifts. It was a morning to lighten the soul, yet I kept thinking of Miss Hillas's words. *There's evil everywhere.* Alden's video had been a poignant reminder.

Before going to bed I'd watched the remainder. It had fulfilled my worst fears. The young girl's so-called punishment had been drawn-out and bizarre, ending with her being spread-eagled on the bed and taken from behind. Or rather raped. Nothing would convince me she was a willing participant. But perhaps that was the point – perhaps, for some, acting wasn't enough. Deviants like Alden would probably pay big money to have it for real.

The thought sickened me, reminding me of the wide gulf between fantasy and reality. Anthologies of sexual fantasies make bestsellers and I, like many others, have laughed, occasionally squirmed, at the outlandish things that turn people on. Yet for most of the raconteurs the fantasy was enough; the idea of putting it into practice aroused genuine horror. Only a few will cross the line. We see them on late-night television – the rubber fetishists, grown men dressed as babies, sado-masochists in leather and chains – and we, the viewers, the voyeurs, watch with whatever emotion such behaviour evokes.

Only a few months before, returning from the pub, Lisa and I had tuned to a late-night chat show and listened to a group of men and women recalling their most extreme sexual encounters, and like naïve adolescents we had giggled, gasped, once or twice been repelled. But we hadn't switched off. Like thousands of others we had been riveted to the screen, fascinated by their unorthodox antics. Afterwards, Lisa had shaken her head.

'Poor bastards,' she said. 'Imagine telling that to a new man. There but for the grace of God and all that.'

Yet there had been nothing harmful in the programme. The participants had been adults, people of like mind indulging in games. Alden's video was in a different league. The girl, I was convinced, had been underage and, I was also convinced, unwilling. Which meant I couldn't let it go. Somehow, I had to tell Simon.

I rang him as soon as I got back and left a message asking him to call. I didn't have the faintest idea what I was going to say.

Late that afternoon I was back on the moor, this time minus Hewitt. Much as I love his company, he's too much of a distraction when I need to work. It was a need that was becoming ever more urgent. The bright promise of the exhibition was fast becoming a black cloud.

Rarely had I felt less inspired. I chose a location I didn't know and began to walk, hoping something would grab. Finally it did; a massive pyramid of rock, a few sheep grazing at its base. They scattered as I approached but not before I'd taken some shots. Circling the stone I was reminded of the video, the way the man in the smoking jacket had circled the young girl. The image persisted and my first few sketches were pathetic. But eventually the power of the scene took over and I became lost in my work, oblivious to all but the task in hand.

The sun was low in the sky when the sound of people shouting jolted me back to the present. I was miles from the road and ravenously hungry, and when I climbed to my feet pins and needles started in my leg. I jumped around, stamping my foot, performing a war dance for the people on the hill.

By the time I reached my car the light was fading, and the air had that metallic, vinegary taste it gets when dew begins to fall. Lights were coming on in distant farms, and high above my head two vapour trails arced like golden javelins through a watercolour sky. I painted it in my mind, a translucent graded wash, cobalt over yellow. To

169

the north, low against the horizon, clouds had fragmented into pink-tinted shards.

There are moments on the moor of absolute stillness. This was one of them. Nothing was moving, not even a distant car. It was as if someone had pushed a Pause button and the world had ground to a halt. Such moments are precious and I leaned against the car, listening.

I heard the birds before I saw them, a ponderous flapping of wings, followed by the soft whoosh of displaced air. They sounded close by, but when I looked up they were far in the distance, two silhouettes high against the blue. As I watched they were joined by others and soon the sky was full of them, mostly in pairs, flying home to roost.

And suddenly I was thinking of Dougie and what we had once shared. Loneliness engulfed me. It was time to go home.

I was a good two miles from the village when I saw the girl. She was running towards me, dark hair swinging to her waist. When she saw the car she stopped, squeezed tight to the hedge and turned her back.

It was the girl I'd seen near the farm, June's daughter. Wondering what she was doing so far from home, I pulled up alongside.

'It's Lorna, isn't it?' I called. 'Can I give you a lift?'

She didn't answer, nor did she look around. Perhaps I'd scared her. These days, I remembered, even women are suspect.

'I didn't mean to frighten you,' I said. 'I'm Gus Tavender. Bob Tavender's daughter?'

Still nothing.

'I met your mum yesterday. Up at Judith's. She –'

I got no further. Suddenly she was off, sprinting down the lane like a gazelle. But not before I'd seen her face. I threw open my door, dashed after her.

I caught her easily and grabbed her arm. 'What happened, Lorna?'

'Nothing!' She twisted away.

'But you're bleeding –'

'It was a nosebleed, right?'

A nosebleed that punched her in the eye?

A sharp kick landed on my shin. I grabbed her other wrist, held her at arm's length. 'Let me see.' She continued to squirm, yelled at me to lay off. But at five foot nothing she was on a loser. I hung on until she calmed down. 'Who did this, Lorna?' I asked gently.

'No one! I fell over, all right?' She wiped her cheek on her shoulder. 'In the lane. I hit my face and it started!'

'Okay,' I said, 'my mistake.' Clearly I would get nowhere unless I played along. I managed to turn her towards me. 'Hey, that's nasty. You ought to get it cleaned up, otherwise it might scar. Look, why don't I drive you home – '

'*No!*' She jerked back so sharply I almost let go.

'Okay . . .' I said. 'How about a friend's?'

'I don't want to go *nowhere*! I'm fine. Just leave me alone!'

'You're not fine, Lorna,' I told her. 'That eye needs attention. Much longer, and you won't be able to see. Besides, I can't just drive off and leave you, my dad would have my guts for garters. You know my dad, don't you?'

More squirming, then a nod.

'Did you know he used to be a fireman? Right up until the time he came here. He spent his whole life caring for people after accidents, so he'd hit the roof if I abandoned you now.' I paused. 'Now that's an idea. Why don't I take you home, let him have a look?'

'Your *dad*?'

'Why not? He'd be only too happy. Besides, your mum says you're Queen of the Revel. A fine sight you'll be if this isn't treated soon.'

My mention of the Revel struck a nerve, and her lower jaw began to tremble. 'I can't be Queen now,' she wailed, as the tears began to flow. 'Not like this. They'll get Hayley Dart instead.'

171

'Not necessarily, not if we can stop the bruising. But we'll need to act fast. The secret in stopping bruising is speed.'

Her head came up. 'You can do that?' She sounded like I'd offered her the moon.

'I can try,' I said. 'But I promise you this – do nothing, and tomorrow you'll be black and blue. It's worth a try, isn't it?'

She sniffed wildly, touched her lip with her finger. 'You sure your dad won't mind?'

'The only thing he'd mind is if I drove off and left you,' I said, putting my hand on her shoulder and turning her towards the car. 'Come on – we might as well give it a go.'

Seeing her in the bright light of the kitchen, I wondered if I'd done the right thing in raising her hopes. Her face was a mess, the bottom lip split, her left eye already closing. How could anyone *do* this?

Dad masked his surprise well. 'Heavens, someone's been in the wars,' he said, when I ushered her in. 'Whatever happened to you?'

'Lorna had a fall,' I said, though I knew he wasn't fooled.

'Dear, oh dear. Well, we'd best get you cleaned up. Come and sit over here.' He drew out a chair, patted the seat. 'What were you doing, running?'

She nodded, though I noticed she didn't meet his eye.

'You youngsters!' Dad tutted. 'Always in a hurry. Gus was just the same at your age.'

'And a fat lot of sympathy I got!' I teased, hoping our banter would relieve her awkwardness. I took some ice cubes from the fridge. 'I'm going to try to stop it bruising. Lorna needs to look her best for Saturday.'

'Of course, Queen of the Revel. Your mum's full of it. I saw her the other day up by the church and she was telling me . . .'

I left him doing what he does best, putting people at ease, and went in search of cotton wool and gauze. He was still chatting when I came back and already she seemed more relaxed. I soaked some cotton wool in the iced water, squeezed it into a pad and gently placed it on her eye. 'Can you hold that there, Lorna?'

She did as she was told. 'Is it bad?'

'I've seen worse.' I sponged dried blood from her cheek. 'At least you're not fair. Fair people bruise more easily.'

She jumped as I touched a tender spot. 'How d'you know all this stuff? What to do?'

'Dad taught me. When I was young.' I rinsed the cotton wool, watched the water turn brownish-red. I saw her wince. 'Head hurting?'

'A bit.'

Dad went off to find paracetamols. Lorna watched him go. 'He's nice, your dad,' she said wistfully. 'I couldn't just – you know – turn up with someone. Mine doesn't like people hanging around. Nor our Gary.'

'What, strangers you mean?'

'Anyone.'

Dad returned with the pills and handed two to Lorna along with a glass of water. She gulped them down, flinched when she tried to smile. When he set about making tea she followed his every move. Another conquest to add to his list.

I removed the last traces of blood, cooled the pad in fresh water and replaced it on her eye. 'Well, that's about it,' I said. 'Try to sit still. The less movement the better.'

She nodded, closed the other eye.

When I started to clear away, Dad followed me to the bathroom. 'Who the hell did that?' he hissed. 'The father?'

'Or brother.'

'Dear God!'

'Think you can find out?'

'I can try. But you know what it's like.'

I nodded. The victims of domestic violence are notoriously reluctant to speak out. Not only are they burdened by familial loyalty, but they fear that by doing so they will incur further abuse. Little wonder it's one of the least reported crimes. Yet I knew if anyone could get Lorna talking it was my father. In the Brigade he'd been renowned for his ability to calm, and if someone was trapped or injured it was him they would send in. To talk them through the trauma, soothe their mind from the pain.

But gaining Lorna's confidence would take time, and it was something he would do better alone. I told him to give it his best and made myself scarce.

It was a couple of days since I'd checked my emails, so I went upstairs and logged on to my laptop. They were nearly all junk. Only one message grabbed my attention and that was from Lisa.

Wish you were here!!!!!! L x x x

Short and sweet. I frowned. Why did she wish I was there? Was something wrong?

I typed a reply – *What's up? Ring me!!* – but the moment I hit Send I knew it was a mistake. I should have rung her.

Picking up my mobile, I remembered Simon. My stomach did a flip. Hell, I had to face it sooner or later. I might as well make it sooner.

He answered on the second ring. 'Furneaux!'

Curt. 'It's Gus,' I said. 'Is this a bad time?'

'What's up?'

'Doesn't matter, it'll keep.' This wasn't something I wanted to do in a hurry.

'Remembered something?'

'No, but –'

'Gus, I haven't got all day!'

'It's just . . . I found a videotape. At the Institute. No rush, but I think you ought to see it.'

'What kind of tape?'

'Pornography. Not kids, but –'

'Why didn't you tell me before?'

174

'I didn't know what was *on* it before.'

'That's not – hang on.' Voices sounded in the background. 'Look, I've got to go. Call you, okay?' The line went dead.

'Shit!' I threw the phone on to the bed. Immediately it rang. I snatched it up again, yelled my name.

'God, you sound pissed,' said Lisa. 'Urine test just turned pink?'

'Like I need one!' I said, relaxing.

'And there's me thinking you were having fun. Don't tell me – you've spent every minute working.'

'Actually I've hardly worked at all. But forget all that. What's up with you?'

'Oh, you know . . .' I heard her sigh. 'Shattered illusions.'

'John?'

'You got it.' She paused. 'What is it with men, Gus? Or is it me? Perhaps *I'm* the one with problems.'

'Want to talk about it?'

'No. But it would be nice to meet up. You doing anything tomorrow?'

'Other than washing my hair?'

'You are now. I'll come to you. A nice drink in a nice quiet pub. Who knows, we might find ourselves a couple of rich farmers.'

'Haven't you had it with men?'

'You're right – thanks for reminding me. Not sure what time, won't be before seven.'

I told her I'd expect her when I saw her, and after a few minutes of mindless chatter we hung up. I imagined whatever was bothering her was a temporary glitch. Come tomorrow it may well have blown over.

Too soon to go back down. I returned to the computer, logged on to Google and did a search on *Alden Chadwicke*. The name scored several hits, all in connection with Sacred Oak. I opened each one in turn, found much the same blurb as in the brochure. Several referred to courses long past. No mention of any history or of a similar institution in the States. Returning to the search page I typed in *Joe de*

175

Zaire. His name brought fewer hits than I'd expected, mostly from galleries in the States, plus a couple of magazine references. One, I noticed, was *dot UK.*

But there was no time to check it now, I'd spent too long reading about Alden. I closed everything down and returned downstairs.

'Ah, here she is,' Dad said. 'We thought you'd gone down the plug hole.'

'Sorry, had to make some calls.' I looked at Lorna. 'Pain easing off?'

She gave a nod.

'Lorna's been telling me about her boyfriend, Kenny Hatch. He sounds like a really nice lad. Lives near Moretonhampstead on his parents' farm. He'll be taking it over when his dad retires.'

'Lucky lad,' I said.

'He also does a lot with Young Farmers. He's even in their tug-of-war team, will be pulling this Saturday at the Revel. I told her we'll be there, cheering him on.' He paused. 'Sad thing is, Lorna's brother doesn't like him.'

'Gary?' I feigned surprise. 'Why ever not?'

'Something to do with the animals, wasn't it? Kenny –'

'You said you wouldn't tell!' Lorna cried, jerking forward and dropping the cotton wool. 'You *promised!*'

'I won't, Lorna. But I can't not tell Gus . . .'

'Oh, I *knew* I shouldn't've said nothing.' She was squirming in the chair. 'Dad'd *kill* me! Never talk about family away from home, he always says, and here's me –'

'Hey!' Dad grabbed her hand. 'It won't go outside these walls. Gus isn't going to tell anyone, are you, Gus?'

'Of course not.' I replaced the pad.

'Sometimes it helps to talk,' Dad urged quietly. 'You know that old saying, a trouble shared is a trouble halved? Well, it's true, believe me. Bottling things up does no one any good.' He gave the hand a squeeze. 'It can't be easy loving someone and having your only brother dislike him. But sometimes you have to put your *own* needs first, Lorna – in this case, yours and Kenny's.'

Her lower lip was trembling. 'It still don't seem right . . .'

'You'd be a strange sort of girl if it did.' He pushed a strand of hair from her face.

She sniffed, wiped her nose with the back of her hand. 'It's not that Gary . . . It's Kenny, see. He cares about things. People say farmers don't have feelings, 'cause their animals get slaughtered, but Kenny does. He says animals have feelings just like we do, and while they're in your care they should be treated well. He feels real strong about it and don't mind speaking out, so when he saw . . .' She broke off sharply, looked down at her lap.

'Saw what, Lorna?' Dad prompted.

She hunched her shoulders.

'But Kenny confronted them?'

She nodded, and I saw a tremor run through her body. 'Dad got real angry. He said it was none of his business. Then our Gary got hold of him and threw him out. He said if I saw him again he'd – you know.' Her hand went to her damaged lip.

Dad and I exchanged glances. The action spoke volumes.

'But I *do*!' she added defiantly. 'In secret. Kenny don't like it, but – well, it's better than not seeing each other at all.'

'That's tough, Lorna,' Dad said. 'On both of you. But all credit to Kenny for speaking out.'

'Have you no idea what he saw?' I asked.

She shook her head.

I made a random guess. 'Was it sheep?'

'Uh?' She gave a shrug. 'Might've been.'

Clearly not. What then – ponies? It wasn't impossible. There've been numerous claims of maltreatment over the years made against certain owners, usually concerning food and shelter during the bleak winter months. Having seen the farm I could well imagine Tom Weblake might shirk his responsibilities.

I thought back to the one time I had seen him, coming out of the barn. Before turning to pee he had yelled at the dog inside to shut, a dog that had been whining.

177

I squatted down beside her. 'Or was it the dog, Lorna?'

'How –?' Too late she realized her mistake. Suddenly she was on her feet, looking frantically around. 'I don't know what he saw, all right? I wasn't there! Now I must go. Mum'll be going spare.'

So suddenly home was preferable.

'I'll drive you,' I said.

'No need.'

I told her it wasn't up for debate.

We drove to the farm in silence, Lorna staring straight ahead, her battered face creased with worry. I wondered how she would explain her injuries to June. No doubt the same way she'd explained them to us, which June would accept, knowing it was a lie. The old, old story, violence explained by carelessness – I walked into a door, Lorna; I tripped in the yard, Mum – year after year, refusing to acknowledge the truth. Because Tom and Gary were family, and you don't talk about family away from home.

My fingers tightened on the wheel. Beating up women and cruelty to animals. It didn't say much for the Weblake males. Nor would such traits have endeared them to Miss Hillas. Was this the evil that had caused such concern?

'Can you drop me at the gate?' Lorna begged as we neared the farm.

I pulled in, cut the engine. The last thing I wanted was to prompt more violence.

She started to climb from the car, then stopped and brought her hand to her cheek. 'Thanks.'

I smiled. 'Let's just hope it works.'

She gave a little wave and vanished into the darkness. I stared after her for a moment then reversed back down the track. I also hoped that whoever had inflicted the injury had had time to calm down.

Chapter Seventeen

For once I had the house to myself. Dad and Monty had left shortly after breakfast for a farm sale near Okehampton. The implements and machinery had already been sold off and today's auction was for the house and contents. The inventory had mentioned some small granite troughs.

'How small?' I'd asked, knowing how much the things weighed.

Dad shrugged. 'Don't suppose it matters, they'll most likely go through the roof. Anything you want me to look out for?'

I shook my head. 'Just promise you won't try lifting them!'

'Don't you worry about me,' he said. 'You worry about your work.'

I intended to, and as soon as he was gone took myself up to my room.

I'm fortunate in having the whole of the top floor. Not long after Dad bought Tynings – not needing the space himself, and anticipating my need for a studio – he had the original two rooms knocked into one, augmenting the natural light with a large Velux window. The result is a bright, airy workspace with sloping ceilings and a sleeping/sitting area at one end. It has to be said his motive wasn't entirely altruistic, any more than my initial response was entirely grateful. He knew if I had somewhere to work I'd be more inclined to stay there, which I regarded as both manipulative and unnecessary. I would visit when I had time, and because I wanted to. That said, it's a room I've come to value, being far more conducive to work than the cupboard-like space at my flat. It's allowed me to work on a far larger scale, which has encouraged me back to painting. It was a painting I was planning now, a large oil-on-canvas development of the pyramid idea.

Or would be planning if I could stop thinking about Lorna, pornographic videos, maltreated animals and old ladies pushed from cliffs. Perhaps I should have asked Dad to look out for a time machine. Not to go back far – just enough to miss the pony rescue, meeting Judith, and to arrange a holiday in the Costa del Sol.

I kicked myself into action and for most of the morning toyed with composition, finally achieving what I wanted shortly before twelve. I had just gone down for lunch when Joe de Zaire rang. Would I like to visit his studio that afternoon, say around three? Apparently he was between pieces so it was a good time to call. Once he got started on a new one he'd be totally out of it.

I knew what he meant, I was in the same position myself. I also knew I should say no.

'Well?' he asked.

'Love to. Is Judith coming?'

There was a pause. 'Hadn't planned it. But sure – why not? You'll have to ask her, though. Too far for me to go to find out.'

I let it ride. If he was planning a cosy afternoon for two, why make it a crowd?

I threw together a sandwich and munched it standing up, poring over the OS map to check the exact location of Holt Mill. It was closer to Higher Verstone than I'd realized, just a couple of miles as the crow flies. By road it was more like six, taking me along the very lane where I had met Lorna. I wondered how she was feeling today, and whether my ministrations had helped. And what kind of reception she might have had when she arrived home.

The more I thought about it, the keener I was to find out, so I decided to leave early and call at the farm. I would use the pretext of buying eggs – and hope it was June who answered the door.

The sun was a fireball in the sky when, for the second time in twenty-four hours, I drew up at the gate. Most places look better in sunlight but here it seemed only to highlight the squalor. Halfway up the drive a large rat scuttled across my path, doubled back and disappeared under a car. Nothing else moved. I was convinced the place was deserted – until I tried to enter the yard. Suddenly, from out of nowhere, a Border collie appeared. It was large for its breed, with a matted coat and the kind of deep-throated growl that rooted me to the spot. I'm not normally afraid of dogs but this one looked mean – and probably was if it had been the victim of abuse.

Crouching low, lips drawn back in a snarl, it inched towards me. I stared it in the eye, hoping it couldn't smell my fear.

'Okay, boy . . .' I took a step forward.

The dog upped the volume and tensed ready to spring.

Now what?

It seemed I had two choices. Push forward and risk being savaged, or beat an ignominious retreat and get bitten from behind. I decided on the latter, improving my chances by walking backwards, keeping it in view. The dog moved forward a few feet then dropped to its haunches.

So far so good – as long as I didn't make any sudden moves. I might not arrive at Holt Mill until suppertime, but at least I'd arrive in one piece.

I'd retreated as far as the barn when I heard the whining. So it hadn't been the collie that was making the noise. From the corner of my eye I could see the door, a chain and padlock hanging loose at the side. Question was, would Cerberus let me open it?

Cautiously I raised my hand. The collie didn't move. Maybe it was only the house and yard that were out of bounds. The latch was primitive, made of gnarled wood

181

grey with age. No lifting mechanism, only your fingers, reached from the other side through a hole in the door. Slowly I reached out and pushed it upwards, increasing the pressure when it didn't move. Finally it gave and, jolting on its hinges, the door swung inwards.

The smell that met me was indescribable. What had they got in there, a cesspit? Flies were having a field day, a million tiny buzz-saws roused by the sudden burst of light. And now Cerberus was on the move.

Dog or smell?

No contest. A smell I could survive.

Once inside I wasn't so sure. The stench was thick enough to cut, like advanced putrefaction. I was convinced something had died. Beneath its corrugated metal roof the barn was an inferno. I'd closed the door behind me to keep out the dog, and the only light came from a small window on the opposite wall, partially covered by a sack. But even in the dim light I could see the junk. Large pieces of battered machinery were half buried by fertilizer sacks, plastic sheeting, old buckets, barbed wire mangled with bailer twine. Rusting drums of chemicals had been thrown carelessly about, many lying on their sides and uncapped. A heap of plastic sacks, covers torn, were leaking their contents on to the already foul ground. It was an environmental nightmare.

Flies batted my face as I stared around. God knows what they were carrying. In the far corner was what looked like a makeshift pen. Was this the source of the smell?

The whining started again as I picked my way towards it, turned to a faint growl as I came up close. Cautiously I peered in.

'Jesus!' Briefly I closed my eyes. No wonder Kenny had lost his rag.

The pit bull was huddled in a corner, lying in its own filth, its body a mess of scratches and ripped flesh. Torn ears, mangled mouth, open oozing sores. The undamaged parts of its face were a patchwork of old scars.

No need to ask the reason for its condition. The

Weblakes were into dog fighting. No wonder they didn't want strangers at the farm. Why the hell hadn't Kenny reported it?

But I knew the answer – Lorna. How could he report his girlfriend's father?

I stared down at the animal, wanting to comfort it. Knew better than to try. The gentlest animal will attack when injured and pit bulls aren't renowned for their meekness. All I could do was fetch help, someone authorized and equipped to deal with it. At least the poor creature had water, albeit in a filthy plastic bowl. Assuming it could drink with such a horribly injured mouth. Assuming it still had a tongue.

Telling it to hang on in there, I staggered back outside. Thankfully the collie had vanished. I leaned against the side of the barn, gulping lungfuls of fresh air, shaking with anger. When sufficiently recovered I started back to my car. I needed to phone Chris Daggett, and fast.

I had almost reached the gate when a man stepped out from behind a van. 'What do *you* want?' he demanded, blocking my path. 'What you doing here?'

It was the man I'd seen leaving the barn. Somehow I summoned my voice, tried to appear unruffled. 'Mr Weblake?'

'What of it?'

Up close he was intimidating. Shorter than me, but with a bull-like body, unshaven jowls, the broken-vein nose of a drinker. Grey hair curled from under a filthy cloth cap, and lay like a pelt on arms the size of my thighs. His fists were like hams.

'I was looking for June. Is she –'

'What d'yer want *'er* for?'

'I thought she might sell me some eggs.'

'Us don't sell eggs.' The meaty fists bunched. No wonder Lorna had thought my father nice.

'Well, now I'm here, if I could just see her –'

'*She ain't here!*' Suddenly he was in front of me, close enough to smell his sweat. He jabbed his finger at my chest. 'I knows your sort! Come 'ere nosin' around, pokin' in other people's business. Just like 'er up there.' His head jerked towards Judith's. 'Well, yer can do yer nosin' elsewhere, 'cause I ain't puttin' up with it. Now bugger off before I set the dog on yer.'

He stepped aside and I continued down the drive. Clearly it was my day for ignominious withdrawals. He followed me to the gate, watched to make sure I pulled away.

I drove as far as the junction, then stopped – thinking of the bunched fists, hoping I hadn't made things bad for June. The RSPCA number was in my address book and, shaking with fury, I punched it into my mobile. No response: I was in another dead zone. The nearest phone was the call box in the village. I put my foot down and returned the way I'd come. Now I *was* going to be late.

Chris wasn't at home – grossly overworked, he rarely is – so I left a message describing what I'd found, gave Dad's number, and said I'd be back in a couple of hours. For the moment that was all I could do.

Still seething I jumped back in my car, did a far from sensible three point turn, and set off once again, forcing myself to drive more slowly. I needed to compose myself for the meeting with Joe de Zaire.

I found him in the garden, sprawled on his back on a harshly modern sun-bed. Essence of Starck, all stainless steel and sweeping grey ply. A similarly uncompromising structure rose above his head, a minimalist pergola draped in a far from minimalist vine. The swelling clusters of grapes looked in danger of pulling it down.

He sat up when he heard me and shaded his eyes. 'Thought you'd changed your mind.'

'Got held up, sorry.'

He waved the apology away. 'Sit down. Grab yourself a beer.'

He slid a cool-box from under the lounger. Budweisers,

icy cold. I took one gratefully; I could still taste the stench of the barn. I only hoped the smell hadn't permeated my clothes.

I perched on the edge of a second bed identical to his own. His choice in furniture surprised me, it seemed so totally at odds with the man. But then, so did the car.

'Isn't this great?' he said, stretching out. 'Reminds me of home. Knew I should've put in that pool.'

'It's not always this good,' I said, swinging up my legs. The bed was more comfortable than it looked but not by much.

'Tell me about it!' He took a swig of beer then lay back, closing his eyes, dangling his arm over the side so the bottle rested on the ground. Again he wore black, this time a body-hugging sleeveless T-shirt and shorts. Brief shorts, revealing long well-shaped legs, a tan that didn't end at the hem.

'So where is home?' I asked.

'LA.'

'Same as the Chadwickes?'

He pushed up on one elbow. 'You know Alden? Great guy.'

'Is that why you're here?'

'How d'you mean? Oh, I get it.' He laughed, adopted a nerd Yank voice. 'You live in New York? Gee, I've a cousin in New York. P'raps you know him?'

'That's not –'

'I know. Fair question. No, I didn't know them before. I met Al a couple of days after I moved here. He came round, introduced himself, next thing I know I'm signed up for some lecture. Not really my thing, but what the hell. He's a great guy.'

'How did it go?'

'The lecture? Okay, I guess. Must've done, he keeps asking me back.'

'And being a fellow American . . .'

'Oh, Al's not American, only his wife. You meet Zara?'

He laughed. 'That is one crazy lady. Anyway, you're not here to talk about them. Wanna see what I do?'

I followed him down wide gravel steps, flanked on both sides by foliage planting. Lots of ornamental grasses, hostas and yuccas. I guessed this was what Wilfie had meant by 'daft'. We wound up at a thatched porch, massive granite troughs on either side. Dad would have been envious.

'Nice garden,' I said. 'Do it yourself?'

'You kidding? I've this old guy comes in. Stinks like crazy but he knows his job. I just say what I want and where.'

The style was in bizarre contrast to the house, a long granite building with all the whimsical features I'd expected to find at Verstone. The thatched roof was almost black with age, and patches of moss were sprouting on the reed. Joe led me around the side. More architectural planting surrounded a small terrace, then ended abruptly as the land sloped away. From there on it was as nature intended, bracken and rocks as far as the leat. The same on the far side, the land curving gently upwards to a line of ancient trees. Below us was a second building, presumably the mill.

'My studio.' Joe nodded. 'Some spot, huh?'

'To die for,' I said, and meant it.

More steps led down to the mill. Not a place for the infirm.

'You didn't bring Judith, then,' he called as he started down.

'Wasn't time.'

He glanced back, smiled.

The mill was cut into the hillside, the ground at the back almost reaching the slates. The door was in the near end. We'd almost reached it when a loud wailing noise came from behind the building.

'What was *that*?' I asked, and Joe laughed.

'I'll show you.'

He helped me down the bank, to the very edge of the

leat, a slow-moving stream at the bottom of deep vertical banks. Leaning forward, he pointed along the building. Near the far end a massive waterwheel hung on a rusty shaft, barely touching the water, barely moving. Suddenly it gave a jolt and let out another squeal.

'Needs oiling,' Joe grinned. 'Great though, isn't it? Ten feet across. This used to be a sawmill though everything else is long gone, including the sluice that controlled the water. You should see it after a storm!' Suddenly he pointed. 'See that?'

All I could see were ripples.

'Think it was an otter. I watch them sometimes from up there.' He nodded at a high row of windows running almost the entire length of the building. 'Lucky, huh?' He grabbed my hand. 'Come on, I'll show you inside.'

The studio was one huge white space, brightly lit by the windows and overhead striplights. A workbench took up most of the leat-side wall. On it were hand-tools, heavy-duty protective gloves, welding masks. At the far end a drawing board was lit by an anglepoise lamp.

The body of the room was filled with machinery – saws, pillar drills, lathes, oxy-acetylene and MIG welders – and racks were fixed to the rear wall, on which lay sheets of metal and lengths of square-section steel. Towards the far end, raised on a dais, was what I assumed was his latest piece. Or should I say feared. It was an abstract construction, all angles and planes, sprayed an ugly viridian green.

There is so much present-day sculpture I admire – the ephemeral art of Goldsworthy, the living sculptures of David Naish, the organic forms of Randall-Page – and I'd hoped to feel the same way about Joe's. I didn't. Not only did the piece seem dated, it also lacked warmth. Fraser would have claimed it lacked soul. It left me as cold as the metal from which it was formed.

I could feel Joe watching me. 'You don't like it.'

'I didn't . . .'

187

'You don't need to. Hey, that's okay. Lots of people don't understand what I'm about.'

'I think I was expecting something less – harsh.'

'Hey, the moor *is* harsh! Wild, aggressive, dog eat dog . . . But you don't see it, that's fine. I make pieces to make people react, and you reacted. So that's great, right?'

'Right,' I said, wondering why I felt so let down. I wandered across to the drawing board, next to which photos of similar pieces were stuck to the wall. Extremely similar. A style that didn't alter.

To the left of the drawing board, almost in the corner, was a door, the latch identical to the one on Weblake's barn.

'Where does that go?' I asked.

Joe grinned and pulled it open, and the sound of water grew louder. I stepped forward. We were almost directly above the wheel.

'For maintenance, I guess,' he said. 'See the old ladder?'

Steadying myself against the frame, I leaned out. A row of rusty metal hoops led down to the water, embedded one above the other in the stone. 'I can see why you've put off oiling.'

He smiled, stared across the stream at the distant trees. 'Amazing, isn't it? When I think of the dumps I used to live in. Never thought when I was earning a couple bucks an hour I'd wind up in a place like this.' He glanced back. 'Good thing *some* people like my work.'

'I didn't –'

'Just kidding. Anyway, now you've seen it. Fancy another beer?'

We set off back to the house. Definitely a place for the young and fit. While climbing the steps, I asked where he exhibited.

'The States mostly,' he told me.

'Not over here?'

'Sure. I've one in a couple of weeks. Didn't Judith tell you?'

'Judith?'

'Her gallery's putting it on.'

188

I stopped in my tracks. 'You show with Kempe Hillas?'

'Have since I got here. Fourth big one. Though they usually keep one or two of my pieces.' He frowned. 'I'm surprised she didn't mention it.'

So was I.

We continued to the house, entered from the terrace through french windows. The interior afforded another shock. I'd expected more postmodernism, instead met an eclectic mix of old and new, mostly European, with hints of his homeland in an Amish quilt, a folk-art painted chest. In a weird sort of way it worked.

The melange continued into the kitchen, painted cupboards rubbing shoulders with state-of-the-art appliances in stainless steel. The *batterie de cuisine* hanging from the ceiling was impressive. Joe opened the fridge – a two-door affair the size of a wardrobe that no American can live without – and took out two beers. We drank them on the terrace, sitting either side of a wooden table, in the shade of a silver-trunked birch.

'So how did you meet Stuart?' I asked. 'Did you approach the gallery?'

'Hell, no. I dropped in on the old lady one day – the aunt who died – and Stuart happened to be there. We got talking, I told him what I'd done. Next time he was down he dropped in.'

Next time? 'I got the impression he didn't visit often.'

'Maybe he was passing through. Anyway, he saw my work, liked it and offered me a show. At the time . . . well, I almost refused. They're pretty small-time as galleries go. Then I thought, what the hell – new country, virtually unknown – and told him to go ahead.'

'And you've stayed with them.'

'No reason not to. Stuart's looked after me well. The guy has some good contacts.'

'Not Judith?'

'Okay, the *gallery* has good contacts. But it's mostly Stuart; he's been in the business a long time, here and back home. I think Jude's more a sleeping partner.'

'Back home?'

'California. He ran a gallery there – and no, I didn't know him then. Anyway, what about you? You show in London?'

I shook my head. 'My most prestigious exhibition to date was a small gallery in Bristol, shared with three others.'

'That where this next one is?'

'Nope – an even smaller gallery in Exeter. Not exactly big-time.'

'Then chat up Judith. You gotta be up *front*, Gus. It's all about who you know, right?'

'Right,' I said, and glanced at my watch.

'Hey, you're not running out on me . . .'

'I'm working, too, Joe.' I slid back my chair.

He pulled a face. 'And there's me about to offer you dinner. Out here – candlelight – sitting beneath the stars . . .'

'Sounds nice.'

'*Nice?*' He gave a hoot. 'You Brits! Sounds *fucking beautiful!* The sound of the water, owls hooting in the trees . . . Did I mention I'm an excellent cook?'

'Did I mention I'm vegetarian?'

'So? Half my *friends* are vegetarian. Now what do you say – stay?'

'I can't, Joe. I've already made arrangements.'

'And do you have *arrangements* for tomorrow?'

'No, but –'

'Then come then. About eight? Hell, come whenever you like, you can talk to me while I cook.' His eyes sparkled. 'I don't mind being watched.'

I sparkled back. And I didn't mind watching.

Dad was poring over a book when I walked in. 'Simon rang,' he said. 'Wants to come and see you.'

'When?'

'Tomorrow afternoon.' He saw me frown. 'Poor Gus. Holiday not going as planned, is it?'

'An understatement. Anyone else?'

'Not since I've been here.'

So nothing yet from Chris Daggett.

'How was the sale?' I asked. 'Get the troughs?'

'You kidding? I could have a week in Spain for what they went for. But I did get these,' he added proudly, tapping the books. 'Tintin, from the fifties. In the original French.'

'Should I be impressed?'

'You should if I manage to read them. I can't believe no one snapped them up.' He flipped back a page. 'So where've you been – Judith's?'

'Holt Mill.'

That made him look up. 'The American's place? How come?'

'He rang up, asked if I'd like to see his studio.'

'Come and see my etchings?'

I glared.

'Sorry. You're not worried about him working at the Institute?'

'Hardly. He's a nice guy. I think he happens to live near by and can provide what they want, simple as that. I imagine he's very good.'

'What's his work like?'

I hesitated. 'Cold.'

'And the sculptor?'

I shrugged and Dad chuckled. 'Thought you had a glint in your eye. Ah well . . .'

'And what's that supposed to mean?'

'Nothing. Now go away, I'm trying to read some French.'

I was happy to oblige and took myself off to my room, flopped down on the bed. A lot had happened in a short time and I needed to think things through. First and foremost in my mind was Joe, and I got a strange tingle when

I thought of the following night. But that could wait: there were other things I needed to consider. Like why Judith hadn't mentioned his exhibition.

And what of the dog fighting? The more I thought about it, the more I was convinced it was this Miss Hillas had stumbled on. I could imagine her horror if, like me, she had called at the farm and found a dog in similar condition. A woman who abhorred cruelty, who wasn't afraid to speak her mind. She may well have confronted Tom – had him laugh, tell her she had no proof.

But that didn't make sense – the dog would have been proof. She too would have called the RSPCA. Unless she had overheard a conversation – Tom and Gary plotting the next fight, or discussing a previous one? If she had *then* discovered the dog, taken photos, threatened to expose them. . .

But it was *Alden* who was being blackmailed. Did that mean he was part of the dog-fighting ring? I shuddered. Perhaps watching animals tear each other apart was just another aspect of his sadistic taste.

'Gus?' Dad's voice came from below. 'Telephone.'

I ran downstairs. It was Chris Daggett.

'Sorry I couldn't get straight back,' he said, sounding excited. 'Hell of a day. But I wanted to say thanks. At least now I might get *one* of the bastards.'

'I never knew dog fighting went on around here,' I told him.

'No, well they don't exactly advertise the fact. And with the kind of locations it happens, it's difficult to keep track.'

'What kind of locations?'

'Isolated farms, mostly, and Lord knows there's plenty of those on the moor. No neighbours around to hear what's going on.'

'What about out in the open, miles from anywhere?' I was thinking of Miss Hillas's photos.

'Possible, I suppose. But unlikely; usually it's in a building. Sound travels; walls deaden the noise. Anyway, about directions . . .'

I described the layout of the farm, the exact location of the pen, then asked when he would be going. He refused to tell me, in case I was tempted to hang around.

'I don't want to worry you,' he added, 'but did anyone see you there?'

'The owner. But he doesn't know I saw the dog.'

'Sure about that? What's he like?'

'Not the sort to meet in a dark alley. Why?'

'They're going to wonder who blew the whistle, Gus. So be careful. Watch your back, okay?'

I resisted telling him I was watching it already.

I had barely pulled on a clean pair of jeans when Lisa arrived. Quickly I combed my hair and applied some mascara. Dougie always said my eyes are my best feature, and when we first met assured me he could drown in them. By the time we parted I wished he would.

A final touch of lipstick and I ran downstairs, gave Lisa a hug. She was looking great in tight-fitting white trousers and a skimpy mauve top, but more make-up than usual covered her grey-blue eyes and I guessed at some point in the day she had been crying. Maybe her problems hadn't resolved themselves after all.

Dad had wasted no time and was proudly showing her the Tintins.

'My brother used to watch the cartoons,' she said, adjusting the scrunchy holding her dark blonde hair. 'He even called his pet rabbit Snowy. Heavens, I can hear the intro now – "*Tintin by* . . ." – oh, what was the guy's name . . .'

'Hergé,' Dad said, giving it his best French pronunciation. 'It was his initials. *Aire-zhay,* for Remi, Georges. Did you know –'

'No, and she doesn't want to,' I said, dragging her away. 'We have some serious drinking to do.'

I took her to the Packhorse Bridge Inn, one of my favourite pubs on the moor. Architecturally it has little to recommend it, but its location is second to none, set beside the ancient footbridge, hemmed in on all sides by heather-covered hills. On a warm summer evening I expected it to be busy, but was amazed at how many had shared my idea. We seemed to walk for ever before we found a spot on the riverbank where we could talk without being overheard.

I say talk, but for several minutes we sat in silence. Lisa had thrown her jacket on the grass and was sprawled on her tummy, picking out tiny stones and tossing them into the river. Since leaving Tynings she had said barely a word. All she had told me was that she and John had split.

'So is it final?' I asked at last.

She nodded, gave a sigh.

'But how come? You guys were like Siamese twins. I thought you were all set to ride off into the sunset.'

At least that raised a smile. 'So did I – that's why it's such a bummer.' She rolled over, sat up. 'Turns out we're incompatible.'

'Oh, come on . . . You told me on my birthday, you got on better with John than with any guy before. '

'I do – in most things.' She began tearing at grass. 'I can't . . . It's a sex thing, right? So please don't ask for details.'

'Okay,' I said, more confused than ever. How could two people who cared for each other fall out about sex? John couldn't be impotent, she would have found that out long before, and I couldn't imagine her complaining that he wanted too much. Suddenly I thought of Alden.

'Is he into something you're not?' I asked, and I saw her tense.

'You're quick.' She took a gulp of beer, spilled some down her chin. 'God, look at me, I'm a nervous bloody wreck!' She rummaged in her bag for a tissue. Following it came a tin of tobacco.

'Oh, Lise . . .' I said, as she dabbed her chin. She hadn't smoked for over a year.

194

'I know. Back to square one.' She feathered out a Rizla. 'Did I tell you John was married before?'

I shook my head.

'Well, he was – two years. That's how long it lasted.' She spread the tobacco, ran her tongue along the glue. 'Eighteen months in he told his wife. She couldn't hack it. Six months later she left. Which is why, when he sensed we were going somewhere, he told me. Didn't want to risk it happening again.' She lit the cigarette, inhaled deeply. 'And guess what? I can't hack it either. Bummer or what?'

I didn't know what to say. Sitting across from me now, glass in one hand, roll-up in the other, she looked like the Lisa I had first met – blunt, exuberant, out to have fun and to hell with the consequences. Marriage? No way! Been there; done that; don't want to go there again. All that had changed with John.

'Remember that chat show we watched?' she said suddenly. 'All those weirdos dripping on about what turned them on, getting excited just talking about it? Well, John was like that. I could hear it in his voice, the same tenseness.' She caught my expression. 'Hey, it's nothing awful – he's not a paedophile or anything like that. Just . . . Well, you know what they say – one man's need is another woman's turn-off.'

'Do they?'

'Maybe I made it up.' She downed the last of the beer. 'Fancy another?'

I watched her walk to the inn, shoulders back, chest thrust out. As usual, heads were turning. A size ten from the waist down, a fourteen above, she has the kind of figure that gets her noticed. I was glad to see she was still flaunting it.

She came back looking brighter. 'I've been thinking of life post-John,' she announced. 'Hell, that makes me sound a sad bastard. But you know what I mean. I was thinking how we used to have fun – concerts, plays . . .'

'We still can.'

'You're not miffed that I've ignored you?'

'I'd probably have done the same.'

'Yeah. Men, huh?' Out came the tin again. 'So fancy a concert? There's this band people are raving about – blues, shit-hot sax player.'

'Lead me to it,' I said. 'When?'

'Tomorrow, eight o'clock.'

'Ah . . .'

'You can't make it?'

I shook my head, told her about Joe de Zaire. Lisa's eyes widened. 'All that and he cooks too?'

'So he claims.'

'So where's the catch?'

'Catch?'

'Oh, there'll be one, count on it! Is he gay – married?'

'Neither, as far as I know.'

She laughed, raised her glass. 'Then congratulations. You've just met the only guy on the planet who's got it all.'

I looked down at the ground. I'd thought *I* was the one who was cynical.

'Sorry,' Lisa said, a moment later. 'That was bitchy. I'm sure he's great. You have fun, okay?'

I nodded. 'What else are men for?'

Chapter Eighteen

I spent the following morning in my studio where, somewhat to my surprise, the painting was going well. Perhaps thoughts of the coming evening were spurring me on. Over lunch Dad informed me he was going up to see Judith, and asked if I wanted to go with him. I told him no – like Joe, the painting wouldn't leave me alone. Besides, Simon was coming and I wanted to be there when he arrived. If Dad wasn't, so much the better!

Or that was the plan. Lunch over, Dad suddenly felt queasy and had to lie down, and not wanting him to fret, I decided to go myself. It was June who answered the door – she had been washing the hall floor – and as soon as she saw me she began muttering thanks 'for looking out for our Lorna'.

'No problem,' I said. 'How is she?'

'Oh, I don't reckon she'll make Saturday, poor maid.' She twisted the mop handle in reddened hands. 'I told her, she shouldn't have been in such a hurry, never looking where she's going, but they don't listen. Might as well talk to the wall.'

Judith had appeared while we were talking and her eyes went up at June's words.

I said, 'She hasn't pulled out?'

'Not yet – wants to leave it to the last minute. But seeing her this morning, I reckon it'll be young Hayley what's queen.'

'Nonsense.' Judith stepped forward. 'Bring her up

197

here on Saturday morning. I'll see what I can do with make-up.'

'*Make-up?*' I asked, and June looked bewildered.

'We can at least try.' Judith motioned me inside. 'But make sure she gets here early.'

We picked our way over the wet floor and she led me to the kitchen. It felt cold and I realized the Aga had gone out. Judith switched on an electric kettle.

'Simple life palling?' I asked.

'The simple life's damned hard work. *Everything* about this place is hard work. Tea?'

I told her if it was quick. 'I only popped in to check you're okay.'

'Which you wouldn't have had to do if there was a telephone! God knows how Aunt managed. Maybe I've spent too long in London.' She leaned back against the sink. 'So this accident of Lorna's . . .'

'Wasn't.'

'How did I know you were going to say that?' She sighed. 'So it's the daughter, too. And June's got the gall to blame it on running! How can she *do* that? How can she remain quiet and let it go on?'

'It's family.'

'It's her *daughter!*' She spun back round, took two mugs from the rack and dropped a teabag in each. 'So how bad is she?'

'How bad's anyone after a thump in the eye?' I frowned. 'You really think you can disguise it with make-up?'

'I can disguise bruising. Swelling's more of a problem.'

'But how do you know what to do?' I realized I was echoing Lorna.

Judith gave an embarrassed smile. 'You might not believe this, but shortly after leaving college I did some modelling. I was actually approached by an agency – did you know they scout cafés looking for the right face? I'm still not quite sure why I agreed. I think I told myself it would be valuable experience, though for what exactly . . . Anyway, I soon realized it was a mistake and it didn't last long. But long enough to pick up a few tricks. Blemishes aren't tolerated on the catwalk.'

'Lorna has more than a blemish, Judith!'

She met my eyes. 'So at times did the girls.'

Oh, happy world.

Over tea I told her about my discovery of the dog and my meeting with Tom Weblake, swore her to secrecy about my notifying the RSPCA.

'It's my guess that's what your aunt discovered,' I said. 'I've been thinking about it a lot and it all fits. The film, the blackmail – assuming Alden's involved – confronting Tom. It was most likely him who sent the note, perhaps via Gary. It didn't make sense at first, the reference to friends. Then I remembered. That first time I came here, on the way back I stopped outside the farm. It's possible Tom saw me. And he may have seen you with Dad. Then when I turned up at the Institute . . .' I spread my hands.

Judith screwed up her eyes. 'You really must rue the day you met me, Gus. Believe me, if I'd had any idea what I was letting you in for . . .'

'Water under the bridge. None of us knew. The main problem is, even if I'm right we still can't link it to your aunt's death. Still, at least now the police will be involved. I suggest we leave it to them.'

Judith didn't reply. She was staring at her mug, her brow furrowed in thought.

'Not convinced?'

'I'm not sure. Oh, Aunt would have been appalled by the dog fighting, there's no question of that, yet I can't quite . . . If you knew the number of times I've heard her, bemoaning blood sports, berating those who take part. Such *cruelty*, Judith, she used to say: how can people be so *heartless*? She referred to them as brutes, savages, inhumane. Yet not once do I remember her using the word evil.' She looked up, gave a fragile smile. 'But I'm sure you're right. It's me being pedantic. And yes, Aunt would have considered it her duty to get it stopped.'

We talked it over some more while I finished the tea, and I was standing up to go when I remembered de Zaire.

'By the way, I saw Joe yesterday,' I said. 'You didn't tell me you exhibit his work!'

'Didn't I?' She gave a shrug. 'I suppose it didn't seem important.'

'He tells me Stuart was in America. Quite a coincidence, three ex-Californians in a small area like this. Four if you count Zara.'

'Stuart doesn't live here. He would never have met Joe if he hadn't come to Verstone.'

'He didn't know him in the States?' It was as well to check.

'Of course not. Stuart wasn't even in LA, he was in Santa Barbara.' She smiled. 'For seven years, which I find remarkable. I'm amazed he lasted seven months.'

'Why's that?'

She looked as if I should know the answer. 'He's so terribly *English*.'

I wondered about the coincidence as I drove home to Dad's. According to Judith, she and Stuart had been married three and a half years. Plus seven in the States made ten and a half. Rayjay had been gone for twelve. Close enough to make him a contender, yet, unless my memory was playing tricks, he no more resembled the photograph than the others. Although he did have a strange mouth. The result of bungled surgery?

Dad was up and about when I returned, feeling much better, and I managed a few more hours' work before calling it a day. Simon failed to materialize. At six thirty I took a shower, blow-dried my hair and applied some make-up. Tonight I intended to look my best.

I was struggling with the zip of an ankle-length navy sheath when the doorbell rang. Hewitt launched into a frenzy of barking, and a moment later Dad called up the stairs to tell me Simon had arrived. Muttering under my breath, I pulled on some flimsy sandals, by my standards fairly high, slipped the cassette in my bag and teetered downstairs. I felt ridiculously overdressed, an upshot of spending most of my life in jeans.

When I entered the kitchen, Dad whistled. 'Well, look at you!'

Simon just looked embarrassed. 'I'm sorry. I've obviously come at a bad time.'

'That's okay.' I waved him to a chair, looked at Dad. He took the hint. When the door closed I pulled out the video and slid it across the table.

'Where did you find it?' Simon asked, getting straight to the point.

'At the Institute.'

'Where *exactly*?'

I swallowed. 'Alden's bedroom, but –'

'I see.'

'No, you don't.'

'It's none of my business, Gus. If you and he want to –'

'Alden wasn't there,' I said, wondering why it was important that he knew. 'Look, this is – kind of awkward. Can we talk off the record?'

'Why would you want it off the record?'

'Because I don't want to lose my job!' His eyes narrowed. 'Among other things,' I added. 'Look, you know why I was there, Simon. To see what I could find out. And after that note, and hearing Alden being blackmailed . . .'

'You broke into his room.'

'Actually, no – the door was open. But yeah, I looked around.'

'And what would you have done if he'd come back?'

I shrugged.

'Taking a chance, weren't you? Or did you *know* he was busy elsewhere. Evacuating the building, perhaps?'

I groaned silently. I should have known he would talk to Leo.

'*Jesus!*' I heard him mutter.

'Look, can we stop discussing how I got it and talk about the content?' I snapped angrily. 'There are two films on that thing, and the girl in the second one is abused, raped, probably drugged and far too bloody young! That's the only reason I've told you, and believe me it wasn't easy. Now if you want to drop me in it, go ahead, I've done my bit.' I jumped to my feet, marched across to the window. 'Oh, and perhaps I should mention there are thirteen more where that came from, no doubt in similar vein. Now, do you want to arrest me or can we sit and discuss it sensibly?'

'*I'm* happy to discuss it all night.'

I spun round.

Simon's expression was unreadable. 'But as you so clearly have other plans, then yeah, let's talk.' He tapped the cassette. 'This tape that's come from an unknown source – how do you think it links to the old lady's death?'

I released my breath and wandered back, more relieved than I showed. 'I don't. But I think one of his other interests might.'

I told him about the pit bull and my suspicions concerning a dog-fighting ring. Simon scowled as he listened, several times wiped his hand over his face. Only then did I realize how tired he looked. I wasn't making his workload any lighter.

'Well, there's one consolation,' he said at length. 'It doesn't sound like Rayjay. Not lucrative enough. Anything he does is big money. These bastards do it for fun.'

'*Fun?*'

'You know what I mean.' He sighed. 'Shit! Looks like I'm back to square one on the Trevor front.'

'Do you still have that photo?'

He pulled it from his pocket. 'Why?

'Judith's husband, Stuart. He spent time in the States. Roughly the right time frame but . . .' I shook my head. 'Not him. Anyway, he lives in London.'

While he was returning it to his pocket, I glanced at the clock.

'Forgive me, I'm keeping you.' He promptly climbed to his feet. 'Actually, I was intending to ask if you'd like to go for a drink. Clearly someone beat me to it. Any chance of another time?'

That I hadn't expected. 'Er – yes,' I stuttered. 'Why not?'

'Good.' He picked up the cassette. 'I suppose I should tell you to enjoy your evening. But then again, maybe I won't.' A smile. 'I'll be in touch.'

I waited until he was at the door. 'Simon?'

'Hm?'

'Thanks.'

Chapter Nineteen

I wasn't the only one running late. Joe answered the door in a bathrobe, wet hair flowing loose around his shoulders. 'Sorry about this,' he grinned, ushering me in. 'I was working on an idea and – hey!' His eyes slid over my body. 'Don't you look something!'

I could have said the same about him.

I followed him through to the terrace and sat facing the sun while he went off to change. The table was draped in a white cloth and laid for two, a small bowl of flowers at its centre. White daisies spiked with violent red nasturtiums, simple but effective. Wonderful smells were issuing from the kitchen – fresh basil, garlic, something impossibly sweet. I closed my eyes and listened to the hum of insects, the gentle sound of water. Why weren't more evenings like this?

When Joe returned he was carrying two drinks, something he'd concocted himself in long slender glasses. He had dressed simply in black trousers and a white shirt, the sleeves rolled back and open at the neck. His ponytail gleamed like ebony.

'Notice anything?' he asked as he sat down.

'It's *nice?*'

He grinned. 'No banshee-wails. I oiled the wheel. I promised you the sound of water.'

'And owls,' I reminded him.

'I'm saving those till nightfall.'

The drinks were delicious. So, later, was the meal, beginning with a chilled gazpacho and ending with a concoction of pineapple and wild strawberries accompanied by an excellent Sauternes. Joe hadn't lied about his culinary skills. Throughout we talked easily, mostly about work, artists we admired, his life in America, and when dusk slid into the valley we turned our chairs to watch the sun grow ever larger as it dipped behind the trees. In its wake came the sunset, fiery bands of orange, gold and red across an azure sky. An owl hooted in a nearby tree, and from across the valley came an answering call.

'Promise fulfilled,' I said, and Joe smiled.

I sipped the last of my coffee and moved to the cognac. Until now the evening had been warm, but with the disappearance of the sun the air had cooled and a light breeze was rustling the creeper. I shivered slightly and rubbed my arms.

'You're cold,' Joe said. 'Want to go inside?'

I shook my head.

'Then let me fetch you something.'

He ran his finger along my arm as he passed. Another shiver, but this one had nothing to do with cold.

Music began to play in the house, a slow bluesy number with haunting sax. Hell, he even played my kind of music. He returned with a shawl and draped it around my shoulders. Embroidered silk, fringed at the edges.

'It's beautiful,' I said.

'Bought it in Mexico.'

I didn't ask who for. He put a small lacquered box on the table, returned to his chair and began to unpack the contents. Out came a bevel-edged sheet of glass, a razor blade, a straw . . .

I looked away – swept at a moth that was fluttering too close to the candle. He cut the powder and divided it into lines. I heard him inhale. Moments later a hand touched my arm.

I shook my head. 'No thanks.'

'You don't do coke? Ah well – shame to waste it.'

The second line went the same way. More inhaling. More cognac. *Ease off, Tavender . . .*

Far away a church clock struck one. I looked up at the stars. The Milky Way was a sprinkling of dust across the heavens, almost close enough to touch.

'Aren't they something?' Joe murmured. 'Kinda weird, seeing something that isn't there. Millions of light years . . .' Then, 'I've shocked you, haven't I.'

'No.' Flakes of powder were clinging to his nose.

'Yeah, I have. Look, it's no sweat, just social. No different than this.' He raised his glass. His other hand snaked out, tipped me under the chin.

'You haven't shocked me, Joe.'

'Good.' The fingers slid up, brushed my cheek. Next minute he was on his feet. 'Let's dance,' he said, and pulled me from the chair, pulled me towards him.

We swayed to the music, a slow seductive number with a sax solo that sent shivers down my spine. So did his first kiss, and a lot more places beyond. The shawl fell from my shoulders and slid to the floor.

The track seemed to go on for ever. I wasn't complaining. Finally it segued to an even slower piece. Unlike the music, Joe was hotting up, in a way that left me breathless. Too fast, too soon. I pushed against his shoulders.

He took no notice. If anything, my resistance seemed to excite him. The pressure on my arms increased, his fingers digging holes in my flesh. Beneath his mouth, my lips were beginning to swell.

'Hey . . .' I said, pushing harder.

He eased back, grinned, grabbed my hand and spun me round. But something was different. His eyes had grown darker and looked slightly unfocused. Had he drunk more than I realized?

We danced some more but within minutes he was at it again, this time backing me against the wall. He kissed me so hard my head slammed against the stone.

'Whoa!' I said. 'That hurt.'

'So what's with a little pain?' His voice was different, too – rougher, more aggressive.

'Just that I'd still like my head in the morning,' I said, trying to keep it light.

'You Brits!' He came at me again.

I dodged to one side. 'Look, I think I should leave, Joe. It's been a great night but . . .'

The hand that yanked me back was anything but gentle. 'Hey, don't get prissy with me!'

I gasped. *Prissy?* 'I'm not going to sleep with you, Joe,' I said, 'not tonight, so –'

Air burst from me as he slammed me against the wall. More mouth-crushing, and this time I tasted blood. Pinning me with his body, he grabbed both wrists, forced my arms to my sides.

Suddenly it was no longer funny. I was beginning to feel genuinely scared. What was *wrong* with the guy? One minute gentle, charming, and now . . .

My arms were being forced behind my back. 'Not like this, Joe. Please! Maybe another time . . .'

I might as well not have spoken. He'd managed to seize both my wrists in one hand, was holding them like a vice. His other hand slid to my thigh. He grabbed hold of my skirt and began to pull.

Definitely not funny. My heart was hammering against my ribs. This was the sort of thing you read about, heard about on the news . . .

I tried to wrestle out from under him but could barely move. He was tugging now, wrestling with the fabric, hauling it above my knees. How did I get out of this one? *Think, Tavender . . .*

I couldn't overpower him, I didn't have the strength. My only hope was to outmanoeuvre. But how? Fighting only seemed to excite him, make him more determined. Perhaps if he thought I had given in . . .

I stopped struggling, hung like a limp rag in his arms. Joe sensed the change. The pressure on my body began to ease and his mouth dropped to my neck. When he let go my arms, I threw them around him, dug my nails into his

207

back. Raising my hips from the wall, I all but helped him lift the skirt around my waist. If this didn't work . . .

Slowly I moved my leg into position – just as slowly snarled my fingers in his hair, wrapped my hand around the ponytail. I waited until his fingers were on my thigh, then, using all my strength, gave an almighty jerk. At the same time I brought up my knee. Joe made a whooming sound and buckled forward, clutching his groin.

'*What the* . . .'

I brought my knee up again, caught him under the chin. Heard a crack.

He staggered backwards, tried to grab a chair, missed and caught the edge of the tablecloth. Bottles and glasses crashed to the ground.

'Bitch!' he growled as he tried to get up. 'You fucking . . .'

He fell back, hampered by cloth and broken glass. Blood stained his hand, he must have cut himself. Or was it one of the flowers?

I didn't wait to find out. Already I'd grabbed my bag and started to run. Choice words came after me as I sprinted from the terrace and vanished into the night.

Sobbing. Gasping. Heart pounding so much it hurt. Somehow I got up the steps, found my way through the darkness. The sandals were slowing me down. The one time I needed trainers.

Was he following? At any moment I expected to be grabbed from behind and thrown to the ground. Please God let him be incapable!

A lifetime later I reached the car. I was shaking too much to unlock it. I dropped the keys and whimpered like a child as I scrabbled around on the ground. Finally I found them and got them in the door, went through the same thing again with the ignition. Staring at the windows, expecting at any moment his face to appear. If he caught me now . . .

When the engine fired I almost cried. Slowly, I told

myself – don't stall. I eased the pedal gently, felt it engage, and when the car began to roll jammed my foot to the ground.

Tears were blinding my eyes and half a mile on I stopped, checked myself in the mirror. I looked like a hooker after a rough night, make-up smeared, lips swollen and bruised. How the hell would I explain this to Dad?

I wouldn't. *Couldn't.* There was no way I would let him see me like this. I would drive to Exeter, make up some story, hide in my flat until the swelling had gone down. I rummaged in my bag for the keys, remembered I had left them at Tynings. And howled like a babe.

And suddenly I understood. All those women like Lorna and June. It wasn't simply protecting loved ones that made them clam up – nor was it the fear of reprisal. It was shame – sheer, unadulterated shame. I felt dirty, humiliated and cheap, and no matter how much I told myself that it hadn't been my fault, I knew I would do anything rather than let it be known. There was no way I would tell my father. I doubted I would even tell Lisa.

Shame too at my lack of judgement. How could I have got it so wrong?

Lisa had been right. She said there would be a catch.

Chapter Twenty

Praying Hewitt's barks hadn't woken my father, I tiptoed to the bathroom and filled the basin with cold water. If ever there was a case of déjà vu. Not that my injuries were anywhere near as serious as Lorna's. My lower lip had split when it crushed against my teeth but the rest, thank God, were fairly superficial – a raw, red chin abraded by Joe's stubble and finger-shaped bruises on my arms and wrists.

I could still smell him, the shampoo smell of his hair, the lemony aftershave, and when I stood in the near-cold shower I scrubbed and scrubbed, desperate to remove all trace. I emerged shivering and towelled myself dry, wishing I had the long fleecy dressing-gown I wore in winter. I felt like howling.

Would Joe have raped me? Yes – of that I had no doubt. Nor that there would have been others before me. Had they, too, been shamed into silence?

I longed for a hot drink, Ovaltine or chocolate, something comforting, but afraid Dad might still get up I went straight to bed. Sleep wouldn't come and I thrashed around, reliving the events over and over, asking myself how it had got so out of hand. Even at times questioning my own actions, fearful that I had given the wrong impression, had in some way led him on.

Ah, the self-doubts of the night. What is it with us women?

*   *   *

Dad was at the table when I came down for breakfast, engrossed in one of the Tintins.

'Good night?' he asked, without looking up.

'Mm,' I replied non-committally. 'Hope Hewitt didn't wake you.'

'I heard him bark.' He turned the pages of a French-English dictionary. 'Damn verbs,' he muttered. 'Never could get to grips.'

I helped myself to cereal, making sure to keep the long sleeves of my T-shirt well pulled down. Olive-toned make-up masked the redness of my chin, but I couldn't disguise my swollen mouth. It didn't take Dad long to notice.

'What happened to you?' he asked, then almost as quickly looked away. He seemed faintly embarrassed, and I realized he was attributing it to a night of passion.

'Car door,' I said quickly, patting my lip. How easily it slipped off the tongue. 'Blame the sandals.'

'You tripped?' he frowned. 'Not like you to be clumsy.'

'Yeah, well I guess I'm not used to heels. At least it happened when I was leaving.' I found a spoon, carried my bowl to the window. Trying to chew. Muesli had been a bad choice.

'So how did it go?' he enquired. 'Good meal?'

'Excellent.'

'And the chef?'

I hesitated.

'Thought so.' He folded his arms.

'What's that supposed to mean?'

'I can read you like a book, Gus. Last night you were up in the air, today you're flat as a pancake.'

'It was a late night.'

'If you say so.' The telephone rang and he picked it up. 'Yes, she is – hold on. It's Simon,' he said, holding it out.

Just what I didn't need, especially with Dad here. But he wasn't calling about the tape.

'This Revel tomorrow,' he said. 'I thought I might come along, take a look around. I wondered if you would like to come with me?'

211

'To point people out?'

'Partly. Also because I've got a day off, I thought it might be fun. Of course, if you're going with someone else . . .'

'No,' I said, rather too sharply. 'That would be nice. Where shall I meet you?'

'Ah.'

He wasn't sure what time he could get there, so we left it that he would find me. When I looked back Dad was deep in his book. 'Other fish,' he murmured as I replaced the phone.

How rapidly things change. At Judith's suggestion that Joe might be at the Revel, I'd let Dad persuade me to join the procession. Now he was the main reason I didn't want to go. But the promise had been made and, not wanting another fiasco, I settled in for some practice. I'd managed a few scales when Dad brought his own accordion and joined in, and together we ran through 'The Pure Lady', a tune peculiar to the Revel, not unlike the Padstow Hobby-horse dance and probably as old. Monty arrived while we were playing and applauded warmly. I caught him looking at my mouth.

'Car door,' I said before he could ask. 'What's that?'

'Mm? Oh, something I picked up at auction.' He handed me the book he was carrying. 'Thought you might be interested. Folk traditions. Mentions the Revel.'

I found the entry under the heading *Lammas Fairs*. '*Lammas*', I read out loud, '*an ancient feast, derived from Hlaf Masse or Loaf Mass meaning the festival of first fruits.*'

'What's it say about Swinlake?' Dad said impatiently.

I found the relevant passage. '*A time of feasting and merriment accompanied by dancing and sports, including wrestling and other feats of strength.* It says it was banned by the Church in the nineteenth century for *encouraging drunkenness and immoral behaviour.* Reinstated 1910.'

212

'Doesn't sound like it's changed much,' he grinned. 'Anything about the Queen?'

'*A local girl is chosen to be Queen of the Revel. Dressed in white, mounted on a white horse, she leads a procession through the village, accompanied by her entourage and a band of musicians playing an ancient melody known as "The Pure Lady". The origin of the title is unknown.*'

'Always assumed it referred to a waterfall,' Monty said. 'Like the White Lady at Lydford.'

'It mentions that,' I said. '. . . *waterfalls, once thought to be the home of Sprites. But – Another popular theory is that the Queen was a "pure lady" or virgin being offered for sacrifice.*'

'Better not tell Lorna,' Dad chuckled.

'It also says Swinlake has a local tradition. Apparently when loaves were baked from the first corn, farmers took pieces and crumbled them in the four corners of their barns.'

'Never heard that one,' Monty said. 'Must remember to ask Old Gam.'

'Wilfie?' I grinned.

'Oh, don't underestimate him, he's a mine of information. Cars, gardening, old customs . . . Your dad tell you he's coming to work here?'

'No?'

Dad shrugged. 'Only half a day. It was after you told me about the Institute. Couldn't resist the thought of some home-grown fruit and veg.'

Saturday morning dawned bright and warm and the village was already buzzing when I walked to the shop for milk. Lines of coloured flags fluttered over the main street, and lamp posts, gates and fences were being decked with garlands of flowers, greenery and woven wreaths of straw. The villagers must have been up since dawn. Children were everywhere, running and shrieking, and men were busy in the field where the ram-roast was to take place, erecting sideshows and marking out the ground. I'd never been to one of Swinlake's Revels – all previous years I'd been on call – yet in a strange way I was looking forward to it. My only concern was de Zaire. I wasn't sure how I would react if we came face to face.

There was one other minor thing Dad had 'forgotten' to mention. The band were supposed to dress up. Two o'clock found us outside the village hall, Dad in a collarless shirt, braces and a red and white scarf, me in the long skirt I'd worn at the Institute and a geranium clipped behind my ear, the best I could do at short notice. With us were the other musicians and a dozen or more children in fancy dress, along with what seemed like most of their families. Shrieks and wails rent the air as mothers tweaked and adjusted costumes. The three foot high carrot had already won my vote.

Inevitably things were running late but at last we heard the clip-clop of hooves and around the corner came a white beribboned pony led by the local blacksmith. A moment later Lorna stepped from the hall. She wore a long white muslin dress and a floral headdress, and was followed by her attendants, all similarly attired. None was as pretty as Lorna.

Dad and I exchanged looks. From this distance, at least, her face appeared unmarked. Judith must have performed miracles.

The blacksmith helped her sidesaddle on to the horse and while the band tuned up a couple of women arranged her skirts. Two drummers moved in front to lead the way and finally we were off, marching to the slow, unrelenting drumbeat. It was hypnotic, magical, and suddenly I was glad to be taking part. For who knew how many years the villagers had walked this path, on this same day, and I was proud to continue the tradition. I caught Dad's eye and smiled.

Crowds jammed the pavements and spilled on to the road, leaving barely room for the procession. People had flocked from miles around. If Simon was among them I couldn't see him, but I did spot Judith, standing at the base of the old stone cross. Next to her, to my amazement, was Stuart. When and why had he turned up?

In the recreation field, stalls had sprouted like mushrooms. We halted in front of a dais and kept playing while Lorna dismounted. Then the drummers continued alone, maintaining the sonorous beat as she climbed the steps to the platform, for all the world like a condemned person mounting a scaffold. For me the sacrificial virgin theory won hands down.

The vicar stepped forward and tapped the mike, then started on about proceeds and church restoration funds. The crowd fidgeted. June, standing beside the platform, kept beaming up at her daughter. So did the curly-haired young man beside her, and I guessed it was her boyfriend, Kenny Hatch. A couple of yards further on, Wilfie was gazing up, nodding happily. He was the only person on the field to have personal space.

There was an audible sigh from the crowd when the vicar at last called Lorna forward to formally open the proceedings.

'Thank God for that,' Dad muttered as people began to disperse.

I frowned. 'Are you okay?'

'Bit tired, don't think I'll hang around. Anyway, I promised to meet Monty in the pub.'

'Want me to come with you?'

'Don't be daft! Stay here and meet Simon.'

I watched him march off, shrugged, then stashed my accordion under the platform with the other instruments, hoping Simon wouldn't be late. This wasn't the sort of event to attend alone.

He finally caught up with me at the wellie-throwing. 'Not bad,' he said, as the boot landed heel first in the grass.

'Thank Hewitt,' I grinned. 'He taught me to throw sticks. Did you see the procession?'

'Caught the tail end.' His eyes narrowed. 'What happened to your mouth?'

'Car door.' The line was becoming jaded. 'And no, I wasn't drunk. Anyway, what do you want to see?'

'Everything.' He clapped his hands. 'Tug-of-war, Punch and Judy – anyone we've talked about . . .'

'Stuart's here,' I said.

'The husband? That's one I didn't expect. But no rush. What say we wander for a while, enjoy ourselves?'

'Pretend we're normal folks?'

He smiled. 'Sounds good to me.'

The smell of fried onions wafted from the hot-dog van as we visited stalls selling cakes, toffee apples, jams and handicrafts. We threw quoits over pegs, guessed the name of a doll, and almost, *almost*, won a coconut. Simple pleasures yet I was having fun, I was surprised at how much. Simon, I was discovering, was an interesting guy, far more so than I'd imagined. He seemed perfectly happy to don his non-policeman hat, which was just as well because the only person we saw was Wilfie. He was sitting on the grass watching Punch and Judy, packed in amongst the children.

'Is it always this crowded?' Simon asked, when we hesitated outside the beer tent. It was full to capacity, people spilling on to the field.

'We could try the pub.'

'Might as well. It can't be any worse.'

We set off towards the entrance. One last stall stood apart from the rest – Guess the weight of the pig. He paused. 'Want to try?'

'You kidding?'

'We can only be wrong.' Already he was heading towards it.

'Yeah,' I called after him, 'by about a ton!'

An elderly man stood up as we approached. 'Gonna guess 'er weight, then?' he asked, his hand already out for the money. 'Want me to get 'er out?'

I looked into the pen. It was divided into two, the front part open, the back a cobbled-together shed that provided shade. I could see the sow through the doorway, a massive mound of pink lying on her side in a bed of straw.

'Don't bother,' I said. 'It won't make any difference.'

He handed us biros and paper. 'Name at top, then weight. Stones or pounds, don't make no difference.'

'What about metric?' I asked.

'What's that then?'

Simon looked away.

I pulled a figure out of the air and wrote it down, and we handed back the papers. The old man read them, nodded, and stuffed them in his bag. 'Not farmers, then,' he observed.

Something told me we hadn't won.

Simon was right, the pub wasn't worse, but nor was it any better. We had to fight through a crush simply to reach the door. Inside, most of the clientele were male, most of them standing. I spotted a couple of chairs near the corner and Simon suggested I grab them while he went for the drinks, joking that he'd see me in an hour. Or I hoped it was a joke.

I couldn't see Dad or Monty but that didn't mean they weren't here. Who I did see was Tom Weblake. He came bursting through the door a minute after I sat down and elbowed his way to the bar. I wondered where he'd been when his only daughter was opening the fête.

Simon was back sooner than we expected and handed me a Perrier. Barely had he sat down when angry voices rose above the din.

I glanced towards the bar. 'How long before there's trouble?'

'Not my problem. Job for the local boys.'

'Hope they're near by,' I said, as the body of people surged.

'Come on, lads, break it up.' The landlord.

'He started it!' came the reply. 'Stupid fuck!' We heard a thwack as fist presumably met chin.

'Okay, that's enough. Out, both of you!'

The crowd parted as the landlord and another man

217

propelled two youths towards the entrance. One had cropped blond hair, pierced ears and eyebrows. Blood was running from his nose. The other was swarthy with an ink-black quiff, arms covered in tattoos. The resemblance to Lorna was startling.

The door slammed behind them and the landlord brushed his hands. Spotting me, he came across. 'Bob's daughter, isn't it? He said to look out for you.'

'Was that Gary Weblake?' I asked.

He gave a snort, glanced over his shoulder. 'Father next, no doubt. Talking of which, yours said to tell you he's gone home. Not feeling too good.'

'Hell!' I muttered, and jumped up. 'I'm sorry Simon, but –'

'I'll come with you,' he said, and climbed to his feet.

Monty was in the kitchen when we arrived, making a cup of herb tea.

'No need to worry,' he said, 'just tiredness. He's having a lie down.'

I hurried to the bedroom. Dad was propped up on pillows. His face looked grey.

'Now don't start fussing,' he said. 'Overdid it, that's all. Good night's sleep and I'll be fine.'

'You sure?' I perched on the bed.

'Positive.' He smiled. 'Good procession, eh? Glad you could make it at last. Is Simon with you?'

I nodded.

'Nice chap. Like him. Is he married?'

'I don't know. Why?'

'Just wondered. Think he'd mind a quick word?'

'What about?'

Dad tapped the end of his nose.

Simon was only with him a few minutes, and came back smiling. 'Your father wants me to take you back to the Revel,' he said. 'No arguments, he says he'll feel worse if

218

you hang around and miss the fun. Says if he needs anything he's got Monty.'

'Was coming home anyway,' Monty muttered. 'Can't stand crowds.'

'Well, it's nice of you both to arrange my life!' I snapped.

'Yeah, he said you'd say that, too,' Simon grinned. 'Anyway, I told him I'd be happy to – after we'd been for a meal.'

We drove to a pub in a neighbouring village. I'd not eaten there before and doubted if I would again. All it had going for it was location, the alfresco tables scattered amongst the trees.

'Anything back on Alden?' I asked, as I chewed through vegetarian lasagne microwaved too long.

'He hasn't got a record, if that's what you mean. Well, not in this country. We're still waiting on the States.'

'What about the others?'

He shook his head. 'Wonder if any of them will turn up tonight?'

'Suppose it depends on how keen they are to know a pig's weight.'

He smiled, and a moment later laid down his knife and fork. 'Gus, about last night – your date. Is that an ongoing thing?'

'No.' I reached for my wine. 'It was a one-off, not to be repeated.'

'So if I said I'd like to do this again . . .'

'I'd probably say that would be nice.'

Nice? It would be fucking beautiful!

I shuddered.

'You okay?'

'Someone walked over my grave. When?'

'That's the problem. It might have to be short notice . . .'

'Busy times?'

He carried on eating. 'Let's just say I smile when I'm told the crime rate's down.'

219

Chapter Twenty-One

Shadows stretched ahead of us as we approached the field, and on the other side of the fence a cornfield glowed red-gold in the evening sun, dotted here and there with the vermilion splash of poppies. Behind us Ver Tor was a dark silhouette against the western sky. The ram-roast was now well under way, the air pungent, a plume of smoke and sparks rising high into the air. Disco music was blaring from loudspeakers, and up on the platform a local band called Fast and Loose was setting up its gear. Watching them from below was Wilfie.

'Want to meet him?' I asked.

'Why not?'

We wandered across and I introduced them, talked for a while about the weather. According to Wilfie we were due for rain.

'I hear you're coming to work for my father,' I said. 'My fault. I told him about the garden at the Institute.' I glanced around. 'Is Mr Chadwicke here tonight?'

'A'n't seen 'un.' Wilfie nodded. 'Seen Mrs Kempe, though. Got 'ubby with 'er.' He scratched his stomach. 'Seen 'un before, up to Verstone.'

'What, earlier today?'

'Nah, backalong. When Miss 'Illas were alive.'

'Really?' I was impressed. If Judith was right and Stuart had only visited once, Wilfie was going back three and half years. 'You've got a good memory, Wilfie.'

'Remembered the car. Never forgets a motor.' He looked up as someone crashed a cymbal. 'Band later.'

'You must have seen a lot of Revels,' Simon chipped in.

'Fair few. Don't change much. More people, mind. Comes from all over.'

I remembered what Monty had said. 'I also hear you know a lot about local traditions. Is it true farmers used to scatter bread in the corners of their barns?'

'Course. Loaves from the first corn.'

Not so green as cabbage-looking.

'Know why they did it?'

The blue eyes twinkled. 'To block up holes, most like.'

'You're winding me up, Wilfie . . .'

His grin revealed two rows of surprisingly healthy teeth.

'So when did it die out?'

'Scattin' crumbs? Hasn't. Farmer Penney, 'e scatted 'em. 'Er's dead now, mind. But Farmer Dart, ee's still alive.' More scratching, this time under his arms. 'Then there's new 'uns.'

'Young farmers are carrying it on?'

'Nah, not farmers. *New* 'uns! 'Im what I works for.'

'Mr Chadwicke?'

'Mr Zaire!' He chuckled. 'Didn't get it right, though. Should'a bin in corners.'

Simon turned away to hide a smile, while up on the platform a young lad attempted a Hendrix riff. Wilfie glanced up. 'That's changed. Used to be Bob Cann, folks dancin' in circles. 'N step-dancing. Ever seen that?'

'Once.'

'Us liked that,' he said wistfully. 'Gone now, though. All gone now.'

We'd started to walk away when I paused. 'Hang on,' I said and turned back.

'Wilfie, that time you saw Judith's husband, when old Miss Hillas was alive. When was it exactly?'

The leathery brow furrowed.

'Quite a while ago. Like three or four years?'

His expression told me time meant nothing.

'But you do remember his car.'

'Oh yeah. Same one 'er's got now.'

'Are you sure?'

'Never forgets a motor.'

I glanced at Simon. 'Can you remember the time of year? Was it winter, summer?'

He thought for a moment, tugging on the lobe of his ear. 'Pussy willow were out, I remembers that. Reckon it must've bin spring.'

'Thanks, Wilfie.' I drew Simon to one side. 'Hear that? Someone's lying. Stuart must've been here around the time Miss Hillas died.'

'How do you work that out?'

'The car. It's less than a year old.'

He smiled.

'Wilfie knows about cars, Simon. Which means either Judith's lying about Stuart only coming here once, or he didn't tell her he'd been.'

'Maybe it slipped his mind.'

'But why *would* he have called? He couldn't stand the aunt. Besides, Judith swears he didn't leave London, was too busy. He couldn't even get away for the funeral.'

'Then perhaps she's setting him up. Wouldn't be the first time.'

'I'm serious!'

'So was I. But okay, let's say the car was here. Who's to say your friend didn't borrow it and come on her own?'

'Wilfie did say he'd seen *him* before.'

'The old chap said a lot of things.'

'But suppose it *was* Stuart.' I was unwilling to let it go. 'He was in debt, right? Didn't know which way to turn. Suppose he came to beg for a loan? In confidence; don't tell Judith. The old lady might have coughed up for her niece's sake, but what if she didn't? All that money sitting there, his wife the sole beneficiary . . .'

'So where does the blackmail fit in?'

I frowned. 'Alden and Stuart?'

'With Gary watching? That's some crowd, Gus. And why not kill her in the house?' He draped his arm around my shoulder. 'Know what I think? You're giving Wilfie too much credence. He might be a great character but he's hardly a plausible witness. He also claimed to have seen this de Zaire character performing pagan rites. *Scattin' crumbs!* It was probably stone dust from his latest sculpture.'

'He works in metal.'

'Then maybe he was putting down rat poison!' He squeezed my shoulder. 'I'll bear it in mind, okay? Now, what say we go see this tug-of-war.'

We were halfway to the pitch when I spotted Alden. He was hard to miss, dressed in an orange embroidered tunic more suitable for Glastonbury than a Devon fête. We followed him to the beer tent, watched him pause outside and stare around. Seconds later he was joined by another man.

'Shit!' I muttered, louder than I intended, and Simon looked at me strangely.

'Who's that?' he asked.

'The crumb scatterer.'

'De Zaire?' He pursed his lips. Then, after a moment, 'That wouldn't be the one-off, never-to-be-repeated, by any chance?'

I gave a nod. I hadn't realized I was so transparent. 'But please don't ask me to introduce you.'

'Don't worry, that's the last thing I want.'

He did however want a closer look, so I hung back in the shadow of a stall while he moved nearer the marquee. While he was hovering a third man arrived – Stuart Kempe. Bohemian, hippy and city slick. They made a bizarre trio.

'Who's the flashy dresser?' Simon asked when he came back.

I told him.

'Guessed it might be. Brave man. Damned if I'd wear a suit like that to a ram-roast.'

'Could you afford one?'

He grinned, again circled my shoulder. 'You're right about the photo. Zero resemblance.'

223

'So you're no nearer finding –'

I was about to say Rayjay. Simon stopped me with a kiss. My eyes widened.

'Didn't want you to say the name,' he said when he drew back. 'Too many ears. Actually, that's a lie. I was looking for an excuse.'

The light was fading when we finally reached the tug-of-war, and two large floodlights were throwing strange shadows across the pitch. A pull had just ended and the winning team were celebrating, clapping each other on the back. We'd only been there a moment when Lorna came running up. I told her she looked beautiful.

'Thanks to Judith.' She touched her face shyly. 'Is it still okay?'

'Perfect. Is Judith here?'

'She was supposed to be.' She glanced around. 'You going to stay and watch? Kenny's on next.'

'Who does he pull for?' Simon asked.

'Young Farmers. Oh, here they come!' she squealed as the teams ran on to the pitch. 'That's Kenny, third one back.'

It was the young man I'd seen by the platform, now dressed in dark shorts and a red and white football shirt. His blond curls had taken on a gingerish tinge in the lights. The men started limbering up, flexing muscles. Several were naked to the waist, their lower halves clad in jeans, shorts or jogging pants. All wore thick-tread boots for grip. Kenny was no weakling, but compared to some he looked puny. The guy at the end of the rope was a gorilla.

'Good anchor man,' Simon said, and when I looked him a question, 'Used to do a bit myself. Works team.'

The men had taken their positions and were leaning back, taking the strain on the rope. The referee aligned the marker. When finally satisfied he raised his hand, and suddenly they were off, straining as if their lives depended on it.

'*Heave!*' Simon yelled. 'Come on, Young Farmers!' and beside me Lorna giggled.

The atmosphere was electric and soon I was yelling too.

The teams were giving it their all, sweat pouring from their bodies, their faces contorting with the strain. Backwards and forwards, a foot one way, a foot the other, faces getting redder and more tortured as they struggled to hold ground. The gorilla was threatening to burst a blood vessel.

All of a sudden Young Farmers gave a massive pull. The other team juddered and lurched forward. Another jerk and they shot forward again. The crowd was going crazy. And suddenly it was all over, the marker had crossed the line. The teams let go the rope and, like skittles after a strike, collapsed on to the pitch.

Lorna was jumping up and down, clapping her hands. 'They did it, they did it! Through to the next round.' And next minute she was gone, running across the grass towards Kenny. He saw her coming and struggled to his feet, laughing as he held out his hands to keep her at arm's length.

Beside me Simon sighed. 'Ah, that takes me back.'

'Tugging ropes or having women throw themselves at you?'

He grinned. Then, 'Uh-uh, could be trouble.'

I looked back to see Gary storming on to the pitch, accompanied by a bunch of mates. Kenny's team were scrambling to their feet. Kenny tried to put Lorna behind him, but Gary grabbed her wrist and hurled her to one side. I tried to run forward but Simon caught my arm. 'Leave it!'

'We can't just –'

'Uniforms'll sort it,' said a voice at my side, and when I turned I saw Phil Twigg, beside her her girlfriend, Susie.

I spun round on Simon. 'Is that always your cop-out?' But already I could see she was right. The boys in blue were swarming on to the pitch, and within seconds had brought Gary to the ground. A young WPC was bending over Lorna.

'Might have known I'd find you here,' Phil said, turning

her back on the mêlée. 'Now we have, how about buying us a drink?'

Sweating bodies, the reek of stale beer, and enough spilt on the ground to churn it to mud. So was the beer tent as we elbowed our way through. The noise was unbearable, everyone shouting over everyone else. By the time we reached the bar we were so squashed together I could have lifted both feet from the ground and remained where I was. Simon waved a bunch of notes in the air to attract a barman's attention, and through sheer persistence finally got served. Then it was another scramble, this time to the side of the tent.

'How long have you been here?' Simon asked Phil, as we huddled beside the canvas.

'Couple of hours. Having a ball, aren't we, Sue?'

'Wild.' Susie twirled an end of spiky black hair.

'Spent most of it in the pub. Waste of time. You owe me one, Furneaux.'

He smiled. 'Don't tell me you're not having fun . . .'

'Read my lips.' She went to take a drink, instead lurched forward as a man catapulted from the crowd. 'Jesus!' She shook beer from her hands. 'And I thought Exeter was rough!'

Simon was staring over our heads towards the centre of the tent. 'It's him again!' he said in disbelief. 'The brother. How'd he get here so fast?'

I stood on tiptoe to see what was going on. Those nearest the dispute had drawn back, but even so I could barely see Gary. He was being overshadowed by a red-faced bull of a man, who was holding him by the shirt-front, waving a meaty fist.

'Who's the troll?' Simon asked.

'That,' I said, 'is his father.'

I'm not sure what happened next, who made the first move. All I remember is a tangle of thrashing arms, a woman screaming, and being caught up in the surge as people battled to get outside. It's a miracle no one was trampled. Drinks went in all directions, glasses shattered, but we finally stumbled out into fresh air and brushed ourselves down.

'Alcohol, huh,' muttered Phil. 'So much for a quiet night in the country.'

Sounds of fighting were still coming from inside. The uniforms were having a busy night. We left them to it and headed towards the platform, listened for a while to the band. Couples of all ages were dancing, doing their best to stay upright on the uneven ground. When the band launched into a smoochy golden oldie, Simon and I joined them, swaying gently beneath the coloured lights.

A balmy evening, in the arms of an attractive man – it should indeed have been 'Wonderful Tonight'. But for me the fighting had soured it. Simon seemed to sense it, and when the number ended offered to take me home. I nodded, and after a quick word with Phil we left.

Monty had gone home, but had left a note propped on the table, assuring me Dad was fine, no cause for concern. I checked on him anyway, found him sleeping peacefully. I went back intending to offer Simon coffee. Instead he suggested a drive.

'Now?' I asked stupidly.

'Why not? A leisurely moonlight stroll . . . Round off the evening nicely.'

Indeed it would.

I needed to wind down, I told myself. Needed a few quiet moments. Dad was okay. Relax. Enjoy the company.

I glanced at the company from the corner of my eye. He was leaning back in the seat, driving with one hand. Disappointed at the lack of results? Or had that compartment been pushed to one side?

He paused at a junction, took the left-hand turn.

'Know where you're going?' I asked.

'Nope.'

I didn't enlighten him. He was heading on to the moor and that was fine by me. He hit a button on the CD player and an old Bonnie Raitt number filled the car. I recognized it at once: Dougie had had the same album.

But that was in a previous life . . .

We continued to climb, the headlights picking out the unfenced road, the fairy lights of villages strung out behind us. Another couple of miles and Simon pulled on to the verge. A cool breeze met us as we climbed out and Simon pulled a jacket from the back seat, followed by a sweater which he gave me to put on. When he slid his arm around my shoulder, I slipped mine around his waist. We walked in silence, listening to the faint night sounds, strange rustling noises at our feet, the whirr of bats overhead. Not much moon, but the stars made up for it, the Plough, Orion's Belt, the Milky Way . . .

Was it really only twenty-four hours?

Rounding the tor, we disturbed a small herd of ponies. One, paler than the rest, lingered to inspect us, then it too galloped away. Simon turned me to face him, brushed his lips against mine. 'I know it's a cliché,' he murmured, 'but I really have wanted to do this for a long time.'

If the air was cold I wasn't noticing. Simon's body was keeping me warm. The jacket and sweater were on the grass beneath us, plus one or two items besides. First date, I kept reminding myself – take it slow. But we *were* taking it slow, enjoying the moment. Why rush something this good?

I moaned softly as he kissed the shivery spot on my neck, and ran my fingers down his spine. Smooth skin, firm muscles. He raised himself up, took my face in his hands.

Six inches from my ear his mobile rang.

'*Shit!*' he muttered, hesitating a moment before rolling on to his side. He continued caressing my shoulder as he checked the number, held the phone to his ear. 'This better be good, Twigg.'

The hand stilled and he jerked upright. 'When? Jesus . . . Okay, I'm on my way.'

An icy shiver ran down my spine. 'What is it?'

'Gary.' Already he was pulling on his clothes. 'Looks like he annoyed one person too many. And they've made sure he won't do it again.'

Chapter Twenty-Two

It was a farmer who found him, a man by the name of Gordon Ayres, the same man who earlier in the day had allowed us to guess the weight of his pig. He had left the beer tent shortly after midnight and, after talking 'for a fair old time' to friends outside, had stopped off at the pen. The pig had been removed earlier, but Farmer Ayres had left a shovel and pitchfork just inside the doorway and he didn't trust them to still be there in the morning.

The pen was set apart from the other stalls, and the area around it was dark. He reached inside but the tools weren't where he had left them, so he stooped over and went in.

'Knew straight away somethin' were wrong,' he said later. ''T'were the smell. Like somethin' 'ad been butchered.'

He hurried back to his friends but they laughed at him, claimed he was drunk, so he borrowed a torch and returned to the pen alone. What he found when he shone the light inside would stay with him for the rest of his days.

Gary's body was wedged in the far corner, his head anchored to the wooden side. He had been impaled by the pitchfork. One long curving tine had punctured his throat; the other had pierced his eye.

Farmer Ayres had staggered outside and thrown up.

'We were on our way home,' Phil was telling Simon. 'We were just coming out of the car park when we saw the blue lights. Thought oh-oh, *serious* punch-up. Anyway, thought I'd better check, just in case, and when we came back there's Dredge strutting about and they're taping off the pen. Soon as he told me what had gone down I called you.' She glanced at me. 'Sorry if it was inconvenient.'

'Anyone see anything?' Simon asked.

'Nothing – too far from the other events. Short time frame, though. Not two hours since we saw him in the tent.'

Where he was being threatened by his father, I thought, sliding the orange tape between my fingers. But surely no father, however abusive, could do this to his son?

'Course, Edge knows who did it,' Phil added scathingly. 'Some youngster called Kenny Hatch. He's the one who –'

'They've arrested Kenny?' I blurted, spinning around.

'Taken for questioning, why?'

I shook my head, frowning. What the hell was all this going to do to Lorna?

'Witnesses?' Simon asked.

'Only to what happened on the pitch.'

Simon clicked his tongue. 'Where's Edge now?'

'Fuck knows. Want to take a look?'

They flashed their IDs and ducked under the tape. I ducked in after them, expecting to be turned back. The uniform must have assumed I was one of them and let me pass.

'Pathologist here?' I heard Simon say.

'On his way. Ditto the SOCOs.'

They skirted around the pen, me in their wake. Already a floodlight had been set up and what had been a dark interior was now blindingly bright. Simon looked at the scene without comment but I was forced to stifle a cry. What shocked me most was the blood, the sheer quantity of it, every surface spattered. I've never got used to accidents. I certainly wasn't used to this.

The body was lying diagonally, legs strung out towards the doorway. The pitchfork handle was jammed against the inner front wall. It had been used with force, spiking the head at a freakish angle. But it was the face that would haunt me, the one remaining eye frozen wide in terror. From the place where the other had been, blood and Christ knows what else had oozed beneath the prong, covering half the face before merging with that from the neck. Gary's shoulder, arm and chest were drenched in the stuff, as was the straw on the ground where it had pooled. The colour confirmed he hadn't been dead long. It was a brilliant scarlet, the colour of the poppies in the field of corn.

Simon turned, saw me, and promptly placed himself between me and the door. 'Okay, let's move back.'

We retreated to a spot well inside the barrier, away from the mass of people crowding the tape. Their excitement was palpable, the morbid excitement that accompanies violent death. Few had left the Revel since word got out.

Phil scanned the faces, I guessed looking for Susie, then turned back and pulled out a pack of cigarettes. 'Weird choice of weapon,' she muttered. 'Think it's ritual?'

Simon didn't reply.

'I *said* –'

'I heard you, Twigg. Wouldn't have thought so. Most likely the pitchfork happened to be to hand.' He glanced back. 'One thing I'd put money on, we're looking for a man. Few women would have strength or stomach for that.'

'Has anyone told his mother?' I asked.

'WPC's there now.' Phil's eyes narrowed. 'You knew him. Anyone hate him?'

'I knew *of* him,' I corrected. 'From what I hear, quite a few.' I glanced at Simon, guessing we were both thinking the same thing. Blackmail can be a powerful motive.

Phil was scanning the crowd again. 'Wonder what happened to Susie? Hey up, Kojak's arrived.'

Kojak, real name Jack Pilcher, was the pathologist, a man I knew by sight having seen him at incidents. It was easy to see how he had earned his name. He was a big man with a big smile, bald as a coot, with a fondness for expensively tailored suits. Though I'd yet to see him with a lollipop.

He ducked under the tape and strode across. 'Thought this was Edge's case,' he addressed Simon.

'It is. We just happened to be here.'

'Night out, huh? Nice way to end an evening. Okay, show me where it is.'

There was more commotion as Phil led him to the pen. The SOCOs had arrived, and soon they would be dusting, sifting and examining every inch of ground, cameras flashing as they recorded the minutiae of the scene. I didn't envy them the confined space.

'What now?' I asked Simon, as they donned the white suits.

'Move on.' He sounded distracted. 'Not my case.'

We were heading towards the tape when a voice barked his name, and a shortish man with ginger-blond hair and a tight little moustache strutted up. DI Edge.

'And who might I ask called you?' he demanded.

'Been here all day,' Simon replied calmly. 'Thought we'd guard the site in your absence.'

He jerked his chin. 'Who's she?'

'She's with me.'

'That's not . . . Where's Twigg?'

'With Jack.'

'He's here? Bloody hell . . .'

Simon stared after him, shaking his head, then put his hand on my back and guided me towards the tape. Immediately he was pounced on by the press, each reporter fighting to get closer and shout louder than the others. Their questions merged in a blur of noise. 'No comment,' was all Simon said.

The rest of the field was almost deserted, just a few less-inquisitive souls clearing up. A group of women were huddled near the platform.

'Don't you want to hang around?' I asked, as Simon took hold of my hand and set off for the entrance.

'No point. Whoever did it will be long gone. SOCOs will find anything there is to find.'

'*You* don't think it was Kenny?'

'Right now I don't think anything.'

I stopped dead, pulling him up short. 'Hey, this is me, remember? We both know who wanted him out of the way.'

'We also know Gary and the boyfriend were daggers drawn. It's called keeping an open mind, Gus.'

'What about gut feeling?'

He stared back towards the murder scene. 'You mean if I had to bet my house, my car and a year's salary? Then no, I don't think it was Kenny. What's back there was contrived – choice of weapon, position of the wounds. . . No, I think if Kenny had killed Gary it would have been spontaneous, the result of a fight, out in the open. But that's only my opinion. Until Forensics have their say, everything's conjecture.'

We were halfway to the gate when I remembered my accordion, so we turned back and made for the platform. It was hard to imagine that only a short time before Fast and Loose had been entertaining the crowds. Now most of their equipment was gone, packed into the grey van standing alongside. One lone figure remained on the dais, winding something on to a reel.

The huddle of women were still there but as we approached they parted and from out of their midst ran Lorna. To my surprise, she hurled herself into my arms. Maybe it was association, the memory of my helping her before.

'Gary!' she sobbed, her frail body heaving. 'He's dead. Someone . . . somebody . . .'

'I know,' I said softly. 'I'm so sorry, Lorna.'

'They're blaming Kenny,' she wailed. 'But *he* didn't do it. He couldn't. I was with him the whole time.'

I stroked her hair. 'I'm sure the police will let him go when you tell them.'

She looked up, tears streaming down her face. All trace

of Judith's handiwork had vanished. 'I *did* tell them. They don't believe me. They think I'm making it up.' Suddenly she stiffened. 'Where is he? I want to see my brother. Why won't they let me see him?'

'I don't think that's wise,' I said, wishing my father were there to comfort her.

'But I want to! I *must!*' She started across the field, but I caught her arm, looked pleadingly at Simon. He stooped down, brought his face close to hers.

'The place where it happened has been sealed off,' he said gently. 'To preserve evidence. Someone killed your brother, Lorna, and we need to find out who.'

She jerked back. 'We?'

'Simon's a policeman,' I told her. 'A detective. He's also my friend. We were having a day out, just like you.' She continued to watch him warily.

'They'll want to talk to Kenny because of what happened at the tug-of-war,' Simon explained. 'And anyone else Gary argued with. So if there's anything you can tell me . . .'

'What did they do to him? How was he . . . how . . .?'

'He was stabbed, Lorna.' It was all she needed to know at present.

It was more than enough. Her lower lip began to tremble and she let out a wail. Next minute she was on the ground.

A woman came rushing from the group and dropped to her knees beside her. 'There, there – you go on and cry.' She looked up helplessly. 'Ellen Smith, friend of her mum's. I've been keeping an eye on her.'

'She should be at home, Ellen,' Simon said, crouching beside them.

'That's what I've been telling her. Reckoned she couldn't leave *him*.' She nodded across the field. Then holding Lorna at arm's length, 'Think of your poor mum, Lorna. At home all on her own. Don't you think you should be with her?'

Another burst of sobbing.

235

'We'll take her,' I said. 'You'll come with me, won't you, Lorna?'

She surprised me by nodding; I'd expected her to refuse. Perhaps she no longer had the strength to argue. She certainly made no protest when we helped her to her feet. Simon took himself a short distance away to put in a call to Phil, while one of the women fetched my accordion. Then, one on either side, we led Lorna to the car.

'Where've they taken Kenny?' she asked Simon when we were free of the field.

'Exeter, I imagine.'

'He didn't do it!' she spluttered. 'I know he didn't!'

'Then will you help me prove it? By answering a few questions?'

She didn't reply. Simon and I were exchanging hopeless glances when she finally murmured, 'Okay.'

He waited until we were in the car, me in the back with Lorna. 'So tell me about the last part of the evening,' he said softly, swivelling to face us. 'Start with the tug-of-war.'

Lorna stiffened. 'You *saw*. You were there.'

'But I couldn't hear, Lorna. What did Gary say when he ran up?'

She shifted uneasily. 'He told Kenny . . . He said he thought he'd told him to stay away from me. Then he grabbed me and – that's when the police came.'

'What happened afterwards?'

'Don't know.' Her voice was little more than a whisper. 'Me and Kenny disappeared.'

'Disappeared?' I prompted.

'You know – hid. Where that thing was.' She prodded the accordion case with her toe.

'You were under the platform?'

A nod. ''Cept when Kenny had another pull. Dave knew where we was and came to fetch us. Dave's the anchor man,' she added. 'I watched but – not up close, you know? Didn't want Gary to get funny again.' More tears at the mention of his name.

'Did Kenny's team win?' Simon asked, and elicited a nod and a weak smile. 'But this time you didn't run on. Was that because Gary had threatened Kenny?'

She smoothed her hands several times down her thigh. 'Sort of. But he wouldn't have done no harm, not really. He just . . .' She broke off, turned her face to the window. 'Anyway, he didn't show up.'

'So when was the last time you saw Gary?'

'When he . . . when the police ran on. After the first tug. Least . . . I *thought* I saw him later but I'm not sure, it was dark and –'

'Where did you think you saw him?'

'The beer tent. Round the side. I was like, you know, keeping out the way, but soon as I saw them I ducked back. But it was just a glimpse. The other chap was stood in front of him.'

Simon caught my eye. 'Did you recognize the other chap, Lorna?'

She shook her head.

'Can you remember *anything* about him?'

'It was *dark*!'

'Try, Lorna,' I said. 'Was he young, like Gary?'

A shrug.

'Taller, shorter . . .?'

'Taller.' She sniffed loudly, wiped her nose on the back of her hand.

'What about build?' Simon asked. 'Was he a big man? Thin? Can you remember what he was wearing?'

But Lorna's resources were exhausted. As she kept saying, it was dark and nothing more than a glimpse. She wasn't even sure it was her brother.

'Do you think Kenny would remember?' I asked, but again she shook her head.

'Kenny didn't see him, he was inside getting drinks. I said I'd wait outside – well, Kenny told me to, because of the crush. And in case someone saw us. But he was thirsty, you know? Always is after a tug. '

'I remember the feeling well,' Simon smiled. 'So he left you waiting outside . . .'

She nodded. 'He was gone for ages. I thought he was never coming back. Must have been at least half an hour.' She looked from me to Simon, blissfully unaware that she'd just blown Kenny's alibi. 'Can I go home now?'

'Of course.' He half turned back. 'You don't happen to know what time it was? When you were waiting?'

Another head shake. 'Last pull was supposed to be eleven, but I think they were running late. I'm not wearing my watch.' She offered her wrist for inspection. 'I know soon as it was over we went straight to the tent – well, after Kenny'd changed his shirt.' She frowned. 'Afterwards he wished he hadn't. When he came back there was blood all down the front. There'd been this fight in the tent, some bloke dripping everywhere. T'was new, too. He only bought it last week.'

Simon caught my eye, then pivoted back, started the engine. 'Let's get you home,' he said quietly.

There were two cars in the farmyard, a police car and Judith's BMW. Earlier in the evening, Lorna informed us, Judith had given her mother a lift home. Presumably she had still been there when news arrived of Gary's death.

Lorna climbed slowly from the car. 'I wonder if Dad's back?' she murmured.

It was something I'd been wondering myself. But when we entered the kitchen there were just the three women – June, Judith and a WPC. Simon quickly introduced himself.

'Perhaps now you'll take my aunt's death seriously,' Judith replied archly.

The room where we were standing was bleak, the walls painted in a harsh yellow gloss. A row of cheap modern units lined one wall. The rest of the fittings appeared to date from the sixties, including the enamel sink unit under the window. The policewoman was sitting at a large table covered in oilcloth, on one of a set of chairs with red PVC seats. The pattern on the oilcloth was almost scrubbed away.

But these were details I noticed later. At the time, all I could see was June. She had pulled an overall over her frock and was violently scouring the Rayburn. She seemed driven by a wild, frenzied energy.

Lorna ran up to her and grabbed her arm. 'Leave it, Mum. That'll wait.'

'Oh, you think so, do you!' June snapped, shrugging her off. 'Work don't stop just 'cause of this.'

'She's been like that since PC Morris arrived,' Judith whispered. 'I suppose it's her way of coping.'

But it was hard on Lorna. Tears were streaming down the girl's face as she pleaded with her mother to sit down.

'Is a doctor coming?' Simon asked.

'I thought you were him. Any sign of Tom?'

'Isn't he here?'

She gave a snort. 'He's probably passed out drunk in a ditch somewhere.' She cocked her head at the sound of a car. 'That's probably the doctor now.'

She went to let him in, and while Simon drew the WPC to one side, I went over to Lorna. She was still pleading with her mother, who had started on the twin copper water pipes behind the Rayburn, attempting to buff them to an even greater shine.

'Why not leave your mum for now,' I said. 'Let her work. It's her way of dealing with the shock.'

Tearfully Lorna agreed and allowed me to lead her to a chair. I waited beside her until the doctor came in, then left them and joined Simon in the hall. He was using his mobile, held up a finger. 'Say that again, Twigg. Reception's crap.'

While waiting, I looked around. Boots were lined up along one wall, beneath a row of hooks holding padded hunting jackets, a couple of macs belonging to Lorna and June. High up four shotguns rested on brackets, and a mounted pair of antlers hung above the front door. No doubt as to where Tom's interests lay.

'Well, the police don't have Weblake,' Simon said, returning the phone to his pocket. 'No one's seen him. But they're sending someone else in case he turns up. Male,' he added pointedly. 'I've sent PC Morris outside to wait for him.'

'So what happens now?'

'Stay for a while. I want to have a word with Judith.' He wandered to the bottom of the stairs, flicked a light switch, looked up at the next floor and flicked it off again. 'Wonder where the bugger is.'

He was walking back when the door opened and the sad little party emerged, the doctor leading June by the arm. Judith followed with Lorna. 'Work don't just stop, you know,' June was muttering. 'Dirt don't just disappear.' The doctor was telling her it would wait until morning.

'I'll be down in a moment,' Judith whispered as she passed. 'I shall stay here tonight. I don't think they should be left alone.'

We returned to the kitchen, where I pulled out a chair, slumped down. 'So the number grows,' I murmured. 'Miss Hillas, Trevor – now Gary.'

Simon was staring at a calendar from a local seed merchant, the only non-utilitarian item on the walls. 'And three totally different MOs.'

'You don't think they were killed by the same person?'

'I didn't say that. It could be deliberate, to avoid any obvious connection. On the other hand –'

He broke off as the door opened.

'I've left them to it,' Judith said, making a beeline for the units. 'God, what a night!' Several doors opened before she found what she was looking for, a bottle of Johnnie Walker and three tumblers decorated with a gold key design. She put them on the table. 'Not my tipple, but it'll have to do. I think we deserve it.'

'How are they?' I asked.

'Sedated. Numbed from the pain till morning. At least there'll be someone here when they wake up.'

'What about Stuart?'

'Oh, you saw him. Yes, he turned up out of the blue. I imagine he's at the house, he has to leave early for London.' She sank into the chair opposite. 'Joe was driving him home. Joe de Zaire, the sculptor,' she qualified for Simon's benefit. 'We're staging his exhibition. That's what they were discussing and I could see it dragging on, so I'm afraid I left them to it.' She took a drink. 'I was on the way to the car when I met June, clearly upset. That's why I offered her a lift. Thank God I was still here when the police arrived.'

I said, 'So Stuart doesn't know where you are?'

'I dashed up quickly and left a note.' She turned to Simon. 'So – another murder. My aunt, now Gary. All roads lead to the Institute, wouldn't you say?'

'Do you know what June was upset about?' He ignored her question.

She hesitated. 'Oh, I suppose you'll hear sooner or later. It was Tom and Gary. Apparently they'd been at each other's throats all day. Eventually June could stand it no longer and tried to intervene, and got a mouthful of abuse for her trouble. When I found her she was in tears.'

'They nearly came to blows in the beer tent,' I said. 'We saw Tom threatening Gary.'

'I'm sure a lot of people did.'

'Were they arguing about anything specific?' Simon asked.

'Tom was accusing Gary of "shooting his mouth off" – presumably about the dog. You do know about the pit bull?' He inclined his head. 'Apparently the RSPCA turned up yesterday and took it away. They're taking Tom to court.'

I gaped. 'Tom didn't think *Gary* reported him?'

'Heavens, no – they assumed that was Lorna's boy-friend. But it was Gary who kept leaving the barn unlocked, which is how Kenny happened to see it. The

241

final straw came when Gary confronted Kenny at the tug-of-war and openly accused him – actually mentioned the words dog fighting. The whole team heard, and when it got back to Tom he hit the roof. Accused him of "letting the whole bleeding world know", or words to that effect.'

I leaned back in the chair. 'So I do the dirty and Kenny gets the blame. Great!'

'It's not your fault,' Judith replied. 'You did what any caring person would have done. No, I'm afraid it's this wretched family.' She looked towards the door. 'Queen of the Revel. What an ending.'

She turned to Simon, 'That's assuming it is the end. It might only be the beginning. I wonder how many more deaths there will be before you find out why?'

Chapter Twenty-Three

We left soon afterwards and headed for my father's, taking the long route around the village to avoid the field. We both sensed that whatever we had started earlier would not be continued that night, yet when he reached the farm gateway Simon stopped, leaned across and took my face in his hands. He kissed me long and hard, only easing back when headlamps swept the windscreen. The second police car had arrived.

He accepted my offer of a nightcap provided I wasn't too tired. In truth I was exhausted, but I knew I wouldn't sleep. I left him in the kitchen while I checked on Dad, and on the way back collected a bottle of whisky from the sitting room. Simon was slumped in a chair, elbows on the table, chin resting in his hands. What he needed was a good night's sleep, preferably with me – or was that a contradiction in terms?

'I wonder what the three musketeers were doing after we left them,' I heard him murmur as I fetched glasses.

'According to Judith, Stuart was with Joe. She didn't mention Alden. *He's* taller than Gary. I bet that's who Lorna saw.'

'Maybe.'

'Oh, come on – it *has* to be him. He's the one with the motive. We know he killed Miss Hillas, probably over the dog fighting, and we know Gary was blackmailing him. He would have had to kill Gary to shut him up.'

'We've no proof Alden even *knew* about the dog fighting.'

'But we know where his tastes lie!' His resistance to the

obvious was beginning to annoy me. I filled the tumblers, pushed one across.

'You think that a powerful enough motive to kill an old lady?'

'Yes, if she threatened to expose him. It would threaten his whole livelihood. Who would visit the Institute if that kind of thing came to light?'

'You still think that's his livelihood?' He washed his hand over his face. 'Oh, I don't doubt Gary was killed to shut him up. The guy was a loose cannon, too much of a risk. I'm just not convinced that's the reason. Where does that leave Trev?'

I shrugged. 'You were the one who mentioned different MOs. Isn't it possible they're not related?'

'Possible.' But not likely, judging by his tone. I could tell he was clinging to the Rayjay idea.

I sat back in the chair. 'Okay, Detective, what do *you* think ties them together?'

He smiled, raised his glass. 'Here's to Saturday nights.'

'Simon . . .'

'Okay, if you want my opinion. Drugs.'

My mouth opened and closed.

'It's been thought for some time that a large chunk of the heroin and coke reaching major cities is coming via the south-west. But we haven't been able to get a handle on it, not its source, nor how it's getting through. Not one runner's been caught, meaning it's a clever operation. Then out of the blue comes a phone call from Trev. Rayjay's back. And Trev winds up dead. Suddenly everything clicked. Stuff lands and promptly vanishes. It's a carbon copy of the time he disappeared.' He pushed back his chair. 'Mind if I use the bathroom?'

Absently I told him where it was, urging him not to wake Dad. Already my mind was racing. About de Zaire and a small japanned box. Recreational coke, he'd told me, which it probably was – he'd hardly be so blatant if he were smuggling the stuff. Even so, it would be interesting to know his supplier.

Thinking about Joe made my heart race, just as it had earlier when he'd appeared at the tent. Meeting Alden and Stuart Kempe, all so buddy-buddy. Stuart giving him exhibitions, Joe giving Stuart a lift home . . .

'I wonder why Judith's husband was here?' I mused when Simon returned.

'Yeah,' he settled back in the chair, 'that's been on my mind, too. How often does he visit her?'

'Not often, I don't think – only if he's passing through. The time I met him he was on his way to Cornwall.'

'What about last month, the time of the fire?'

'I've no idea, why?' But as soon as I said it I could see where he was heading. Wilfie put Stuart here around the time Miss Hillas died. He was here today and Gary died. If he was here when Trev was killed . . .

Hair rose on the back of my neck. 'He's Judith's husband!' I blurted.

'Desperate people do desperate things, Gus. As I said before, Rayjay pays others.'

I grabbed my glass, downed half the contents in one. God knows I hadn't liked the guy – but a hit man?

'Of course, I could be way off line,' Simon conceded. 'My money's still on Chadwicke. I'm damned sure that Institute is a sham.'

'A sham?' I echoed.

But of course it could be. It was the perfect cover. An ever-changing clientele, for the most part genuine students, some highly respected lecturers. Filter in an occasional impostor, someone like myself with just enough nous to get by . . .

Or not. How did I know Mr Silent was a GP?

I tuned back in, realized Simon was following the same lines. '. . . quasi-religious courses. Who's going to question people like that? They come for a few days, inspect the merchandise, load up and scatter like the four winds. They could come back time and again, who's going to know?'

'Jenny,' I said quietly, 'one of the women. She'd been several times. And Fraser had been at least once before.'

245

'There you are. And neither would find it odd that the other was there because they'd returned themselves.'

I shook my head, realizing he was right. Hell, he was probably right about everything. Judith's one reservation with the dog-fighting theory was her aunt's use of the word evil, but I had little doubt she would have used it to describe drug trafficking. How she could have learned about it I couldn't imagine, unless she too had overheard a conversation. Not at the Institute – maybe at the farm? Or out on the moor, the speakers unaware of the distance sound travels . . .

Suddenly I remembered the photographs. 'There's something I want to show you,' I said, and fetched them from upstairs.

Spreading them out, I explained what Judith had told me, pointing out the grid references and dates. Simon stood beside me and together we pored over them, and I felt his fingers run up and down my arm. Briefly I closed my eyes. If Dad wasn't down the hall . . .

'Anything I'm not seeing?' I asked, hoping my voice didn't give me away.

'If there is, I'm as blind as you.' He picked one up. 'Is that people?'

'And in a couple of others. Think they're important?'

He shrugged, then brought it closer and squinted. 'Any idea where they were taken?'

'They're all within a couple of square miles of each other. I plotted them on a map. And all within walking distance of the Institute. I thought at first they might be sites where dog fights had taken place, but the RSPCA chap thought that unlikely. Now . . .' I paused. 'You don't think they could be meet-up points? Presumably at some point the drugs change hands.'

'Possibly, but . . . No, I can't see that. Why travel so far? There are enough lay-bys and pull-ins on the moor to meet without drawing attention. In fact, I'd say it's highly *un*likely. Too exposed. Someone planning a clandestine meeting is going to want cover, not somewhere they can be seen for miles around.'

'So why did Miss Hillas take them?'

Another shrug. He tapped the print against his hand. 'Mind if I take them with me? See what the experts have to say.'

I told him Judith would be delighted.

He straightened up as I collected them, rotated his shoulders and neck. His face split in a yawn.

'You should be in bed,' I said.

'Correction, *we* should be in bed.' He kissed me lightly on the lips. 'But not tonight.' Suddenly he became serious. 'Promise me you'll stay out of trouble?'

'I promise.'

'Why am I not convinced?' he murmured, running his finger down my cheek.

It was as if Gary's death had in some way angered the rain gods. I awoke next morning to sunless skies, rain lashing my window. The temperature had dropped by several degrees. Not surprisingly I had overslept and I found Dad already in the kitchen, hunched over a cup of peppermint tea. He looked up at me through rheumy eyes.

'What a state!' he muttered, his voice adenoidal. 'No wonder I felt awful. Monty insisted on calling the doctor, for whatever good that'll do. He's supposed to be coming this morning.'

I bit my lip. It was probably no more than a summer cold, to most people a minor irritation. But not if your immune system has broken down.

'Why don't you go back to bed,' I said. 'Have you had your medicines? Is there anything I can get you?'

'No, yes, no and stop fussing!' Angry. 'I'm not *totally* incapable. And I'm not going to die of boredom stuck in there!'

I backed off. It wasn't the first time I'd seen him like this. His anger was born of frustration and fear, in roughly

247

equal quantities. The best thing, I knew, was to leave him alone, try to act normally.

I went to the counter, started to make myself breakfast.

'So how was the Revel?' he asked, as I dropped bread into the toaster.

I hesitated. 'Okay.'

'Okay. I see.' His tone made me glance round. 'A guy gets murdered and you tell me it's okay? It was on the *radio*, Gus! They're full of it! Did you think you could keep it *quiet*?'

I sighed. Clearly it was a day to tread carefully.

I filled him in over breakfast, not bothering to keep anything back. The grisly details would have spread through the village like wildfire. Dad white-knuckled the mug as he listened, and I knew exactly what he was thinking. Who's going to be next?

'So what does Simon think?' he asked brusquely.

'It's not his case.'

'Doesn't stop him thinking, does it?'

I shrugged. Wrong response. Dad banged his mug on the table. 'Don't play ignorant with me, girl! We both know where Gary worked. How do I –' He broke off to sneeze, burying his face in a handkerchief. 'God damn it!' He wiped his nose. 'What I want to know is, are you in danger? Because if anything should happen to you –'

'Nothing's going to happen to me!' I snapped back. 'And now who's fussing?'

'Well, pardon me for not wanting my daughter to end up the same way!' He reached for the box of tissues. 'You should never have gone there, never got involved. Didn't I tell you not to go back?'

'Spilt milk, Dad.'

'And now there's spilt blood!' He blew his nose loudly. 'Well, thank God you've got Simon to keep an eye on you. Christ knows I'm no bloody use!'

Which was precisely what all this was about. I sipped my coffee, waited for him to calm down. For both of us to calm down.

'I'm sorry,' Dad said at last. 'But I keep thinking of the lad's mother. How do you live with something like that?' He shook his head. 'Think Simon will be brought in?'

'I imagine so.'

'Good. He seems to have his head screwed on. Nice chap, I like him.' He sipped his tea. 'Know if he's married?'

'You asked me that before, Dad.'

'And you didn't answer.'

And I still couldn't.

Dad insisted I continue with my artwork. Fat chance. I busied myself around the house, getting under his feet, like June taking refuge in housework. The doctor arrived at midday and they retired to Dad's room. While they were there Simon arrived. I hadn't expected to see him so soon, had wondered how I would feel when I did. The warm flush of pleasure took me by surprise.

'How's your father?' Simon asked as I tried to calm Hewitt.

'The doctor's with him now. Probably just a cold but . . .'

'Cause for concern?' Something about the way he said it made me look up. 'He told me about the HIV, Gus. Must be hard.'

'He copes. Remarkably well, as a matter of fact.'

'I meant for you.'

The closing of a door cut off my reply. The doctor was leaving. I excused myself and went to show him out. When I returned, Simon was making tea. 'Hope you don't mind, but I haven't got long. What did the doctor say?'

'Told me to keep an eye on him. Like I'm going to do anything else!' I snatched milk from the fridge.

'Is it serious?'

'Watch this space.'

Too snappy. I counted to ten. 'Sorry, but the truth is I don't know. It's a disease without rules, every case different. Dad's still not developed full-blown AIDS, but

249

anything that weakens his immunity further . . .' I spread my hands.

Simon was frowning. 'Forgive my ignorance but . . .'

'How long before that happens? Who knows?' I leaned back against the worktop. 'Compared to some – many – Dad's been fortunate, if I dare use such a term. I mean he's been like this a long time. But you have to remember his immune system is already damaged, so an infection means it's having to work harder. In time it will become exhausted.'

'So a simple thing like a cold could, what – push him further?'

'Not necessarily. It's not that simple. Hell, nothing about this blasted bug is simple! People can show symptoms and recover, while others . . . As I said, every case is different. The only sure thing is that it's there, multiplying away, slowly destroying his defences.'

I saw Simon's eyes drop to my hands. I was threatening to crush the mug. 'Sorry.' It seemed to be the word of the day. 'You're in a hurry. Now's not the time.'

'Doesn't mean I'm not interested.'

'I know.' I crossed to the table, lowered myself into a chair. 'I take it you're here because of last night?'

He nodded. 'I've just come from the Institute. Been interviewing the Chadwickes. We're talking to everyone Gary worked for, including Stuart Kempe.'

'Stuart never employed Gary.'

'Aunt-in-law did, that's reason enough.' He followed and sat opposite. 'Alden was politeness itself. Shocked beyond belief. Anything he can do to help, etcetera, etcetera.'

'Loved Gary like a son?'

'On the contrary. Considered him a rough diamond, not entirely trustworthy. Claimed certain things had "disappeared". No proof, but they were keeping an eye on him.'

'Clever,' I said, offering a tin of biscuits.

'Extremely.' He pulled out a bourbon, dunked it in his tea. 'The caring employer wary of a light-fingered employee. Speech was planned of course: they would have known we'd be coming. Wifey hardly said a word throughout, just drifted in like some new-age hippy in a trance.' He helped himself to another. 'I wouldn't mind betting she's a user.'

'*Zara?*'

He laughed. 'Probably not. All part of the act. Still, at least now I've seen the place.' His hand went out again.

'Would you like me to make you a sandwich?'

'No time.'

'You can eat it while you're talking.' I got up, went to the fridge. 'So how come you got to interview him and not Edge?'

'Edge, God bless him, is concentrating on farmers. Victim was killed with a pitchfork; farmers use pitchforks; ergo, victim was killed by a farmer. But you'll be pleased to know they've released Kenny. Nothing to hold him on.'

'But the blood . . .'

'They've traced the guy it belonged to. A fight, just like he said.' He gulped some tea. 'I saw Kempe too, caught him just as he was leaving. God, that is one arrogant prick! Yet interestingly, he checks out. Stuart Milton Kempe, originally from Surrey. Croydon, to be exact.'

I smiled. 'I wonder how he wound up in America?'

'Easy. Went after he lost the family business. That was failure number one – unless you count dropping out of university and some disastrous dabbling on the stock market.'

'You *have* done your homework.'

'Not difficult if someone's legit. It's the others that pose problems.'

I jammed a second slice on a mountain of cheese and tomato and carried it across, told him to excuse the doorstep. He kissed his fingers, told me I was a star. It was the first thing he'd eaten since the pub.

'So what was the family business?' I asked, sitting back down. 'Don't tell me, a gallery.'

'Not even warm.' He held up his hand while he

munched. 'A small manufacturing plant, electrical components. Kempe inherited it when his father died. By that time he was dabbling in artworks but he dropped all that to run his inheritance – or rather run it down. Messed up monumentally – five years and it was down the tubes. So off he goes to America where he runs a gallery called, wait for it – Travi Arta.' We both grinned. 'Four years later, when that bombs, he heads north and opens one of his own, the SKA Gallery in Santa Monica. When –'

'Hang on – headed north?'

'Travi Arta was in LA.'

I sat back.

'Anyway, when – no big surprise – SKA goes the same way, Stuart comes running back here. And opens another, in a pretty high-class area. Which begs the question, where did he get the money?' He took another bite. 'Know if your friend was independently wealthy?'

'You think Judith put up the money?'

'Somebody did.'

The sleeping partner . . .

'It would explain why Stuart's in such a funk,' I said. 'Imagine persuading your partner to part with that much cash, then making some God-awful cock-up that threatens to lose it. '

'Yeah, I don't imagine he sleeps too easily.' He checked his watch. 'I must go.'

'What about the others, Chadwicke and –'

'Not yet.' He stuffed the remains of the sandwich in his mouth and stood up. 'By the way, they found Tom Weblake. Your friend was right, drunk as a skunk halfway across a field. He's Edge's latest suspect.'

'You're kidding!'

'Would I joke? Several witnesses heard him tell Gary to shut his mouth or he'd shut it for him. For good.'

'Which he's probably said a hundred times.'

'Right. Except this time someone did.'

*   *   *

252

Following Simon's departure, my mood took a fall. I'd been low before; now I was blue as yesterday's skies. Before leaving, along with further warnings to take care, he'd said he might not see me for a few days. 'Work?' I'd asked, but he'd brushed the question aside. Which left me wondering. In the short time we'd had together I'd learned little about him, only that he was thirty-nine and had had a French grandfather. Why was he so reluctant to talk about himself? I didn't even know where he lived, or if he lived alone. Was there a wife, a live-in lover? Children?

Somehow I didn't think so, yet my heart gave a little flutter, proving that I cared. *Nice work, Tavender.* The first man since Dougie to arouse more than a passing interest and I had chosen a walking enigma.

Dad wasn't hungry so I ate lunch alone. Soup: it was that sort of day. Afterwards, loading the dishwasher, I dropped the cafetière, sending slivers of glass in all directions. Swearing under my breath I swept them into a heap, extracted the larger bits with my fingers, and dropped them into an empty dog-food tin. Inevitably I cut myself. As I said, it was that sort of day.

Holding my finger under the tap, I groped in the drawer for plasters. More déjà vu. This was how I'd found Dad after my first visit to Judith, after some thoughtless ignoramus had dumped glass in a letterbox hole. I could imagine how carefully Dad would have cleared up, every last piece, concerned for those who might follow.

Without warning, my eyes began to swim. I punched the sink top. 'Bloody illness!'

I told myself to get a grip but the tears kept coming. It was all getting too much. It wasn't just Dad I was worrying about – it was myself, Judith, Lorna and June, the whole damn convoluted circus. Ever since that first fateful meeting, events had been building up, but only now had I realized the full extent of the danger. When Judith had first expressed her fears I'd been sceptical. Later I'd come to accept them. But in my heart I'd been thinking manslaughter rather than murder, her aunt's death the result of a tussle, an argument that went wrong. Most likely over local issues: dog fighting, inheritance, the issue of a loan. Even Simon's suggestion of a tie-in with Danner Road, with its tenuous links, its hazy reasoning, hadn't fully hammered the danger home.

The discovery of Gary's mutilated body had. That, and the subsequent conversation with Simon. They had forced me to confront a far greater nightmare, the world of major crime. It was a world of which I knew nothing, where stakes are high, the rewards colossal, and with unspeakable penalties for getting in the way. Which I, in my ignorance, had done my damnedest to do. The note and the rock-fall had been warnings, which for the most part I'd ignored. Because I hadn't known what I was up against. Now I did.

Outside, Dad's garden was taking a battering. During the morning the rain had eased but once again it was coming down in sheets, like someone was emptying a bath sideways. Shrubs were beaten low, stems snapped, once-beautiful flowers lying prostrate on the ground. If ever there was a day for curling in front of the fire . . .

But first I needed to shake this mood. I finished what I was doing, scribbled a note for Dad and grabbed my keys.

Despite the weather the village was heaving. The curious had come to gawk. I edged between cars, wondering why there were so many until I remembered it was Sunday. A chance to savour horror on the day of rest. I paused at the turning to Judith's, wondering how Lorna and June were coping, until an impatient toot from behind forced me to move on. Minutes later I was on the road to the moor, the same road I had driven with Simon. The memory prompted a pleasant shiver – until I remembered how it had ended. And suddenly I was back at the pen, staring at the spill of red, the one terrified eye . . .

To hell with the rain, I needed to walk!

Up on the high moor, wind buffeted the car. I found a lay-by and pulled off the road, zipped up my jacket. The wind caught me as soon as I climbed out and threw me against the wing. It was all I could do to stay upright. I turned my back and let the gale blow me along, head down, running rather than walking when the gusts became too strong. It was wonderful, exhilarating, just what I needed to blow the blues away.

I walked for maybe half an hour, found myself in a flat featureless wilderness not unlike that in the photographs. Everything was grey – grey, grey and more grey, as far as the eye could see. Apart from one tiny spot of yellow. Another walker. It seemed I wasn't the only one prepared to brave wind and rain.

A blue jacket popped up beside it, then both dipped from sight. It didn't take an Einstein to know what they were doing. Even in this, I thought, smiling. Did nothing deter the inveterate letterboxer?

They must already have found what they were looking for because a moment later they moved off. I fixed the point in my mind and headed towards it. Still I had trouble finding the box. They had disguised it well, jamming sprigs of gorse in front of the stones, and had I not been searching I would have passed it by. The letterboxers themselves were a far easier target. Their jackets shone out like beacons, making them visible for miles around. I knew what Simon meant about the sites being too exposed.

I pressed on, for some reason keeping them in view. Then paused. Suppose the fact that you could be seen was the whole point?

But why would someone *want* to be seen?

I glanced to my left, at the raised ground lying to the west. A watcher on those slopes could take in the whole vista. He would know the minute someone arrived – someone he was waiting for?

I felt a shiver of excitement. It was turning the whole thing on its head. Anyone watching would also know when no one else was around. No other walkers to see what they were doing?

But as Simon said, why come this far? They could meet

at any of a hundred pull-ins to hand over the stuff, without ever setting foot on the moor. Unless . . .

I spun round, wind whistling in my ears, and stared back at the letterbox. Suppose it *wasn't* being handed to a person? Suppose it was simply being left?

My heart had begun to pound. *Not one runner caught . . . no idea how it's getting through . . .*

No – it was too far-fetched!

He'd also said it was a clever operation . . .

Next minute I was pulling out my mobile. It worked perfectly – another advantage of an open site. Simon's recorded voice was barely audible above the noise of the wind, but I managed to catch the beep.

'It's Gus,' I told him breathlessly. 'Those photographs. I've an idea what they might be.'

Chapter Twenty-Four

'Letterboxes,' Simon said, managing in just one word to convey impatience, incredulity, and more than a smattering of Tavender's-lost-the-plot.

'Dartmoor letterboxes,' I said. 'They're –'

'I know what they are.'

I stared down at my cup. I didn't blame him for being sceptical. The idea that had seemed so plausible out on the moor had, as the hours passed, left me less and less certain. Now, sitting across from him in the coffee shop, I wished I had kept it to myself.

Muzak was playing in the background, a bland, barely recognizable version of a Beatles' song. 'Let It Be'. If only I could.

I fiddled with the spoon. 'Look, I know it sounds crazy but – yesterday I was out walking, ended in a spot not unlike that in the photos. Despite the weather, I wasn't alone. Off in the distance were two letterboxers. They stood out a mile, just as I'm sure I did to them – just as the three of us would to anyone watching. Which got me thinking. Suppose the very openness could work to your advantage? And I realized it could – *if* you wanted to make sure no one else was around, that you had the place to yourself. I remembered what you'd said about drugs, put two and two together and thought – well – suppose they're using them for the drop?

'It's not as stupid as it sounds,' I added, knowing full well that it did. 'Those people in the photos . . .'

'Walkers.'

'Exactly. Nerds in anoraks to most people, who you wouldn't suspect in a million years. There are hundreds of them out there, humping rucksacks, burrowing around in holes. Well, what if some of them are leaving more behind than a stamp?'

'Like a few kilos of cocaine.' Six words this time but the message was the same.

I shifted in my chair. 'You're right. Stupid idea.'

He didn't contradict me.

I sipped my coffee, avoiding his eyes, staring instead at the salmon pink walls, the stainless steel fitments, the mostly empty tables. The coffee shop changed ownership as often as most shops change their window displays, and I wasn't surprised this latest incarnation had limited appeal. The last time I'd been here it had been cosy wood and plum-coloured walls.

'Let me get this straight,' Simon said. 'You're claiming that runners, disguised as walkers, hike Christ knows how many miles across hazardous terrain to dump X kilos of coke under a pile of rocks for the next letterboxer to find, is that right?'

'No, for *Alden* to find – or whoever he happens to send. But you're right in that it's ridiculous. I'm sorry I wasted your time.'

He grinned. 'Don't throw your frock over your head, Gus, I haven't got all day. So how are you saying the hook-up works?'

'Does it matter?'

He raised his brows.

'Okay, for what it's worth . . . Someone, possibly Alden, is watching through binoculars, perhaps from a nearby tor. The runners – maybe he gives them a signal, I don't know. Anyway, they wait till the coast is clear then leave the stuff in a prearranged spot. When they move off, the watcher moves in, loads up and carries it back to the Institute.'

'Wouldn't it be easier to bring it by car?'

'Not if you want the final destination to remain secret. This way there would be no connection, to person, vehicle or place. Even if the runners were caught, what could they tell you? They wouldn't know where the stuff had gone, *or* who to. Besides, cars can be pulled in for routine checks, speeding, they can be in accidents. This way the stuff spends virtually no time on the road.' I paused. 'Didn't you say you'd never caught a runner?'

'Ye-es.'

'Well, perhaps you've been looking in the wrong place. And another thing,' I added. 'Letterboxes. It would take a local man to know about them. A clever man, an original thinker . . .'

'Yeah, yeah, I get your drift. But – hell, it's too crazy. If I went to the Chief with that, he'd have me certified.'

Yet I could tell he was considering it. His brow was furrowed and he'd caught his lower lip between his teeth, a habit I'd noticed when he was deep in thought. But a moment later he was shaking his head.

'It's too far, Gus. The stuff comes in – let's say on the south coast – and gets stashed, probably somewhere close by. That much I'll go along with. Sent out in small quantities? Perhaps: I can see the advantages. But on foot all that way? No chance.'

He had a point. 'What if it's just the final stage?' I suggested. 'Drive so far, walk the rest. No car to be followed, no direct link with the Institute.'

He thought for a moment, still chewing his lip. 'Makes more sense,' he murmured.

My eyes widened. 'You're not laughing me out of the shop?'

'I probably ought to. But with Rayjay I rule out nothing.' He scratched the corner of his eye. 'Stupid as it sounds, in a way it's got his mark. Bastard always went for the bizarre.'

I sat back, shocked he was even considering it.

'Look, leave it with me, okay? I need to toss it around.' He checked his watch, drained the last of his coffee.

'I've just thought of something else,' I said. 'The dates on the photos –'

'Don't worry, I'm ahead of you.' He slid along the seat. 'Incidentally, I got a couple blown up. Two mauve jackets. Different photos, different days.'

'Same person?'

He rolled his hand.

'But you don't believe in coincidence.'

'Do you?' He kissed his finger and touched it to my mouth.

I left soon afterwards, emerging on to a street jammed with shoppers. Shoppers and glum-looking holidaymakers, searching for something to do on a rainy day. The end-of-season sales were on and I treated myself to a couple of T-shirts, bought a replacement jug for the cafetière, then stocked up on art materials at the shop in Cathedral Green. It was embarrassing how few I needed, a stark reminder of how little I'd done.

I arrived at my flat to unaccustomed silence, then remembered it was signing-on day next door. I collected my mail and checked my phone for messages. Nothing that wouldn't wait – nor was there anything from the estate agent. With no good reason to hang around, I locked up and headed back to Dad's.

I arrived to find Wilfie at work in the garden. The ground too wet for digging, he was busy clipping a hedge.

'Says he doesn't mind the rain,' Dad said, as we watched him through the window. 'If he didn't work all weathers, he'd never get things done.' He chuckled. 'Talk about a sight for sore eyes. Looks like a refugee from a labour camp.'

He wasn't far wrong. Wilfie's black wellingtons were barely visible under a black oilskin reaching almost to the ground, and an old sack was draped around his shoulders to protect his back. A bin-liner covered his head, knotted under his chin like a scarf.

'Vivienne Westwood eat your heart out,' I grinned. 'So how are you feeling?'

'Damn sight better than yesterday. I think it was just tiredness. Always used to sneeze when I was tired, and I don't suppose anything's changed.'

Personally I thought anxiety was the culprit but I wasn't about to argue. Let him believe what he believed.

'So how was Exeter?'

'Wet.' I unpacked the glass jug and fitted it in the holder.

'Get your art materials?'

'I did.'

'Going to use them?'

It was a fair question. It was now the second week of my holiday and so far I didn't have much to show. I took the stuff upstairs, stared at the unfinished canvas, knew full well I wasn't in the mood. Perhaps that's what marks the professional, I thought wryly, someone who's able to switch tasks at the click of a finger, to ignore outside influences and demands. If so, I was failing on both counts.

It was then I remembered Magalie Vosper, her inspired use of music, and next minute I was rummaging through my CDs. I found some Vaughan Williams and sat myself down, and as the lark ascended began to draw. Marks. Lines. Angry stabs. Christ, I was tense. But slowly the music worked its magic and I began to relax, the jabs mellowed into gentle curves. Before the final notes had died I'd laid down the charcoal and moved to the easel.

I achieved more in the next twenty-four hours than in all the previous week, and by Tuesday afternoon the painting was – well, not finished exactly but well on its way. Not only that, I was excited by the result. It was darker than my usual work, more dramatic. My sombre mood showing through?

The price for my labours was a headache. Too much concentration; too long in one room. I decided to drive up and see Judith. I'd not seen her since leaving the farm, had heard nothing about Lorna and June. Nor, come to that, had I heard from Simon. Was he taking the letterbox idea seriously? Somehow I doubted it. The more I thought about it, the more far-fetched it seemed. Dumping quantities of coke in a hole in the ground? Come on!

Water was streaming through the dip in the track but it didn't look too deep. I eased through, tested my brakes, and with a few slips and slides made it to the house. Judith wasn't there. I wandered around, peered into the conservatory, waved to Geoffrey when he called hello. A magazine lay open on the table beside an empty glass, and one of the cats was asleep on a chair. No sign of her car, which meant she'd probably gone shopping. I wondered if she would call at Dad's on her way home.

She did.

'About five minutes ago,' Dad told me. 'Wouldn't wait. She was off to see that sculptor chap.'

'*De Zaire?*'

Dad looked at me strangely. 'Any reason why she shouldn't?'

I gave a shrug. 'She say why she was going?'

'Not really. Something to do with something her husband had said, I think. To be honest, she seemed a bit distracted.'

'Perhaps there are problems with his exhibition.'

'Perhaps – though it's more likely this whole Gary thing.' He frowned. 'I wish to God she wasn't up there alone.'

After dinner Monty came around and we spent the evening playing Scrabble. French Scrabble, another sale acquisition, from the same lot as the Tintins. We were all as rusty as each other and short words like *le* and *un* predominated, though Dad did manage to impress us with *caillou*, a stone – until he confessed he'd looked it up in the dictionary earlier in the day, having come across it in one of the books.

Wednesday passed in much the same way, with me in my studio until late afternoon. Then for the second time I drove to Verstone. It had been raining all day and the ford was much deeper than when I'd last seen it. Much more of this and the track would be impassable.

Judith's car still wasn't there but the glass and magazine were, exactly as I'd seen them the day before. The cat too, only now it was watching me from the window sill, opening and closing its mouth in silent miaows.

'Where is she, Geoffrey?' I asked as the parrot turned somersaults on the bars of his cage.

Ignoring the downpour, I circled the house and tried the back door. No reply. Nor was there to my knock on the window. I stood back, wondering if I should be concerned. Magazines have been known to lie open at my flat for weeks on end, I told myself. So why was I feeling uneasy?

I knew why – because of who she had been going to see. Not that the circumstances were in any way similar. De Zaire would hardly try the same trick with the wife of his friend.

Even so, the unease persisted. Maybe I would come back later, just to make sure.

I returned to yet another empty house. There was a note propped against the kettle. *Gone to my club (forgot it was today). Bore them about my latest hiccup! Back about nine. Think I'll get extra Brownie points for braving the elements?*

I smiled. Dad's club. No leather armchairs and ironed newspapers there, just plastic chairs and tea from a machine. It was the local support group for sufferers of AIDS and HIV. With all that had been going on, it had slipped my mind too.

I fed Hewitt, then made a ratatouille with Monty's tomatoes. While it was simmering I watched the news. Flash floods in the south-west and two motorway pile-ups. Dad didn't deserve Brownie points, he deserved a medal.

Shortly after seven Simon called. He was using his mobile and almost immediately it began breaking up. 'I can't hear you,' I shouted. More static, a few snatches of words and the line went dead. I shrugged. If it was important he'd call back.

I loaded the dishwasher, tidied around, put some washing in the machine. Thinking about Judith. Should I drive up there again? A glance out of the window decided me. It looked more like ten o'clock than eight, with pelting rain and a wind that was bending the trees double. I told myself it could wait until morning and went up to check my emails.

A few minutes surfing the net stretched into half an hour. Funny where time goes. I logged off and went downstairs, poured myself a whisky. The Scrabble was still on the table; so were the Tintins. I pulled one across – *Le Trésor de Rackham le Rouge*, by Hergé. A pseudonym derived from the author's initials, as Dad had again informed us last night. *Aire-zhay* – R-J.

'R-G!' I corrected myself. G for Georges. The French pronounce G, *zhay* and J, *zhee*, something I'd always got muddled at school.

I jumped as something crashed against the window. The wind was getting stronger. I started sifting the pile of letters I'd collected from my flat. I'd been putting off sorting through them but now I did, wincing at the number of bills. I wrote a few cheques, addressed the envelopes, and got a buzz of gratification knowing I was up to date. For me, paperwork rates like housework.

Nine o'clock came and went. Still no Dad. I wasn't unduly concerned: he'd seen enough accidents resulting from adverse weather conditions to know to drive slowly. I poured another whisky and returned to the Tintin, struggling to make sense of the antics of Capitaine Haddock and the rest of the crew. Hewitt padded up and rested his head on my knee. '*Ash-tay*,' I said, fondling his ears, 'Hewitt Tavender.' He looked up adoringly, as if I'd just uttered something profound.

And suddenly I was playing mind games, attributing French pronunciation to initials of people I knew. *Zhay-tay*, my own. *Bay-tay*, Dad. *Zhay*, no *zhee-kah*, Judith. Absently

I turned the page. *Ess-ef*, Simon, the same as in English. Lisa Lambton, *ell-ell*. Except the French wouldn't say it like that, not according to Dad. He'd been showing off when he laid down *caillou*, spelling it out as he went. *Say, ah, ee, deux-ell* – at which point Monty and I had groaned. But ten out of ten for remembering. He'd even got the liaison right, pronouncing it *de zell*, double L. Anything that began with a vowel, I reminded myself – *deux-ell, deux-ess, deux-aire* –

Deux-aire?

My heart gave a jolt. *De zaire* – double R.

'Rampant rapist,' I muttered bitterly. Then froze. That wasn't all the letters stood for. They were also someone's initials.

'Rayjay Rickards,' I murmured, and Hewitt nuzzled my thigh.

I shook my head. Coincidence. How convoluted could you get?

But yet again my heart was racing.

No way, I told myself. De Zaire looked nothing like the photo, probably didn't even speak French. The guy was a sculptor, had exhibitions, sold work . . .

Could pass himself off as anything . . .

I thought of the photographs. Within walking distance of the Institute, I'd told Simon, but the sites were equally close to Holt Mill. And the Institute wasn't the only place to have a constant stream of visitors. Artists would too – buyers, journalists, agents . . .

Gallery owners?

Judith had visited de Zaire because of something Stuart had said. I'd assumed it concerned the exhibition. But suppose it was more than that, something he'd inadvertently let slip? Hadn't Dad said she was edgy? Perhaps that was *why* she had called, to let us know where she was going. In case something went wrong? Suppose there'd been a drop. Suppose she'd arrived unexpectedly and inadvertently caught them with the goods. What would they do to her?

Into my mind flashed the image of Gary.

Hewitt barked as I leapt from the chair. 'It's okay, boy,' I said. But it wasn't okay. It was far from okay.

I snatched up the telephone, had begun tapping Simon's number when I realized the phone was dead. The storm must have brought down the lines. I dashed upstairs and grabbed my mobile – but as soon as I saw the signal knew I was wasting my time. Back downstairs I leaned against the dresser, closed my eyes, took several deep breaths. My heart was crashing against my ribs. *Cool it, Tavender . . .*

I told myself I was overreacting. All this because of a name? De Zaire was probably who he said he was, Judith safe and well at Verstone.

Probably?

'Hell!' I ran to the hall and grabbed my Barbour. I had to find out. Storm or no storm, it wouldn't wait until morning.

Chapter Twenty-Five

I was half soaked by the time I reached my car. 'Go, you bastard!' I yelled when it refused to start. Eventually it caught and I screeched away. Would Monty hear me over the wind? Would he tell Dad?

The village was deserted. No one but a fool ventured out on a night like this. Was that what I was – a fool? I prayed so. Nothing would please me more than to find Judith curled up by the Aga reading a book or listening to the radio, wondering what all the fuss was about. Well, she wouldn't be staying there, not tonight. I would bring her back, drag if necessary, and she could remain at Dad's until this whole damned mess was over. Or at least until I had spoken to Simon.

I couldn't believe how the track had deteriorated in a few short hours. The ford had become a swirling black torrent, and as I nosed the car in I begged it not to stall. Mercifully it didn't and I started up the other side, finally skidding to a halt beside the high stone wall. The house was in darkness. So what, I told myself, she'll be in the kitchen. I climbed out, the wind almost tearing the door from my grasp. Up here it was blowing a Force 9. I switched on my torch and, bent almost double, made it up the steps. I didn't bother to knock but went straight to the rear. The kitchen was in darkness.

I banged on the window, calling Judith's name. The wind snatched my words and funnelled them away. Was she in bed? Had the power failed? I should have looked for her car. Normally it was parked around the corner, often with its nose poking out. Tonight I hadn't noticed it.

Leaning into the gale I retraced my steps, crossed the terrace and peered over the wall. The space was empty.

My guardian angel must have been with me when I raced back down the track. Twice I hit the bank, the first time losing a wing mirror, the second graunching the wing. But at least I'd skidded the right way. The other and I'd have ended in the Cleave.

I knew exactly where I was going. Holt Mill. Not what I would do when I got there, but I would play that by ear. It depended on what I found, whether Judith was there, whether she was there willingly. At the junction I called Simon. The phone was as dead as last week's sun.

As nightmare journeys go, the next hour scored high. The lanes were littered with debris and branches, and three times I was forced to reverse, twice when the road was flooded, once for a fallen tree. Each time meant sticking my head out the window while searching for somewhere to turn, and each time left me colder and wetter. The detours added miles. I kept trying Simon but with no better luck – it wasn't a night for cell phones. But I'd be insane if I didn't let *someone* know. What the hell did I think I could achieve on my own?

I had one other option – the radio. I quailed at the thought of using it. It's strictly for Brigade use, a low-band VHF, meaning anyone with a similar device could be listening in. Not only that, but every word spoken is recorded at HQ. If my wild idea was wrong . . .

But what other choice was there?

I snatched up the handset. Busy pips warned me to wait my turn. Brigade radios demand a strict procedure, because only one person can speak at a time. While I was waiting I thought of what I would say, how I would phrase it, couching everyday phrases in Brigade jargon. A small branch landed on my bonnet and jammed against the wiper, and instantly rain blinded my vision. I threw down the handset, braking sharply as I wound down the window. Reaching out to dislodge it, I felt water trickling down my neck. Only a fool . . .

When I retrieved the handset a voice was speaking. '. . . closing on pager contact, over.'

The reply from Control was patchy. 'Rog . . . two . . . QD standing by.'

More pips, then silence. I was free to go.

I pushed the button. 'QD from Hotel three-one, over.'

A pause, then, 'Go ahead, . . . tel three-one.'

A different voice. Lisa's? I cleared my throat, enunciated clearly. 'QD, can you relay the following message to DI Furneaux – I repeat, DI Furneaux at Police HQ.' I waited a beat for them to type it up. 'Message reads – the man in question is de Zaire.'

'Hotel three . . . can you repeat . . .?'

I was dropping into a valley. The radio was breaking up. Should I stop, or keep going and risk it? I decided to risk it.

'The man in question is de Zaire,' I shouted. 'I spell – Delta, Echo, Zebra . . .'

'. . . ith . . . t . . . ic . . .'

Shit! 'Alpha, India, Romeo, Echo,' I completed, praying they could hear me. 'Message continues, I am proceeding to Holt Mill – I repeat, Holt Mill, over.'

Nothing.

'QD, Hotel three-one, do you read, over?'

But it was too late. The signal had gone.

Adrenaline is said to induce colossal feats of strength and courage, allowing ordinary people to lift cars to free trapped bodies, or plunge into raging torrents to rescue drowning men. I can only assume it was fuelling me that night – or was it blind stupidity? If I was right, I'd seen what de Zaire was capable of, first in Danner Road, then at the Revel, and the memory of Gary's body would haunt me to the grave. Had it not been for the storm I may well have turned back, but I was too busy concentrating on my driving, avoiding hazards and keeping the car on the road, to imagine what lay ahead. My only concern was Judith, the fear that she too would suffer at his hands. Maybe the fuel was blind rage.

I reached the Mill from a different direction and almost didn't see it. Just in time I noticed the gate. No sign of Judith's BMW, but that didn't mean she wasn't there – did it?

My stomach lurched. Misuse of Brigade radio, wasting police time . . .

It was too late to worry now.

The storm had some advantages. It masked the noise as I crashed down through the garden. Not daring to use the torch, I was tripping over branches, veering into shrubs, sprawling over the metal pergola that had been brought down by the gale.

A faint light from the house was guiding me. It was coming from the hall, filtering through an open door into the sitting room. The curtains there were undrawn and cautiously I peered in. The room was empty, but showed signs of recent visitors. Bottles and several glasses littered the table and an ashtray was piled high. A couple of cushions had tumbled to the floor.

So where were the guests? Had Judith been one of them?

A thought flashed into my mind – Judith and de Zaire upstairs in bed. Ridiculous? Not if he kept the violence under control. He was an attractive man, her marriage shaky, it wasn't inconceivable that she would have an affair. If so, I was about to make myself the biggest prat of all time, barging in and attempting her rescue. Her knight in soggy Barbour. At any other time I might have laughed.

Yet somehow the image didn't ring true. If there *was* something between them, I was sure I would have noticed.

I hesitated by the door but was afraid to knock, instead fumbled my way around the side. Better to try the french windows. I was almost at the terrace when I heard the scream. For a moment my blood ran cold. Then I remembered – the wheel. The rising water would be forcing it to spin faster and again metal was grinding on metal. I stared towards the source of the sound. Was that where I would find de Zaire?

Shielding the beam, I flicked the torch on and off, and started down the steps. Did the same when I reached the door. Below me I could see water, now a treacle-dark torrent surging between the banks.

See? Something was illuminating it. A light must be on in the studio.

I slithered down to the bank and looked up at the windows. A faint light was coming from the far end. Too dim for striplights – probably the anglepoise over the desk. Had it been left on by mistake, or was somebody in there?

More doubts assailed me. De Zaire's guests could be fellow artists, or people interested in his work. How natural to invite Judith to join them. A few drinks at the house, a look at his studio. Then what – out for a meal? They could be there at this moment, laughing and chatting in a cosy restaurant, while I, idiot that I am, was soaked to the skin, dreaming up wild and improbable –

I caught my breath. Suddenly all was brightness. The striplights had come on in the studio above. I could see the floodwater, just inches from my feet, the grass on the opposite bank. Moving across it were two shadows.

They vanished almost immediately and the lights went out, and a moment later the door began to open. I leapt back against the wall, pressing myself flat as a flashlight spilled across the ground. Two men wrestled their way out. Briefly the torch lit on the face of one of them but it was no one I recognized. 'Fuckin' wind!' the other shouted.

They were less than ten feet away. The speaker was battling to close the door. If the torch swung my way . . .

It angled towards the water and I closed my eyes. When I opened them it had swung upwards and away, and I almost wept as I released my breath. The men were

271

heading towards the house, two silhouettes bulked out by waterproofs. Neither one was de Zaire. But nor did they look like art connoisseurs. Who then – his henchmen?

My heart was in my mouth. Something *was* going on. I thought of Simon's warning, how Rayjay would do whatever it took to protect his interests. And there was no question things were starting to go wrong. First Miss Hillas, then Trevor – the first death dismissed as an accident, the second far enough away not to draw attention. But killing Gary had brought things closer to home. They must know the days of the operation were numbered. What they couldn't know was that Trevor had talked. They wouldn't be sitting around drinking and smoking if they thought the police were on to them. Perhaps they were here to wind things up, planning one last shipment before removing all traces and moving on. If so, and Judith had walked in . . .

I shuddered. They would kill her – they had to. The same way they had killed the others. They would dispose of anyone who got in the way. Would probably hide her body, make sure it was discovered long after they were gone. She could be in there now, locked up, terrified . . .

I scrabbled up the bank, tried the door. The men had locked it behind them. Did that mean they weren't coming back? The only other door was the one over the wheel, the only way to reach it via the leat, and even in my hyped-up state I wasn't *that* crazy. Which left the windows.

I slithered back to the water's edge and stared up. The sills were a good twelve feet above my head. A flick of the torch showed a wall of smooth stone, slippery with moss. No handholds, only a horizontal row of iron spikes leading towards the wheel. They had been driven in at two foot intervals, roughly at the height of my chest. Had I a plank to lie across them the problem would be solved. Like life's ever that simple!

Still no sign of the men. I ran the torch further down the wall. Two feet from the water the weeds began, nettles and ferns, sprouting from gaps in the mortar. But no gaps large enough to take the toe of a boot. Below the weeds were the remains of a walkway. *Not in your wildest dreams, Tavender!* The framework was almost submerged, the torrent licking the base of the few remaining planks. Even if I held on to the pegs . . .

No way! The boards were slimy, obviously rotten, the spikes rusty, probably loose, both too far gone to take anyone's weight. I might as well hurl myself into the stream now and get swept away.

I turned my back, kept thinking of Judith. Suppose she *was* inside? Thought too of my father's words – '*It's not about fighting fires, Gus, it's about saving lives. There's nothing more important . . .*'

Oh, crap!

Heart in mouth, I looked back at the framework. The least I could do was test it. I grabbed hold of the first spike and tugged. It held. So by some miracle did the next. Keeping one foot on terra firma, I swung my other over the water and placed it on a board, making sure it was above the support. The surface was like glass. Slowly I leaned forward, transferred my weight. Another miracle. Tempting fate? How long would my angel hang around?

I brought my other foot to meet it and shuffled sideways, reached for the next peg, trying not to think of the water surging beneath my feet. Instead I pictured myself in a burnt-out building, feeling my way, testing each section before giving it my weight. Familiar procedure – apart from the wheel. No room I'd ever encountered had ten feet of shrieking metal at its end, threatening to suck you into its maw.

The nearer I got, the more terrifying the wheel seemed. The force of the paddles could crush a skull, most likely sever a limb. Still I edged towards it. Now I could feel water from the buckets sloshing over my head, though I was so wet already it made little difference. The noise up close was deafening.

The flailing paddles were barely three feet from my head when, without warning, the board I was standing on gave

273

way. Suddenly I was up to my knees in water, strung out sideways by the force of the flow. My boots filled with water, turned into lead weights. I clung to the spikes, praying they would hold, promising that if I ever got out of this alive I would rival Phil in my work-outs. My only hope was to find the ladder. I hauled myself as high as I could, let go one hand and groped wildly up the wall. Almost wept when my fingers hooked over the ring. One last gargantuan heave and I was able to grab hold. I dragged myself higher, let go the peg and reached for the next.

Only when my feet were clear of the water did I dare switch on the torch. A seven foot section of walkway had vanished. There was no going back.

For a while I didn't move, simply clung there, marvelling at the fact that I was even alive. But I still had to get in through the door.

Lashed by water I began to climb, telling myself the ladder at least must be sound. De Zaire must have used it when he oiled the wheel. I tried to count the rungs – five, six, seven . . . I had passed the uppermost paddles when the rungs ran out and my hand slid over a ledge. The base of the door. But how did I get on to it? With the door open it would be easy – lean over the ledge, slide into the room. But closed?

I fumbled around. The ledge was no more than a foot wide. Needing something to hang on to, I again risked the torch. A pulley was projecting just below the eaves but too far out of reach to be useful. There was nothing except the corner of the wall. Pushing against it, I leaned into the opening and stepped up another rung.

If the walkway was a bad dream, this was the nightmare. I was virtually hanging in mid-air, at the mercy of the wind, and not for the first time I was glad of the darkness. It prevented me from seeing what lay below.

Another step up and I got my knee on the ledge. I ran my hand up the door. Still I couldn't reach the latch. Nothing for it, I would have to stand up. I groped at the corner of the wall, found a gap in the mortar, clung on, and hauled up my other knee. This was insanity! Squirming in the narrow space, I raised myself on one leg, stretched upwards. Thankfully it was enough. My fingers found the hole, slid in and lifted. Next minute I was falling forwards, sprawling across the floor. If anyone *was* in there, they would certainly know I'd arrived.

Nobody rushed to grab me. I sat back on my haunches and peered around. I'd been right about the anglepoise, it was shining over the desk. The far side of the room was in shadow but from what I could tell it was empty.

'Judith?' I hissed.

No reply. But she might not have heard me over the noise. I scrabbled to my feet, forced shut the door. Water was running from my coat, leaving a tell-tale puddle on the floor. I shrugged it off and stuffed it under the desk. I didn't want to leave a trail.

'Judith?' I called more loudly.

Still nothing. I snapped on the torch and shone it around. The floor inside the main door was also wet. I could see leaves and muddy footprints. A trail of muddy footprints, leading off behind the central bench. Hair standing up on the back of my neck, I tiptoed forward, boots squelching, fearful of what I might find.

The trail led to the end wall, where a heavy pillar-drill had been pushed to one side. In its space was an open trapdoor.

But of course there was a room below. The wheel-shaft entered beneath the studio, and would have led to belts, pulleys, whatever else was needed to drive the ancient saws. Slowly I crept forwards. The torch lit up a flight of concrete steps – new concrete, edged by a breeze-block wall. Purpose-built, and recently.

I hesitated, wondering if I dared go down. If the men came back and there was nowhere to hide . . .

But I hadn't come this far to chicken out now.

The steps were steep, turning sharp right at the bottom into a narrow passage. No forks, no recesses, just a door at the far end. A solid iron door with ornate hinges and studs, totally out of place beside the modern blocks. I pressed my ear against it, heard nothing – but a door like that would suppress all sound. It didn't mean Judith wasn't behind it.

The handle was a ring of plaited iron. I had already grabbed it when, somewhat belatedly, it occurred to me she might not be alone. If this was where their operations were carried out, there was a good chance others would be inside. De Zaire could be there, Alden . . .

Suddenly I was having trouble breathing. I leaned back against the blocks, closed my eyes, took several deep breaths. Above my head a door banged.

I lurched forwards. Footsteps were coming towards the stairs. Frantically I looked around. I was caught like a mouse in a trap, the door the only exit. With nowhere else to run, I grabbed the handle and turned.

Out of the frying pan – and into a living hell.

De Zaire looked up as I entered. I don't know who was the most surprised. His shock was at seeing me. Mine was at what I was seeing.

I recognized the room straight away – the leather armchair, the wall sconces, the small high window with the iron bars. The bed was still against the wall, though now it was draped in white linen, the frills and flounces virginal as snow. As virginal as the robe of the woman stretched across it. Judith.

Chapter Twenty-Six

It was de Zaire who recovered first. 'Looking for me?' he asked unctuously.

I couldn't answer. Fear had taken my tongue, the horror at what I was seeing. Slowly, but slowly, the reality sunk in. Judith was their victim – she was being abused – like the women in Alden's video. It had sickened me that he watched them. Never had it occurred to me that he made them, too. But the proof was laid out before me – the cameras and microphones, the spotlights, the grisly array of props. My revulsion must have shown because de Zaire lifted his brows.

'Not what you expected?' He grinned, looked me up and down. 'I take it it's still raining. British summers, huh?' Then, beckoning with his finger, 'You might as well come in now you're here.'

My feet were like clay. Somehow I shuffled forward. I was vaguely aware of the men behind me, of a second man already in the room. I didn't look around. Nor did I look at Judith. I was too afraid. One glance had been enough to see the blood on the sheets, the lines on her wrists and ankles where the cuffs had cut in.

Yet every second I was aware of her. She'd tried to sit up when I entered, fixed me with terror-filled eyes. Now once again she lay prone, her face as pale as the gown rucked up around her thighs. Deep in my gut, anger welled.

'You sick bastard!' I growled.

He pointed to his chest as if to say, Me? 'A little harmless role-play. You should try it.' He picked up a bottle. 'Drink?'

I didn't reply. He shrugged, hoisted his hip on the corner of a table. 'So what brings you here on a night like this? Don't tell me – you're regretting your hurried departure the other evening, hoping to continue where we left off.' His laugh cut through me like ice. 'So how did you get in? Those assholes leave the door open?'

'It was locked,' a voice said behind me.

De Zaire jerked his head. 'Go check. Make sure there's no more.'

Footsteps retreated. His eyes hadn't left my face. 'Though my guess is you came alone, right?'

'Let her go,' I said, ignoring him. 'Judith's done nothing to you.'

'Yeah, well that's not strictly true.' His hand settled around a glass. 'See, yesterday she walked in when we were – conducting business.'

I curled my lip. 'You call this business?'

'Hell, no – this is the fun bit.' He brought the glass to his lips.

'Oh, I *see*,' I said. 'She walked in on the drugs.' The eyes narrowed fractionally. 'What was it – heroin, coke? Is that how you get your supply, by smuggling the stuff?'

He glanced behind me and I heard the iron door close.

'You're well informed. I wonder how you found out?' He reached behind his head, adjusted his pony-tail, then sidled towards me, brought his mouth close to my ear. 'But you're right, that's exactly what she saw. Coke. Charlie. The big C.' He blew in my ear, stepped back laughing.

'So art won't support your lifestyle. Shame.'

'Ain't it just!' Closer again. 'But what the hell. The other brings money beyond your dreams.'

'And death to thousands – young people, kids. But I guess you can live with that.'

He didn't reply, just stepped back, and this time he had something in his hand. My heart slammed against my ribs. I was staring into the round black muzzle of a gun.

'In case you were thinking of leaving.'

I couldn't take my eyes off it. I'd never seen a gun

278

before, not this close, certainly not from the wrong end. I felt myself sway; my legs had turned to water. I willed myself to stay upright.

De Zaire retreated to the table, poured an inch of Jack Daniels with his left hand. 'So how did you find out? Who's been talking?'

'Not Gary, if that's what you think.' I cursed the tremor in my voice.

'Why would I think that?'

'Isn't that why he was killed? For shooting his mouth off?'

'So I hear.' A smile. 'Who then, the old girl?'

From the corner of my eye I saw Judith squirm, heard her mumble something behind the tape covering her mouth.

'Is that why you killed her?' I demanded. 'Because she found out what you were up to?'

'Uh-uh. You can't put that one on me.'

'Like hell! Christ, what kind of animal are you? She was eighty-two, a harmless old lady –'

'*Harmless?*' He jerked forward. 'She'd been spying on Gary's lot for months, pissed about the dog fighting. Like it was *her* business! ' He jiggled the gun. 'No, I don't reckon it was her. She'd have gone to the cops.'

'Maybe she did.'

His face split in a grin. 'Nah, they'd have been here long before this.' He glanced at the bed. 'Hell, what's it matter?'

'It matters that you killed her!' I snapped, anger overcoming my fear. 'Oh, not you personally, you're not that stupid. Rayjay never does his own dirty work, isn't that right?'

The glass stopped halfway to his lips. Another glance at the door. A nanosecond and he'd composed his face. 'Rayjay, huh. And who might that be?'

'Like you don't know!'

'You think the guy's me?'

'I do now. At first I thought it was Alden.'

'*Alden?*' For some reason that seemed to amuse him. 'And now I've got the honour. How come?'

'Your name.'

The tanned brow furrowed. 'What the fuck's my name got to do with it?'

'Nothing – in English.'

'English? What the fuck are you on about?'

'In French they're your initials!' I yelled. '*Deux-aire*, double R. Rayjay Rickards!' I added, when he still looked blank.

His eyes widened. Then he bellowed a laugh. 'Is that right? Shit! So all this time . . . What was it again, *deux* –'

'Very funny.'

'Lady, if you knew how much! *Jesus*! Of all the crazy – Hell, I don't even *speak* French.' More laughter, this time shaking his head. 'Oh, I changed my name, I grant you – but not from Rickards.' He spun round, gave an exaggerated bow. 'Joe Desmond, that's me. Originally from Chicago.' He grinned a bit more, then opened his mouth and goggled, mimicking my expression.

I had good reason to be shocked. I believed him. So much for my brilliant idea! Yet he had recognized Rayjay's name, that was clear from his reaction. So who the hell was he?

He'd scoffed at Alden. Stuart? One of the men? Or were they all just pawns in Rayjay's game, front men, shielding him from recognition? My eyes drifted to the bald man half hidden by the camera.

'You haven't a fucking clue, have you?' de Zaire taunted. 'Who're you going for next – Eddie, here? Frank?' Another glance past my shoulder. 'Shall I put her out of her misery? Hell, why not.' He jerked the gun. 'Look around if you're so interested. Rayjay's right behind you.'

Slowly I turned. A man was leaning to the left of the door. Next to him stood Zara. Her presence appalled me – the very fact that she was involved. How could one woman condone the suffering of another? And this a woman who preached goodness and spiritual awareness.

But I didn't dwell on her long. My attention was on the man. How could it not be? He wore a long brocade waistcoat and satin britches, white stockings and buckled shoes, a white Prince Charming wig tied with a velvet bow. The last time I'd seen him he'd been wearing a smoking jacket.

Rayjay a porn star?

I frowned. This couldn't be right. The guy was too young, thirty at the most. I spun back on de Zaire.

'Is this some sort of joke?'

'You still don't get it, do you?'

Get what? I turned back round. Zara smiled and pushed herself from the wall.

I gasped. *'Zara?'*

'Got there at last.' The voice was deeper now. Still the twang – but he'd been in America a long time.

I staggered backwards. The one person we hadn't considered.

Can pass himself off as anything . . .

Why had we only considered men?

I watched with grim fascination as he moved up beside de Zaire. He had had plastic surgery, but I could still see traces of the old features, the high cheekbones, the fine straight nose. The robes had hidden what couldn't be disguised, an Adam's apple, a man's hands and feet. I wondered if he'd taken hormones to remove excess hair.

'Sex change?' I asked, when I'd recovered my voice.

'Please!' He flipped the cap on a Perrier. 'And not be able to revert to red-blooded male? No, Zara was an interlude, a means to an end – as it turned out, a highly successful one. Sure you don't want a drink?'

I shook my head.

'Wise girl. Keep a clear head. It'll make it all the more interesting.' He exchanged grins with de Zaire. 'Frankly, I'll be glad to see the back of her, these frocks are a pain. Still . . .' He swigged from the bottle. 'So how did you learn about me – the boyfriend? Inspector now, isn't he?' More smiles, gloating at my shock. He reached for a cigarette. 'Didn't know he knew I was back. Thought you and he were just –'

'He knows I'm here,' I blurted.

'Yeah? What, sent you as vanguard, did he?' Laughter from the men. 'Oh, I don't think so. He doesn't have a *clue* who I am.' He accepted a light from de Zaire. 'I must say I enjoyed meeting him again. He came to interview us, you know – after Gary's unfortunate death.'

'Don't you mean fortunate?' My fists clenched. 'Don't deny you had him killed.'

Zara/Rayjay shrugged. 'He was becoming a liability – drinking, mouthing off. I couldn't allow that.'

'And blackmailing. Or didn't you know about that one?'

He didn't flinch. '*I* knew. But I'm surprised you do.'

'Sound carries,' I said. 'So who killed him – Alden?'

He chuckled nastily. 'My dear girl, Alden was purely a voyeur. Sadistic, true, but only to a degree. He liked to watch, play a few mild games. He didn't have it in him to kill.'

Liked, didn't . . . Why was he using the past tense? 'Where *is* Alden?' I demanded. 'Where is he now?'

Rayjay hunched a shoulder. 'I expect he'll turn up.'

The man by the camera gave a snort.

'Jesus . . .' I breathed, squeezing up my eyes. 'Him, too? *Why?*'

'Oh, I think you know the answer.'

Of course. The blackmail. He had let Gary find out.

Anger burst from me. 'It's all so easy, isn't it! Kill off anyone who gets in the way, who speaks out of turn. But you're wrong about one thing. Alden *did* kill. He killed Miss Hillas. That's what Gary was blackmailing him about. I heard him – up at the Institute. He said, I know about the old . . .'

I broke off, catching my breath. Stared. Suddenly I knew I had got it so wrong. I had heard what I expected to hear, made assumptions . . .

'The old lady,' I murmured. 'Oh God. He didn't mean Miss Hillas, did he? He meant *you*, the so-called wife.'

Rayjay had begun a slow hand-clap. 'Congratulations – you're absolutely right. Alden's "old lady". My, er, late "husband", after rather too much drink, made the monumental mistake of referring to me as "he". And Gary – remarkable for someone with one brain cell – picked up on it.'

Things were beginning to make a horrible sort of sense. Almost. 'But why didn't he blackmail *you*?'

'My dear girl, it was *me* he was threatening to tell.'

Of course. Gary wouldn't have gone to the police, he was too deeply involved. But he knew what would happen if he told Rayjay. As did Alden, which was why he was paying up. But Rayjay had found out anyway and, true to form, had ensured their silence. Doing what was necessary to protect his interests. But if it wasn't Alden . . .

'So who did kill Gary?'

Rayjay turned to the man beside him.

De Zaire shrugged. 'He had it coming. Guy was a klutz.'

Bile rose in my throat. To think I had once fantasized about this man.

'You have to admit my friend is inventive,' Rayjay grinned, patting him on the shoulder.

'Inspired,' I replied icily. 'Unlike his sculptures.' The sarcasm fell on stony ground. 'So how many are we talking about? Is Trevor Collins on the list?'

'Poor Trev.' Rayjay arranged his face in mock sympathy. 'Must have been a shock finding his body. He thought he could siphon off, sell on the streets. It doesn't pay to get greedy.'

I felt myself sway. 'Shame you were too late,' I replied shakily. 'He'd already spoken to the police.'

'Oh, I guessed that. What did he tell them, that Rayjay was back? Can't have been more, he never saw my, er, *feminine* side.' He chuckled as he stubbed out the cigarette. 'Bet it riled Furneaux. Must have had him jumping up his own arse!'

He had an answer for everything. I was running out of ideas. I glanced at the bed, saw Judith watching me, pleading with her eyes.

'And Miss Hillas?' I asked.

'For fuck's sake . . .' De Zaire slid to his feet. 'That wasn't me, okay?'

'I'm supposed to believe that?'

'Lady, I don't give a monkey's shit what you believe!' His eyes travelled to Judith. 'Perhaps you should look closer to home.'

'Judith didn't kill her aunt!' I cried.

'Did I say it was her?' His eyes snapped round as the door behind me opened. 'Anything?'

'Nah, clean as a whistle.'

'How'd she get in?'

'Door over the wheel.'

De Zaire let out a hoot. 'You've more guts than I thought. We could have used you on the team.'

Before I could think of an answer, Rayjay clapped his hands. Suddenly all was business. 'Okay, let's move it! Frank?' He jerked his head at the rear wall, and somebody shoved me from behind.

'You do know you're finished here,' I blurted as I stumbled forward.

'Tomorrow we'll be gone, sweetheart.' His eyes were darting round the room.

'The police will be here long before that. They know I'm here.'

Another shove.

'I'm serious!' I cried. 'I rang before I left.'

'Yeah? What on?'

More laughter.

De Zaire grabbed my arm and slammed me against the wall. 'Shut it, okay? Or we'll tape you, too.' He pointed the gun at my face. 'Don't think I won't use it.'

He didn't need to worry on that score.

Frank, the man in costume, had taken up position beside the bed. Rayjay marched towards him – no gliding now – and started gesticulating, directing his next moves.

'Period drama?' I asked.

'Shut it!'

I closed my eyes as the room began to spin. 'Eddie?'

284

I heard Rayjay yell, and when I opened them the lights had changed, banks of spotlights had come on. On the bed Judith began to squirm. I tried to turn away but de Zaire grabbed my chin, jerked it round, hard fingers digging into the bone. 'Better watch,' he leered. 'Might be your turn next.'

My turn?

The one called Eddie flicked some switches and the lighting changed again. He picked up a clapperboard, moved in front of the camera.

'S.B. Scene three, take one.' The board snapped.

Frank lifted something from the table and held it up and I saw light glinting from a blade.

'No!' I screamed, and a second later there was a bang. I thought for a moment the gun had gone off.

'Fuck!' someone snarled, and I almost wept with relief. One of the spotlights had exploded. It was a respite – but for how long? How long did it take a bunch of psychopaths to change a light bulb?

'What's so fucking funny?' de Zaire growled, and I realized I was laughing. From shock. From horror. From the knowledge that Judith was about to suffer unimaginable pain and I was powerless to stop it.

'Nothing,' I told him, but the bubbles kept rising. The gun he pressed against my stomach killed them dead.

Rayjay came storming back, his face thunderous. 'Would you fucking know it! She behaving?'

'Think she wants to join in.'

'Why not? Reckon we can fit in one more.' He looked me up and down. 'What d'you reckon, Bluebeard?'

'Cute.'

He snatched the gun. 'Go check outside.'

I was trembling like a leaf in a gale, the wall the only thing keeping me upright. I was vaguely aware of something digging into my leg.

'This film have a name?' I asked, summoning a bravado I was far from feeling.

'Sleeping Beauty.'

'Yeah, right!'

'You think they're dressed like that for their health?' He gave a laugh. 'We have some very discerning clients, in this case a European gentleman with a penchant for fairy tales. With a twist,' he added pointedly.

'Client? You mean someone pays for this shit?'

'This *shit*, as you call it, is much in demand.'

'It's a sick old world.'

'Ain't it just.' He glanced across at Eddie.

'Bit of a step down, isn't it? Porn flicks?' Something told me to keep him talking.

'Not the kind I make.'

'What's so special about yours?'

'Exactly that. Specially made for specialist tastes.'

'Sadistic tastes.'

He didn't reply.

'So why fairy tales?'

'How the fuck would I know? Probably got his first hard-on when nanny was reading Perrault. Who gives a shit as long as he pays.'

'And does he?'

'Oh, yeah – big time. Especially for ones like that.' He jerked his head at the bed. 'Class – he likes that. This one even *screams* posh.'

Anger, white hot, flared in my stomach. 'Can't be easy, finding women who fit the bill. What d'you do, advertise?'

'Nah. We wait for them to climb in over waterwheels.'

Laughter from the nearest man.

The door opened. De Zaire was back. He retrieved the gun, grinningly informed us there was 'no sign of the cavalry'. Rayjay's attention shifted to Eddie. 'You got problems over there?' he yelled, and started to walk away.

'What happens when this is all over?' I called after him, desperate to keep him talking. 'When you've tortured her for some sadistic pervert's amusement – what happens to her then?'

He stopped in his tracks, slowly turned round. 'You still don't get it, do you?'

And in that instant I did. There wouldn't be a 'then'. Because this was no ordinary porn flick. By the time the camera stopped rolling . . .

I let out a cry, felt my legs buckle under me. Next minute I was on the floor. My guts were roiling. Not that; *please* not that. It would be the ultimate humiliation.

'Get her up!' Rayjay snapped, and de Zaire grabbed my arm. I knocked it away, somehow struggled to my knees, using the thing that had been digging into me to pull myself up. I saw vaguely it was a fire extinguisher, an old model, bolted to the wall.

'Keep her quiet,' Rayjay ordered and spun on his heel, and from a million miles away I heard Eddie's voice.

'Scene three, take two.' The clapperboard snapped.

I closed my eyes.

'I said watch!' de Zaire growled.

I did what I was told and stared straight ahead – at the flames leaping in the sconces, the way the light fell on the velvet drapes. Anywhere but at the bed. But I couldn't block out the sounds. The tape had been ripped from Judith's mouth and I could hear every whimper, every futile plea. Her scream was drowned by one of my own.

My reward was a back-hander from de Zaire, and for the second time in his presence I tasted blood. I steadied myself against the extinguisher. Somehow I had to halt the filming. If I could just create another diversion . . .

And then what – hope against hope that Simon would arrive?

Who was I kidding! The radio had broken up, he hadn't got my message. He didn't even know I was here. All a diversion would do was prolong the agony. And what did I hope to achieve with a gun pointing at my chest?

Another scream. My hand fastened round the cylinder. If I could rip it from the wall, turn it on . . .

Like they were going to let me! I'd be grabbed the moment I moved. Or shot. Right now, that seemed the better option.

Hell, if they were going to kill us anyway . . .

I ran my hand over the cylinder. I thought I recognized the type. It was the sort where you swing up the nozzle while extracting the pin, then point and squeeze. But first it had to be unhooked. How long would that take?

A damn sight longer than it takes to squeeze a trigger. It probably wouldn't work anyway; it was too old. Hell, I didn't even know what the thing contained.

So was I going to just stand here and watch Judith being tortured? Patiently wait my turn?

I risked a glance at de Zaire. His eyes had drifted to the bed. When he looked back I saw the savage excitement. He was getting off on the action, the same way he was getting off on my fear. If I could hold back, wait for him to become totally absorbed . . .

But still I needed that diversion . . .

Seconds crawled into minutes, minutes into a lifetime. Every second brought Judith further pain. Was that the price of saving her life? Both our lives?

Still staring ahead, I let go the extinguisher and shifted my position. While doing so I slid my hand into the back pocket of my jeans. I was aware of de Zaire's eyes flicking round, but my own didn't waver. When he was again drawn to the bed I withdrew my hand, bringing out a fifty pence coin. I tested its weight. Would it be heavy enough to make a noise?

De Zaire was no more than three feet away, the gun still pointed at my chest. The cameraman a few feet beyond that. A little to his left stood Eddie. Furthest away was Rayjay. Did he have a gun too?

Maybe they all did. I no longer cared. Soon it would be too late to matter. Taking several deep breaths, I flexed my fingers and adjusted the coin.

All eyes were on Judith. Frank was kneeling over her. He brought his hand over her mouth to silence her cries. In the sudden quiet I gave a flick of my wrist. I felt the coin leave my fingers – heard it land somewhere near the door. As de Zaire spun round I tugged at the extinguisher, felt it come free.

288

And suddenly everything was chaos. Shouts rang in my ears as I held it up, raised the nozzle. De Zaire was turning back. The gun came up as I pulled the pin.

Point, squeeze . . .

The blast of powder hit him square in the face. He reeled back, choking. There was a loud crack as I surged forwards, and something whizzed past my ear. But by then I'd turned the jet on the cameraman and Eddie. They disappeared in a cloud of white.

Blasting the powder before me I ran forward, tripping over cables and equipment. Where were the others? The fine dust was searing my throat, hampering my breathing. It was like being in a blizzard, visibility nil. I found Frank when I tripped over him. He was writhing on the floor, gasping, fighting for air. Had the same fate befallen Rayjay?

I could only pray; the cylinder was empty. I hurled it to the ground, fought my way to the bed.

'Keys!' I croaked. There was no time for compassion. 'Where are the keys?'

Judith was choking too. 'T-table.'

I found them by a tray of surgical instruments and snatched them up, started on the cuffs, at any moment expecting to be grabbed by Rayjay. Or would another bullet come flying through the air?

Judith was all but naked. I swung her legs off the bed and half-dragged, half-carried her towards the door. Strangled noises were coming from the ground. If we didn't get out soon we would be down there with them.

The air in the passage was blissfully clear. Judith sank to the ground. I hauled her up, dragged her to the stairs. I was wondering how to get her up them when something crashed overhead. 'Down there!' someone yelled, and feet hammered across the floor.

Men were running down the stairs. I saw boots, uniforms. I collapsed beside Judith and took her in my arms.

'Jesus!' said a voice, and when I looked up Simon was rushing towards me. He tore off his jacket, draped it around her. I think briefly he took me in his arms. But everywhere was noise – pounding feet, thumps, yells.

'Rayjay,' I gasped, 'Zara . . .' Or did I only say it in my mind? I no longer know. Whatever had been keeping me going had suddenly shut down.

What I do remember is Judith's face. She was ghostly white, catatonic, staring straight ahead.

Not even blinking.

Chapter Twenty-Seven

'Five minutes,' the nurse told Simon.

He nodded, staring down at me in the hospital bed.

Hot tears swamped my cheeks. 'Judith?' I croaked.

'Sleeping.' He pulled forward a chair. 'Feel up to talking?'

I nodded, tried to sit up. There were so many things I wanted to know. Simon helped me plump the pillows.

'Did you catch –' I lapsed into a fit of coughing. My throat felt like sandpaper.

'We caught them.' He passed me a glass of water. 'Thank God your message got through.'

'I didn't think it had,' I said, when the coughing subsided. 'I told them I'd called you. They didn't believe me.'

'Of course not, the phones weren't working. Lines were down across half the county.' He paused. 'Lucky you had the radio.'

I nodded. Why couldn't I stop crying? 'Sorry,' I said, blowing my nose.

'Don't worry, it's aftermath. Shock. You'll be fine.'

He went on to explain how they had got there so quickly. It seemed a raid had already been planned on the Institute, and the advent of my message had made it all systems go. All that changed was the venue.

'One team went there anyway,' he informed me. 'Place was deserted. Looks like Chadwicke's done a bunk.'

'He's dead,' I said, and Simon's eyes widened. 'De Zaire killed him. And Trevor, Gary –'

'De Zaire?' He jerked forward. 'But I thought –'

'De Zaire was the hit man!' I cried. 'Zara! Did you catch –'

But already Simon was on his feet.

He rushed out to put out an APB, came back looking thunderous. In the far corner of the cellar they had found a door, hidden behind the drapes. It opened on to the riverbank on the far side of the wheel. A little upstream they had found two ropes, strung one above the other across the water. A commando-style escape to the opposite bank.

'Must have had a car waiting,' Simon growled. 'Bastard could be anywhere.' Then seeing my face, 'We'll find him, Gus. He won't get far.'

Like the last time?

He dragged his hands over his face. He was looking more exhausted than ever. 'What I don't get is why you thought it was de Zaire? What made you suddenly take off like that?'

Sheepishly I told him about the Tintins, the French pronunciation. 'I should have known it was too convoluted,' I added. 'Why do I come up with these stupid ideas?'

'Hey, they're not all stupid. You were right about the letterboxes. Even down to it being the last leg, car left on the road. We've had people on the moor since the photos were blown up. Undercover anoraks.'

I smiled. It was a nice feeling.

'They witnessed the drop and the stuff being collected. Not sure who by, short guy, we think it might have been Eddie. Then unfortunately they lost him – probably had his route carefully planned. Exposed bit for the drop; cover for the return. Difficult to keep track, as Rayjay was all too aware.'

'And you assumed he'd gone to the Institute.'

'Hence the raid.' He paused, sat forward. 'Gus, about what happened in the cellar . . .'

Slowly I nodded. The time had come to relive the ordeal.

I'd reached the part where I dragged Judith clear when the

nurse returned. She grudgingly granted an extension when I assured her I was okay. 'It was difficult to see anything,' I continued. 'Like being in a blizzard. The powder stings your eyes and it's almost impossible to breathe.' I paused. 'The men. Are they okay?'

Simon hesitated. 'De Zaire got it worst. Damage to his eyes but they think he'll recover. Mostly it's skin irritations.'

'And?' There was something he wasn't telling me.

'One didn't make it, Gus. Frank, the one in costume. Seems he was asthmatic and . . .' He hunched his shoulders.

I swallowed, turned away. Stared at Simon's reflection in the darkened window. Remembering how I'd last seen Frank, writhing on the floor, fighting for breath. For a brief moment I felt self-reproach – until I remembered the surgical instruments, heard again Judith's screams. His death was something I could live with.

I realized Simon was speaking again. 'Sorry, I didn't . . .'

'I said, did de Zaire kill the aunt too?'

Vaguely I shook my head. 'He claims not. Was quite adamant. He suggested I look closer to home.' I met his eyes. 'I've a horrible feeling he meant Stuart.'

'Shit!' Simon pinched the bridge of his nose. 'I've just been talking to him.' He dragged himself to his feet. 'For Judith's sake, I hope the bastard's wrong.'

I left hospital next morning and returned to Tynings. I'd expected my father to be over the moon; instead he was strangely quiet. When I finally asked why he took my hand.

'I'm angry, Gus. Fuming, if you must know. Talk about bloody stupid! Taking off like that, with not so much as a note . . .'

'I didn't think.'

'Damn right, you didn't!' He glared for a moment, then lowered his eyes, squeezed my hand more tightly. 'It's knowing how close I came to losing you. But that's me being selfish. If you hadn't done what you did – well, Judith might not still be here. Hell, I'm proud of you, Gussie. Just don't do it again, okay?'

We hugged. More tears. Christ, I was getting emotional.

He left to answer the doorbell. Yet more flowers had arrived. The place was beginning to look like a hothouse. If it wasn't the door, it was the telephone – the press, people I'd barely heard of enquiring about my health. Those who wanted to visit, Dad politely dissuaded. Apart from Simon there was only one person I wanted to see. Lisa drove out on the second day, armed with chocolates and some books. It was the first and only time I've known her speechless.

The press were the biggest nightmare. They hung around outside, tried to peer through windows. Day and night we kept the curtains closed. Lord knows what they wrote, I refused to look at the papers, though I know Dad was following the news on TV. Simon called when he could, though the aftermath left him little time. Sleep looked like a distant memory.

It was on one of his visits that I learned the identities of the men. Eddie was Eddie Pisano, an Irish-Italian from the East End with a history of violence. The cameraman was Ian Playstow, one-time cameraman for Westward TV, and they were checking for a West Country link. The one who died – Frank Tuttle, aka Freddie Turk, aka Frankie Wang – had been another Londoner, a porn actor since his teens, again with a record of violence. He'd moved to California to boost his career, presumably where he met Rayjay.

But the most surprising history belonged to de Zaire. He was who he claimed, Joseph Desmond, but like everything else in his CV, the impoverished background was a myth. He'd been brought up by a respectable family, one of three adopted children.

'He was trouble from the start,' Simon told me, 'but it was in adolescence the real problems began. When he almost raped his sister, his parents washed their hands.

There were two later pull-ins for a similar offence, but both times he produced an alibi. Before the days of DNA.'

I looked away as my heart began to race. The anger would be with me for a long time. 'And Alden?' I asked.

'No body as yet, but we think we know who he was. Alan Chesney, former teacher at a girls' school in Oxford. Left when some parents discovered certain extracurricular activities. It was all hushed up, hence no record, but his career was finished, at least in this country.'

'So off to sunny California.'

'You've got it. Where he met up with the rest of the crew.'

'Rest?'

'*All* of them.'

And that was when he told me about Stuart.

The initial search of Holt Mill had turned up nothing. House and studio had been torn apart and sniffer dogs sent in, but apart from de Zaire's private stash, no drugs had been found. Until someone thought to look in the sculptures. They found them inside the metal sections, bag after bag, welded in. Bound for the exhibition at Kempe Hillas Fine Art.

Stuart's part had been simple. On the opening night, certain pieces were given red stickers, indicating they were already sold. A few days later the 'buyer' would arrive and take them away.

'Claims he didn't know what was in them. Thought it might be diamonds,' Simon said. 'Didn't want to know, more like.' He sighed. 'Looked at one way, he's just another victim. Before this, the only thing he was guilty of was wanting to be the big-time entrepreneur and not having the wherewithal to carry it out. Then he met Rayjay. From then on the only way was down.'

'So Miss Hillas didn't introduce him to de Zaire?'

'He let her *think* she did. Strange as it might seem, I think Kempe's meeting Judith, her aunt living close by, *were* coincidence. One of the few things Rayjay didn't plan, and still it worked in his favour. Bastard must have laughed like the proverbial drain.'

'But how did he get Stuart in his clutches?'

'By bailing him out of debt. Hefty loan, hefty interest, which he knew Stuart couldn't pay. They met, according to Kempe, when Rayjay *happened* to walk into his gallery one day. Like Rayjay just *happens* to do anything! My guess is he had the whole thing planned, Stuart was the final link. When the time was right Rayjay called in the loan, and when Kempe couldn't honour it, he offered him a way out.'

'The London gallery.'

'Right. The perfect drop-off, slap in the heart of the city. Judith thinks hubby's put up the money; we thought it was Judith. And all the time it was that –' He stopped himself saying the word.

'But the fake painting . . .'

'Stuart trying to be clever, allegedly to get Rayjay off his back. Says he knew deep down it was a copy but thought he could get away with it. Imagine his panic when the shit hit the fan – in debt to Rayjay for a second time. Not just that. If it went to court there'd be massive publicity, police involvement – and by now he knows what Rayjay's capable of. He knew Rayjay wouldn't risk him talking, hence his desperation. So he starts borrowing more, trying to keep it under wraps. When all the usual sources dried up, he appealed to Judith's aunt.'

'And the appeal fell flat.'

'Not at first. He'd already had two pay-outs. It was the third request she refused. And this time she threatened to tell Judith what a useless piece of shit she'd married.'

'So he killed her.'

Simon nodded. 'Soon as we confronted him, it came pouring out. Seemed almost glad to get it off his chest, that the whole thing was finally over. Not one of your natural born killers.'

'Unlike de Zaire,' I murmured. 'Judith said his personality had changed.'

'Hardly surprising with Rayjay on his back, and having just murdered his wife's only relative.' He pulled a face. 'That's where his story gets weird. According to Kempe, he told the old girl he'd deny ever having been there. Reckoned Judith would believe him, would be convinced her aunt was gaga. Next minute out comes the camera and she's got his picture. He realized later he should have snatched it then; instead he stormed back to his car and drove off. After a few miles he had second thoughts and came back. No one at the house. Then he sees the old girl off in the distance, guesses she's got the camera with her and sets off in pursuit.'

'So why didn't he kill her nearer the house?'

'Precisely what I asked. Claims it took him that long to catch up. The aunt was a seasoned walker, dressed for the moor: he was a city boy in city clothes. Reckons he was wearing hand-made shoes with leather bottoms. If so, it's a miracle *he* didn't go over the edge.'

'And he just happens to catch up with her at the top of a hundred foot drop? Come on . . .'

'That's what he says. Swears all he wanted was the film but she refused to give it up. He tried to snatch it, Miss Hillas steps backwards . . . Suddenly he's got a dead body on his hands. So he goes to the bottom, extracts the film –'

'Whoa!' I said. 'No way! I've been to that quarry, Simon. It's difficult enough reaching it in summer in walking boots.'

'He did say he almost didn't make it.'

'And you believe him?'

He shrugged. 'Question is, will a jury? If they do, he might get off with manslaughter. But add that to the drugs charge . . . He's going to be away a good number of years.' He rubbed the back of his neck. 'Right now I think he wishes he'd gone over with her. He's lost the one thing he cared about.'

'Money?' I asked cynically.

'His wife. When I asked why, if he was in so much shit, he didn't take the easy way out,' he put an imaginary gun to his head, 'Kempe said he would have done had he been alone. But he knew if he did, Rayjay would go after Judith. In his own way he was trying to protect her.'

I sat back in the chair. 'So there was no way out.'

Simon shook his head. 'But when Rayjay's involved, there rarely is.'

I didn't dare think what Stuart's involvement would do to Judith. Physically, I'd been told, she was recovering well. It was her mental state that concerned me. Since the ordeal she had barely uttered a word, spent most of her waking moments staring at the walls. But when I next saw Simon there had been a change. He had spoken to her that morning.

'How is she?' I asked.

He hesitated. 'It's going to take time, Gus.' He pulled out a chair, sat opposite. 'I told her I would be seeing you. She said to tell you, the books are small reward.'

'Books?' And then I remembered – the Dulacs, the Louis Wains. I'd forgotten they even existed.

'I must visit her,' I said, scrabbling to my feet.

'Gus . . .' His hand shot out, grabbed my arm. 'This may sound hard but – she doesn't want to see you.'

'*What?*'

'Sit down.'

'What d'you mean, she doesn't want to see me?' I snatched my arm away. 'She must! I'm the only one who knows what she went through.'

'Maybe that's why. Sit down and think for a moment.'

It took me a while. Finally, in some strange way, I began to understand. I had been witness to her humiliation, her pain, all manner of degradation, and seeing that knowledge in my eyes would be more than she could bear. At least for now.

'She says she'll write,' Simon said gently.

I nodded. But would she ever recover? Could anybody? She had lost everything – her aunt, her husband – even her dignity. Her future, too. She loved Verstone, hoped one day to live there. Now all it would hold were reminders.

I clenched my fists. 'And all because of that bastard!' I said out loud. 'I don't suppose . . .'

'Not yet. But we'll get him. This time we have finger-prints *and* DNA.'

'DNA?'

'They found a small amount of blood near where you said he was standing. Doesn't belong to the others. We're guessing de Zaire winged him when he let go that shot. The place where they found the bullet lends credence.' He risked a smile. 'Better send de Zaire a thank-you note. That's probably why he didn't come after you.'

I told him I would pass. 'I keep wondering how many others there were – films, girls. How did he find them, Simon?'

'Runaways, most likely, young girls heading for the bright lights. They're easy prey. They arrive in the city, get addicted to crack, next thing they're working the streets. Thousands arrive every year and many are never heard from again. Just one more faceless statistic.' He grimaced. 'But it was worse than that. Sick bastard was using them for the drop. Clever, huh? Two runners, one a regular who knows the route, the other the budding actress. Bring her down to the West Country, dress her like a walker and off they go. Regular leaves, girl stays, and gets collected along with the dope. They were delivering themselves right into his hands.'

I shuddered. 'The Path of the Dead.'

'What?'

I shook my head. 'They wouldn't *all* have met the same fate, would they?'

'Possibly not – I guess some got away with the stuff Chadwicke watched. I suppose it depended on the client. That's where the money was, in the fact that the films were tailored. Rich perverts script their wildest fantasies, Rayjay brings it to life. Or death. Christ, there are some sick minds out there!'

He looked up at the ceiling, and I saw a muscle working in his neck. 'And I let him go, Gus. Having *spoken* to him. Hell, I *sat in the same bloody room!* And now he's out there, we don't even know in which country. Christ, we don't even know which *gender* he's using . . .'

I could imagine his frustration, part of which I could share. Along with the anger. But Simon, I knew, would work through it in time.

A short while later he stood up to leave, but first he paused at my side.

'I haven't forgotten that dinner, Gus. When you feel up to it.' He squeezed my shoulder. 'We're not all monsters, you know.'

I stared down at my lap. 'I know.'

Seconds later I heard the door close.

They found Alden's body the following week, washed up on a beach near Salcombe. He'd taken a bullet through the brain. Of Rayjay there was still no sign. Roadblocks had been set up, guards put on ports and airports, but somehow he had slipped through. Simon believed he was still in the country, living at some pre-arranged location under yet another name and disguise. Waiting for the fuss to die down.

As the days progressed, the horrors at Holt Mill became old news, were overtaken by political scandals, a major train crash, an oil spillage in the North Sea. Birds were dying in their thousands. With the departure of the press I started walking again, spending entire days out on the moor. I followed the West Dart to Rough Tor, visited the ruins of Bleak House, and the remains of Teignhead Farm. Even made it to Cranmere Pool, the long way via Hangingstone Hill. Soon I would return to work, face my flat,

300

the noise, the everyday hassle. But first I needed to spend time alone. We all have our ways of coping.

I was leaving on one of my walks when the post arrived with Judith's letter. I started to open it, then changed my mind – instead took it with me, finally opening it at the top of Kes Tor.

My dearest Gus,

What can I say? All words sound feeble, inadequate. Little did I know when I first sought your help where the path I was treading would lead. I hope you can forgive me – hope also that you can understand why I found it impossible to see you. Something tells me that you do.

You will know by now how my aunt met her death. Perhaps it came as no surprise. To me it was devastating. Would I have acted differently had I known the truth? Ah, the power of hindsight. I have thought much, too, of subsequent deaths, asked myself if our actions in any way precipitated them. Truly, I don't believe they did. Having spoken long hours with your friend DI Furneaux, I've accepted that tragedy of some kind was inevitable, with or without my/our intervention. Perhaps that is what we should hang on to.

I don't suppose we'll ever know exactly what my aunt knew, nor how she found out. But her words keep coming back to me. 'There's evil everywhere . . .' How right she was.

As you know, I had hoped one day to live at Higher Verstone. Not any more. Shortly the house and everything in it will be sold. All I shall keep are my aunt's paintings. The books I promised you will be left with my solicitor. Please have them; they're small enough recompense. (Unless like me you want no reminder?)

June has kindly agreed to feed the cats until the house sells (though I understand the Weblakes themselves are moving). With luck the new owners will take them on – if not, for the tamer ones, she will endeavour to find homes. But my main concern is Geoffrey. I always intended to keep him, but having now decided to travel, to settle I know not where, this is neither practical nor fair. So I'm going to beg one last favour and ask if you, Gus, would find him a home – perhaps with the help of your friend in the RSPCA? (Unless, of course, you know someone already?) I do know you care enough to make sure the home is a good one, which will allow me to rest more easily. He has a special place in my heart.

As do you, dear Gus. You will have my love and respect always.

Your friend,
Judith

I lowered the letter, stared out across a moorland made hazy by tears. So she hadn't relented. I wouldn't be seeing her again.

Such a short friendship, begun with a favour, ending with a favour. A home for a parrot with attitude. Nice one, Judith!

I knew exactly what she meant by a good home – one with love, constant companionship, someone to amuse and be amused by. And of course I knew someone already, as Judith knew only too well.

I refolded the letter and placed it in my bag. Went home to break the news to Dad.

Author's Note

Those familiar with the Devon Fire Brigade will notice I've taken several liberties. Gus's job as I've portrayed it does not exist, and I've drawn on details past and present to give an idea of this ever-changing Service. So too with the geography, and apart from well-known landmarks all places are fictitious. It goes without saying the people are too.

I would like to thank anyone who helped with the shaping/making of this book, including my editors Krystyna Green and Imogen Olsen; Stephen Buss for his advice on Fire Brigade procedure (any mistakes are mine); and Tracey (TAG) who unknowingly gave me the idea for Gus. Finally, a special thank you to my agent, Michael Motley, whose support throughout has meant so much.